Lesley Chamberlain is the author of many books on literature and philosophy. Her work on Russia, particularly her book, *The Philosophy Steamer Lenin and the Exile of the Intelligentsia*, has been highly acclaimed. Over half a century of writing and travelling, she has approached Russia through food, philosophy, music, literature and history. She has travelled the length of the river Volga to try to understand that mysterious and perplexing country. *The Mozhaisk Road*, her fourth work of fiction, is the culmination of a lifelong project exploring why Russia both attracts admirers across the world and is greatly feared.

Lesley Chamberlain

THE MOZHAISK ROAD

Russian Heart of Darkness

AUSTIN MACAULEY PUBLISHERS®

LONDON * CAMBRIDGE * NEW YORK * SHARJAH

A CIP catalogue record for this title is available from the British Library.

ISBN 9781035868254 (Paperback)
ISBN 9781035868261 (ePub e-book)

www.austinmacauley.com

First Published 2025
Austin Macauley Publishers Ltd®
1 Canada Square
Canary Wharf
London
E14 5AA

The cover image incorporates Ida Kar 'The Queue for Lenin's Mausoleum', courtesy of the National Portrait Gallery, London.

The people in this story are real, please remember that. The road is real too, and it just goes on and on.

The road frightened me. I had come to Russia in hope, among the last of my kind, for few had hope after me. I wanted for nothing to divide rich and poor—and for my own country—any notion of an 'own country'—to vanish, and then I would have a place in the world.

For I had nowhere to go. So you see why Russia attracted me. The dream that the road might lead somewhere.

Russia was where you found yourself, back in the last century. You fell in love with the stories that vast country told because they spoke to your soul. Russia's wide-open spaces and its soulfulness promised a new life where your origins didn't matter, only your good intentions. Russia, magnificent, holy Russia! People like me lapped up thousands of pages of its heart-piercing history of faith and disappointment. Laughter, cruelty, hope and self-sacrifice held out a light and showed us the way. Ours was the road to revolution, Russia our new Garden of Eden.

So, I went there and these people were real. Please remember that.

On *Anyone's Game* (2012)

'Sophie's pursuit of freedom, self-knowledge and a "home" in a "rational world" takes her to Constantinople, Scotland, Moscow, London, Cambridge and Paris. This unpredictable journey unfolds amid political unrest and economic distress in the decade after the First World War. One of the many strengths of this absorbing novel lies in the unsentimental characterization of Sophie…'

– Susan Civale, TLS

'The difficult life of Sophie Asmus is thrilling, not least because her own liberation comes at a cost. She is a remarkable and haunting creation.'

– Jennie Erdal, *The Independent*

On *The Philosophy Steamer* (2006)

'The persecution of free-spirited intellectuals and artists in the Soviet era has become, in many respects, a familar tale. Numberless novels and memoirs have described, in nightmarish detail, the varied forms of coercion and punishment it adopted — whether in Josef Stalin's prison camps or Leonid Brezhnev's psychiatric hospitals, through public shaming or private harassment. Yet there is an episode in this chronicle which is less widely known, even though it occurred at the very beginning. With her new book, 'The Philosophy Steamer', Lesley Chamberlain makes an irrefutable case for its significance in the intellectual history of 20th-century Europe.'

– Oliver Ready, *The Moscow Times*

'Those who sailed on The Philosophy Steamer, the countless others whose names have not been remembered -they were like a mythical tribe from a lost world. Chamberlain retrieves their stories in a narrative that is compelling, laudably unsentimental and deeply significant to the history of ideas.'

– Frances Stonor Saunders, *The Guardian*

'Lesley Chamberlain has a rare gift for animating philosophy through intensely human stories…she movingly describes the experience of exile in ways that echo the great exiled novelist Nabokov himself.'

– Michael Burleigh, *The Sunday Telegraph*

On *Motherland* (2004)

'Chamberlain tries to explore Russian philosophy neither as the passive victim of political repression, nor solely as the origin and motor of a ruinous totalitarian ideology, but as "a story of hope and belief" with its own internal impulses, achievements and pathos.'

– Rachel Polonsky, TLS

'With echoes of Simon Sebag Montefiore and Orlando Figes intertwined in her narrative, Chamberlain tells the story of over 200 years of Russian thinking…this intelligent assessment of the great Russian minds will provide readers with an unparalleled insight into Russia's spirit.'

– *Good Book Guide*

On *Girl in a Garden* (2003)

'Lesley Chamberlain has done a brilliant, delicate job with this vivid novel set in the post-war atmosphere of 1961.'

– *Daily Mail*

'Chamberlain writes with such clarity and understanding about human pain that she effortlessly reaches the hidden child in all of us.'

– Lucy Beresford, *The Literary Review*

On *In a Place Like That* (1998)

'As a veteran of both Bezzakonia [The Country without Laws] and the New Russia, I found this book immensely absorbing, as though it had been written just for me, Fellow veterans will immediately recall what it felt like to stand in a queue in order to buy a kilo of tomatoes, to be admitted to a Russian's flat, or to emerge triumphant from a clash with some petty official. Perhaps they too seek in vain, like Alice, for the way back into that frustrating and insane, but enticing Wonderland, experiencing a sense of loss when the key can no longer be located. Lesley Chamberlain's brilliant book is a touching and humorous requiem to a lost world.'

– Lindsay Hughes, TLS

'Lesley Chamberlain's great love for Russia has led her to acquire a Russian sensibility, and some of her episodes have the economy and sense of humour of Mikhail Zoshchenko. She is a wonderfully observant writer, constantly noticing little things. She writes of the fad for wearing T-shirts with meaningless foreign slogans on them; she remembers with nostalgia the grey horror of a refectory meal…Love or hate them, such experiences are not easily forgotten – and were well worth recalling. Chamberlain's atmospheric fictions are a delightfully revisionist reminder of what the Cold War was really like for the footsoldiers in the front line.'

– Richard Gott, *The Independent*

On *Volga, Volga* (1995)

'…her voice is always original. Combining journalistic skills with careful research and imaginative flair, she extracts the condition of post-Communist Russia from the shell of everyday experience and detects the historical and cultural resonances of the Volga lands…Most importantly, the author never loses sight of the fact that her views of Russia are glimpsed through the veil of Western culture. I was relieved, after a spate of "Russians are just like us" books since 1991, to read one which acknowledged and explored the differences…Free too of the opposing baggage of Slavophilia, she despairs frankly of the lack of public honesty, the constant shifting of goalposts, conceptual trickery and the "historically unhinged" quality of the country. The result is a sad, enlightening book about the trauma which underlies Russians' deep love for their homeland.'

– Anne McElvoy, *The Times*

On *In the Communist Mirror* (1990)

'Why don't British leftists write about eastern Europe as well as [Timothy Garton] Ash, [Lesley] Chamberlain or [David] Selbourne? Because they have been too embarrassed by the sheer fact of Soviet-type socialism to listen to east Europeans and learn from them.'

– Mark Thompson, *City Limits*

'Lesley Chamberlain's diary-style memoir – quite beautifully written – [describes] travelling in Eastern Europe in the early to mid-eighties when communism was still firmly in place. Now that the ideology has vanished the sensitive traveller and individualist – especially one like Lesley Chamberlain, with a conservative and romantic disposition – may feel a paradoxical sense of loss. For, while its monstrous form destroyed certain types of life, it protected others; guarded them from the onslaught of change and the drearier models of Western progress. Lesley Chamberlain's discreetly erotic memoir is in its own way a work of conservation, of commemoration – imbued with the melancholy poetry which always comes from the contemplation of ruins.

– Mark LeFanu, The Observer

On The Food and Cooking of Russia (1982)
'I read it from cover to cover as one would a novel…'

– Paul Levy, The Observer

Other Titles by Lesley Chamberlain

Fiction

In a Place Like That

Girl in a Garden

Anyone's Game

Selected non-fiction

The Food and Cooking of Russia

In the Communist Mirror

Volga, Volga

Motherland A Philosophical History of Russia

The Philosopher Steamer Lenin and the Exile of the Intelligentsia

Arc of Utopia The Beautiful Story of the Russian Revolution

Ministry of Darkness How Sergei Uvarov Created Conservative Modern Russia

'He had seen decisive moments in men's lives. He had witnessed a scene in Red Square when demonstrators were arrested, and when an ordinary citizen, an accidental passer-by, had suddenly gone across to join them, and been arrested too…He had never truly lived in places where duties were terrible and their consequences life-destroying and long.'

'These are the great actions of the century. These are our real heroes. These are people whose courage and devotion to goodness goes beyond any dream of one's own possibility.'

– Iris Murdoch, *An Accidental Man*

Part 1

One

You know that feeling, when you aren't expected. It's the way we humans are, animals really. Among animals, strangers are not welcome. They have to serve out a time of trial and sometimes they're never accepted. Instead, they get pecked or kicked to death. I'd taken a taxi from the airport and just turned up at Howard Wilde's office, hoping he would let me stay for a while. My motives didn't matter to the guard on the entrance, a tall anonymous-looking man wearing a smart grey military greatcoat and an astrakhan hat. With his eyes focused straight ahead, his job was only to protect the motherland. He let me in. His actual task was to stop Russians entering the Western compound. But I was so obviously a Westerner, in my fashionable clothes, I was no threat. In my brown boots made of good leather, he watched me go, his eyes on the boots. The heels were too high and narrow for a Moscow winter.

I picked my way over the potholes in the car park, carrying a small heavy suitcase and struggling with my balance. Climbing the steps to the raised pedestrian level that ran along the single inhabited side of the courtyard, I stopped at the entrance to the first of the four staircases and looked around. The accommodation for the few Westerners officially allowed to live in Moscow was arranged like you found it in a Cambridge college, arranged by staircase, with rooms, or flats, set either side of the stairs, and one above the other. In case I'd got the address wrong, or I couldn't get Howard Wilde to accept my stay, I left my suitcase outside and entered the first *vkhod* (for this was not Cambridge). There a massive iron lift cage—really, Gustaf Eiffel would have been proud of it—resembled a moving prison. It made my heart turn over. Imagine, they'd put you in there and you'd go up and down the five floors for the rest of your life, between bowls of kasha shoved through the bars and glasses of tea. Rather than take a risk, I clacked my way up the first two flights of internal stone steps. There, to my relief, the door to the LGN office stood open.

In some sense, for visiting Westerners, the LGN office was a public place. Perhaps even a refuge, because from there you could imagine sending a message out. Also you met people like you, of the same broad origins, all capable of speaking English, although I have to say no one was like me.

Howard Wilde objected to my intrusion and it was an effort for him to smile. I knew what he looked like from his black-and-white photograph, and I couldn't immediately see a difference. Largish man, curly hair, tricky mouth. He knew I was coming and tried to smile, but his lips were forced out of a position unnatural to them and soon reverted, as if they'd had an unpleasant dream. But I could be like that too. I have these goals I set myself and no one is part of them, and sometimes I smile and sometimes not.

'I wanted to see for myself.' I hovered in the doorway of his office, not smiling too much but hoping he might like the look of me. (I'm a woman and I freely admit to resorting to such hopes.) There was a faint cabbage smell in the air, otherwise everywhere paper and books and three typewriters, two more than were presently needed, I surmised. 'I won't get in the way.' In a very real sense I obviously would. The room was small and cramped. Howard Wilde too looked at my boots. Was he fond of women, I wondered.

Howard Wilde though—he was quite a name. He was an accredited Western newspaper reporter. With his professional legitimacy in mind, his assured position in the order of things, I assigned myself to him to carry out my experiment.

The Soviet city too, another suspicious, clannish animal, only grudgingly welcomed strangers. There were many reasons for that, but the end result was Westerners felt uneasy if they didn't club together and now and again visit the LGN office to renew their sense of family, or tribe, or some such unchallenged belonging. I was about to slot myself into that network, become part of that Western family, to give myself a legitimate reason for moving about the city. I had to see if it wasn't a place to give me hope.

Moscow was a city that liked to boast it was the finest in the world. It didn't want criticism. So you could stay there so long as you didn't voice a sense of anything wrong. Their expectation that you would come out with some terrible judgement of what you saw meant pressure from every official person you encountered. It meant suspicion and shyness from just about everyone else. What Russians feared most was having to defend the indefensible, but this I learnt only much later. For now I was only on guard at the strangeness of everything, and still, even more, for that reason, I was full of hope.

To get away from the pressure to be admiring or silent Westerners liked to congregate together, and joke, and—in a way—imagine they were somewhere else. I knew this already because as a promising Western linguist, destined for who knew what prestigious job, I had spent time learning the language. I had already spent a month in the company of official Russians, and puzzled over their ways. In those days Russia ran courses in its sonorous, seductive language, and those schools for Westerners were situated on the very fringes of its Western Empire as well as in Moscow and Leningrad. Our course was in Vilnius, in Lithuania, which hardly looked like Russia at all, except for the propaganda, and the nameless shops, and the official institutions intimidatingly lining the streets. I think the director of the institute where I learnt Russian must have had good connections in Moscow to make his Vilnius school happen, for it was a great boon to that forgotten Soviet corner. It brought exotic young people like me and, with them, wallets full of hard currency to be spent on anything we could find. We brought dollars or pounds sterling with us, as opposed to the humble, domestic Russian rouble that couldn't be traded on the international market, and we spent them on what we could, which was almost nothing, except ice creams and outings. As students we were polite, we offered the teachers at the institute our cheerful, careless, noisy, wildly-dressed exoticism freely, and they must have known we laughed at them and made comparisons when we were out of the classroom.

But then Howard Wilde *lived* in Moscow, at the heart of the empire that made the periphery as it was. He was *supposed* to be there. He had a registered address. He was officially allowed to try to understand Russia in its latest incarnation, as a new civilisation. I wanted his privilege. I needed it, if I was to go ahead with my plan. I'd written to him, long-hand, by post. My father's secretary had also telephoned, she assured me. Yet by his unyielding face now who knew if he got the letter, or took the call.

It was the connection to my father that made it impossible for him to smile.

My father was a hugely wealthy man. He was also Howard Wilde's boss. 'Friends in the Kremlin, has your Daddy? I don't know how else you'd get here.'

I shrugged. Every day of my life since I was fourteen hostile people had invited me to take responsibility for my father. I hated that.

'It wasn't hard. I caught a plane.'

I had a visa of course. For Moscow every foreign visitor needed a visa. The difficulty was few visas were issued. Usually you had to have a job—of which there were even fewer—and I wasn't even posing as someone's nanny at the embassy. Or you were someone's relative. But that's where my father had stepped in.

'My Dad's your boss. I'm sorry you don't like him. Don't hold it against me.'

Howard had scrubby hair and his rosy cheeks burned with indignation at my provenance. No photograph could capture what he was really like in that moment, not the black-and-white photos of those days. I didn't find him bad-looking and kept hoping, as in those days a woman in my position had to hope, that the feeling would soon be mutual.

'I mean that my Dad always knows someone. How else would I get here?' I could see Pa's great jowly face, which I had tweaked with joy when I was a little girl; and I could smell the tobacco on him. Because he was overweight he looked better in tailored suits than in casual clothes. The tailors of Saville Row know how to cut their cloth to disguise the results of years of self-indulgence. He was a wild man. He didn't like being told what to do and who to be. He would force himself on others, if need be. He wore a leather bomber jacket with slacks at weekends and looked so much a mixture of worlds and nations and social classes that outsiders were simply baffled. In some of this I was like him.

That weekend outfit never flattered him, by the way, though it did make him look more of a family man and possibly more approachable. I started to step back and notice just how wild and selfish and powerful he was when I was about fourteen.

And how do you feel about *that man*, I could see Howard wanted to ask, as if holding him up in miniature as a specimen of all things vile. How do you feel about your famous, powerful, wealthy father who controls my destiny, and so many more.

'At least working for him gets you *here*. Here's the place to be, isn't it?'

'You seem to think so.'

'I've done a lot of reading.'

'God save us.'

I guessed that deep in his heart, but also close to the surface, Howard Wilde hated being in someone's employ; anyone's; loathed the fact that anyone had control over him. I guessed that because I felt the same. Which made three of us.

'Look, I won't be any trouble. He didn't send me. I was in Russia last year. I wanted to come back.'

'In Russia?'

'In Vilnius, learning the lingo.'

Should I try some way to charm Howard Wilde? To suggest somehow that, with a man like him and a woman like me, this could be an auspicious meeting? We were both young, or in his case youngish, and possibly unattached, and not bad-looking. But no. This was serious and the deal between us should be reasonable. 'Pa just made it possible. He hopes I'll mend my ways. Get my life together. Something like that. Have you got children?'

He shook his head and there was some concession in some flickering memory of what might have produced children; love affairs that had led nowhere perhaps. So I smiled, fractionally, hopefully, just for him to accept me as younger than him but of his kind. I was a freelance person, a one-off, who could do anything and nothing, who felt at once hobbled and free, and I had this foreknowledge of Russia.

Which probably made things worse because he remained thoroughly irritated. 'So you'll take the guest flat upstairs. It's hardly a suite at Claridge's but it'll have to do.' Was that a sneer on those enigmatic lips? And a hateful passion in the blood that flushed his cheeks? I thought so.

The hostility was too much. I was my own person and could resist. He had to accommodate me, as he well knew, as the daughter of his boss. 'Something along the lines of the Intercontinental would do fine,' I retorted. 'Decent double bed, shower, bathtub ideally, space to move, bookshelves, and if you could throw in a view—'

His answer was to pull up his iron-framed typewriter like a shield. 'Guest flat. Floor up from here.' He opened a desk drawer and half-standing handed me a key in a worn leather fob. 'Now I must get on.'

'Of course you must.' Something in my upbringing, all those years ago, made me respectful of men and their work. Work was important. Women mostly didn't have it. (I mean my mother was a complete doormat.) Still I wasn't quite comfortable and I didn't like the way he was treating me. 'But, er, Mr Wilde, Howard.' I felt myself looking at him directly for the first time, still standing as I was in the doorway, for he hadn't asked me to sit down, or even come in. 'The Second Russian Revolution. Didn't you write it was coming?'

I had wondered in the midst of my reading whether that was Howard Wilde's secret, or did everybody know?

'Where the hell—'

'In the newspaper of course.'

My putting him on the spot only added to his annoyance. 'I'm hardly alone. It's a common view of this country today—why, you'll even hear it on the BBC.'

'I listen to the BBC. I have heard it there. But *you* said it first. That was what interested me.' I'd seen his byline. I'd followed his reports, since I came back from those three bizarre weeks in Lithuania when it struck me Russia was a tragedy. The Soviet Union, properly speaking, it was that I had visited; but to us then it was all just 'Russia'.

'On my head be it then. You grew up and wanted to become a Russia-watcher and your Dad, my boss, fixed up for you to come here.'

'A good way to put it.'

'Thanks. I'm a wordsmith by trade.' More defences. Poor fellow. He ran his eyes over me, cool and practical. 'What about your bags?'

'A suitcase downstairs. The rest to follow in a few weeks. I wasn't sure—'

'Of course, you weren't. Now you go off and leave me alone.'

I retreated into the stairwell, admiring the vast thickness of the office front door, padded with leather on the inside, as I went. Howard Wilde's work protected him against some unimaginable cold; or some other threat.

He was still at his desk when I reappeared an hour later. I tried to read his face. He was supposing I'd 'freshened up'. He was nine years older than me but something about Howard Wilde reminded me of an older generation. Or was he just being stiff and remote with me. I was twenty-six, by the way.

'It's great. I'll be happy there.'

'It's got nothing to do with happiness. You can put that right out of your mind. Hah!'

'I speak Russian. I should be able to get about.'

'Makes it worse if you know what it all means.' He gestured vaguely through the dirty window.

'All?' I probably tipped my head to one side when he said that because I found it so bizarre. 'Look, I've heard Russian for "thank you" actually means "God save you," so as an atheist I can't use it. But you know I'm grateful. *Spasibo*.'

He shook his head.

'I suppose this is a very traditional society, under the surface. Very religious. Under the red banners.'

'You did hear they had a révolution first time round and it made them all atheists, I suppose?'

'Even so.'

'The only thing I can say...' and here he appeared to be making a huge concession to me—'Is that everything here means something else. At least, not what you think.'

I pounced. 'That's exactly it. It's what I've come to find out, that what.' God save you Howard Wilde, though. I didn't say the last part.

He looked at me as if I was very strange, but that he would accept it, because at least that wasn't my family heritage.

The *spasibo* thought stayed with me. 'I wonder what being saved by God would feel like.' I said this out loud. It was, after all, everywhere in my reading.

'Happy, I daresay.' He lightened for a moment. 'So maybe you have come to the right place.'

'Thanks then. I'll try to leave you in peace.' I smiled. Just a tiny fraction of a welcome was enough.

I took the first two weeks to say hello to our neighbours in the foreigners' compound and establish my presence. Yes it was true I was from London and that I knew Russian. So many people and all the women shot covert glances at my boots that I certainly got that message. They may have been expensive but they really weren't suitable for the cold, icy, erratically paved city where I'd arrived on the cusp of deep winter. But then it was made known to me that I could buy Western goods by mail order from Frankfurt or Helsinki and thus replace them with something more suitable. I gave as if I would do that and the conversation moved along. Howard Wilde was a nice man and a good colleague and he would see me right, they said. My Japanese neighbour took me in her car and showed me where to buy groceries at the foreigners' supermarket, using a kind of monopoly money that Howard had provided. I would need to buy that special foreigners' currency from him. We would sort that out. In the supermarket I felt for a moment I could have been anywhere. Except no, we don't put foreigners in compounds and make them use special money, so that we can extract an extra profit from their daily existence. The streets down which we drive our cars don't drown in the sulphurous reek of low-grade petrol and somehow there's less dust, even in London. The Moscow streets were as ugly as

I remembered streets in Vilnius, away from the official centre. But then maybe that was the first truth about Russia in those days that I gleaned on the ground, that materially it was so ugly it inclined you to spend your time imagining paradise at the end of the rainbow. 'You'll go mad if you go on like that,' said Howard, and by about day seven we were capable of conversation.

The potential second revolution that gripped Moscow was still in its early stages. But it had sympathisers, and admirers worldwide. To every creak and grind in the old mechanisms—every sign and signal that Howard Wilde and the BBC man and a few diplomats could detect—the so-called free world was listening. It was free by Russian standards. But I'd come to understand why there had to be such a difference. Or what Russia's secret was that it didn't *want* freedom. I was hungry to see and hear for myself whether Russian taste—call it taste—was changing. *La Russie va-t-elle subire une nouvelle revolution? Gibt es heutzutage wirklich eine Freheitsbewegung in Russland?* Translators across the West, not only in England, not only in the United States, suddenly had a new topic.

'How…?' I began, for I wanted everything Howard could tell me from the beginning, and from before that. I ached for some grip on a new, bold Russia, closer to what the books told me it should be. If it's possible to ache for rebirth, I ached inside and pressed him to help me.

'You can read of little changes more than you can feel them.'

'Read the press? I can do that. But Howard, wouldn't most people expect change to happen the other way round. I mean, first you'd feel it on the street and then you'd start to read about it?'

'Didn't I tell you everything is different here?'

' Of course you did. But maybe you could spell it out. You don't read about the seasons. They happen. Isn't revolution like that? Somehow inevitable?'

'All I'm telling you is you can't judge by the mood of the people. Moods aren't allowed here.'

'I don't understand.'

'I mean theory reigns here, and theory comes from above. First the theory changes then the life can.' He paused. The topic evidently interested him. 'It's a very peculiar thing but it happens to be true.'

'Go on.'

'Theory means something to them that it doesn't to us. It's like a constitution, or a set of laws. They interpret it, they debate it in the newspapers and just maybe someone dares to hint at a new direction—'

'But you're watching them as if they were a strange tribe…'

'Indeed. We might just as well be anthropologists as reporters. We keep our eyes and ears open. We hear things and see things, or think we do. We try to find equivalents back home.'

'All because it's not democratic.'

'Something like that.' He sighed.

'You meet people and they talk. Is that how it goes?'

'There are a few honest and brave people willing to talk to us.'

'Oh, my. That's the clue. You'll let me tag along when you meet them?'

He shrugged. 'I don't feel I have much choice, Gels Maybey. I really don't.'

'*Spasibo*, Howard.' I wasn't used to having God on my side. That's what it felt like for me to be in Russia, that maybe God would change his mind.

In that moment I was so excited. If we have privileges in life like those I was born with we must use them. I sometimes feel I have magic powers. I'm here to make a difference. I'd like to see that revolution happen. My privileges can help with all that, just by getting me here. But don't tell Howard that.

Hurrah! Hurrah! I'm so happy to be here.

Howard's chief contact and informant was a man called Alexander Razumovsky. He was a modern Hercules who took this whole tragic country on his shoulders, so that it might yet be set right. I, Gels Maybey, would get to know Alexander Razumovsky first of all.

'I will. I'll be overwhelmed and embarrassed but I will come with you to see the Razumovskys.'

'The police might arrest you.'

'I'll tell them who I am.'

He laughed. '*Nu ladno*, as we say here. OK. Perhaps your Dad knows someone in the KGB too.'

As the world waited for signs of the second revolution, some arc of concern stretched from Moscow to Washington, Pskov to Paris, Leningrad to London, for Russia was in such distress, and the hope was a great country would learn to swallow its pride and ask for help; stop pretending that the great Communist experiment hadn't gone wrong, but with that not all was lost; for when the second revolution came it would be a revelation of an enduring moral truth, that Russia had tried and failed to secure goodness on earth. A decent world, more moderate in its ambitions, would vibrate in sympathy at a confession of that failure, and perhaps a willingness to settle for something slightly less; for we all still looked upon Russia as a moral place. Anyway that was how I saw it as we set off that evening to hear Razumovsky address Moscow, and with Moscow the world.

Across the city Natasha Razumovsky took off her glasses. The thermometer on the balcony read minus three degrees Celsius, so nothing special, dress as normal. Back in the bedroom she pulled over her head a thick, warm tartan skirt. Its red and black squares nestled against her whiteish grey nylon slip. Adding a red sweater she glanced at herself in the hall mirror. She was older, but still a woman.

Meanwhile she was married to a good man, so brave that… No. Don't think of it. The large orange-framed glasses from Helsinki cast a glow over her sallow winter skin. They didn't flatter her small heart-shaped face but they spoke of the West. The West she both admired and resented. It was easier to live in the West. You could buy anything you needed. But then, poor darlings, after they'd finished shopping what task did they have in life? She sneered at that slack-minded West. Her daughter Tatyana had gone to America and now what? She dyed her hair and did a lot of shopping. Natasha would never succumb. Streaked with grey, her own thick, wiry hair crowned the head of a thinking woman with a life of her own and more or less eager—she sometimes faltered—to serve her country in need.

So strong was her self-conviction over that mission, except in rare moments of doubt, that it gave her—she glanced at her face now, removing the glasses—an expression so deeply attentive and so powerfully insistent that officials in her country quailed. Razumovsky, Natalya E., as they wrote her name on their smudgy typewritten lists. They preferred not to deal with her. For she let her enemies know they were fools (as opposed to, say, amongst the cruellest men on earth) and they didn't know what to do with that.

You mean me, lady?

Got it in one, you idiot. *Ty durak*! You nincompoop. You dolt. All of you bastards, making us live like this.

Birds were rejoicing on the balcony, and inviting their friends, and squabbling over the bread. She tiptoed closer. People found Natasha fierce, but that was what they always said about strong women.

'Ts, ts, ts, birdie, it's only me.'

Still what a debt one paid for being alive in Russia! *Bozhe moi*. Dear God. It heaved you this way and that.

Birds just exist to fly and sing, said Tolstoy. And that's how we should be too. Not let those bastards lock us up and keep us silent. Nice that the birds are out there. They squabble over the bread. But then they're only human. So much did she adore them that for a moment fear crept across her thoughts like a dark shadow. No *cat* can get up here, five floors up. I'd throw any bloody cat overboard with my bare hands. Prowler, murderer, destroyer of beautiful life!'

The door lock snapped back. Sasha returned out of breath from the phone box. 'Sshshsh! Idiot! You'll disturb their tea.'

Idiot he was too and he'd only come in the door.

How she talks to a man she's supposed to love! whispered the neighbours.

Well, yes, it's not right. Him being an Academician too.

But it just comes out like that, she confessed to no one but herself. 'Heeeeh,' he wheezed. 'Heeeee.' Followed by the little cough she knew by heart.

'For God's sake, Sashenka!'

He was bent double, holding on to the piano. His face was flushed, his eyes wayward and his lips protruding.

'You've not been taking your pills. How many times must I tell you...'

'That I'm not immortal,' he groaned. He meant to take the pills. He was a rational man, who perfectly understood the need to dilate the arteries. Not an idiot then, only one not interested in his conduits. 'Don't *fuss* so, my dear!'

She put two pills on a saucer and brought him lemon and honey in a glass. 'Drink up! You'll need your voice tonight.' He would have preferred the luscious amber of tea to this maiden's water, but she said tea dried out the vocal chords, so sweetened lemon it was.

She yelled at him. She needed him alive. Russia needed him alive. 'For God's sake you must take care!'

Her head was on his chest, her arms around his head.

He thought himself perfectly well. 'Aah, you're wearing the red sweater!'

'Yes, darling, I am.'

So the evening would go well. He squeezed her hand. The sweater had some meaning between them.

The first tablet fizzled on his tongue. An American journalist, Arthur Zimmerman, gave Razumovsky vitamin C to help him through the winter. Funny thing the Cold War was! Half the world wanted Razumovsky alive, the other half would have preferred him dead, only not by their own hand. All battles, and there were battles in that war, ongoing thirty or more years now, were disguised. War by other means, it was.

The Razumovskys thought well of Arthur's principles. Explained Sasha: 'You and I, my dear, we are this way because of ...our country. But Arthur Zimmerman's principles would be absolute anywhere.' Which was to say that they respected him but didn't quite find him congenial. His wife Harriet was the more overt warrior, but also somehow sentimental. She didn't have enough Russian for them to get to know her, or they didn't try.

The second tablet was nitro-glycerine. 'I am dynamite!' Razumovsky cried, as he tipped back his head and swallowed his second cure. Perhaps there was some nitrous oxide in there too, for he started laughing as she cuddled his tilted head.

'That's it. You are *explosive*. You are the *bomb* we all need. Without you not even a *spark*.'

'No wonder they want me to peg out.' He was laughing, laughing, a kindly man, a good husband and a man of peace. Why didn't they kill him? Well, he knew why. He'd become too famous.

'Natasha, are you not over-preparing for tonight?'

'Sasha, *durak*! You can never be over-prepared in our country.' She called him a fool for the second time in a matter of minutes and that was the thing about Natasha. You could never criticise her. She *knew*. And she was prepared to *fight*. Fight to change Russia, and in that she was rather like Arthur and Harriet Zimmerman.

'Our country is not predictable,' he began, more gently, a touch ironically, as if he were starting to retell a familiar story.

'I would say, as a woman who has lived here for forty-five years...' she glanced out of the window at the grey and the mud and the two policemen sitting in the yellow car below, 'that our country *is* entirely predictable. So we prepare. I'm right. I know I'm right.'

'Is there more honey tea, my sweet love?'

'Honey and hot water do? The lemon's been squeezed so many times it's like our whole economy. Flavourless and three-quarters dead.'

'Lovely. Just what I need. By the way I adore you in the red sweater.'

'You do? First it was papa's and then it was mama's.' She posed, spreading her arms. 'It's served in prison, in bed and in the marketplace.'

Papa's from his mistress and mama's when she needed something warm in prison, the sweater was. Such was a Russian inheritance. You couldn't be too choosy as to what it had been through; what principles might have been compromised along the way.

'Now they'll see a photograph of it in Washington, and Bonn, and Tokyo.' Which was a nice thought, although the reality was newspapers in those days were still black and white.

As the chemicals went to work on Razumovsky's heart, he could meanwhile reflect that actually you would need 30,000 bottles of nitro-glycerine pills to produce a small spark. Natasha and Sasha both had knowledge of chemistry. Moreover, the Soviet medical industry was as short of nitro-glycerine as the whole country was of lemons from Cuba. So yes, their talk was often ironic, and that was why. Because they knew so much.

In that vein Sasha Razumovsky continued to reflect (and there was the structure of a logical consideration in that "actually...moreover ..."), that you would need raw alcohol and access to a laboratory to extract the active element from the dormant pill. He could probably still get into a lab, but now, excuse me, but who has a bottle of ether on the shelf in these Russian days of ours? Raw alcohol is permanently in deficit because people drink it. They tip it down their throats, for the burn, and the oblivion. Everyone knows that. Our Russia is amusing, isn't it? Funny haha. Side-splitting. On the other hand we have a culture. Not like the Americans. Americans, people say, the general run of them, are so desensitised by their capitalism it's just like a drug anyway. Moreover, they don't learn from irony and suffering. All they do is eat and grin and waddle about.

Not Arthur Zimmerman, it's true. He's active and anxious. But they don't send their typical people to Moscow. Only the cleverest, and the most dedicated to a cause of which my wife and I are just one tiny part.

Sasha Razumovsky surveyed the home in which he had lived quite comfortably, albeit (these days with more difficulty) up five flights of stairs, for the last quarter of century. Natasha had joined him fifteen years ago, when his first wife died. Was she only thirty then? How young she still looks! In sum, whatever happens tonight and tomorrow and next week and next month a renewed lease of life will suit me very well.

He'd made her laugh about the national shortage of raw alcohol. But good things like bananas were *defitsitny* too, she added. So were tomatoes. So was cockroach powder. Everything was in short supply, including kindness. Not to mention justice.

'By the way, did you get through just now?'

From his trouser pocket he had fished out the pile of thin grey coins he had taken to the phone box and made a perilous small stack of them on the bookshelf. 'I did. All the reporters will be there, and some diplomats.'

She was cramming things into a small bag. He saw soap and a toothbrush go in, one set each. Unpredictable but predictable, what lay ahead.

'I've put in a couple of hard-boiled eggs.' A hard-boiled egg contained enough calories to energise a suffering man for an hour. 'A bird by comparison'—more logic—'can survive two days on eighty calories,' she ascertained. 'It would be easier to be a bird, up to a point, though once one of those ruffians got hold of you—I mean, if that malign feline upstairs did make it on to the balcony…right, that's it.' She glanced in the mirror again, saw Sasha out ahead of her and locked the door of the flat.

The neighbours on all six floors registered their departure, as the infamous couple continued to bicker. But then the neighbours were dolts, dopes, nincompoops, what could they know.

'Let me carry the bag.'

'No!'

The two further dopes in the yellow Volga sprang awake just fast enough to notice a tall man in a *shapka* and a smallish woman in stout boots and muffled in layers leaving the building. They seemed old to the young policemen trained to despise them.

Natasha tossed her head in their direction, equally dismissive. 'Posing as a taxi,' she muttered. 'You're not very bright, are you?' It was already dark, and one goon had the saloon light on and was reading.

'Good that they read at least.'

'He's a dolt. He's just pretending.'

Sasha's sensitive face twitched. The guards were thugs. But still human. Somehow to be saved.

'Vels called them the Morlocks,' he said eventually. 'I suppose he agreed with you, my dear. It's the end of the human race, when people behave as they do. But it doesn't have to be like that. Vels was just writing a story.'

Vels? Howard had once scratched his head. Ah you mean H.G. Wells. The British writer had a place in the Russian canon because he was a socialist? Not at all! It was because his science-fiction was so damned useful to understand the human catastrophe that followed the first revolution. Morlocks were brutish but otherwise sheep-like people who just did what they were told.

Still Sasha was almost a Christian, in his kindness and respect for others, even for the young policemen, so he felt a qualm when he gave into such despair about the consequences of 1917 sixty years later. Vels was extreme. It's a temptation to be extreme when you write stories.

Sasha looked across at the surveillance team and wished them good evening and then he quipped to his wife: 'At least we'll get *there*, if THEY are not detaining us *here*.'

Haha. Side-splitting, she muttered. But she did smile a fraction.

Her Sasha remained optimistic about humankind. Idiot, *durak*, that he was.

But he was hers.

It was five thirty in the afternoon. For a while each retreated into deeper thoughts.

'Why are they so afraid of us? I am not afraid of them.'

Sasha Razumovsky was steeped in his optimistic hope for a great reconciliation and a new start in that moment. A longing to see Russia restored to health; a yearning for people not to be divided one against the other; that spurred him on. He even proposed that present ways could be analysed, genuinely to find a different path into the future.

Natasha snorted. 'Who wants to *study* our society, Sasha, dear! It's quite enough to live in it.'

'No, no! Darling!' His wife ought to give Russia a chance. She pecked at it like one of those birds she fed. He stopped still and drew a breath. 'Our scientific colleagues are in the forefront of the reform of our culture. We must support them. Find a way to build our community again.'

She glanced at the delicate gold watch on her wrist, which, like the red sweater, was a family heirloom. 'Don't stop like that in the middle of the pavement!' Sasha tended to stand still if he really wanted to make a point. 'And don't talk! We have to get there.

'What you have to grasp, my dear husband, professor and member of the Academy of Sciences of the USSR is that if science spells out what a mess this place is it will only make more people want to leave.'

'That's enough, Natasha! Don't talk to me like that and don't talk like that!' He had difficulty sounding angry, but now he was. Frustration, not only his weak heart, flushed his face red. He loved his country, and he loved his wife, but nothing added up and he was worried about the evening ahead.

'Only a fool would have hope,' she muttered, from under the orange glasses.

'It's not foolish at all. There's nothing to stop this country being transformed.' A streetlight shone on him.

'Come over here!' She hooked her free arm in his to shift him sideways and so they descended the wet stairs of the metro. 'That streetlamp doesn't agree with you. Now just come on. *Poekhali*!'

Heh-ho.

Below ground he felt an odd relief. He didn't say so because she would have made a miserable joke out of it.

Truth was he always loved the modern metro station at Pervomayskaya. It was modern*ist* to be exact, and he loved it because it spoke the same language as his hope for the human future. Citizens, all we need is reason and goodwill! Two lines of tall thin rectangular marble columns took the weight of the two-track tunnel. Fine square-edged porticos lined the broad platform. Good engineering and good design were part of the good future. Indeed, in the architect's clean lines lay a lovable expression of everything Sasha Razumovsky wished for in a more humane, more dignified, more efficient Russia, someday.

The stations in central Moscow were kitsch. But here was modern style indicative of 'our society's great promise.' Here, where the crude and bombastic leadership descended less often, the whole tunnel was tiled in pristine white and the people were decent and they honoured the rule of goodness and each other's dreams.

'Let me interrupt you there, nitwit! My hope is for my sister and her family, that they'll one day get to the West, like my Tatyana. Nothing to do with science or clean lines in architecture.'

'Natasha! How can you say something so trivial? How can I have married a saboteur of the greatest of human dreams? God help me, how could I?'

'I want justice for people living in *this* miserable country now. That's why…'

But someone's ears pricked at the word 'justice' and moved away from them, along the platform, and they became self-conscious.

'But you know this,' she concluded, as someone or other, another Morlock-type detailed to keep them under surveillance, finally caught up with them and made a fresh note of the target.

As already noted, but sloppily, by the policemen outside their home, the Razumovskys comprised a large man somewhat hunched, in a huge padded jacket and a Russian fur *shapka*, and a younger woman, wearing orange foreign spectacles, but otherwise conventionally dressed in thick stockings and boots, a woolly hat and a knee-length grey coat, with a flash of something colourful beneath it. They boarded a Line 3 train, and changed at Revolution Square.

Boris Marlinsky, a student of maths and philosophy, was also on his way to the meeting when something happened to him too, not predictable but not wholly unpredictable either. A man needed his help. Boris had taken his usual short-cut to the tram, past several low-rise apartment buildings, over the grass between those dwellings and the pavement. Lawn was a grand word to use in Moscow in December, but say it was a lawn, and on it lay the body of a man. He was fully clothed, but hatless and without an overcoat, as if he had wandered out by mistake, or left his outer garments somewhere. Light snowflakes settled on him as the afternoon light faded. 'God in heaven!' Marlinsky thrust his briefcase under his arm and dashed across. He held his ear to the man's chest. Almost at the same moment a woman appeared, in slippers and a floral overall.

'Dead again?' She rolled up one of the man's eyeballs.

'We're in time. Quick!'

'He's not mine,' she replied, with a lift of her nose.

Marlinsky, still young and kindly, smiled out of embarrassment. 'So where is he at home?'

'No 6.'

Marlinsky got hold of the unconscious body and with difficulty dragged it by the armpits to the lift. At least the woman propped open the door. As they stood waiting for the lift both of them stared at the trail the dragged man's feet had left behind him, as if a car had skidded on the white-flecked grass. 'Will someone be in, do you know? We can't leave him in the corridor.'

'She's given up on him. He's always plastered.'

An eye inside inspected Marlinsky, a stranger, through the keyhole.

Unpredictably the door opened. The eye must have liked what it saw. 'Comrade—'

'Yeah, yeah, in there. On the bed.'

The comatose man's eyes flickered open with the change of temperature. 'A stranger has saved your life again, Dad. You ought to be grateful.' The young woman waved towards the would-be corpse dismissively. 'He stinks. He's not worth the effort.' She turned her attention to Marlinsky, who stood there in his duffel coat and dark wool cap. He was a slender young man, of something over medium height, with dark hair and a slightly olive skin. He didn't look as if he drank, and she liked that. If this one smelt of anything it was of carbolic soap, at least not of piss. She looked Marlinsky over so blatantly as a prospect that he was once again embarrassed and declared he must be going. She pulled a face. 'See yah then. We can always do with your help at No 6.' She closed the door to her flat, as the other neighbour, she whose hands were better suited to making dumplings than peeling back the human eye, also watched him go.

In the tram Marlinsky automatically plunged into his reading. Everyone did. It was what made the tram magic. He was reading a new novel of which the title alone was impossibly bold. It was called *Journey of the Dilettantes*, and played on the closeness in sound of the imported French word 'dilettante' to the equally foreign word 'dissident'. It was published in an apparently harmless journal everyone knew, called *The Friendship of Peoples,* but it was dynamite. How had the famous author and singer dared go so far? It was perhaps the case, unpredictably, but also somewhat predictably, these days, that THEY did acknowledge the talent of this or that writer, and so let him, or her, get away with it. Maybe something was changing. Marlinsky looked out of the dirty window as the tram sped past a few straggling cars, beneath buildings with banners exhorting the people to behave well. Whatever THEY offered there were always strings attached; but when you considered what they looked away from and what they secretly envied it was possible to hope.

A Prince in the reign of Tsar Nicholas I was disappointed by his life. He was an intelligent and attractive man but he hadn't been lucky. His story of stymied courage and destroyed love, of being betrayed by his friends, and losing the few companions he loved, was gripping and bitter. Barbarism on a massive scale had crushed his soul. The novelist reached into the dreams of the least civilised tribes in the history of the world to represent the local and present nightmare Boris Marlinsky knew too well.

But then, as the tram sped down one of the city's main arteries, everyone was reading, withdrawn, absorbed into their private realities, or, with laden bags piled on their laps, they stared out of the window glass; not able to dream as vividly as the great writer Marlinsky was absorbing, but equally troubled.

Howard Wilde wasn't looking forward to the predictable outcome of this evening's event. So often his heart wanted to break in this country, out of disappointment. But he had to get out and about, and to know everything he could. He steeled himself with music in the car. Beethoven reduced him to tears, so now he listened to 'All You Need is Love'. He pictured John Paul George and Ringo on the album cover. Goodbye to the imperial past of England, with its fatuous military dressing-up! To the great conservative pantomime that masked a painful decline: rump a diddle da! Stick that up your tuba. He was better away, immersing himself in satire. He didn't like England at all. Ten minutes from home he took a right on to the Petrovka boulevard and a left at the far end. After a few hundred yards he parked.

'Is this the place?' asked Gels Maybey beside him.

Her presence still irritated him, bringing with it the fear he would lose his focus.

'Just round the corner.'

His ear flaps dangled in time with his purposive gait. She jogged a few steps to keep up. He'd had a heavy lunch, and couldn't rid himself of the lingering taste of fish and raw onion. She was witness to that discomfort too.

'Russian food can be heavy, people say.'

'The church puts on big spreads. Good food is rare here. It makes me greedy.'

'There they are,' he added. At the top end of the vast parade ground known as Pushkin Square a little crowd was forming into a horseshoe. There were about twenty protesters, although some must have been policemen. More people were still arriving.

Arthur Zimmerman, the man from *The Globe*, greeted the woman he didn't know. 'Hello, Mam.' With greater ease he patted his colleague on the shoulder and inquired what Howard had recently enjoyed.

Howard, whose garlicky midday feasting had been courtesy of the Moscow Patriarchy, backed away in anguish. 'Carp in aspic and hot mushrooms in cream…'

'The Synod made you welcome then.' And, reverting to Gels, 'And this is?'

'Angela. People call me Gels.' She was dressed fashionably like an English 'mod' of the day, in a long green army parka, and a fur hat from the Moscow foreigners' shop. To Zimmerman who was in his forties she looked barely out of her teens.

'Good to meet you, Angela. Here for a holiday? In December?' The American, dark, rough-shaven, had a worried, purposeful face and seemed to find it hard to joke, though he wanted to.

35

'I'm told Russia is the place to be. That it's destroying itself for something new and better to emerge. But what's the Synod?'

'Wow.' Her question was ignored. 'Gels is staying with me. Her father—'

'My father is Howard's boss. It's a pain for both of us. By the way most people do call me Gels.'

'Gels it is. You must meet my wife Harriet.'

Men, she thought, are very keen to pass you on to their wives, if they have no personal need of you. 'Great. I'm keen to watch what happens here tonight. But do tell me what the Synod is, one of you.'

But Arthur wanted to confer with Howard, so I left them.

They talked about the point of Howard's lunch, which had been contact with the church high-ups. The Synod was the Politburo of the Russian Orthodox Church. Arthur pictured the obese Russian clergy, their bulging bellies in their scruffy black cassocks, and the plastic shoes their long robes couldn't hide. Of course they had white and gold robes to dress up in when they bestrode their magnificent painted and gilded churches, on gala occasions, but they were a shabby bunch outside.

'A story about ever more churches closing, about the horrors of a truly atheist state,' Howard explained. 'They wanted to tell me more churches are closing now than…in the worst times. On the other hand why come up with this report today of all days? I haven't sent it to London yet…because I fear it's a deliberate distraction. I might just hang on to it for a few days. Depends what happens tonight.'

'I'd better look at it all the same. Send it over?'

'Of course. It's all yours when I write it.' The Moscow reporters had a habit of sharing their reports home, whether they were true discoveries or distractions of government origin, like this one. To discern the truth of what was going on was just too difficult for Howard and Arthur to have to compete with each other in addition.

'You've got a good contact among the priests, I suppose?'

'Father Sergei. Somehow I like him.' It was the priest's sad brown eyes that did it. 'Even if I don't trust him.'

'That's what makes us tragic heroes, that we can't trust anyone here. We want the best but we're cursed by the gods. We can't totally trust anyone. We wander about half-blinded.'

(They were tragic. Russia was tragic. What was this country, and our situation within it?)

'On the road from Thebes to Delphi? On The Mozhaisk Road.'

'I trust Razumovsky. He's my one hope.'

Arthur conceded the uniqueness of Razumovsky. Howard tasted fish again. '*This* meeting is the big one. They're just trying to confuse us with that statistic about churches closing.'

'We will not be moved!' Arthur vowed to give tonight's story all he could.

To that end every few minutes his eyes swept the square like searchlights. 'Heh isn't that that mathematician Charodarsky?'

'Dargomyshsky.' Howard too was alert, as Gels, sidelined from the conversation, watched him.

'Where do I know him from?'

'Out at the Razumovskys.'

'I remember. He's the heir they don't want.' Arthur gave a little wave to Gels and moved off. She lifted her curled fingers in response, inside her gloves. Howard glanced out again at the vast square, fringed by birch trees. It was named after the poet whose mighty statue gave it a presence in the darkness. It was a barely disguised military facility of old, but by night Pushkin came out to inspire events like this.

Gels followed Howard's eye. 'I like the lamps.'

'Kitsch,' he said. But to Gels they were traditional, four-sided street lights gently tapered in wrought iron, and faintly they invited passers-by to imagine a more beautiful world. She said so and insisted:

'I can't see what's wrong with that. All the drab places you've taken me to so far. So far, it's all been nasty functional buildings and propaganda banners and traffic fumes.'

'You're not blighted by bourgeois middle-class taste, are you, Gels Maybey? I thought you wanted the real Russia.'

'Am I blighted? Goodness! Something of the real Russia I wouldn't mind.'

'The real Russia!' he scoffed, unrelenting. 'Over the counter, would that be? Done up in gift-wrapping? It's not a commodity for your salvation, you know.'

He liked to trip me up and there was sometimes an anger in him that seemed to me to come from nowhere. So, not to have intimated any of that, I stood as if chastened, hoping to restore the possibility of normal conversation between us.

The milling 'Friends of Human Rights' had spread out a banner with their cause on it but I watched the figures themselves. 'Who's that young one?' I cried. 'Is he one of THEM? I saw him offer Razumovsky his hand just now.'

'His name is Boris Marlinsky. He joined recently, with his friend Aleksei Gerasimov. Gerasimov's the taller one.'

'And they're *dissidents*?'

He hated my naïve questions. I protested I had to start somewhere. I was acting a little to make him talk.

'So yes, they think differently and that's not allowed. It turns them into anti-government protesters.' Howard sounded painfully didactic, even to himself. We had fallen silent when a rather formal but passionately informative English voice sounded out of the darkness.

> We're standing in the most important public meeting-place in Moscow on the occasion of an historic unofficial gathering under the statue of the greatest poet. I have to say, Joanne, that it's very odd that there are no *uniformed* police in sight. The authorities can't let something like this happen without policing it.

Someone close by was doing voice to camera addressing Joanne in the studio.

'Patrick from the BBC,' Howard said.

'Oh but he's famous.'

'He'd be pleased to hear you say that.'

With a light touch on the shoulder of her parka Howard excused himself. 'It's the US ambassador. He's someone almost as important as your father. I must go over and say hello.'

'Do leave my father out of it!'

He left her to mill about. Actually she admired his resistance. He seemed the rebel who wasn't quite sure of his cause, so he hit out here and there, mostly at middle-class life back home and at her, as if she were part of it. That was the impression she formed.

Now she was alone again for a moment she noticed how the bundled-up protesters were silhouetted against the tall thin leafless trees, to the soundtrack of an occasional passing tram. Mesmerising. But then whenever she had gone out in Moscow so far she had been astonished. Day or night there was almost no human sound on the streets and never a smell of food and drink, because there were no cafés and no shops of the kind where you would browse and linger. You weren't allowed to show appetite or temperament or mood in this country. You weren't allowed to have appetite in any real, deep sense, such as might hunger to keep you alive. Moods were inadmissible because they too expressed longings and fantasies and were, in the end, personal and ungovernable, so it was absolutely forbidden to have clubs and restaurants and films and theatre that might correspond to those secret moods. Amazing. As if all the bees had been packed back inside Pandora's Box, five thousand years after Greek mythology had said such a human feat was impossible.

But, here suddenly, at a legal-illegal demonstration, some desire for something, some unusual feeling, was cautiously emerging. Russia had come to a crossroads, and she had come to see it happen, because she wanted to know what things mattered.

'Hello again!' Arthur passed, notebook in hand, as she stationed herself under one of the bijou lamps and felt for the notebook in her own pocket.

The small man over there was indeed the American ambassador, Arthur confirmed. 'Hard-liner, served here before. Hates the Soviets.' The hard-liner's face was muffled by a red scarf and his head was buried in an astrakhan hat rather like the *militsioner*'s outside their compound, but he looked very elegant in a dark, fitted wool coat. The best-dressed man in the whole of Russia, in that moment. Truly a visiting foreign dignitary. Beside him stood his Italian counterpart. Arthur said politically they were chalk and cheese, the Italian almost a Communist. 'Of their Italian kind.'

'Mr Ambassador! Cavaliere!' Howard addressed them. Howard had received a good education, Gels decided, while feeling shy of the American whose name was Heffernan and awarding the Italian the descriptions 'plump', 'untidy' and 'probably quite nice.'

Half-listening to the ambassador's lament about the new Democratic administration in the US, and the Cavaliere's own lilting tale about a European country, *his* country, beset by terrorism on all sides, from the Left, from the Right, revolutionaries and fascists, his own bel*ar*-ved *I*taly, the anguish of it, not knowing how to pull itself out of its Fascist past, Russia was peaceful by comparison, Gels kept looking around. Take away the few cars passing on the far rim of the square, and the clank of the trams, and you could believe yourself in the nineteenth century, with Tolstoy occasionally visiting the Asiatic Russian capital from his country estate.

(Tolstoy mostly travelled by train, I knew.)

Arthur Zimmerman said to Ambassador Heffernan: 'Look at this demonstration, Sir! I hope the President will take heart.'

'I'm not counting on it,' muttered the depressed envoy. 'My new president who loves the whole world is a *hippy,* for Christ's sake! He's also a socialist at heart who thinks the government here is humane and progressive. He's got it completely wrong. Off the record, of course.'

Zimmerman shrugged. 'It's the problem of anyone decent across the world, Sir. They fall for Soviet propaganda.'

'You must be a Democrat, Mr Zimmerman, to be so indulgent. The President of the United States needs to know what this place is really about. Please tell him the truth!'

'I'll remind him Russia can never be a good place with these old men in power.'

The envoy's inscrutable eyes flickered.

Seeing the portly Italian had disappeared, Arthur began afresh: 'But Ambassador Russolo's a sympathiser. So how do you two get on, Sir, if I may?' The ambassador unwound the red scarf and laughed. 'We're diplomats. *Pok-ah,* Arthur.' It was the Russian word for ciao.

Ciao. *Pok-ah.* The world is in a mess but we can't solve it tonight.

By day—and I had read every propaganda sign in Moscow I had found—the avowal that terrified me most was that THE PARTY IS THE MIND, THE HEART AND THE CONSCIENCE OF THE PEOPLE. So now quite rightly and never soon enough the dissidents were contesting the truth of that ridiculous claim to authority over the Russian people. Propaganda was designed to make sheep of the Russian people. It existed to make them conform to one flock. But that was an outrage. They had their own minds and their own conscience.

One of the dissidents, I thought Howard had said that one's name was Marlinsky, was now telling the crowd this country had a great future. He spoke through a megaphone and I understood his Russian quite clearly. That a different human coinage needed to be created. A precious metal, not a debased alloy. The human soul was worth more than *dvushki. Dvushki* were the near-weightless little grey coins that ended up in your pocket if you ever used the public telephone: halfpennies; dimes. Right. That's exactly it.

As, having spoken, the young man moved back closer to the group, holding his torch at an angle to the ground. Gels hurried over to listen in where she could. A middle-aged woman in green with stunning auburn hair softly framing her face, from beneath a grey hat, greeted him. 'Boris Mikhailovich,' she began, 'This is my friend Anna Lunina. Anna, this is Boris Marlinsky and his friend— my nephew—Aleksei Gerasimov.'

'How do you do?'

The woman in green was Galya Obolenskaya and she was a famous translator of Dickens into Russian, for everyone loved the novels of Charles Dickens. She was also Gerasimov's aunt and Anna Lunina's old friend from university.

'Aleksei Igorevich, have we met before?' asked Lunina of the handsome, broad-shouldered nephew.

'Probably not. I usually stay beneath the radar.'

'That sounds like a waste. May there be many more times, dear friend.' Galya noticed the attraction jealously. She felt it herself even though it was her nephew.

Women always fell for Gerasimov. Wordlessly, without an introduction, Gels also shared this appraisal of a very attractive man and his dark, good-looking, sweet-tempered friend in the duffel coat and black cap who seemed a little unworldly.

As Razumovsky now finally produced the paper he was going to read from someone hushed the group again; someone else clapped hands, and the crowd paid attention again. Coming up was the most important performance of the evening.

'Dear friendth, we are gathered here today...' the world-famous dissident began, with the characteristic lisp.

Howard, in the crowd, felt Pushkin, high above, shift his declamatory pose and harken. You couldn't still call yourself a human being if you didn't listen tonight.

'Hell, I can never properly understand him,' muttered Arthur. 'I'll need a transcript.'

To Gels the protesters looked like Carol Singers. They were like persecuted Christians in the last days of the Roman Empire, though the date was Christmas 1978.

Howard appearing beside Gels had also got the impression of Carol Singers. 'Why do we think that?' she asked.

'Because we're Brits and we like Christmas. The dissidents are an especially good story at Christmas. Nothing the Soviets can do about that.'

'A new star appeared in the sky. Nothing would ever be the same again.' He sounded astonished.

'But you're an atheist!'

'For me it's the words. *When they saw the star, they rejoiced with exceeding great joy.*'

What could he say other than: 'By the way, aren't you cold?'

'Not tonight.'

She conceded an army surplus parka was more fashionable in London than suitable for Moscow in winter. But this evening not snow but sleet had started to fall and as it turned to rain it dripped from Pushkin's African curls. She wasn't cold at all.

Razumovsky concluded: 'We are here to draw the attention of the world to...We appeal to President James Earl Carter, and the United Nations, and all the decent people of the free world...help us!'

Howard cast up a hand at the harkening poet.

She cried: 'But what are you—I mean we—going to *do*?'

'I will report *exactly* what has just been said and describe this whole occasion. So will Arthur. So will Patrick. It will go out on the BBC World Service on the hour. Soviet dissident Alexander Razumovsky said: "We appeal to President Carter and the United Nations and all the decent people of the world." Everything will be documented.'

'And how will the world respond?'

'Feel bad. Not much else they can do.'

And the second revolution, I wondered. Perhaps it was in the hands of on those two young men. I walked around to stand closer again to the protesters.

Natasha Razumovsky was talking now. 'We are here to draw attention to...and there is the case of the poet Shaginyan...and of the student Anna Prishvina...and the misuse of the psychiatric hospitals...as well as the misuse of the law that is supposed to govern our country. Where are our human rights? *Gdye nashi gumanicheskie prava...*'

But that was the phrase that set the other side off. Suddenly the people Howard called Korsakov's men had had enough of this STUNT. It was as if the wind had suddenly gone round. THEY had a phrase of their own. *Tryukov khvatit*! Enough of these STUNTS!

Howard watched in anxiety and contempt as the round-up began. Here come Pavlov's bloody dogs!

'Impossible! How can...' Gels began. 'Tell me, Howard...' But he wasn't there to be her teacher. He had his work cut out.

Two official black cars arrived, with a 'Black Maria' van close behind. The Soviet cars were black Fords with flashy wings and lots of chrome, refashioned on licence in Russia.

(Maybe not give the Soviets the blueprint for Western cars, if their politics are so cruel?)

Howard kept his eyes everywhere. The riot squad didn't use guns, but they were rough.

Natasha Razumovsky was rough back. 'Move your meddling mitts, Comrade! Put your paws where they belong! Up yours, you brutes!' Razumovsky, even as he was being lifted bodily into a van marked 'People', blenched at his wife's ferocity. '*Natasha, ne nado...*'

'Numbskulls! Nitwit nobodies! Can't you see this country has no freedom!'

'Shut it, granny, or else.'

With one car ahead and one behind the van drove off in a convoy.

Howard counted six minutes. As the Westerners rallied, a handsome Danish TV journalist, his flowing golden locks squashed under a French beret, complained he had had his camera blocked. Someone asked what the Communist journalists would report. 'Polly, heh Polly...' Howard had caught sight of Apollinaria Montenari, correspondent of *L'Unità*, close to her ambassador. But by now she had vanished. Generally the Euro-Communists kept a low profile.

'The European Communists can't write up protests. They have to be super-subtle.'

'They have it on their conscience,' said Arthur.

'It's difficult for them. They want to keep a foot in the door. Who knows, we might be grateful for their contacts one day.'

But then everyone knew Howard had a 'thing' with Polly and even Gels would find out soon.

Howard ran towards where he had left the car. He wanted to tail the convoy. He wasn't fit. He sweated under his gargantuan sheepskin and that bloody fish kept repeating on him. 'Which way?' He yelled to Arthur, passing him again with the driver's window down.

'Left onto the Ring.'

Gels watched the red MG speed off. Mentally she clapped.

Howard got lucky following his colleague's vague gesture. Over the river and on to the Leningradskoe Shaussay he had the convoy in sight. The city like this thrilled him, his role in its strange life. In the dark the long empty boulevards yawned. He could race through their space. Lighted windows in the older apartment blocks made you think people up there were even living well, having a good evening, with music, and wine, making love. No one looked out. Maybe they were already in the throes of passion. Still it was true even if he had spun off the road and his engine had exploded they would have pretended to hear and see nothing of a foreign car travelling at speed about eight o'clock at night. The foreigner was definitely alone heading out of town in pursuit of a KGB posse that had arrested his dissident friends. The police, the political police, he would explain to his readers, were driving the protesters somewhere unknown, to do God knows what to them. He felt strong, with the whole decent world behind him, and he felt excited. Had he not had this job to do he would have been one of the ardent lovers, six flights up, with the lights replaced by candles and the body of his woman taut and soft beneath his hands. Polly, dear Polly, he was never together with her often enough, because she was so busy, or she didn't feel like it, or she couldn't make it tonight. So he waited, and hoped. So his ardour expressed itself in driving the MG, a lightweight, zippy little car, the best of post-war England, something he could love unreservedly, and he raced it now and felt its throbbing content at being free to run.

With the tail lights of the second Ford now in sight, he slowed a touch and began to write his story in his head. 'Russian plain-clothes police tonight broke up a dissident meeting and drove away prominent figures including Alexander and Natalya Razumovsky in a police van. They took them...'

Sirens screamed and blue lights flashed behind him. And then in front. He stopped, cut the engine and sighed. Bastards. His heart was thumping and his engine was hot with exhaustion.

It was the GAI road police who boxed him in. As he watched its representative approach, through his rear-view mirror, he mouthed the full title of the State Road Inspection Service. 'Not doing a service to me,' he muttered. He lit a cigarette and watched in his mirror.

A bloody conspicuous car, Arthur said. Indeed! Howard agreed. A visitor from outer space! 'But then maybe they won't touch me. Maybe people will watch from their windows, from the bus stop, in the end. They know people have cars like this in the West, and it makes your ordinary Russian curious, and envious, and if they happen to be policemen they can easily forget that their job is to reinforce the law. Why not? You can manipulate them a bit.' It was a definite advantage to being a Westerner to drive a car like this and you needed all the advantages you could muster.

The cop now level with his window was a flabby titan of a man from the waist up; of a size and unfitness that only the overfed clergy could match. The MG Midget—basically a cockpit taken from a wartime Spitfire bomber and stuck on to a saloon car chassis—couldn't have accommodated this bastard. He would have had to rape her, to take possession.

The *militsioner* delivered a message into a walkie-talkie as he approached, and then leant in to Howard and spoke to him surprisingly politely.

'Your rear offside wheel is loose, Sir.'

'You stopped me to tell me that? Bollocks. That's bollocks what you're telling me.'

The policeman, a real one now, not a goon, in the face of Howard's hostility reneged on his politeness and regressed to a grunt and a lifting of the chin and a narrowing of the eyes. He gestured and frowned. 'Really, you don't believe me? Get out and have a look!'

Rule number one. Don't get out of the car. Bastard. But Howard did get out, and the policeman stepped back and pointed knowingly.

Howard exhaled into the night air. I know which is my rear offside wheel, thank you. 'Can't be,' he said, for it was like giving evidence in court whenever you talked to those kind of people. You kept it as brief and unforthcoming as you could.

Occasionally another car passed on the sleeted road.

Now the policeman got down to business. 'Heading out of town, Comrade? Why would that be?' Howard imagined the questions that would have been asked of so-called ordinary citizens. Why would anyone have a good reason to head 'out of town' at eight in the evening in mid-December 1978? There was, strictly speaking, no out of town, just the end of Moscow, then emptiness. No wayside inns, no AA lanterns, no signs to country pubs. This wasn't England. The Soviets weren't bad at cities, but they didn't do countryside. Something to do with the ideology, that.

The GAI man's blue lamp winked, but still no one came to a window above them along the boulevard. Had this been an act of murder no one would have looked out at Howard Wilde's screams; or they would have looked out, and turned away again.

A crudely fancy watch spanned the mottled flesh outside the tight cuffs of his uniform jacket. As if he'd snapped himself into a single handcuff. There were military epaulettes on his broad shoulders. Built like a brick shithouse was the phrase that came to mind. With pips on his downpipes. Shining his torch into the interior of the Midget, the policeman inspected it with greedy boyish eyes.

Having calmed down, Howard took pride in the car. The policeman marvelled: 'It's a real old-timer! Look at that leather! Feel that polished wood! Phouar! They say our president has a secret collection of Western old-timers. A Jaguar, a Mercedes, a Lancia. Good for our president! Give our country the prestige it deserves. But he has nothing as sexy as this.'

(The car as a trophy wife.)

'You shouldn't have stopped me, Mr Policeman. If they hurt one hair on Alexander Razumovsky's head tonight I'll kill you with my own bare hands.'

The policeman made a clumsy job of not recognising the name. 'You have our assurance, Sir, that there is something wrong with your vehicle. We don't want you to come to harm in our country.'

Howard swore and slipped back into the driving seat.

The policeman laughed. 'Just drive home, Sir, and do the right thing.' He tapped the wing of the Midget. Meanwhile Howard, in fact faintly afraid, began to drop his guard within as he turned the key in the ignition, and everything he felt and had suppressed rushed to the surface. He hated every officious, semi-polite lying word. He wished he didn't understand Russian, not for these ugly sounds to mean anything. 'It's Christmas, you know, very soon. That means something where I come from.' But that was a stupid thing to say. He was weak, weak up against Leviathan, and sweaty and he had no force left in him.

'No need for reinforcement. It's only a religious lunatic,' the policeman explained into the walkie-talkie.

'No I'm not, I'm fucking not religious!' Howard did a furious U-turn, tyres screaming. 'Religious' apparently came from mentioning Christmas.

A song called 'Staying Alive' helped the wounded Moscow correspondent of the London Global News (LGN) make it back into town. *Stayin alive. Stayin alive. Life goin nowhere. Somebody help me. Somebody help me, yeah. Life goin nowhere. Somebody help me, yeah. I'm stayin alive.* He protested and rebelled for twenty minutes, until he arrived back at the so-called compound where he lived; where he allegedly led a life, and where Gels Maybey, roving daughter of his newspaper's proprietor, had been billeted upon him. Fuck there's nowhere to park. No spaces left inside the arch. He found one outside, on the street, and trudged up the stairs home.

Inside the unmarked van Natasha wiped the goon's fingerprints from her spectacles. 'Now then, my friends: "We Shall Overcome."'

The detainees filled their lungs with air and it lifted their spirits.

'What is this song they are singing?' asked the Major. 'It sounds like one of our Russian ballads.'

'Maybe because it's Christmas,' said the young driver.

The goons were three, squeezed into a cab for two. Eight more policemen accompanied them in the two squad cars, but the Major wanted to be immediately on hand, given his cargo.

'The American black men sing it, against their exploitation by the white men,' continued the official adviser between the Major and his over-eager driver.

'Ah!'

'They really are scum. Just before Christmas too.'

'What's Christmas got to do with it? That's the second time you've mentioned it.'

'Nothing, Comrade. I just thought—'

'Well, don't! Drive slowly. Our parasites are going for a night outing.' The Major couldn't silence a song like that. But who could hear it anyway, out here beyond the city limits. Eventually they'd get tired. What he was engaged in reminded the Major of his wife taking the baby out in the pram, round and round the block, when it wouldn't stop crying. Eventually, it would.

'If there's an interrogation deny everything. Then they've got nothing to work with.' Back inside the van the mathematician Dargomyshsky, a big energetic man, was telling the assembled company seated on benches how to handle questions. Compared with the gentle Razumovsky he was the furious type.

'Natasha and I have had some practice before, my friend. But there won't be an interrogation. This is just a rerouting of our excursion.'

'Nothing is predictable.'

'But there are some things we know, out of long experience, you see?' insisted Natasha, before turning to her husband who was hot and uncomfortable. With a bottle of water from her supplies she mopped his brow.

'Habeas corpus. It's not legal,' observed Galya Obolenskaya, her lovely green eyes flaring as Gerasimov lit a cigarette.

'One crime among many.'

'What the Decembrists asked Nicholas I for we still haven't got,' said the slight brunette, Lunina.

She mentioned it because the years that had passed since 1825 were the real anniversary, the one that mattered to them. For they were all in their way historians, trying to keep track of what had happened to their country, which otherwise lived in a severely edited version of its past. A hundred and seventy-two…no three….

'De facto we have the legal constitution our forefathers asked for.'

'De iure we haven't.'

'Why are we speaking Latin?'

'Because THEY have even commandeered our Russian language.'

'Pushkin didn't give in.'

'All the same, we can't change Russia with poems.'

'With love we can. "Perfect love casts out fear." John's Gospel chapter four verse eighteen.' That was Dargomyshsky again, reaching for authority.

Sasha Razumovsky sighed. 'Don't go religious on us, Myshii. Love can perfectly well stand on its own two feet.'

'Doesn't mean to say the gospels aren't true, my friend, and that if we are not afraid that must be a great problem for our masters.'

The second part of that statement was true, but the first part? Hell. Razumovsky hoped that, if he died, when he died, Dargomyshsky would not be his successor, because he, Alexander Razumovsky, was a man of the Enlightenment who hoped for a rational good future for his country, even now; whereas Dargomyshsky was a mystagogue.

'When I die,' began the ailing scientist.

'Stop talking nonsense,' shrieked Natasha beside him. 'It's shameful. Far too much is expected of you. It's terrible.' And then, after a pause for breath, she yelled, just in case he could hear. 'Up yours, Major! For doing this to an ill man.'

'So this is scientific socialism,' proclaimed Galya, after a particularly vicious bump in the road. Everyone laughed except Razumovsky who only smiled.

'You know what I think,' Razumovsky said. 'There have been mistakes. But they can be corrected.'

'This is where you are absolutely wrong,' boomed the tireless Dargomyshsky. 'How can you, Alexander Nikolaevich, be an optimist after all this?'

'Reason is the short answer, Myshii, and I won't be giving you a long one this evening.'

They sang, and they sat in silence, and the van rocked them from side to side.

'What time is it?'

'Just after eleven.'

'They're waiting till public transport stops. Then they'll let us out to find our difficult ways home.'

'It's hot in here.'

'Sasha, take another pill.'

Natasha hammered on the side of the van.

Eventually it stopped and the back opened a crack. 'What, woman?' A policeman jerked his chin in her direction. She could see two militia cars parked behind the van.

'You'll kill him. Is that what you want? Think what THEY' ll do to you if you embarrass THEM like that. The whole world will say *you* killed him.'

The policeman sucked savagely on his cigarette before tossing it away. 'And so?'

'Let us out.'

'Not yet.'

'Leave the door open so we can breathe then.'

'*Ladno.*'

The fresh damp air seeped into the cramped space.

Half an hour later, the van started up again. It stopped, and one was released. Then it travelled again, and another was freed. All in different places on the perimeter of the city.

They forced Natasha out before her husband, despite her vocal protests, and his too. 'No, no, you leave her alone, comrades. She is my wife. Where she goes I go. Let me out too!' He struggled to raise his voice as they slammed the door shut again. 'Let me out too! I want to be with my wife.' He slumped back. 'This isn't kind, comrades.'

'Kind? Are you barmy, Comrade Professor? Our orders are to treat you as scum.'

Razumovsky took a deep breath and closed his eyes.

He heard her call to him: 'Don't worry, Sasha, I'm wearing my lucky sweater, remember? Red for luck. My mother survived.' He covered his eyes with his hands. The tears that trickled down his tired face touched even the guard.

'Don't worry grandpa, she's just going for a walk.'

Razumovsky shook his head. Galya put a hand on his knee and tried herself to reassure him. He apologised for his weak moment.

'Like Hecuba mourning her son Hector,' Galya said. 'Tears are allowed. Everyone remembers Hecuba's tears. The finest tears in world literature.'

'My wife is not dead.'

'No. I didn't mean that.'

Even as her fellow protesters were being unloaded in different parts of the city, Natasha, very much alive, hailed a lift from a passer-by. Climbing in she did a rare thing for her and lied. Instead of trying to convert the Latvian driver, who was a Party member, to the dissident cause, she pretended she had been visiting a sick auntie and had missed the last bus. She was perfectly plausible; vivacious even; she ought to be careful with strange men. Razumovsky, now fully himself again, stopped a Volga taxi, and had it drive him to within a few streets of Pervomayskaya.

Howard opened his office to file a brief report along the lines he had outlined to Gels a few hours before: Moscow, December 14, 1978—Soviet dissident Alexander Razumovsky said tonight: "We appeal to President Carter and the United Nations and all the decent people of the world...." and then went upstairs to bed, waiting to be woken. Which happened, predictably, when the phone beside the bed rang just after 2am.

'Are you sure you're both all right?'

'Never better. Things are always good with us.'

Howard chuckled. 'You're indomitable. So I wish you a good night and thank you, Alexander Nikolaevich, for ringing.'

He went back to the office and searched the Russian wire for what had to be the counter-statement, put out by the official news agency, and so he put his second story of the night together, with the date of a new day.

> Moscow – The Communist Party today defended the Soviet Union's record on human rights, accusing the United States, Britain and other Western countries of abuses of the 1948 Human Rights Charter.

> The statement followed the traditional 14 December demonstration by human rights activists in Moscow's Pushkin Square to mark the anniversary of the Charter.

> About twenty protesters, among them Professor Alexander Razumovsky, the veteran campaigner against Soviet psychiatric abuse,

were removed by security police and detained for several hours shortly after they appeared in the central square.

The Soviet commentary attacked the United States, accusing the administration of suppressing individuals and groups opposed to its policies. It said security police in the United States persecuted ordinary people and that the punishment handed down to dissenters included solitary confinement, hard labour and routine deprivation of 'necessary human emotional and physical comforts.'

And so on and so on. He could have gone on writing for another fifteen minutes, but there was a limit to how many words London would accept. He signed off. Howard Wilde. Moscow.

I watched him sitting at the teleprinter in his pyjamas, drinking whisky, by the smell of it. The teleprinter was in the miserable hovel that was the back room of the office, and his drink in a coffee mug was perched perilously on a stool drawn up beside.

'Everything ok?'

'Never better.' He waved his drink at me, offering and not. Someone give you a lift back?'

'Harriet Zimmerman.'

'Good. Good for Harriet. Better get some sleep now.'

'Sweet dreams, Howard. And thanks for taking me along.'

Two

Howard Wilde had to decide whether Russia was a profound truth or a contemptible farce. Or I presumed that was the question. There was no time for a guest.

So I took time to acquaint myself with the long thin flat set that LGN, my father's company, offered those who did manage, on some pretext or other, to make their way to Moscow. The intention was evidently to disappoint, even to repel, as if LGN agreed with the authorities here. But that couldn't be right. I had simply entered an area of neglect. In the bare living room where it seemed only rarely a visitor had ever stayed, the décor was a desert. Now, everyone who has arrived to live in such a space must think of themselves, and use that self to make it warmer and kinder.

In that space, every morning, I stretched my arms, torso and legs. If you want to put your life together and achieve your goal, make sure you exercise. Holding for a count of fifty, I felt enabled. I recalled my time in Lithuania, the little country that is an innocent participant in this story. Compelled to be Russia's friendly neighbour—indeed I knew it only as 'Russia'—it became my launch pad. My university, a very good one, I must admit, despatched us abroad brooking no objection. No linguistic workout with native speakers, no degree. Looking back I suppose I think how magnificent it was that our universities in those days hurled us into contemporary history. University told me to grow up and get out there. Someone had to tell me. The stringent syllabus led me to two men. One was Johannes who lived with his large dog in a small flat. The other was the director of the Institute who presumably had such good contacts in Moscow that he was able to set up such a lucrative foreign-language business in his much more romantic, much more Western outpost. My men, I say. My men don't usually don't become my lovers. Johannes was an exception.

My room in LGN's Moscow guest flat had nothing Russian about it. The furniture comprised a Scandinavian table made of birch, and four stick-backed chairs, each with its own bright yellow cushion. Along with the sofa it had all been pushed back by some cleaner onto the periphery, as if to make way for an event in the church hall. Even when I rearranged it more to my taste the selection spoke out the pages of a catalogue. I would have cleared it all out and started again. But then I wasn't in Moscow to hone my skills as an interior designer.

The walls were white and covered up the only history that would have grounded the place at all. (I wonder if that's why people so often paint their walls white, not to have a past.) I had this strange passion for Russian history: a feeling that I myself must put it right. I might start with the archaeology of those walls. I ran my hands over those cool blank surfaces looking out over the car park, and all along the dark corridor on the internal side of the flat. My hands and legs stretched out like a clockface, it was as if I were looking for the entrance to a secret passage. I didn't expect to hear the sea through a sea-shell but somehow to feel the reverberations of time in a building that at its heart was untouched from before 1917. Before the Revolution wealthy merchants had these apartments built. After the upheaval, when they were chased out, or reduced to poverty, their only trace remained somewhere among these stones, covered with masonry a century old, and now in a box carved out of the whole, called an apartment, providing a Russian roof over my English head.

I sat on the modern sofa superimposed upon a lost room, in a lost building. Upholstered in dark turquoise, the sofa had the same would-this-suit-a new-way-of-living question about it as the matchstick chairs. Like Russia in 1917 the West belatedly and excitedly asked that question between the wars: in films, in books, in architecture, in furniture. The choice I had inherited from circa 1975 was smart, expensive even, still echoing that futuristic dream. But still, as the dream became industrialised and flattened out, the whole room looked as if its contents had been ordered by the teleprinter at the back of Howard's office. It was no one's particular taste nowadays. It could have been a safe house for spies, or an investment no one lived in. I wanted my life to be peculiar to me and not all flattened out like that .

And so I became one of the Westerners lodged passingly in the city that became the Soviet Russian capital, sixty-one years after the Revolution, trying to understand where history had arrived and what had disappeared. An image of a pyjama-clad Howard at the great iron writing machine, at midnight, with a triple whisky in his coffee mug, made me feel an instant affinity for him. He was writing the story down. He was our leader and would be my inspiration.

I moved to the kitchen. All the rooms except the bathroom led off the left-hand side of the corridor, like a train carriage. In the T-shaped kitchen at the end I filled an enamel kettle with water from the vast white porcelain sink and set it on the stove. Something had changed since 1917 but not much. Johannes the museum-keeper in a city on the far Western edge of the Soviet empire would have washed his dog Buster in the nineteenth-century rustical sink while pondering what makes human beings stop wanting to live. Countries too, Johannes had told me, could develop a death wish. Russia after its Revolution failed had that wish, he said. Curse their Russian souls for inflicting their failures on us.

(Did I say? Johannes had converted his flat into a Museum of Suicide.)

Pouring the boiling water over a filter cone full of freshly ground beans—at last a use for the electricity—I wondered what kind of man was LGN's man in Moscow, for having taken on the job I admired, the huge task behind it. The scrubby light brownish hair and reddish face I've mentioned. But what can they convey of a man's soul. Whoever he was on the inside, to my eyes he was tallish, and had an educated manner. He made a good but anti-social impression. He was mightily abrasive and unfinished.

I guessed he was not inclined to be part of 'the system', any more than I was, and that was why he was so irritated to find that it had sucked him in nevertheless. In those days 'the system' was how the world worked. My father was 'system' if anyone ever was. Papa was Establishment. Even more than that he was Power. Howard disdained those privileges. A journalist quite deep into his soul, he felt his task was not to have privileges but to witness them. Reporters see true things on all our behalf and for that some of them pay by living on the margins. Either they choose to be down-and-out or their nerves give way. But then, as I myself know, self-relegation is painful, so, if you have the choice, you might be tempted to give in. That was my account of the mystery of Howard Wilde for the time being.

You see how instantly interested in him I was. (And the homework I'd done in London told me he might just accept me.) He gave off an air of always and only ever doing things on his own terms. Which is why he minded my presence, but not entirely, and he would get used to it, I reassured myself.

Howard Wilde, aged 35 when I met him, was resisting and continuing 'the system' at the same time and it was pulling him apart. The system for him was my father, and of that I was a constant reminder. I only hoped he would notice the same irritant was at work in me.

'I don't think about it,' Howard Wilde claimed pathetically, when I asked him the question head-on where he belonged. 'I just get on with the job.' But then he could always impress me if he stated that the job was to report on the coming of the second revolution.

I teased him. What if it doesn't come. He shook his head and waved me away.

What might make it happen? What might stop it? Capitalism had triumphed in the West, against Russia's claim that it had invented an alternative. That set up the fundamental contest. Which way is better? How many lives are improved because people are better educated and better housed with social help, instead of having to compete all the time to make money? Make up your mind. Read the statistics. I know. There's no way of deciding. So your choice will be a leap of faith. Either Russia is the world's greatest present danger to our Western way of life, or it is the best humanitarian hope in our universe. The point is you can't measure happiness, which is at the heart of things. I guess if you're not happy in the West, if you can't find your place, your options may well tend eastwards. But then most people are not thinking about things like that. They want a house, a job, a partner, a car, and food on the table and they don't mind being flattened out. But I did, and I knew Howard did too.

The Russian dream had a power over me through my reading. Tolstoy and Dostoevsky, Dostoy as we students said, made the West look trivial. What was the point of being so materialistic? We should open our hearts and change our minds.

So it was a shock when Johannes had added a third option for thinking about Russia. What if its twentieth-century incarnation was a mistake? What if it was killing itself? Then Howard and I were destroying ourselves too.

The LGN flat had one small bedroom at the far end from the kitchen opposite the front door. It just accommodated a high-off-the-ground, old-fashioned double bed with a varnished dark oak headboard. When I felt miserable that dark, heavy furniture anchored my existence, because it made me think about the big questions which bedevilled me. Even while I wondered about the empty space beside me; the second pillow that no head dented; even while I explored the unoccupied space that allowed my legs to touch both sides of the mattress, I went on thinking of the hope Russia held out. Depression too is a kind of anchor. At university I'd been writing about a German philosopher called Schopenhauer and about Tolstoy. One was a pessimist and the other an optimist. It was obvious which one I was.

I admired great literature and I had faith in the power of the Russian word. Literature was the last defence against homogeneity, falsehood and evil. I'd even brought it with me into my temporary lodging here, on the edge of history. In the small suitcase I brought by hand to Moscow copies of banned Russian books filled the space between jeans and t-shirts and sweaters like a layer cake. I hoped to give them away. Meanwhile they would live in the suitcase pushed under the bed. Like Bibles! It was as if I were preparing to distribute contraband Bibles in the land of their origin.

The books were illegal and so made me a smuggler. But then for the offence of smuggling to be an offence there have to be borders. Borders are strange things you have to learn about in life. They are about prohibitions and closed doors. Maybe also about tariffs and advantages, if you pursue an economist's way of thinking. But that wasn't the case here. The prohibitions were moral. Like the Catholic church's list of banned books. I've said before it was hard for just anyone to arrive in Russia, and what that meant, at the airport, because the border was moral, or the Russian side thought it was, was that bags were searched brutally. They would have scoured your inner life if they could. Someone with thoughts like yours is not welcome here. It reminded me of a teacher of mine, really years ago, out of a different century, who, if a boy swore (and it mostly was the boys, in those days) he would be made to wash his mouth out with soap. But I think on internal examination they would have wanted me in Russia, because my mind was not made up.

The day I crossed Moscow's threshold from London, a young customs officer, a woman, had stopped an African couple in the queue before me. There were quite a few Africans in Moscow, then. They were diplomats but most were students who had been offered a free education. All they needed to do was accepted it would have a Moscow slant. Many were trainee doctors, for the human body is what it is, not much of a slant possible. The aim was to make Party types out of them, prepared to take the Communist system back home and make Africa Communist too. While Africans also came to the West for jobs they often struggled, and so the aim was to give them an easier time in Russia and so spread the alternative way, Communism, not capitalism, Communism, not democracy, across the globe.

Otkroete! *Davaite otkryt'*! The guardian of Russia's border, her thick blonde hair spilling like coils of wire out from under her navy serge cap, thrust her capable hand inside the Africans' huge, bulging, unsubtle suitcase as if to disembowel a chicken. It was an unintendedly obscene gesture, but what she found was obscene too: reams of silk underwear; lacy bras, sleek panties in wonderful hues of peaches and cream that as she drew them out fell from her hand in a seductive heap, as of if some woman willing to perform a striptease had long ago shed all for her man, or men. 'You are going to sell these for profit, I think,' declared the young border guard severely. Surely so. Surely the intention was to sell them to Russian women to brighten up their lives. Or to sell them to any individual who would pay. Not to feed prostitution, but who cared if it did? But no, it was a crime, to intend to do any kind of business on the black market in a country where a market of any kind was taboo. That was the 'moral' issue. It was a law, and the incomers had no answer, except the woman tried again, to say she needed these aids to the good life in the bedroom, with a wink at her man. Their life as a couple relied on these lubricious textiles. But what severe and puritanical Russian border guard could let into her pure country such deviant ways?

So there's another fact to reckon with. If you are a people who decide to live without profit, effectively without the *power* of money, and try in myriad other ways to be *pure* and *good*, then you have to live in a closed world.

And this was how the poor customs inspector, disgusted with her work, disgusted with the role she had to play on God's earth, came to wave an anxious, sweating, solemn-looking Gels Maybey, and her forbidden books, through the control-point at Moscow airport. She wouldn't police another inner life.

In that moment Gels became the guard. She wanted to tell her she was not wrong. Gels would not give up the secret books that might become triggers for the second revolution. She would run the risk. But she felt sorry for all those who did not know what was at stake.

Harriet Zimmerman had told her, on their way home from the demonstration in mid-December, when she recounted the incident at the border, that officials sometimes enforced the rules, and with a brutal rigidity, and sometimes utterly ignored them, so that you mostly felt at the mercy of their moodiness.

Gels said: 'People do it in our country too. They make themselves moody to stand out. The psychologists (she had had one) call it a disruptive character trait. But people make themselves moody or the system swamps them.'

'The system, Gels?' The older woman smiled. 'But then it's not so long ago that you were a student, am I right?'

As a newcomer Gels Maybey had to keep telling the same story, that she was looking for something different.

'The trouble is only Marxists talk like that. You're not a Marxist, are you? You'll put people off here if you talk like that.'

Gels wondered if she cared even to answer, but then she was destined to like Harriet, so she replied: 'I'm just myself.'

Harriet looked attractive at the wheel, as if she were born to driving. She changed gear smoothly and with some evident satisfaction. The driving seat in the Chevvy didn't dwarf her and she knew her Moscow streets, which included executing an unexpected U-turn on the Ring Road.

'All perfectly legal,' she laughed. 'They have their own system of driving too.'

'Actually I don't know what I am,' said Gels.

'Can that be?'

There was something in Harriet invited Gels's trust, to do with being an older woman, not quite her mother's age, but a good way there.

'I thought Russia would help me sort it out.'

'Russia as a soul doctor, that's crazy! I think you're down on the West, because something happened,' she added, kindly, and shot her passenger a glance. 'Steady, girl! Steady!' Harriet now consciously positioned herself as older and wiser. 'Don't go too far. You've your whole life ahead of you.'

Gels sighed. 'At the moment it's all one great spectacle I've come to watch. Like starting to read *War and Peace*. I don't know how it'll turn out.'

'You keep a notebook?'

'Of course.' Gels wasn't sure whether this was condescending, whether Harriet Zimmermann, whom she had just met, was treating her as a child. But then she confessed she kept one herself, for so many things were strange. Russians behaved in unpredictable and bizarre ways.

'You've only been here a few days.'

'Plus three weeks in Vilnius last year. Same world. Same culture. It worries me it's been forced on them. How would I manage if I were born here. Who would I be? What would I be?'

'They are an oppressed people. It does affect their behaviour.'

Gels liked Harriet, instantly she liked her, but that remark made her scoff silently.

It was a pretty backstreet they headed down now, with the road paved either side of a tree-lined park. The trees were bare and the benches empty, but there was a promise of life there.

'I feel some kind of purgatory has been forced on them. Their world has forgotten what dignity feels like. You have to be able to feel you matter to yourself, that you are someone, to defend dignity. That's why I told you the story of the woman at the customs. Can I tell you another story?'

Harriet grinned.

'Last year too. I wanted to go to Leningrad. I had a ticket too and a visa. There was this train guard stopped me on the platform. He could see I was a foreigner.'

'We Westerners *are* conspicuous.'

'Rule number one, I never tried to disguise myself.' She thought for a moment. Something to do with footwear? 'I only refuse to wear plastic shoes. Ha.' She grinned. 'Anyway, there the guard was barring my way. Waving his enormous pink finger.'

'At least it was only his finger!' They laughed at the enormous pink thing that surfaced in Gels's recollection.

Harriet added: 'But they don't have the same humour as us either. They're not at all Freudian. But go on my dear. He waved his patriarchal finger at you.'

'The thing was I *had* a ticket. He just decided that didn't matter. So then at the very last minute, when the train had already started to move, he let me on. And then I realised that whole set of theatricals was so I could be grateful to him. And of course it worked. It's more than twelve months now and I've not forgotten him. Not because I was grateful but because it struck me he was desperate to make some impression on me. As if I would carry the memory of a good man after all back home with me, back to the West.'

'It's a good story, Gels.'

'I never forgot that man's desire to be a someone, even a good someone, and not a no one. No one wants to feel they are just part of a system, where they have no freedom to act. There must be millions of people in this country like that.'

'Waiting for you to set them free.'

Gels quailed inside at the faint perception that she was perhaps rather silly.

The American, with whom she would obviously be friends, continued: 'But no, you're right. If that's what you mean by the effect of "system" on people then maybe I can agree with you. I can tell you a similar story. It was in a provincial hotel—in Novgorod.'

'Novgorod. Lovely name. Only I can't remember—'

'Northeast. It's got a white Kremlin and not much else.'

'I'd still like to go there.' Gels dreamt with all the zeal of a missionary.

'Well, anyway it was in Novgorod that a foreigner lost the key to his room.' Now they sat talking in the stationary car. It had been a short journey back from Pushkin Square. Harriet had parked the car outside the compound where Gels had moved into Howard Wilde's newspaper office and taken the spare flat.

'I've mislaid my room key,' he told them at the desk.

'There's nothing we can do about that, Mr Foreigner, Sir.'

'But I need my things. I need somewhere to sleep.'

'Just a shrug came by way of a reply.'

'I can imagine.'

'He sat in the bar for six hours until it was already late. Finally there came a voice: "Mr Foreigner, Sir—"'

'They never let you forget you're not one of them.'

The key had been found by a fellow hotel guest. The American tourist buried his face in his hands. He shed tears of relief. Which was just what they wanted. 'Because you know what happened, Gels? The hotel people were the ones who stole it in the first place. It was all a stunt.'

'God. *Bozhe moi*, as they say. It's a kind of wickedness, to manipulate people like that. I'd say people who do things like that are profoundly *bored*.'

'There's something in the culture here,' Harriet observed, 'that makes them think cunning is a virtue.' Harriet had been in the country nearly three years.

'In truth I don't know any real Russians yet. I hope it won't be like that.'

Harriet shrugged. 'I love them all the same.'

'I'd better go. Thanks for the ride, Harriet. Thanks for the welcome to Moscow.'

'Tell Howard to take care of you! I hope we'll see more of you.'

Gels closed the door to the passenger seat, and Harriet drove off. The guard watched both of them, but when she sought his eyes he turned away.

Back in her room she made notes.

So I know what will be the task of the second revolution: to tell the truth about this country even if it is …what it is. What a burden! What a task to expose it!

The Irish writer Victor Pritchett said Russia in the twentieth century broke his heart. 'It's one of those countries which…break the heart and ruin the minds and lives of the logical foreigner.'

Then she slept in the empty, solid, comfortable bed, with the books beneath.

Next morning she gazed at the few clothes hanging in her wardrobe. She had with her nothing light enough to carry her out of winter, whenever winter ended here—and it had only just begun in its full severity—and nothing warm enough, alone, to sustain her in the cold. Her trunk had yet to arrive.

Well, so what if it doesn't. So I'll manage. People have too much stuff. She was on a campaign. She liked the idea of surviving, bivouacking, making-do.

There wasn't a television but a transistor radio came with the flat. Fetching it into the kitchen, plugging it into the wall above the draining board, she tuned the dial and adjusted the volume and listened while clearing her breakfast. Pipers were playing a bold and merry tune. Indeed a tune so lively you could almost see the puffed cheeks of the bagpipers and the marching soldiers twirling their batons. She laid her somehow fragile mug and plate in the surprisingly hard sink. Re-situating the set in the bedroom, yanking out the plug in one room and sticking it back in in another, missing only thirty seconds of the transmission, she continued to listen. As she slid her sleek limbs into her soft jeans—quite unsuitable for Moscow in December—she heard a clean clear male voice speaking perfect English announcing 'This is London.'

The first thought was who am I. The second was a more rational: 'Oh, but the news is all about Moscow! Where *I* am.'

The BBC was reporting as its lead story that Alexander and Natasha Razumovsky, leading protesters against the Soviet regime, had been briefly detained at a public rally in central Moscow last night. A few minutes later a commentator was asked if this meant that the Soviet regime was pressed to open up to 'the free world'.

Yes, he said, in an equally English voice (for people all tried to speak in the same orthodox way, in those times.) 'But it could take years.'

She exploded with anger. 'Of all the cowards of this earth! Doesn't that creep want to commit himself? Bastard's so busy being an expert that all he worries about is his reputation.' At first, not knowing where the anger came from, she was furious. 'Do they know what it's really *like* to be in Moscow at this moment?' But then she knew of course. It was the system. You had to be outside your own system to know.

She made a fresh coffee and took it down to the LGN office. In her head now the British soldiers kept marching. Du dulla dur. She marched in surly fashion the other way.

'Your words about the old couple,' she said, as she browsed the room. 'I've just heard them verbatim on the radio.'

'Verbatim, eh? I'm here to serve. Oh yes and good morning!'

'Morning. I didn't know you stood on ceremony. Patrick not mind?'

'What? My story on the BBC? Of course not. We're all in this together.'

'Of course. You said.' That was the system too, but maybe a good side of it.

The office of her father's newspaper was, via the iron-caged lift, or a short dash down the cold staircase of polished stone, just one floor beneath the guest flat. The space it occupied under Howard Wilde's tenure was not exactly a mess. Some purpose resided there. But every surface was occupied. It reminded her of her essay-writing days. The more complicated the topic the more furniture and floor were covered. Only here it was as if Tolstoy were re-enacting the battle of Borodino. Three tables had been run together to make a capital-I shape and create as much writing surface as possible. Chairs and filing cabinets hugging the walls provided refuge and information respectively but left almost no space to walk in. She looked up at the mouldings on the now yellowed ceiling. Like her flat this room had once seen a grander style of life—an existence led, enjoyed, relished, suffered, by people of a certain ilk. Good people, bad people; all of them now officially consigned to a rejected past. History clung to the mouldings. Among its past occupants had been bourgeois pleasure-seekers who disdained the common people (though who could really know).

'So this is Moscow after the Revolution.'

'It was a while ago now.'

'I don't suppose much has changed. Take out all the office stuff and what would be left?'

'A dirty messy empty space. What kind of mood are you in this morning?'

Uncertain. Nostalgic, she might have answered. Nostalgic for other people's pasts. Outside these very windows and doors had stood the angry people, stirred up against the bourgeoisie. Well, had they? History said there was a moment when the angry common people, so-called, finally called time on the old order.

When tempers snapped. That's why certain people liked Russia, because it showed that systems are not eternal. You want them to end and they do.

The old injustices generated rage in the streets. And, if in truth the rage was not quite so fierce and quite so well-organised as it might have been, had it come truly from their own hearts, this common population of Russia was instructed from on high to be so powerfully angry at the ways of the old privileged classes as made no difference. First the grand houses then the whole country was commandeered by the mob at the behest of those political officers who thought on their behalf. *Politruki* they called them these days. Without a name back then they were a cross between political mentors and activist organisers, and it was they who made the revolution—back then—and established a different way of life; and imposed it on the people. A way of life that had come to this, now: a place where you could never be sure of your next step and where it was better not to have your own thoughts and your behaviour was squashed into a mould of perversity. Now state propaganda hung from every building and was spouted from every newspaper; on the TV and the radio. Exhortations to build Communism and despise the West spouted from every source. And all these truths made people all the more uncertain because no one believed them anymore, because the second revolution was coming and quietly Russians in the street were signalling it to Westerners.

'I had such a good talk with Harriet last night.'

'It certainly seems to have stirred you up.'

'I'm *here*, Howard. I'm just getting a taste of this place.'

Her eyes strayed back to the mouldings on the ceiling. 'It must have been a shock, that's all I'm saying, to have your house and all your possessions confiscated. And to become the enemy, because you had a comfortable way of life people envied.'

'It was dangerous, I'm sure.'

'And unfair.'

'Is it fair that some people have a lot and most people have nothing?'

She shrugged. They both knew there was no answer to that. Or if there was neither he nor she could immediately give it.

'What frightens me is everyone being made to *think* the same.'

'After the Revolution people learnt to keep their heads down and not say what they meant.'

'Which is why people with a true message now have to shout to be heard, like the Razumovskys last night.'

'They also need to be exceedingly brave.'

'So do you think it will come soon, this second revolution?'

'We can hope.'

'Do you hope? They won't all want it.'

'Something has to happen.'

'Because this country is sick? I had this friend last year who said the whole of Russia now has a death wish.'

'Could be.'

'Oh stop being so bloody non-committal! I'm your friend, aren't I?'

'I didn't know you before a few days ago. Who knows who you are! Gels, I'd better get on.'

'I brought you coffee.'

'Thanks.'

He stabbed at his typewriter and she took refuge on one of the chairs.

Howard Wilde, paid to report on how Bolshevik Russia was faring, sixty years after its invention, sits in his headquarters like the captain at the helm of a grand ship, at the centre of the large table that runs not quite the width of the cramped portion of a nineteenth-century drawing room he has commandeered as his office. Every day he reads and writes and practises describing life here, so that when the second Russian Revolution happens he can describe it. Can you describe this? I can. He will be its first historian and have the honour of awarding it capital letters.

On his right, on the small table running crossways, a clipboard marked Outgoing holds together everything he has reported in the last few days, printed on rough paper.

'It's a great job you have. A great job you do.'

'Is this my annual inspection by head office?'

'I get the impression that this whole country is depressed and suicidal.'

Can't you tell the world *that*? Shouldn't you?'

'I could. But then so what? Nor would it be the whole truth. Some 200 million of them look glum but a man like Razumovsky *wants* to live here. He believes there's a good life to be had.' And some fierce aggression leapt into Howard's heart as he said that. He added as an afterthought. 'It's only his wife wants to leave. And even that, I'm not sure it isn't an act, to stoke her anger. To keep them going. They live in opposition. But they don't live in misery.'

Gels sat for a while on a bundle of newspapers to see the office from a slightly different angle. Howard typed with the peculiar fluency of a man who had never learnt the keyboard art but whom unorthodox practice had made semi-perfect. He only became clumsy when he was interrupted, or something made him self-conscious, and he was left searching for b or open quote marks.

He left her sitting there feeling superfluous. 'All male reporters here?' she finally asked. 'I've met Arthur, and Patrick.'

That and the rising tension of having her in the room, interrupting him, asking so many questions, made him explode. 'For God's sake don't give me any of that feminist nonsense!'

'What are you saying? Have you got a male chauvinist hang-up or something?'

He sighed. He was short of sleep after his 2am conversation with the Razumovskys. But actually he wasn't sorry and just wanted to be alone.

'Anyway we're not all men. There's Christina from Sweden, for instance, she's a marvellous observer of daily life. Has fluent Russian. The only qualification is to be pretty damn good at the job.'

'And Polly from Italy?'

'Indeed. She's brilliant.'

'And Harriet.'

'Yes indeed, she has great insight, and concern, although it's difficult for the wives.'

'She told me she teaches at the Anglo-American school.'

'She's also phenomenally well-read.'

'Presumably you're pretty damn good at the job too?' Gels put him on the spot in order to place herself.

Of course he was.

'Where did you go to school?'

'It was a grammar school, if you must know. Not like—'

'Not like me, no. I went where my Dad could afford to send me. The best, of course.'

'And now MY newspaper is your finishing school.'

'I'm not a debutante, Howard. There haven't been any debutantes since almost my mother's day. People don't live like that anymore.'

'But they'd like to, wouldn't they, the rich bourgeoisie? Keep all the best things for themselves?'

'You'll have to ask them yourself. I can only speak for me.'

Did he have a chip on his shoulder? He didn't seem the type. It made her uncomfortable and she really hoped they would be friends. 'Howard—couldn't you forget my background? I won't get in the way.'

'Difficult to see how I can,' he persisted 'And how you *can't* get in the way.' As if, right now, she should have vanished from the stack of newspapers into thin air.

'Pax,' she cried, crossing her fingers. 'Peace, ok. Anything wrong with the coffee?'

'I just forgot to drink it.' He tilted the mug and drained it of its cold contents.

The office came courtesy of her father's wealth, but, against that, Howard Wilde lived at some level like a student. There was a torn poster advertising the allure of the Italian city of Arezzo, and a reproduction of a famous painting by Kazimir Malevich. She forgot the name of it but she recognised it as a late work, after that revolutionary painter of genius had lost hope. THEY had ordered him to curtail his exuberant modernist style. You have to avoid individualism, Comrade. So, not understanding what THEY meant, but undoubtedly feeling threatened, he just blanked out all the faces.

Not Morlocks but zombies. No. No. People still, but people afraid to stand out and be remembered. Or, as things went on, for Malevich last painted in 1935, people so intimidated that, deep down, needing to be individuals and not daring to be, they became whimsical, and deeply untrustworthy, and perverse.

'Because there are no truths they can trust in their world,' said Harriet.

The office seemed Howard's creation, and yet she could well believe this was how he found his paper's Moscow headquarters, as bequeathed to him by his predecessor, two years earlier. As if the debt to history also touched him; as if somewhere evidence had to accrue of the actual passing of time: layers and layers of stuff, untouched. Unreformed documentation of what happened in Russia, day by day, as he and his predecessors had been able to lay their hands on it over the last twenty years. Not sixty. But twenty was already something, the time in which Westerners had been let in, after the war, to see how the first revolution was progressing; or the great experiment failing.

The seriousness impressed her. The office was like a temple devoted to gathering facts. Here was history at work, devotedly practised. Howard's work table was the nave of this secular church, and the teleprinter in the far room the secret altar. Meanwhile the walls of that cramped office, once a reception room made for receiving high bourgeois guests in style, were now packed with information like the contents of a future guidebook. The information, a vast number of clues as to the nature and meaning of the Cold War between Russia and the West, clues to what kept the two civilisations apart, and clues to what drew them together, was filed in ugly green metal cabinets with sharp corners. When she tried a drawer it rolled open with a faint roar. He looked up.

'Sorry. Don't mean to pry.'

'You do. You damn well do! But, hell, be my guest. I've no secrets. Only don't leave anything lying about. You never know who might wander in here and poke about. And make sure it all goes back *exactly* as you found it.'

'I'll do that.'

He had a copy of *Pravda* newspaper, the broadsheet of the Party, folded and quartered to the left of his typewriter, and was alternately reading and pounding the keys. His work was reporting a war after all. It wasn't a joke.

She had a thought to walk over to the window and, where the second narrow table crossed the main workspace, bend over it and look down. The office was on the second floor and so it must look out over the car park below, inside the courtyard, as in her own flat. Yes, she could see the cars, a mixture of colours and models and brands, which was to say, a normal European car park. The yard itself was watched over by the unfriendly sentry, who had his hut and the red and white barrier he operated just on the far side of the old coaching arch.

'I like the arch. It's pretty.'

(Indeed, she would soon write in her notebook, you could imagine Count Andrei Volkonsky arriving in his carriage to attend the Rostovs' ball, nimbly alighting onto the raised pavement which saved him having to wade through—and thus lose his dignity—the ground-level deep snow. Now he was racing with agility up the grand staircase to the ballroom where he would see the angelical Natasha. All this before he was called to go off and fight Napoleon. But alas, poor Russia, you could also imagine Dostoevsky's Underground Man lurking in the basement, rising up in the lift cage, making a ferocious face through the iron bars, trying to catch you out; just to have something to laugh at.)

In the LGN office what made the vintage parquet floor—quite suitable for ballroom dancing by new generations of Natasha Rostov in other circumstances—difficult to navigate in December 1978 were the dusty piles of old newspapers, now in Cyrillic, now in English, that she had been sitting on.

She liked newspapers. Her father's newspaper was a British institution. As a student she had read *The Times* every weekday. Yet there were other perspectives here in Moscow. The neatly laced bales of British newsprint were relieved by a stack of the orange-fronted German news magazine *Der Spiegel*, and the glossy covers of *Time* and *Newsweek* and *U.S. News and World Report*. The books began on the shelves partly obscured behind the newspaper stacks, and then towered above them. From the red-brown row of Soviet yearbooks of official statistics she pulled out 1976, the last available.

'All lies!' he cried, for he couldn't help watching her. 'Well, not quite. Some tell-tale disasters. This is a huge country and yet two years ago they couldn't even feed themselves!'

'My father would say that's because they got rid of all the businessmen.'

'Hmm. Well, he would say that, wouldn't he? A man like him? A capitalist? An apologist for the bourgeoisie?'

'You work for him but you don't pretend to like him.'

(Meanwhile, yes, all lies; how do you live with that without going out of your mind?)

'I take your father's shilling. That's what you want to say. You've come here to make a fool of me.' He released his hands from the folded paper, and the typewriter, and pressed them to his lips. Whatever were Howard Wilde's obscure passions, obscure to her, it was a moment of truth.

'Nothing of the kind. Please believe me. If I want to get away from him I can imagine you do too.'

Not be part of the system. And yet he had to be. And Harriet had told her she had to be too. Stop being so naïve. You're not a student anymore. You have a future ahead of you in which you want to be happy.

Actually it was the growing rumour that when the second revolution happened Russia would become overnight a rich free country, like almost everywhere else. She said that and it made him furious. Who was she to arrive from her tidy little, privileged England and pronounce on a country's fate.

'I don't know who I am. I just feel caught up in …all this.'

'It's certainly hard to pin you down.'

'I could say the same about you.'

Whereupon he bridled and wondered what right she had to know the least further thing about him. But then he softened and confessed, because he quite liked her after all: 'The truth is, Gels, I'd be sorry if capitalism turned out to be the solution here. Russia's special.'

What was Howard Wilde? One of the kind at university who were constantly demonstrating against the system but who didn't include her because she felt it differently? A Communist even? That unheard of thing. But she didn't really know. Only that he felt this loyalty to Russia which made him angry when anyone attacked it. Only he was a devoted admirer of Razumovsky, who did want Russia to change, but to stay good and pure and decent and different.

'Can I ask you just one more thing, Howard? My friend Johannes told me this whole country was committing suicide. Running itself into the ground. Poisoning itself. That people here keep burning their own houses down, he said. Metaphorically, I mean. Not exactly killing themselves but practising a will to self-extinction. I don't know. What do you think? Won't they all be dead if change doesn't come soon?'

(It struck her later, when she made a note of their talk, that her version of Russian history sounded like the plot of an obscure and powerful opera, with a vast chorus of battered, impassioned people. Russia was an epic stage and she was in the audience. She liked that and she awarded Harriet and Howard honorary places alongside her.)

'Christ, isn't it a bit early in the morning for all this?' Resorting to a very English trick of ducking such seriousness, he picked up the empty coffee mug from beside him and waved it.

'Can I get you another?'

'No need to go upstairs for it. There's a coffee machine in the back room. Help yourself while you're there.'

Oh. It quite took the wind out of her sails that her offering of the morning had been entirely superfluous. On the other hand anything to placate him; because without him, in truth, she couldn't stay. Furthermore, now she was here she felt quite his equal.

'I'll explore.'

The filter coffee machine, which meant you didn't need to boil a kettle and pour the water yourself, lived adjacent to the teleprinter. It was quite a new invention in the West, and she herself admired it, never having owned such a gadget. Yet it also seemed rather American, compared with the chic solid metal coffee pots that made hot very thick expresso in France. Johannes after her visit to his museum had made her coffee after their *Liebesnacht*, during which he had explained to her quite what he thought of the Russian death wish. He had made the coffee in a French pot which he said reminded him of a Cubist version of a woman's body. Quite so. With a tiny waist. (Her modest volumes and slight curves just fitted that model, though she didn't have a tiny waist, and was more of a boyish girl, body-wise. Had Johannes minded? No, she didn't think so.) But now this American coffee-maker in place of the French cafetière. You could think that Americans were not very sensual people, to produce industrial paraphernalia like this: a bulky jug, the glass of no merit, standing on a hotplate and anchored in a plastic house which spouted a one-armed conduit for steam.

Beside the imported, characterless, ugly electric coffee-maker, was a sink— this one too small for Buster, but still nineteenth century—and a separate electric ring. There was a small fridge too, with rounded corners, and beside the coffee machine a garish orange plastic coffee grinder, like a miniature lighthouse. (She had bought, for herself, on the outing with her Japanese neighbour, the same model in white.) A wooden tub said, in Russian, 'Butter from Vologda' but when she lifted the lid it turned out to hold the coffee beans. The brew that now dripped through into the jug transformed the whole office into—

'An Italian coffee bar!'

'Nice thought.'

'It also takes away the unpleasant smell that lurks here, don't you find?'
He raised the mug in a toast of thanks, already in a better mood. 'There are a lot of smells here. One way or another. But I think there's especially a farmyard smell about Soviet newsprint.'

'That farmyard smell is just what I always thought Soviet chocolate tasted like.'

'Like coffee?'

'Worse.'

He laughed. A genuine laugh. She might one day get him to like her. 'There's something in it. It was recently a rural society.'

'There's definitely *something* in it. Make a nice little piece.' He meant for the paper. Western readers would find it amusing. A bar of Cadbury's or Hershey's wasn't heaven but it didn't remind you of diarrhoea.

When she came back with her own coffee he lifted his hand and finally gestured at a chair at the far cross-table. 'This a place for me?' Mercifully there was that small window she had aspired to beside it. She would have daylight. The light in Howard's office was poor. She could see him screwing up his eyes all the time. It probably accounted for why they looked red.

'But that's great.'

(Things I admire, she made a mental note: transistor radios, windows that let the light in and that I can see out of, maps, paintings framed to demand my attention, architecture, design, the smell of coffee, and literature and classical music. Makes me bourgeois too, I suppose, she reflected as she sat down. But then Tolstoy admired hundreds of thousands of things in his own time. The *things* around us *are* our lives.)

The nineteenth-century casement window was in two parts to keep out the cold, with a kind of no man's land in between, where dust collected and insects died. A dried-up woodlouse lay stiffly on its armadillo-like back, with its eight feet in the air. It hadn't wanted to die. Most people and most countries don't want to die. In fact they resist it strongly. They rather want the world to change so they can stay the way they are. Even Johannes hadn't been ready to give up, that one night she'd spent with him.

The office did indeed look down on the car park below. Volvos, Volkswagens and Toyotas mainly, now she looked closer: all good sturdy saloons to cope with the weather. She liked cars too, without knowing why, except, well, like a radio, they help you know the extent of things. What's possible. What's likely. Where is beautiful, and not. How far you can get in the right direction.

'In Moscow you need a car that can deal with potholes. Potholes in all the bloody roads, even right in the centre of town. As for venturing beyond...'

She looked through the window for Howard's red MG and couldn't see it, but surely that sleek, low-slung roadster felt the bumps more than most. 'Did you drive far last night?'

'I gave chase, shall we say. Look...' and he was saying it to himself because in the end, he liked talking, 'I must get on.'

'I'm not here.'

'But you are. You are!' he cried desperately.

She could tell he meant it, and so she set herself to read the news. The office paid for the Reuters file, and though that vital resource was printed in faded ink on a continuous roll of poor-quality paper, because of the office budget, the result seemed weighty and important; the same way the BBC news was. She tore off the latest batch of reports, cut them with a ruler to the size of easy-to-read pages and held the whole file together under another bulldog clip. Its place was on the cross-table at the other end from her own.

'Amazing the way those Malevich figures have no faces. You'd think the officials would have found it all the more subversive. The censors, I mean.'

'It was early days. They probably didn't know what they were looking for. If they weren't told specifically.'

'Doesn't make it less frightening.'

'Amazing he saw the way things were going, so early.'

'Communism's been a disaster. Is that true, Howard? It's what my father says.'

'It's cost millions of lives. But...' And once again, his hands flew from his typewriter to his lips, in the form of a warning, or an admonition to himself. 'You just have to remember, Gels Maybey, that if you meant that stuff about not being a capitalist before, and being not only your father's daughter, but your own person, that it doesn't do to be anti-Communist either. You can't go about saying you're anti-Communist.'

'Arthur Zimmerman does, and Harriet.'

'They're a special case.'

'They're nice people.'

He whispered. 'They're a special case because they're American. No really I mean it. People forget, Russia is in Europe...'

(Like the coffee pot, she thought.)

'...In that way it's like us. And the Russians are doing socialism, which lots of us admire. So to be anti-Communist in Europe—in our West—is a problem. It's the socialists who are the nice people, wherever. Except possibly here, where they're only pretending. Though they also pretend in other places too.'

She was listening hard to all those -isms, which categorised people, but which, as Howard used them, did make a kind of sense.

'So you take care what you say, and to whom, about Communism being a disaster, Gels Maybey! Razumovsky doesn't think it's the wrong road for Russia. The system just needs reforming.'

'So I should be careful what I say to Harriet Zimmerman?'

'And to Arthur.'

'But I liked her a lot. Her experience of being in Russia seems to have been rich and varied. She's thought a lot about it.'

'I like them too.'

Was he giving her a warning? Was he announcing something like 'walls have ears'—as the authorities did during the actual war? He couldn't mean that. Just socially to show a certain political good manners.

'There was this 'commentator' on the BBC, this morning. After they carried your report. They said Russia has to change now to survive, don't you think? And all he could do was hedge his bets. I hated him for it.'

'Hate's pretty strong.'

'He was fudging. He needed to commit himself.' Her whole face seemed to ask Howard the question she kept repeating. He had to offer her his view, so she could form her own. And so he tried.

'This country will collapse, it will change, Gels. We feel it now. But maybe it still won't happen for a long time, so I can't tell you how it will be, Gels, whether capitalist or something else. What is relevant now is the West waking up and *realising* that the present Russian system is collapsing. And the Russian intelligence services and the diplomats and all the other experts here are listening to what *we* broadcast about *them*, and reading what *we* write. They know that we know they're collapsing, and the fact that we know gives them an idea about themselves. *That*'s relevant. It's like the West offering a new kind of friendship in adversity and the Russians wondering what to do.'

The Malevich, awash with emptiness and bewilderment amid the ravishing bright colours of the new life, held her attention while she digested Howard Wilde's verdict.

'Funny friendship when one of you has to be the winner.'

She added, after a long pause, 'In Vilnius, I knew the director of the institute. No, not like that. But he noticed me and so I got to know him a bit. He had a face like that, empty. He willed it that there be *nothing* about him, *nothing* to see into, *nothing* to see through, *nothing* to smile or frown about, *no* eyes in which to seek trust, or see fear. But at the same time he was in agony at having to suppress so many feelings. Because human beings do have faces and feelings. That's what the Malevich reminds me of. It was ridiculous over there. The institute was called VIRILE, can you believe it. The Vilnius Institute of Russian Instruction in Life and Everything Else. You couldn't make it up.'

Russia was funny. Side-splittingly funny, when you got to know it. Except that it was desperately sad too.

But that sounded condescending.

(Among the forbidden books Gels was looking to give away, so that Russians could understand their country better, she had Solzhenitsyn's *Cancer Ward* which, hell, was a damned appropriate metaphor for a dying country; and his other great novel *The First Circle*. Dante's First circle of Hell, that was. Is that the way the world is, she wondered? Almost everyone is sick, but then the writer survives to tell the true story? Almost everyone has tumbled into the diabolical pit, except the writer who has climbed out and is now signalling to the world? Me, maybe?)

Howard stood up, swinging his mug, to stretch his legs and orate: 'The management class here, the *nomklats*, are blundering fools. Idiots of the first order. Ours are too—

'Our salarymen back in England?' (A Japanese-ism of the day.)

'The difference is ours get paid to do a job, and if they do it badly they get the sack, whereas here everyone just hangs on, and on and on.'

'It ruins people's lives. I knew this man—'

'Gels, I must get on. There's the midday deadline…'

Right. Enough! 'Sorry. I know you have work to do.'

'For your papa not least.'

74

Three

Howard Wilde is in Russia to invent his own utopia. But in fact all he can do is observe the plight of those around him and wish them something better. He's a good writer and he can describe what he sees. Like me he makes sorties out into a world that isn't his, and, like me, his mission is to describe it. As for me, I am haunted by the simple anxiety that I am not a good person, given what I have come from, and I keep hoping Russia will make me better. Where is goodness, if not here?

It was a December morning still before Christmas when Howard was interpreting Soviet comments on nuclear arms control. Half the world regarded it as the burning issue of the day. A madman might detonate the whole of mankind. He might be a dim-witted American president, he might be a perverse Soviet General Secretary of the Communist Party. Both had to be interrogated for the meaning of their every word and gesture.

I was writing notes on the tumult of events in my early days in Moscow, increasingly bringing my notebook down into the office, when a man appeared on the threshold of the office. Good God, his physical bulk would have blotted out the sun. A smell of snow wafted in with him from outside, shocking the unbearably fuggy office into a new moment of wakefulness. I paused in mid-sentence.

'Ah, Grisha, let me introduce…' Howard got to his feet. A sort of standing to attention, it was, and a salute. 'Gels, this is Grisha.'

Howard sounded so proud, as if this man ten years older, twenty, maybe, were his son. 'He's my driver, officially. I've promoted him. The office can't run without him.'

I could imagine that but couldn't quite work out what to say.

'*Zdrastvuyete*,' pronounced the huge man in a muffled voice meanwhile. I thought of offering my hand but perhaps that was bourgeois, so I just greeted him a bit louder. *Zdrastvuyete* was really the simplest Russian. I boomed out z-drast-voo-yet-ye in return and felt nervous.

The cannonball head, outsize, vast and indistinct, may have nodded. It was hard to tell. He had thin pale hair and almost a boy's face. He had the head of a blond monster, but his shy puzzlement made him look like an angel. Perhaps I was a puzzle to him. Why not? A strange woman in the office. But then he seemed to find something funny. I ended up staring at him, whereupon he looked my way, vaguely, but then like a child, or a pet, was impatient and wanted Howard, his owner.

'Boss, they've stolen your windscreen wipers again, boss.'

'Bugger it.'

'*Tak tochno*,' said the driver. That was exactly it. Someone had taken the *dvorniki* off the MG windscreen.

Rather an admirer of Howard's car, a bright red streak of engineering in a forcibly becalmed grey land, I felt an unexpected concern. Who would steal windscreen wipers? Grisha insisted the perpetrator had to be Russian. It's our people do that sort of thing.

'Why can't they buy their own?'

'That's the point, Gels. There are none to buy. It's—their circumstances.' Howard bemoaned the state of a divided world in which objects vital to everyday life were short. *Defitsitnyi*, as he had taught me to say. I thought of the contraband lingerie, the missing hotel key and the invalid though perfectly valid train ticket. Nothing here was in its normal moral order.

'Circumstances. *Da*.' The big man understood some English; and how solemn he made Russian for yes sound! Like the fourth note of Beethoven's fifth symphony. Your fate, and mine. It hangs over all of us.

But suddenly they both laughed and I joined in. Grisha's deadpan, Howard's gentle consternation, my genuine shock at this petty larceny, and my uneasy sense that the tale was about something else, all dissolved. Released from my shyness by the shared laughter, I went over and shook the huge soft hand of the newcomer and thought he might be able to help me, for I was on that quest Harriet had encouraged in me, and who better to meet than a man who mediated between the two sides.

'*Gospozha*,' he wheezed.

'Dear foreign lady. Pleased to meet you.' So greeting me, with the lumbering precision of a small crane the huge Russian lowered his bulk into a place opposite Howard—the third of the office's three chairs.

'What do you do for Howard, Grisha?' Should I call him Comrade? It seemed an affectation. Sir wouldn't do either, and we were hardly co-citizens. Just use his forename? But that wasn't the Russian way.

'*Ya ego assistyent*,' the huge man squeaked, in his tiny voice. Turning his seated body was difficult.

'Right!'

'I need an assistant.'

'You damn well do, Howard Wilde. I'll tell my papa when I get back what a mess there is everywhere.'

'I do. I do. My ways are terrible,' Howard shook his head. I was pleased to see him like that. I already loved him a bit.

'*Eto pravil'no.*' Grisha agreed.

I remember that harmonious moment when I knew we would be a family of sorts. It made me happy. It was another launchpad.

Howard wrote a story about how, whenever Western governments accused Russia of human rights abuses, the Kremlin turned round and accused America of exactly the same thing. America was its other half. And its scapegoat.

> Letters from families did not arrive, the Soviet newspaper said, and many U.S. political prisoners were given poor food, insufficient exercise and made to work long hours, all of which was designed to break down their health and morale.

> The Soviet Union has itself come under repeated criticism for its treatment of dissidents by Western governments and independent human rights organisations, which have accused it of ignoring the spirit of the Helsinki Accords on human rights signed with the West in 1975.

> But the Soviet newspaper said today that the behaviour of the United States and Britain made the fulfilment of these accords impossible, and were 'a setback for the progress of humanity, enlightened by reason and goodwill.' It said the concept of détente, 'so painstakingly elaborated' at the Helsinki security conference, was in danger of degenerating into fiction.

Britain too then. The West was to blame. Howard returned the typewriter carriage, it pinged, and he began a new page.

U.S. Embassy officials in Moscow said the commentary had been expected. 'December 14 is always an embarrassment to the Soviets,' one diplomat said. 'We have come to expect this kind of mud-slinging. A lot of it is hot air.'

Professor Razumovsky had previously told journalists that the suppression of yesterday's demonstration underscored Kremlin unease on the human rights issue. He drew attention to twenty-four known cases of Soviet citizens convicted in the past year on charges of 'anti-Soviet slander', 'parasitism', 'criminal activity harmful to the state', 'printing and distribution of subversive materials', smuggling and other breaches of the criminal law. He said these charges were used to stop Russians criticising the Kremlin's domestic and foreign policies. They were used to deter people from demanding freedom of speech, movement and belief.

The dissidents were also marking the 152nd anniversary of the Decembrist Insurrection, when critics of the tsarist autocracy pressed for a constitution in Russia for the first time in the country's history.

So, that was how the Moscow story reached newspapers across the world. And still surely you had to be here to feel the truth of it, with all these trivial inconveniences, these little searches for personal identity, the snatched chance to exercise minimal power over another human being, going on besides.

'Tit for tat, exactly. Gels, if you want to "feel the truth of it" let me tell you what happened just last summer when the American embassy here caught fire.'

'Caught fire!'

'Well, yes, you can imagine. There was the US representation blazing away. It lost its whole top storey to flames. The two sides blamed each other. But it was the Americans who looked ridiculous. The Russians really rubbed it in. Think you can win the Cold War? You're so clumsy you set fire to your own embassy. We did NOT. You caused it. You Commies. You Bolshies, threatening the world, trying to make us look weak. Well.

'Some Russian guy showed up in a Mercedes playing 'Burn Baby Burn!' on his tape deck. Now that really hit the target. Heh there, you Amis! Think you're the cleverest and most powerful people in the world? You had it coming to you!'

'A Russian in a Mercedes!' My mind was jumping. First Grisha, now this!

'But then you know that same guy came back and he was a different person. He said he wanted to help the Americans. There were families out on the street.

Surely he could help, with his big German car. No one knew whether to trust him. He was a boy of sixteen.'

'Heavens!' What else could I say. There was Grisha and now there was this unnamed boy, both of them spanning both sides.

But there was another reason why I liked Grisha. He reminded me of yet another significant man in my life. Yes, there had been so many, on my journey to replace my papa. I was sixteen when I ran away and took a job as a waitress in a Bolzano café on the strength of a middle-school qualification in Italian. The pavement café was in the run-down chic area of the city, close to the university (for, perversely, I would always think I belonged there), and it paid me just enough to rent a bleak one-bedroom flat in an unmodernised building. I had no sense of history when I stared at blank walls in those days, and my nights alone were new and all the more painful. I was just waiting for life to happen to me. Every day I was a waitress in the café. Every evening I went to bed early, short of money. Beside me, when I fetched orders from the tiny kitchen, a big man washed the dishes. His bulk took up half the space, which is why I remembered him now. Squeezed together, we scrupulously avoided touching, amid the tall fridges and the service sink and the foetid sprawl of used dishes. He, with his hands immersed in soapy water, seemed to stand dreaming of whatever lay beyond the frosted back window. I found a new pleasure in myself I hadn't known before, wishing him those dreams. I was discovering the human soul. Now and again as he stood there, as tall as one of the fridges, he seemed even to invite my questions, but then no word passed his lips, as if the soul must remain a mystery. How busy we were in the café and how hot it was, I finally exclaimed, a feeble, flabby teenager, resorting to banalities. He snapped open a bottle of chilled Fanta, popped a straw in the neck and thrust it into my hands. As I poured that fizzy orange nectar (which might in that moment have been the blood of Christ) down my pampered throat he too tipped his head back, opened his mouth and pointed inside to half a tongue. He was mute. I laid my cheek against his t-shirted belly. Truth was there.

It's all a question of not being afraid.

Grisha, not mute but a mystery, silently collected daily what the postman brought. That was his first job in the morning. Higher powers sifted our mail first, so letters from the West went on long extra journeys for unpredictable amounts of time. I feigned expecting something, or perhaps I really hoped for a letter from Edward. (I know, I know, so many men, this one almost the age of my papa.) But that was over. Papa might write? Unlikely, but more likely than Ma, who never thought of anyone but herself (married to my papa, perhaps a fair preoccupation). Papa's secretary would send me a birthday card but that was a way off. Otherwise nothing to wait for.

So I watched the world around me. Occasionally Howard got a letter from head office in London, or some aunt he claimed to have in Chichester, but though a plausible occasional envelope arrived, carefully hand-addressed, I didn't believe him. Perhaps it was an ex-wife. Was Howard like me, with an ex here and there, even rather a lot of them? The equivalent of an Edward and a Johannes, women who had in turn left their messages imprinted on his heart? Who knew?

Mostly what the postman brought were distant newspapers from across the Soviet Union. As if the personal affairs of the likes of us, Gels Maybey and Howard Wilde, wherever we had arrived in life, mattered little beside these exotic, and it had to be said, malodorous, printed papers which might yet contain, here and there, the revelation of a half-secret, pointing to a possible second revolution to come.

Grisha returned from the postbox with an armful of people's despatches from afar and descended into his chair. Scandinavian but not made to take so much Soviet Russian strain, it no longer rotated. So what. Chair nil, Grisha one. His job was to mark up interesting items in the long-distance press, so the reporters could investigate. For how else could Howard, Patrick and Arthur, and the woman from Sweden, if you say so, Howard, even pooling their resources, keep tabs on the further reaches of the empire.

The sheer extent of the Soviet empire, which people compared to ancient Rome, was surely a weakness. I had read Gibbon and I knew Gibbon would have pounced on it. The fence could never run the whole way round. The border must have holes in it; gaps where something unofficial could get through. A chink of light. A break in the wire. Surely that happened.

(And I had to wonder why I was obsessed with gaps, ways through, people who worked on both sides, if it was not that, uniting those alienated sides, my parents and me, this country and the world, was not the essence of my plan.) In those further reaches of the USSR aeroplanes crashed, local officials were executed for corruption, foodstuffs were short, and whole peoples banished east. Far away detainees, dissidents and even real criminals were sent to rethink their social misdeeds in so-called correction camps. (Gulags we called them, and translated them as prisons, but there were always a few souls who begged to be sent there, to seek to correct their errors. The human soul is a strange thing, not shy of self-inflicted pain.) Eventually, beyond the Ural Mountains and on and on, was the Pacific Ocean, and, frankly, a seaboard which changed everything, for the horizon was open and bright. How could one power keep hold of all of that and force people to like their prison? I would find a way through, find the secret and release all the prisoners.

The news printer chuntered on. To order its output I had to squeeze past Grisha, who grunted in embarrassment and tried to slide further under our shared side of the table. I forgave him his body, as he forgave me mine, for it was surely provocative. I couldn't help it when a man was around.

The task was to tear the news reel into sections and shuffle the package so it sat neatly on the clipboard, under the metal clip's tight jaws, to the left of Howard's left elbow. The clip was so tightly sprung it somehow added to the seriousness of all those global facts it held together.

'So Grisha apropos of the wipers you'd better go down and see our man at SOVAVTO. You could tag along, Gels.'

'Get me out of the way. Howard?' But I was longing to step out of the window beside me, breathe the fresh chill Moscow air and take the tour, with Grisha as my guide.

*

Grisha drove the office Volga, a yellow version of the police cars that had escorted the dissidents on their journey to nowhere the other night. Of that saloon car that the Ford Motor Company had sold to Russia, the Russians had tweaked a version they loved, in endless duplication, more than any other car in their universe. Every police car and every taxi in Russia was a Volga.

The Cold War was this mirror game; a story of brazen imitation never acknowledged; a story of help and its denial; of trade under the counter; of an eastern country claiming to flourish but on a life-support system, and of western countries claiming an individualist way of life but always anxious that even now collectivist Russia was proving them wrong.

'It's a beautiful city.'

'*Da.*'

Beautiful because parts of it were old, parts majestic, and much of it lay on a great river. Sandy golden houses from the early nineteenth century ranged along tree-lined boulevards. Solid blocks of flats from the 1890s, when there was an economic boom, and again from the 1920s and 1930s, when there was great need, suggested civic virtues, civic pride even; yet the word was that whole families lived in one room, especially in the nicer, older parts. People passed you in the street and you concluded their days were short of grace and respite. Clothes were cheap and crudely machine-dyed and -patterned. Variety was hard to come by, so the streets in winter were a mass of human bundles in darkish overcoats and boots, the heads wrapped in fur hats. Little Fiat saloon cars, called in their Russian reinvention Zhigulis, offered a glimpse of private travel, but otherwise it was trams that dominated the streets, and further from the centre, buses. Both seemed old-fashioned to a Westerner, as if they belonged to a European street scene thirty years earlier.

'Not many people have cars then?'

'*Net.*'

Minutes later we skirted the momentous Communist Party Central Committee building, a bureaucratic fortress, a palace of a thousand windows, that just went up and up and on and on, doing its job to administer and intimidate.

(Propaganda is everywhere. Not only the famous old slogan, COMMUNISM EQUALS THE PARTY AND THE ELECTRIFICATION OF THE WHOLE COUNTRY, which even here must seem antiquated by now, but also, remember that recruiting sergeant's pointed finger demanding British loyalty in the Great War? Well, that's how it is here all the time. THE PARTY IS THE MIND AND THE HEART AND THE CONSCIENCE OF THE PEOPLE. 1914 in England. 1978 in Moscow. Has not the world changed in between? How strange it is not to be able to answer this question with confidence.)

Grisha drove slowly and Gels Maybey strove to take in the view from every side.

'Are you a Party member, Grisha?

'Of course.'

'Of course. I suppose everyone is. Wouldn't work otherwise.'

(Perhaps being a party member was like going to the same school. You could draw on residual loyalty. But to hold this vast country together with that? Some people hate their school.)

He didn't say, though I thought I heard some odd noise.

The giant Rossiya Hotel loomed. Another giant in a world of individuals forced to be pygmies.

It was a recent construction of concrete and glass and looked like a stage a hundred yards long. The concrete curtain, the same incredible length, was firmly down and could never be otherwise. All the rooms allocated to foreigners were bugged.

What kind of architecture was that? A monstrous fascistic façade screening off an anthill.

(The stuff you read about in spy stories, it's all real here. Bugs screwed into the light sockets, fixed under the table. In all the Western offices and embassies too. No one in their right mind would have a sensitive conversation indoors, Howard said.)

Gels was mindful of the bugged tourists. 'THEY keep listening to us. THEY must care so much what WE think of THEM!' Two powers at war, of course.

Grisha chuckled or clucked or harrumphed.

'THEY think all foreigners are against them.'

'Dear lady, foreigners when they come only steal from Russia.'

(Maybe that's me. Maybe I've come to steal the secret of happiness.)

'I hope that's not true.,' She'd seen more of Harriet meanwhile. They'd sat over a long watery coffee with skimmed milk in the draughty new-build Marines' Snack Bar in the US embassy. It was such a nasty beverage it should have been illegal to call it coffee.

'Can we talk?'

'Of course we can, Gels.' Harriet laughed. 'This is the United States, remember?'

'Maybe your own people listen in?'

Harriet smiled in a kindly fashion. 'I sure hope not. *I* am not my country's enemy. I have nothing to hide. As for you, Gels, what a muddle you are! You don't like money and you don't like privilege and you think the United States is spying on you.'

(She made me feel silly.)

'Our English world, your America. It's all rotten.' Gels became a child in Harriet's presence, as if complaining to her mother.

'Have you ever been to America, honey?' said Harriet compassionately. 'No I thought not. Aw hell, it's always the same with you Brits. Everything you don't like about America you like about Russia. That's how your famous double-crossing spies stitched us up. And you're still like them. You and Howard.'

(That was another episode again which Howard and I had talked about. It never went away because the notorious Philby was still alive. Burgess and Maclean were dead but Philby lived in Russia not to be in prison in England.)

'I hope we can be friends, Harriet.' As if across some human abyss, Gels struggled, but she had the suspicion all human relations happened across a great divide.

'Sure we can. Just remember the system in my country is democratic. It's fair. It's the best in the world.'

Gels was speechless. Harriet sounded like a proud Russian. (But I didn't want to spoil our growing friendship.)

Grisha drove on. The city of Moscow had its own weave of sackcloth and gold thread. You could wear Moscow now as a prison uniform and now as a ball gown. The Metropol Hotel had such charm, as if left over from the French belle epoque.

(In my first week in Moscow it had already lured me to go dancing there alone, a painful episode. What had that meek, silent, middling kind of man in a nylon shirt wanted of me, except to stop me talking to, or embracing, others who might have had something more interesting to whisper in return? You could arrive in a strange place and think intimacy was the easiest, perhaps the only, way in, and perhaps for a moment I did hope that evening to climb into bed with any Russian man, before my flesh began to creep with horror in that nylon-clad ballroom embrace and my mind took stock.)

By comparison, Gels disliked the Metropol's near neighbour, the temple of the Bolshoi Theatre. The Bolshoi harnessed culture to power and prestige. It bespoke Establishment. Who wanted that, in the name of culture? No, no, not anywhere. Now they were passing the little village of the Kremlin towers, which beckoned from behind the compound's menacing protective wall. All that was missing was a fairground tune ground out by an organ-grinder. The Kremlin was an extraordinary Russian extravagance built by an Italian. Its ornate, exotic towers burst into colour against the winter grey sky. But when the bells rang they twanged savagely.

Howard meanwhile had reeled the last page of his three-page story out the typewriter with a final flourish. He headed for the back room, where he punched the text on to the teleprinter. The teleprinter was the fourth member of the family, like a giant pet kept outside in its own back room.

'Thank you for that, Gels.'

84

'Well, it is, like an Industrial Revolution all of its own.'

Cold and uncomfortable to live with, she mused. Half monster and half useful friend, it was a vast, loom-like, seemingly nineteenth-century construction; a horrible confabulation of iron and telegraphy. Yet if you wanted to be poetic it set the clock back and brought the kind of writing Howard did close to manual work.

Note for the future: in 1978 *this* was how texts crossed the world! Automatic typewriters across the globe took each other's instructions in the form of a ribbon of code. Howard typed words and they came out as a lacy paperchain punched with holes. This intermediary language was tactile like Braille, and an experienced user like Howard knew exactly how far the machine had reached in sending his text, as the ribbon fed through, or broke, and had to be restarted. He had the ribbon as a record of what he had sent, and sometimes wore it round his neck, a laurel crown of his own making, while, at the other end of his despatch, the receiver would feed the code into his machine, and produce a message sent from Moscow and received in London.

So this is Moscow! Gels exclaimed. Yes to the Pravda newspaper house then, a masterpiece of 1920s Constructivist architecture, when Russia believed it had a vital modernity to offer the dying bourgeois world. Yes to the Posts and Telegraph House, for communication *is* exciting, of people and peoples over huge distances, by telephone, by telegraph, by teleprinter even, not to mention cars and planes and trains. No to the tall, cheap, flimsy blocks of flats built in the 1960s and named after Nikita Khrushchev, the Soviet leader who banged his shoe on the table to make a point at the United Nations. What a gesture! We peasants have taken over your bourgeois world. Get used to it! (Soviet politicians had a reputation for being what her papa called 'peasants'.) But back to her list of good and bad. No to the shops here which are only known by a number, and, for want of goods inside them, have window displays made of fifty examples of the same tin of condensed milk, or deep-sea fish. Yes, surprisingly, to the thick-walled apartment blocks built in the 1930s in a neo-Classical style. They are architecturally reactionary, after the Modernism of the previous fifteen years, yet they have solidity.

(I could live there. That would be my balcony and in summer I would transform it with geraniums and imagine I was back in Bologna.)

Now they were crossing the river, which was a majestic sight. You could look up and back to the Kremlin rising above the water, or forward to the far bank, where a handsome eighteenth-century residence stood. Gels had just discerned the Union Jack when Grisha mumbled something. Either her Russian was rusty or he didn't speak very clearly. Finally he steered them across another bridge, and then they were on a small side road, with nothing much to see. No shops, no flats, just low-rise, unlabelled warehouses and light industrial workshops. He had slowed right down, so Gels could read the name: Car Factory Street.

(Great name! Like a relic of some passion from the past; a trace of that moment when the new world after the revolution had to be named. Machine Building Street (1) and Machine Building Street (2) though, come on! That's a bit much. Either the city engineer had no imagination or he was in too much of a hurry to build the new society to have a trivial care to distinguish one street from another.)

Grisha didn't bother to indicate. Nothing was coming. He turned right and they pulled up in front of a ten-foot-high fence. A surveillance camera poked out above it. His MOS-registration number identified, the rusty iron gates clanked open. But then she thought the gates might not have been automated at all, and the camera was fake. More likely when the Volga drove up an eye went to a peephole in the planks and recognised a friend.

(Not for the first time Grisha made me feel Moscow was a village of cunning peasants, who really believed cunning was a virtue.)

'*Priekhali*,' he announced with satisfaction. 'We've arrived.' Gels was enthusiastic. Everything new thrilled her.

The depot, for that was what it was, was where the new owners of Zhigulis came to collect their car. There were no private garages in Moscow, no car showrooms, and no official private sales. If you wanted a car you put your name on a three-year waiting list, which at least gave you time to save. Whether your application was accepted depended on your political record.

Howard told Gels Natasha Razumovsky would have liked a car—and had the money from her daughter Tatyana abroad—but knew she need not bother to apply. Sasha though was quite glad they had no car and almost happy they were denied a telephone.

'How do you like all these cars? Maybe you'd like to buy one? The boss said…'

Howard, Gels thought with irritation, has no idea how much I do NOT want to own a car. I will not isolate myself driving around in a tin chrysalis. That's not the good life.

And that was what she was pursuing, after all. A better life.

A sea of identical Fiat cars, all the same sandy-mushroom colour, stretched out before her. 'Must be hard to find the one you want. When they're all the same.' But the sarcasm was lost on her companion.

'*Nu ladno,*' he said.

(I mean I liked cars, as transport, because they take you to places, take you away, make it possible to touch new limits. But then I could say that of trains and aeroplanes too. Trains and boats and planes, as the song went.)

'And now?'

'Now I'll go and get some wipers.'

She stood beside the car watching him go. Having heaved himself out of the Volga, he waddled, and bottles bulged from each side of his jacket. It was a Western-style sports jacket in what must be an extra-extra-large size—perhaps Howard had bought it for him in Frankfurt or Helsinki—and the two unshapely pockets were an obscene sight, each with a silver cap just visible, each one like a teat in a fat man's flank. He headed for a corrugated obtrusion in the centre of the compound, like a small aircraft hangar. It had no signage, and there he disappeared.

I banged my hands together and stamped my feet. The clear, bright days were colder than I expected. This one was minus 10 on the thermometer outside the office window. The cars stood in their rows, shiny and obedient and somehow shorn of the excitement people—men—wanted from cars in the West. How would it be to buy—let's think of a number—registration number MOS 02-572. 02-546. 02-539. It was like looking for a grave in a huge cemetery where all the graves were the same. They *were* all the same, from the outside. A thousand beige cars all the same model.

(Two boys sat watching me from the top of the perimeter wall. They sat with their legs dangling, gazing down. Eventually I noticed them and somehow my heart turned over. Not men this time who would help me close out my story, but boys. They couldn't have been more than twelve. They looked like characters from a children's story. Doing something unusual and provocative. Not practising surveillance but watching and learning, or perhaps spying too, for whoever could make use of what they saw. One had a maroon cap and navy training pants, with a stripe. The other was in grey and black.

'*Zdrastvuyete, mal'chiki*. Hi there, boys? Which car should I take?' Anything to make contact with the other side, which wasn't at all an other side, just more variations on the human soul, variations I hungered for. I waved up, shielding my eyes against the winter sun, grinning. The one in grey raised a hand but the other stopped him.

I gestured, and shrugged, but I couldn't get anything out of them.)

After a while, with her face stinging with cold, she went back to the Volga. In a Russian magazine borrowed from the office and stuffed into her bag were recipes and beauty tips. What women needed. She always fell for them and tried not to. Finally, giving up on the prospect of reshaping her eyebrows, which left uncared-for might have belonged to a badger, she looked at her watch. Grisha had now been gone for forty minutes.

She walked over to the aircraft hangar and tapped on the door. '*Ellyo? Mozhno k vam?*' A bit too polite, she sounded, but to acquire Soviet gruffness was a skill. 'Can I come in?'

There was no answer so she pressed the catch on the door—just corrugated metal in a wooden frame—and entered. The space was dark, with a low ceiling she could just make out, but then there was some light beyond. And there sat Howard's driver with three companions, all in the customary brown cotton overalls of the skilled working class. They sat around a wooden table and before them lay a feast: of raw onion, of dried fish, of salami, of black bread. With their food they were drinking vodka from tumblers.

'Oh, I've gatecrashed a party!'

Grisha raised his glass as she approached. '*Zdrast-vuyet-ye!*' he boomed, that red-faced, blond-haired monster-angel-boy, and the way he said it sounded as if he were singing it out in pure parody of all that was and was not Gels Maybey. 'Why hello there! *Zdrastvuyetye*, idiot stranger!' He repeated, and his whole face seemed to bulge with alcohol and merriment and to dismiss any other concern in life.

His companions smirked and shifted. The eyes of the nearest one to Grisha bulged behind his big square spectacles. He quite looked the part of a man caught out in a moment of private vice. The other two, embarrassed, cowered a little. A foreigner had caught them in dereliction of duty, and they felt terror. It helped her to imagine who they were, and thus to bury her own humiliation.

She knew what they feared. In the main bookshop on Gorky Street, the most important bookshop in the country, posters warning workers not to get drunk and fatally tangled up in their machines papered the walls where once books had been sold. Not to arrive at work at all or to be at work and get nothing done was almost a capital crime; or it was bad behaviour; everything, your life, even, depended on the whim of whoever that day was your judge. It was funny, but Soviet law had a lot to do with etiquette, at certain moments, because the task of the whole state was to re-educate people and strengthen their self-discipline. If you were lucky you'd get a judge who saw it like that. Comrade citizen, your task is to commit to the state! Pledge yourself daily, and never neglect your duty to build Communism! But then with a different judge you might get sent east. They feared their complete disdain for the state, especially in front of a foreigner.

'This is our mechanic,' Grisha introduced the thin bespectacled man in his specialist's tan overall. Who knew how old he was? Forty perhaps. 'And these two, they're drivers like me.'

Gels nodded.

'Welcome to our little club,' he said.

A home within a home. A country within a country. Half a secret. Different pledges. Few duties.

She accepted a vodka; sipped it in ladylike Western fashion, in the company of Moscow's official drivers. They were the ones who drove the Politburo members. They were the ones who serviced their cars. She saw the chink in the fence.

'Anyone of you know a Russian who drives a Mercedes?'

'*Yeshcho by*! You must be joking.'

'But it happens, doesn't it? So I've heard.'

(The grinning, flushed, merrymaking Car Club members resembled a trio of Falstaffs disguised as shop floor managers. Shakespearian rustics shifted to the Soviet city, they were carters who now fixed combustion engines in the name of Communism. Got you! I would ask them a favour and it would lead to a revelation.)

Four

The sense all the time was that what you saw was often not real, and in any case not the whole story. This Russia was all around you. You could touch it and smell it, it could crush you, and yet it wasn't real. Yet we in the West thought it possessed a special truth, and we set out to find it like the Holy Grail. (A strange thing had happened in Vilnius when I had asked if our class might visit the Museum of Suicide. I'd heard it was one of the attractions of the city.

'No such museum exists.'

'Really? I heard—'

'It's under repair.'

The director of VIRILE had stood there, flanked by his two lieutenants who immediately contradicted each other. Like Jesus and the two thieves they hung there in a terrible parody of *anno domini* humanity. But then in the director's eye I thought I saw a faint glimmer of sympathy and amusement, as if he had the same thought. Life is absurd. Everyone in Russia knows that. He was one of those men who made me understand the boundary I had to cross and what then I had to report.)

'Did you think you might buy a car while you're here?' Howard interrupted her reverie. The day was colder than ever, and the great padded door to the office was closed, creating a feeling of togetherness, if you liked it, and stuffiness and frustration if you didn't.

'Mmm, well maybe I could go down there with Grisha again. I've got an idea—'

'I see. You'd like Grisha to be your chauffeur.'

'No, no! That's just while I'm still deciding.'

'*Nu ladno.*'

A return visit to the car pound was nothing special to Howard and, wedged in his chair as he listened to the conversation, Howard's *assistyent* just said ok.

Green biro in hand, he carried on working. Eventually, pushing it in Howard's direction, he announced a dangerously diminishing number of bears in the Kamchatka peninsula.

Howard grinned. 'And you're saying my—our—newspaper should be interested in that? We're not the World Wildlife Fund, my friend.'

'Don't be so quick to arrive at your Western conclusions, boss!' Soon we were a family again, laughing together.

(I loved those moments.)

The big driver explained that this factual report, in the broadsheet *Bulletin of the Union of Soviet Huntsmen*, was actually a veiled criticism of the leadership.

'You don't say!'

'*Da*!'

Gels half-stifled a laugh, only to burst out in unstoppable mirth. What a farce!

The point was that the *nomklats* who ran Grisha's country liked nothing more than a day's shooting.

'Our leader buys his shooting clothes from Crombie, Ffion and Belvedere in Jermyn Street.'

'Hah! That's where my Dad goes.'

'Why am I not surprised?'

'Our leaders like to pass themselves off as English lords.'

'Hah! But that's so *funny*!' She couldn't speak for laughter. She was choking, 'You mean, Grisha, ha, they dress up like *us* to feel special? While we pine over their Russian souls? Ha!'

'Krombee ant Fy On and Bell Vedder,' Grisha repeated. 'Maybe you know it?'

'Gels does. She used to go with her Dad on Saturday mornings.'

Ha! It turned out the *nomklats*—the administrators of a sombre proletarian state—craved to be rich. They wanted to be aristocrats. Jumped-up fakes!

All the while there were fewer and fewer bears. Sad that was how they showed they were wealthy. Trying to be like us! Ha!

'Does HE really shoot bears? I thought it was wild boar.' Howard was referring to the great leader, the General Secretary of the Party, the collector of foreign cars and, as such, the idol of that bastard GAI policeman who stopped Howard pursuing the arrested dissident demonstrators, after the December 14 demonstration. The point was wild boar weren't in deficit yet.

'It's possible, from a certain point of view, to say that he only shoots wild boar—' said the *assistyent*.

'I see. HE does shoot bears then, at some other time. Gotcha!'

'Ha!'

Grisha looked up at the possible device in the pretty nineteenth-century ceiling rose and fell silent.

Nomklats eh, mused Gels, and their corrupt leader who liked to dress up as a rich Western landowner! Recovering from the comic interlude she registered the tragedy; the terrible distortion wrought on the human soul, for a country and its people to communicate like this. And for Russia to communicate with its Western foe using such an absurd sign language. The word *nomklat* was borrowed from the late Latin *nomenclatura*, to describe the corrupt ménage surrounding the emperor. Westerners coined it and the Russians liked it so much they borrowed it back. They didn't mind being called Imperial Romans by another name, and seen as English aristocrats, shopping in Jermyn Street, in another disguise, because all the world was only a stage.

'Are you going to shame the Leader, Howard?'

'Ridicule him more like, Gels. This is a shameless country.'

'*Da.*'

Untrue, unreal, shameless: the indictments were stacking up, and yet Howard and Gels still hoped.

Grisha refocused his eyes on the ceiling rose: the abusive conversation was straying into dangerous territory. *Ostorozhno, molodtsy!* Careful how you go, my friends! It was twenty-five years since the last mass executions for wrong thinking, let alone wrong deeds, had taken place, mostly down in the basement of the Lubyanka prison, with a shot in the head, or a shovel to the skull, but you never knew how much of the tragic past lay ahead; if and when the present comedy died down. That might even *be* the revolution, not even to be wished for at all.

Another of Grisha's stories that morning was that somewhere out east THEY had sentenced to death a SOVKHOZ manager. Was he guilty? Don't you believe it! Cried Howard. A SOVKHOZ was a state farm on which food production depended. Production was patchy. People were even hungry. Or fed up with eating just kasha and bread and horsemeat salami. So every now and again the Party swooped down from the idyllic blue sky above the propaganda banners fluttering in the wind and plucked a victim, somewhere between Minsk and

Vladivostok, and blamed him for the failures of production. THEY picked someone in a certain locality and made him (nearly always him, in those days) a national example.

'Everyone's corrupt so it doesn't matter who they choose.'

'The order comes: "We need an example, comrades." So they choose someone hated in the factory. Or a man chooses the *podlets*, the bastard, who slept with his wife. Or a woman gets rid of her rival in love. To accuse someone of economic corruption is a very useful weapon.'

'He fiddled the books. She faked the invoices. No one asks for proof.'

'Everyone's corrupt so it doesn't matter who they choose.'

'You see, Gels, you have to read between the lines. A man is charged with corruption but everyone knows that's not why there are only a few apples and no oranges in the shops. Or it's never the whole story.'

'I get it. But it frightens me. There's a lot of vengeance in this country.'

(I would learn the truth of that at the far end of this tale. Vengeance and fear, nothing else. Vengeance and fear.)

Corruption. Incompetence and carelessness. Purloining of state resources for private gain. If the official harvest failed most workers didn't care a jot. Distribution failed the nation too. Not enough vehicles were fit to be driven. Or if there were lorries available the drivers weren't sober enough to pass the straight line test.

'Add that to the cunning—the heroic cunning they salute as virtue—and the untruth. The second revolution won't be pretty.'

'Who says it's untrue? Paperwork covers it up. This whole country runs—or doesn't run—on paperwork. What gets written on the paper and what doesn't no one can say.'

(Which meant even the act of writing, even the keeping of records, the very desire to know *exactly* what was the case, was impossible, even for us.)

'It's like a fairy tale with a bad ending.'

'It's a nightmare.'

(It wasn't the first time I thought—who was it said that sometimes the closest you can come to the truth is a lie? I've heard it said there are situations even the novel cannot cope with, but I will try to write what I know.)

'Howard, did you say *I* could write something for LGN?'

'Certainly. I'd be delighted.'

'It would have to be something positive. Listening to all this I feel I'm living in the first circle of hell. I mean I love the metro. What about a story on the Moscow metro?'

'I like that idea.'

'It's like a stately home down there.'

(And immediately I said that I knew whatever I wrote wouldn't be the truth at all, because my imagination would intervene. We all have imagination. It's what saves us. I have the imagination to tell you a story of what the *nomklats* were really up to and I will. But not today.)

'Today Gels Maybey will talk to you about the Moscow metro, which by now tens of thousands of you have seen for yourselves, because you've come here as tourists (and had your hotel rooms bugged).

'It's like some grand ballroom, all marble and chandeliers. You pass through it to catch your train.

'Actually it's a burial vault down there. They buried the aristocracy in surroundings they would be familiar with. Like Egyptian kings, in their chambers full of jewels. No, listen, Howard! Imagine, you were a sort of Nabokov (a writer-aristocrat from the old days, a real one). You were used to the grand marble-and-chandelier whirl in your palace. Or, I don't know, you were Tolstoy and lived too long. One day you took the escalator up to the surface. You found this wasn't palatial old Russia anymore. It was the mouse-grey Soviet Union. You wanted to go back down the escalator but you couldn't. You were trapped. Not in one place or the other.'

'It is a good *story*. But you can't write that for LGN.'

Gels pondered. 'Seriously, what were those *nomklats* doing, who usurped the past?'

Howard rested two thoughtful fingers on his lips. 'Well, I suppose, they *thought*, with a bit of tweaking, that *everyone* could share the wealth, and the graceful living, if they got rid of the tsar and the landowners and princes and princesses. There would be wealth for everyone, except the corrupt few they'd just got rid of.'

'The people were duped.'

'But who were the people? Who are they? They'd be the same if they had the power. It doesn't really matter who comes out on top here. Only that someone does, to take the place of the tsar and his princes, and carry the old luxuriously corrupt life on.'

'So the country's just as it was, until it's time for a second revolution.'

'It can't come soon enough. The day of reckoning.'

In the industrious silence, with Howard and Grisha doing real work, Gels, who was not, because from that day on she knew her work was elsewhere, continued her forensic examination of the office. Howard's real books must be elsewhere. On his shelves were only those dreary Soviet yearbooks which could tell you what the Party resolved in '72 and '76, and a few random paperbacks—the story of those Russophile British spies of the 1950s who betrayed the Americans in the name of the Communist ideal. Yeah yeah. They hated their own privileges.

(Harriet thinks I'm like them.)

Prominent on the shelf was also a well-thumbed copy of Robert Conquest's *The Great Terror*, on which Gels pressed Howard, as if the fact that he owned that great work meant he should also take responsibility for disseminating its contents worldwide.

'How many died?'

'Seven hundred thousand.'

'My God. A drastic pruning of the Soviet Garden of Eden. Another day of reckoning. I suppose that's also how you avoid another revolution. Make everyone too scared. My God.'

'Stalin forced people to confess. The ONE truth was his own. They had to confess that they doubted that truth and for that they had to pay with their lives. And they had to agree that was only right. If with their pissed-upon, bamboozled souls they didn't die in the cells they died in the camps. Stalin didn't interrogate them in person, of course.

(What a find that would be for the historian, if that fact were wrong.)

'But it seems as if he was there in person, because the men who carried out the executions were next in line themselves to become his victims. As if he was always the ultimate supervisor and executioner. This country had become a killing machine and HE was the only one not in line for punishment because he wasn't part of the turnover. People died because the guards were cruel. Or because their fellow prisoners were psychopaths. People died because there was not enough food, and no medicine. They died because of poor planning. Or they fell foul of wrong thinking. As if a devil had got into the works. And people like them were also the executioner's executioners. So the system used them, and used them up. And only the Leader and his One Truth endured.'

'No one can know what's in someone else's head.'

'Stalin decided he could. He could tell what your thoughts were and how they deviated from his ONE good idea for the country's future.'

'That's sick! What kind of a story is that! The drains got clogged with human hair and gristle. I read that.'

'The Lubyanka prison was everyone's nightmare.'

'The one next to the children's toy shop?'

'That's THEIR humour for you.'

When Gels lifted her shoulders to her ears and screwed up her face and battled these terrible thoughts she looked to Howard terribly young. Yes. Twenty-six. Nine years younger than him, and not having faced any of life's great tests.

(The dream, my dear, the dream! Howard said and I cried. Grisha uttered a sound that came out like Bvaaaaaa.)

Gels sat in her allocated chair, musing that surely not everything *could* be so bad. There must, somehow, be a way to live in Russia; some expertise that people acquired; some defiant counter-logic. She would sooner or later meet someone who would teach her the otherness of Russian souls. They could not all be so vile.

Then Howard reverted to her writing a piece on the strangely beautiful underground railway: 'Tell you what. You could start at Pervomayskaya. Razumovsky loves that station. I'll pick you at 1pm outside and you can tag along. He wants me to go and see him this afternoon.'

In which case she needed to set off now. But before that she had to ask Grisha a favour, so before she left she paused in the back room. There was a huge map of the Soviet Union on the wall beyond the teleprinter. She often stood there, trying to improve her geography, her nose right up against the vast continent. What was the name of that province with the bears that were dying out, Grisha? she called out. 'Kamburov? Kamchuria? I just can't find it.' The *assistyent* manoeuvred himself out of his chair and into the back room like a stiff puppet. Like a human tree, she noted down, his arms and legs stuffed into a suit-like jacket and trousers and branching out sideways from his trunk.

Once he was beside her she put a finger to her lips and whispered: 'I need a list of all the owners of Mercedes owners in Moscow.'

'That's not possible.'

'I think it is. A list of all the Mercedes imported in the last five years. Your friends at SOVAVTO will know. They're drivers. They know the *nomklats*.'

'Not possible.'

'Come on! There can't be so many. I haven't seen a single Mercedes in the streets.'

'That's not where they drive them. They drive them where people can't see.'

'But that boy who was driving the night of the Embassy fire—'

'He wasn't allowed. He was misbehaving.'

'I need to know his name. I want to talk to him. I think your Drivers' Club can help.'

'Impossible,' he muttered. But she knew he knew he had no option. She had him over a barrel. For what was the Drivers' Club but a nice little earner? The Moscow Drivers had a lucrative sideline reselling stolen Western automobile parts because they stole them themselves.

Five

The Razumovskys, whose heroic actions had persuaded the Westerners to believe the second revolution was coming, lived a few minutes' drive from the metro station, close to Ismailovsky Park. They were heralds of change, and especially Howard Wilde loved them, was indebted and in awe.

In normal times theirs would have been a good address, not right in the centre of the city, but civilised, still with a trace of history about it, with plenty of solid older housing and close to transport and green space. It was just what you might expect of a professor who was also an Academician, married to a talented pianist with a degree in chemistry. The Moscow middle class before the Revolution had acquired a knowledge of how to live and the Razumovskys were among its descendants. Their forebears were people with good manners who went to galleries and concerts and read many books in several languages. Not immediately visible to the naked eye, in the Razumovskys the bourgeois life-form lived on. In fact all across Moscow you could see traces of how, despite the imprisonments and the poisonings and the evictions, a refined culture had adapted to sixty years of official hostility. The aristocracy had gone but the bourgeoisie, withdrawn into its shell, was almost intact. The Soviet regime didn't like individuals like the Razumovskys, and like their friends Galina Obolenskaya and Anna Lunina, who had also turned out for the December 14 protest, because these were people, who, however difficult the *nomklats* made their daily existence, could still make fine judgements about art and morality and discern the truth for themselves; people who preferred self-cultivation to ignorance. By whatever name you called them, those good people endured. Anna Lunina worked at the Tretyakov Gallery and Galya was a translator of Dickens.

Howard and Gels parked on the hard shoulder that stood in for a courtyard. It was raining and Howard—in that dirty sheepskin which smelt rather like Soviet newsprint when it got wet—covered his head with his bulging briefcase.

Gels turned up the hood of her parka. It was so capacious that when she wore it in London it had shielded her from the world around her that wasn't hers at all, she felt. She often turned her head like a baby into a blanket into the soft mass of warmth and darkness of that hood. But now her eyes faced outwards. Russia had given her courage.

The ground was slippery and the day, as usual, grey. They climbed the five flights, she proud of her fitness, because, as she told herself, she was vain and proud and arrogant, while he acted out being not so impressed by his own. He wasn't in good shape. Too much sitting around, she said, the beginning of the unhealthy body in which the mind rots. Yeah, Gels, I must do something about it. I knew you'd come to watch over me.

'It's only us,' he called, as he tapped at the door already ajar. Natasha had buzzed them in downstairs.

There, in a modest fifth-floor flat, one bedroom and a living room that had space for nothing else, stood the grand piano that had come down through Natasha's mother's family. 'Hell, what's happened?' they cried in one voice. Everything in the Razumovskys' flat was upset and upended, as if burglars had been overtaken by burrowing rats. In that same room, and in the bedroom, and in the half-room, not much bigger than a cupboard, that served as Sasha's study, books straddled the floor, like paving stones after an earthquake. Compulsory classics read in schools for form's sake, now cast aside at random. Cherished works of literature long ago taken to heart now tossed away. The Party didn't care. Only that the book as a physical object might conceal something.

It's a physical object, a book. You can break it.

'Our policemen paid us a visit.'

'Not that they can read themselves, the bastards!'

'Natasha, *golubchik, ne nado*!'

But Howard would not take offence at Natasha's whiplash tongue. It saved him an outburst of his own.

Pushkin, Lermontov, Gogol, Tolstoy, Dostoevsky—all the classic writers who were still, in the West, the good face of Russia, were they not?—were suspect to the present regime.

The West loved those dead writers. They were the hope of a second revolution.

But that wasn't why they lay battered and squandered on the carpet. The trouble with books, if you were a nomklat policeman was that they got in the way of transparent citizenship. You know, all the thoughts they share invisibly with their readers. No one can police that.

No, Western lady, but we can break their spines. Their readers' too.

How shameful the present regime was! *Kak im ne stydno*! Gels cried, remembering a useful grammatical construction drilled into her in Vilnius.

(That's why we love Russian literature. Because truth always fights back. Pushkin had a gift for puns and satirical squibs and poisonous double-entendres. Remember Pushkin, the rain dripping from his stone curls, last week in central Moscow? Remember Gogol? Gogol invented Grisha, in the moment I caught him out feasting with his friends in the Car Club.)

'So what happened?'

Gels was on her knees in front of the bookcase beside the window, beyond the piano, teasing the spoiled volumes back into shape. They'd emptied the soil from a pot plant over the poetry of Mandelstam. She fetched a cloth from Natasha's kitchen. Mandelstam wrote a marvellous poem about a tram trundling along the road and then rerouting itself into the sky. The last place that's free to go. Oh, and yes, and he wrote a squib about Stalin. It wasn't even published, but then, fool that he was, he got drunk and recited it at a party. Whereupon some Soviet Salieri denounced him and that ended his life. Vengeance is mine and I will hurt you.

(What I had to learn. I was a student of Russian literature and I was on my knees.)

The poem desecrated by soil could have been Lermontov's 'A Solitary White Sail' or Pushkin's 'I loved you once'. There is a good human sensibility, wide and deep, which flows like a river and will continue to the end of our days. They were trying to kill it here.

Howard was working with a dustpan and brush; and with a second moistened cloth was rubbing the carpet. It was probably water from the flower vase, but you never knew. He lowered his head and sniffed.

'What happened?'

'…retaliation for all the bad publicity worldwide they got from our December 14 meeting…'

'That's right,' said Natasha, listening to them. 'I understand perfectly your English.'

But they reverted to Russian to show sympathy.

'But it will just go on, a never-ending cycle, because now Howard you'll report what they've done to you and it will be on the BBC, and it will annoy THEM more…'

'Whoever gets tired first will stop,' said Razumovsky with a faint smile, watching them and it was embarrassing because they'd made him superfluous in his own flat, with their zeal to clean up.

'*Were* they looking for something, Aleksander Nikolaevich? Or just making a mess?' For both interpretations were possible.

Howard remarked on some burnt photographs.

'My mother. But I remember what my mother looked like,' said Sasha, standing over them as they wiped and sorted, and swept and scrubbed the rugs, and the parquet in the bedroom and the hall.

Trampled stationery!'

'Nothing must get out of this country. Letters tell tales. Postage stamps have wings.'

'You shouldn't forget, Miss Gels, that our policemen are idiots.' Obviously that was Natasha.

Three empty glasses stood on the piano. Howard sniffed. The idiot marauders had toasted themselves in vodka.

'There must be DNA on those rims,' Gels said, as her colleague—she had chosen him as that, to make a start on her real life—carried the shot glasses into the kitchen.

'Unfortunately drinking Professor Razumovsky's vodka when he's not at home isn't a crime, Gels. None of this is a crime. It's just routine surveillance.'

'Dear Mr Howard, give me that bottle! I knew it! It was the vodka Mrs Dargomyshsky gave Sasha for his birthday.'

'Lemon vodka? I hate the stuff,' Razumovsky replied quietly. 'Don't make so much fuss, dear one.'

'All the same it was *yours*. A present to *you*! Shall we sit down? Gowart? Mees Dzhellsa?' Chastened, Natasha softened towards the Westerners, with the occasional welcoming gesture she was capable of. 'Would you like tea? I'll make tea.'

The two of them perched on the brown sofa which was hard, with wooden arms, and probably served as a guest bed.

The tea glasses in their pretty metal holders looked enchanting, with their delicate silver-coloured handles; so enchanting you thought you were missing something about what was real and true in Russia. Just for a few minutes you held a tea glass and got to touch a simulacrum of the true country. The holders were cheap Soviet aluminium, but they were magical, evoking the precious past.

'What really matters is that they took the report we've compiled on the *psykhushki*,' Sasha blurted. Suddenly, he had his face buried in his hands. Possibly he was sobbing. His life's work gone.

Howard got his feet. 'No! No!'

Gels looked to Natasha. 'Should we call an ambulance?'

'I'm not sure I can go on,' the old man sobbed. He was breathing heavily. '*Podozhdi*!' Natasha cried. Wait! Don't die yet! She fetched the nitro-glycerine from the bedroom. 'So far as our work goes it is a terrible setback…' the old man wheezed.

Howard wrote the couple's last two sentences down. 'You can't go on, you say. Sasha Nikolaevich? These Party men really are beasts.'

'We will need your support more than ever.'

'We will help you all we can,' Howard replied.

'I've lost so much of my work,' Razumovsky bellowed.

But then, so saying, Razumovsky regarded the ceiling rose and led their gazes upwards with him. The performance was over.

Gels opened her mouth to speak but Howard put a finger to his lips.

Surveillance only amounted to sound, in those days, and so the silent movie was reinvented, side by side with the talkie.

'Still, we're forgetting it's Christmas.' Howard brought out the mince pies and the Christmas cake he had wedged in his open shoulder bag and set them on the table. The cake came in a festive tin from England—some visitor to the British Embassy had set up the usual seasonal bridge between Fortnum and Mason and dissidents in their Moscow flats. Likewise someone at the embassy had baked the traditional pies. Charity, you see.

'Where were you two, by the way, that let them get in here last night?'

'Away, visiting my sister Yelena in Gorky.'

Razumovsky, somewhat exhausted by his performance, nevertheless, sat and listened to his wife.

'They're watching us all the time—which means, of course, that no *real* burglars ever get in here.' Razumovsky chuckled.

Natasha thundered. '*Grabiteli*! They're all *thieves*. They steal from the Russian people to buy themselves fancy food and cars. And keep this wall around Russia so no one can stop them. And twist the psyches of the people so they too cannot judge for themselves anymore what is true and what should be.'

Howard and Gels had also brought tangerines and nuts from the foreigners' grocers.

While Russians had meagre rations Westerners could buy the very best food. 'My sister knew a woman who worked in one of those *places* that sell special food to the Westerners,' observed Natasha grimly. 'She sold her soul, that one, just because she was greedy.'

'I'm so sorry,' Gels said at last, 'I'm so, so sorry. I mean the way *we* are caught up in this. It's difficult.'

Howard came back to the main point: 'What will you do now?'

'Start our work again, what else?' Since that remark was once again meant for the device in the ceiling for a moment they all looked up and smiled. It was like a toast they drank to all their good efforts prevailing.

'So you'll write a report, Gowart?' asked Razumovsky, standing on the threshold in his slippers to see them out into the long since dark late afternoon.

'Of course.'

'Happy Christmas to you. And you, young lady.'

She looked too young, and too fashionable for a man of his generation to take seriously. But Razumovsky meant well. She shook his old man's hand.

Back in the car Howard switched the tape deck on automatically.

'No, no, don't. Not Beethoven, Howard. It's too much. Fuck THEM, Howard! I mean fuck THEM!'

The rain had turned to a foul icy drizzle in the premature evening and the wipers were desperately scouring the windscreen to keep any surface in this contaminated city clear and clean.

'Fuck them! Squalid bastards! For making this place the hell it is.'

'How was the metro ride?'

'Right. Yes. Full of people carrying huge objects. I saw two men with a fridge. The lady at the bottom didn't mind a bit. She just got on with her knitting.'

'She sits there making sure people behave.'

'It's kinder than trashing their lives.'

'We find her charming and exotic, at least. But it's all the same in the end. Repression Repression Repression. Fit in or be punished.'

Gels was mulling over this miserable truth when a question that had formed in her mind a few hours earlier resurfaced. 'Howard you say the secret police attacked the Razumovskys. But isn't there some *one* person we can hold responsible?'

They waited at traffic lights which, as everywhere in Moscow, were high in the sky, compared with London. She was sure she would have missed them. So then they were talking about cars and roads again. 'I take care because traffic offences are a way they can get at us.'

'I admired you the other night. I would chase after them. Besides, your lovely car.'

'Just doing my job. And letting off a little steam.' He laughed at himself, and they were on the move again. 'There is a man though, yes, in answer to your question. His name is Vladimir Arkadevich Korsakov. He's my boss here, and a lot of other people's too.'

'I want to confront him!' She sounded childish to herself. She could hear it. 'I don't see how *you* can do that.'

'I will.'

Once past the big intersection with the Red Army Park, as they turned off the main ring road, there loomed the old merchant complex they called home. Again Howard had to park on the unpaved mound outside the compound. 'Whoops, don't slip.' He grabbed her arm. The rutted mud was stiff with frost. 'You need different boots.'

'I know. But I like these.'

'I like them too.'

'So I'll keep them.'

Gels took his arm as they stood under the arch, gently moving him out of the earshot of the sentry. 'I wanted to ask you something. About the wipers.' He had them in his hand. 'The other day. You didn't forget the wipers, Howard, did you? You let them be stolen. It's a favour you do for Grisha ever now and then. So he can earn some money and cultivate his friends.'

'I don't know what makes you think that.'

'I visited SOVAVTO and you're not a good liar.'

He smiled and stared ahead of him. 'We all have our ways of helping. It pleases me to play a silly game.'

They climbed the cold stairs. The lift in the blue-painted central iron cage passed them coming down. 'I'm always afraid of it.'

She kept on liking him. But really this Moscow was a nightmare. Howard was lying too. Everybody was lying. Even Razumovsky.

Grisha had locked the office door and left. When they let themselves in the world news was spilling out over the floor. Spain had become a democracy. The

Shah of Iran had handed his country over to popular rulers, after forty years of dictatorship. The Americans had abandoned Taiwan and become friendly with the Chinese. It was almost another strain of the Moscow disease, to view the world in terms of enormous power blocks, tilting and shifting like tectonic plates, spoiling lives here and there, occasionally offering people something THEY called democracy but didn't resemble Howard and Gel's idea of it at all.

She was by now very efficient at dividing up the endless bulletin into readable pages. Howard was in the back office looking for editorial messages when she heard him curse.

'Bugger it!'

'Something wrong?'

(Reverting to our old conversation about Stalin I was wondering about having my mind cut out in a *psykhushka*.)

'Match it!' The London office wanted him to lambast ATHEIST COMMUNIST RUSSIA! GODFORESAKEN RUSSIA! As if nothing more were at stake. 'I have to write that fucking churches story Sergei gave me because some lowlife tosser for the London Evening News got hold of it.'

'You just have to keep the good end in sight.'

'The end of the Cold War?'

'Freedom for these people. Freedom and true democracy.'

'You sound like the Zimmermans.'

'You know what I mean. Something better than living in a nationwide prison. Anyway I'm going up. I'm going to lie in that Russian bath installed in 1900 and reflect on what I've seen today.'

When she went back down, as she pushed open the heavy leather-padded office door, she found him typing.

DISSIDENT HOME RAIDED IN REPRISAL ATTACK. REPORT ON ALLEGED PSYCHIATRIC ABUSE STOLEN.

She read over his shoulder. She was very close to him.

Howard's words, even now lining up on his typewriter, would be heard tonight on the BBC and appear tomorrow in the International Herald Tribune. Something was good.

'Shall we have a drink when you've finished?'

'Glad to. Give me ten minutes.'

(And that, probably, should have been our night.)

Six

On Christmas Eve the Zimmermans, viewed as nice people but hardliners when it came to the Cold War, threw a party for colleagues and friends in their flat. In the West the festival was becoming difficult to hold together. What once had been a time of unity and celebration was now the occasion of mild dissent. Jews, Hindus, Muslims, Shintos, Buddhists, even Russians, had their own, different, holy days. Many more people, including most of the expatriate community in Moscow, were not believers at all. A national holiday normally meant a quiet time for the news media. But the journalists were jumpy. If the West relaxed the Kremlin would take advantage. They'd done it in August 1968, deep into the Western world's summer holidays, by invading Czechoslovakia. Now again in December 1978, when the once Christian West was overfed and tipsy, would the Russians make some dastardly move to upset the world order? So the correspondents stayed in Moscow over the festivities, were briefly at a loose end, and felt obliged to celebrate somehow. An international crisis rather than five days of overeating might have been easier.

Gels noticed Natasha Razumovsky had found the mince pies a curiosity rather than a delight—often the way with another culture's 'specialities'. The Christmas cake made by the defence attaché's wife had a greater capacity to cross borders, especially if, like a Christmas cracker, it contained, instead of jokes, secret communications. But Howard said that was the wrong way round and it didn't do to be paranoid, 'even here'. The box of clementines found most favour with that brave, not at all motherly woman Gels would come deeply to admire. Here was real fruit, not just a vitamin C pill. Besides, the colour and glossy sheen were painterly, and Natasha Razumovsky had an artistic sensibility, long buried under the weight of political responsibility, but not lost. At this level contact between the two women, with such different burdens, truly incomparable, was made. Gels worried she would herself prove inadequate.

But now, always with the season of good tidings and great joy in mind, unless you were a Kremlin predator – (Were there other good Russians? If they existed, like the young man, she would find them) – now it was time to think of Grisha. Howard bought him at least one gift from the foreigners' mini department store, which sold electrical goods at seductively low prices. Gels said she didn't want to hand Moscow extra hard currency by shopping in such despicable places. Howard found such a view prissy and disgusting, and declared he would do his bit to ward off Russia's bankruptcy.

'The Soviet Union running out of cash! Lord! I'll put that top of my wish list for 1979.'

'It could happen,' he reflected with a twisted smile more aimed at Gels than how things stood in the world. Whatever his motive and his true view Gels felt glad. The initial hostility had gone.

The gift for Grisha was a Toshiba 45/78 rpm turntable to which, with some forethought, having imported them from Frankfurt, Howard added vinyl recordings of Chet Baker and Thelonius Monk. Presents were exchanged at a Christmas ceremony in the office, late in the afternoon of the 24th. Taking Gels by surprise, Howard laid two crackers at each place on the I-shaped conglomeration of desks. One, two, three, *Raz, dva, tri,* go! When they pulled them it sounded as if they were shooting at each other. 'Finally a real war! Heh!' Cried Howard. Grisha's turnip face cracked from side to side. He went red and held his sides and had to sit down on the long-suffering swivel chair. Bang. Bang. Bang.

Tipped off by her Japanese neighbour as to where to go, Gels bought Howard a Chinese teapot and a packet of Jasmine tea. He thought she was trying to refine his taste. Women were often like that, with him. He wondered did it happen with other men, or had he let himself become gross. All in the name of the task at hand.

He gave her, unwrapped, a copy of Baedeker's 1914 guide to Russia for travellers, which silently took her breath away.

'Nabokov would have known of it, I suppose.'

'It's outrageously kind. I don't know what to say.' The office felt overheated as usual but she was also blushing. To walk down streets before all this greyness happened! To take down the banners and replace them with coloured lights! To give every shop a proprietor's name instead of an anonymous bureaucratic number. And still those were trivial changes, not what the Razumovskys were campaigning for.

Several glasses of Soviet champagne helped diminish her anxiety and turn her brain to mush. Howard even brought flutes down from his flat, an improvement on the tumblers he generally reached for when guests came. It was a gesture in sympathy with the legendary Soviet proletariat, she guessed, or was it some political battle he was fighting in faraway England, which, as he had told her almost as often as the number of days she had been in Moscow, he disliked.

Igrivoe they were supposed to call it, on World Trade Organisation orders, but most people still called it *Shampanskoe*, which sounded better. It was the stuff she'd drunk in the Metropol Hotel, on that night she went dancing alone and made her first clumsy attempt to know the other side. With alcohol comes melancholy. Brain mush accompanied by acute emotions.

She clinked glasses with the boyishly overwhelmed Russian, who, yes indeed, would have preferred his wine in a tumbler, and with Howard, whose glass actually held only mineral water. He'd stopped drinking alcohol, he muttered. The more ready to do battle? She wondered. and said nothing, until he smiled sheepishly, as if to say sorry but there's nothing I can do about this moment on the calendar, nor about my new t-total ways; as if the season itself were making him nostalgic and kind.

The record player came with two speakers that slotted into the top to form a unit for easy portability. 'So, plug in, put the record on the turntable—hold it at the edge with your fingers, don't *smudge* it, Grish—move the arm back *gently* till it clicks free and there you are. At one touch of the needle on the record you have music.'

'Magic!' cried the Soviet man-boy. The central toyshop next to the secret police headquarters had nothing to rival it.

The sound was tinny, as if the true energy of the music were locked in a neighbouring room. Also Gels didn't think Grisha was musical. His enthusiastic foot-tapping had nothing in common with the pulse. His thick paws would never manage those surfaces correctly. But he was happy and so was Howard.

'Five minutes!' Gels cried, and ran up to her flat to butter some black bread.

(As my head cleared I laboured already old thoughts. I had inspected empty shops and joined food queues in the street, hence my discomfort in our privileged shops for foreigners, for we were forced into replacing the old aristocrats as a despicable spectacle. The truth hurt like a loose tooth that I agitated back and forth with my tongue. Painful and yet I wanted it.)

'Here,' she set the plate between Howard and Grisha. 'Help yourselves. Howard, I was just thinking. The *nomklats* of our days live like lords—like us!—while the ordinary folk queue for a bit of meat. And you say these Korsakov types don't find anything wrong about that and the people don't complain. I don't understand. In any other country there'd be riots.'

'*They* want to be Western consumers. *They* want to be rich. It's their *revenge* against the revolution. And except for a very few people like the Razumovskys the rest of Russia simply says good luck to them. We'd be the same if we had the power. Our whole country would be the same.'

'I'm not going to accept that. We have to confront these awful types.'

'Do that and you'll be in the Lubyanka in a specially selected cell without a view of the toyshop, my dear Gels. I'll do my best to get you out but I can't promise.'

'Sticks and stones may break my bones—'

'If you were Russian, they'd break you so never a word more would come out of you.'

'They wouldn't do that to a Westerner. They wouldn't dare.'

'I said if you were Russian. But whoever you are they can arrange some way to get rid of you. Car crash. Some such. Gels, you can't fight them alone.'

'But I can. I can be a witness.'

In truth, indeed, she craved action. 'Anyway, where is this Korsakov bastard? Let me see him!' She poured herself another glass of the Russian champagne which as it turned out was quite impervious to black bread and butter. It just went on lightening her head and foaming over her hand. 'Whoops!' On the desk too.

Grisha, watching them—for he was a witness too—packed up at his usual hour of 1630 and went home, whatever he thought of her tipsy outburst.

'Where does he live?' She asked, with something like a bad taste forming in her mouth. She fetched a mug of water from the cold back room.

'God knows. Out somewhere.'

'Family?'

'No idea.'

'I'd better get ready. Seven is it?'

'On the dot. They're Americans after all.'

'I'm looking forward to it.'

He watched her go. Unexpectedly he was too.

She drank a lot of water and had a bath in the big enamel tub from the cusp of the century. To have a bath was to indulge in a kind of spiritual punctuation. She submitted to it often, as the sentences formed and reformed in her head. She lay there for an hour.

Restored, in her pyjamas she did some stretches to carols being relayed on the World Service. Her fitness would help her campaign against Comrade K. She saw herself, energetic and determined—manic, Howard Wilde would have said—reflected in the glass doors that separated the living space in the LGN guest flat from the dining room. That end of the room housed a table she didn't eat from but used as a desk.

It was time to dress for an unusual occasion. The date was late December, but bearing in mind that all Moscow flats were overheated, she chose a little black dress with a plunging neckline, for, as a woman, she was not totally modest. The parka and a silk scarf would see her over to the Zimmermans, while barely keeping out the draught.

Outside when she joined Howard again the rain had passed and the sky was almost clear. It was cold, of course it was cold. But she always enjoyed a break from the indoor fug. Howard had on a black shirt, no tie, under the sheepskin, and some pepper-and-salt body hair showed in the neck which caused her some pause. In the dark, as he opened the passenger door to the MG, the only smell was of fuel from the ring road. That diabolic sulphurous residue she would never learn to ignore. Foreigners and the secret drivers of imported Mercedes could get hold of premium fuel. But domestic cars and lorries ran on the cheapest possible petrol and the whole city stank as if God were underlining this was the fuel of hell. There was little traffic though and that was a blessing. Psyching themselves up with 'Saturday Night Fever' on the way, they arrived, Gels still pretty febrile from the afternoon, on the dot of seven.

'Great. You made it.' As if Moscow were always a test.

'It's not snowing or anything.'

'No. Not what I mean. Come in!' Arthur appeared behind Harriet and disappeared again.

Another music was playing from what had filled their ears and eased their anxieties in the car. It was Scarlatti for harpsichord. Not Alexander Scarlatti père, but Domenico, his better-known son, and it just seemed like a facetious ornament on the waning hours of the day. How many functions music has, she reflected. I suppose this is diplomatic music. You can always say you didn't hear words that were better unsaid.

'How do you know about two generations of Scarlattis?' he whispered, far too close to her ear for it not to be disturbing.

'A paid-for education, Howard. You know that. Don't keep rubbing it in. Harriet! Great to see you again!'

'Gels! Good to see you. Howard's been hiding you.' Yes and no. It had been all of seven days.

In the shelter of the spare bedroom Gels whispered tipsily: 'You know what, Harriet? I think he quite likes my company.'

'He'd be a fool not to,' said Harriet, finding a coat hanger for the parka she would otherwise have thrown on a chair, and perhaps in her present state have missed in her aim, and watched it slide to the floor.

But then something happened which changed her life and she would say she had been sober ever since.

'Oh, what's that painting?'

It was when they went through to the sitting room, and it was presently half-obscured by a Christmas tree.

'Call me a philistine but there was just nowhere else to put the tree.'

'No, no, I can see it, if I stand here.'

It was a work whose manifold black surface, a thick, oily impasto, teemed with light beneath. Fire was spreading under the black lid of night.

'You want me to tell you about it now?' asked Harriet proudly.

'I do. It's magnificent!'

'We were patrons of the painter, Anatoly Mundt, before he left.'

Gels read the title. '"Communism equals the Party plus the electrification of the whole country". Of course. What else could it be?'

'THEY wouldn't see it that way. They don't like being made fools of.'

That famous slogan of the first revolution was here being ridiculed.

'They'd have to understand it first.'

'I suppose they did. That's why they got rid of him.'

So they made Mundt leave?'

'They pushed him out and took away his citizenship. All because he was such a fine artist.'

'Lord!'

(Even as I ogled the black surface it wasn't enough. I wanted to put my cheek to that black belly. 'So the country's been electrified but there's been a short circuit and now everything is in darkness. Except for the memory, smothered but still burning. Maybe the painting just needs viewers to…for the sparks to kindle the fire.')

'Personally I think it's good that Mundt left. He couldn't have survived.'

'But Harriet, what if all the good, honest, talented people leave? What will this country be then?'

'Then this country will die and we will have won the Cold War.'

'Oh.'

(Did anyone ever talk about human bankruptcy? A place where all the good people have left?)

'But I for one don't want it that way. I want Russia to come to its senses. To heal.'

So Harriet wasn't the Cold War warrior Howard made her out to be. Or she had different sides to her, all of them worth knowing. 'Gels, how can anyone want the culture of two hundred million people to die off?'

'They seem to want it themselves. I had this friend who told me a death wish had seized the whole of Russia. It's in this painting too.'

'Now that's an idea.'

So powerful was the painting that Gels just stood there, while the Scarlatti played on and the doorbell rang and glasses were refilled. Arthur was holding the fort.

Then came a thought about that faint glow showing beneath the darkness. 'They're in an evil situation but there are little good things they can do, almost in stealth.'

'I know that. I can imagine someone among the *nomklats* who told himself he wanted to save a great artist and the only way was to expel him from Russia. He—or she—persuaded themselves that was the only decent option. That's the sort of nonsense the ones with a conscience will tell themselves here.'

Harriet said: 'It's all the wrong way round. Mundt was a political problem. He found a loophole in the constitution and made fools of them. And so most of them hate him. Even his would-be saviour must have known he couldn't paint abroad. So was he trying to save him, Gels, or was it redoubled malice? It happens a lot here. Somewhere amid the mixed motives is the fact that truth has no value and no power is worth resisting. Unless you're prepared to die for it.

'You know how Mundt made fools of them? Not with this painting. The message is too veiled. No, it was only having that outdoor art show you've surely heard about. Artists can have indoor shows, so long as they have permission. But Mundt and his friends never got permission, so they set up their work in the open air. In a car park.'

'And the show was broken up with a digger. I saw the picture.' It had been sensational, and appeared on front pages round the world, of a man, Mundt himself, it turned out, swinging from the digger's blade by one hand, suspended in mid-air while the driver decided where to dump him.

'Out of the country! Outside the walls of fortress Russia!'

'Harriet, what madness possessed THEM to send in a digger and bulldoze an art show? They can't be so brazen. They can't be so careless of what people outside think.'

(The tears were running down my cheeks. I was sobbing on her shoulder. I couldn't take my eyes away from that stifling blackness with its smothered fire.)

'We'd better go back. Arthur will be needing me.'

'It's magnificent. I'll…' There was probably a handkerchief in the parka pocket, or she'd find something. 'I'll follow you.'

Finally she rejoined the party.

Was that a wink from Howard? 'You've got Christmas tree in your hair. May I?'

The tension between them was mounting, and people noticed, but didn't know how to gauge it, especially not the Zimmermans, who knew Howard of old.

After some diplomatic agonising, they had invited Howard and Gels together on the same piece of 'At Home' white card. But Harriet had to wonder: were they, in any sense, "together"?

Arthur, in a fine mood that evening, suggested Christmas Eve in Moscow, in 1978, was still not a Henry James novel. 'They won't be offended to be on the same card.'

'I do worry about Howard.' Whose first marriage must have fizzled out, Harriet guessed. What was such a decent, intelligent, good-looking man doing alone?

Well, yes. Gels asked herself the same question.

Harriet continued to watch. Her other question was what was Gels doing in Moscow with no job.

'And this is Patrick and his wife Mary. But I think you've already met.'

Scarlatti was racing up and down the keyboard, rhythmically, repeatedly: a delicate drill to fit their souls for a cordial Christmas Eve and conceal the turbulence within and all around.

'I know who you are,' said Gels. Patrick Wormold's voice was familiar from the night of the dissident rally and his face from many appearances on television. She only hadn't seen him without his *shapka*, she said. His trademark fur hat, though they all wore them.

Patrick, though he performed on camera every day, now in private seemed embarrassed at his fame. He twisted his head to one side and tightened his lips. It was as if all he could do was apologise for his distinction.

'It does actually keep his ears warm,' said Mary, defusing what surely was a familiar situation, when her husband was hailed by his viewers.

'Hi Mary. Gels.' It was a moment of instinctive mutual warmth and relief. Patrick with his upturned eyes and bashful smile turned out to be a charmer.

Away from the screen and the microphone he was a smooth, silken-voiced producer of himself. Gels would have immediately disliked him except she couldn't because she instantly so liked his wife. Besides, he made such an amusing drama out of his self-pity. On top of that, his performances brilliantly served the home country and the Corporation. So she was pleased to meet the Wormolds.

They were talking about his reporting. Poor man! No one ever let him get away from that.

'Howard tells me it's hard to get at the truth here.' A totally banal thing to say, Gels!

The charmer's eyebrows shot skywards. With an imaginary hand of cards held close to his chest, away from prying eyes, he mimed 'secrecy' as if he were playing a game of charades.

Gels smiled.

'On the other hand, is truth what our viewers want? Don't they *expect* cliches about snowflakes and samovars—'

'It's your bosses who want the cliches, Wormy,' said Mary, using her affectionate name for him. 'The viewers themselves are bright. They don't deserve a condescending journalist. Or politicians of the same ilk.'

'I second that.' Since it was praise, Patrick nodded.

'What's Russia about, Patrick? Can you tell us in three minutes flat?' She mimicked interviewing him for a change. He played ball.

'I'll tell you, young lady. It's about being a third-world country, but with bloody NUKES.'

'Oh God yes,' said someone. 'There have been *four* nuclear weapons tests this month.'

'Semipalatinsk. We've all reported that,' said Arthur, passing with canapes made by Mary.

'Try, Gels. These are seriously *vkusno.*'

'Brynza and herring. Just Gastro stuff I put it together.' But Mary was pleased with her inventiveness. 'Brynza's like Greek feta. You can do anything—'

'But NUKES!' someone said.

'It's great.' Tasty indeed. Sweet, sour and creamy all in one bite. Gels turned to talk to Mary alone. They seemed to like the look of each other, and that always mattered, as well as their ease of talking. Patrick's wife was slender, with wavy auburn hair, and her manner was spiky and attractive. Gels was strong-looking and funny, and she wore her trendy clothes well. Mary had seen her enter, in the parka. Now the reddish silk scarf was wound round her neck above a neat black dress. Her accompanying tights and ankle boots were, once again, quite unsuitable for outdoor life in Moscow but sexy indoors.

'Back home there are two Russias in people's minds. One is sentimental and speaks to the heart. It comes from the novels and makes you want to live. The other one is savage and—'

'But *how* to say that?' writhed Patrick, back with them. 'On screen, for God's sake? They'll all switch off. Besides, mixed truths are the hardest.'

'I'll second that,' said Howard, drifting over with a kiss on the cheek for Mary.

'What's your new sidekick here actually *doing* in Moscow?' Patrick suddenly jibed.

'Wormy!' said Mary. But clearly everyone wanted to know. No job, Gels thought, that's what they mean. But I have got a job. The one I've chosen.

'I was writing a thesis and I got fed up with it.' She added: 'I did my degree in Russian. *Ya govoryu po russki.*'

'She does. She's pretty damn good,' said Howard.

'I wanted to see what it was like here.'

'Good for you,' said Mary.

'Just decide on something and do it.' Patrick, Gels thought, remained sceptical.

Gels took Howard aside. 'They actually bought that painting?'

'Isn't it superb?'

'Poor Mundt.'

'Poor man indeed. Russian artists depend on Russia and yet they can't live here.'

'Mary, you're a genius.' Arthur was back, handing round the last of the *zakuski.* They were everything from 'little bits and pieces before a meal' to a full-blown smorgasbord table and the foreign community loved them. 'No Russian has thought of sweet herring and brynza together before.'

'Hell, Arthur, they must have done!'

'That's not the case. Minds here are in chains. Even in the kitchen.'

'Except when they write novels,' said Gels.

Arthur shrugged and smiled.

'So something about Russia is good news,' said Mary. The Scarlatti had stopped and now people had had a few drinks the room no longer needed a background tinkle to hold it together.

'The power of the writing. The films.'

'We all agree on that.'

It was somehow a sad moment, to think of Russian art beside Soviet reality.

Like the mismatch between ancient and modern Greece.

Harriet, with the help of her Russian maid, Dusya, had gone to much trouble though and they sat down to a fine menu. Perhaps in the end Russian food, the real thing, could be added to the list of novels and films. The beetroot soup, with sour cream, had an outstanding depth of flavour, because Dusya had boiled beef shin to make the stock, and added dried mushrooms for extra pzazz.

Pikeperch *quenelles* followed.

'Kennels?' whispered Howard, so tantalisingly close.

'It's French. A classic French dish they used to like to borrow. When they were aristocrats.'

'It must be a curse to be so well educated.'

'Being able to put a name to a thing can be quite useful, Howard. And no I didn't go to finishing school.'

Mary and Patrick looked amused to see their colleague and his neighbour—was she just his neighbour—bickering.

Harriet picking up the drift said the recipe came from Julia Child. 'You don't know who Julia Child is either.'

'Actually I do.'

'I don't,' said Patrick. 'There's one love in my culinary life and that's Elizabeth David.'

'Elizabeth who?' said Howard, feigning ignorance.

'Actually, Gels has run away from home. But then you know who her father is.'

'Howard, that's not fair.' And Gels really minded, as if her wealthy and powerful father—to escape from whom was her particular way of emerging from England—would always count against whatever she proposed of her own making.

With the *quenelles* they drank a white wine from Soviet Georgia called Tsinandali. Mention of Georgia recalled once again the name of Stalin, who had killed—Gels had since double-checked in Conquest—roughly three quarters of a million of his own, plus a few thousand foreigners caught in the wrong place at the wrong time, because, Gels had decided, his imagination was diseased. His imagination about imagination meanwhile was totally wrong. The very thought that he could smash that glorious capacity, that lifeline in every last human being, out of the heads of those he suspected did not agree with him, that the mind in the man was like a snail in a shell…and could be hammered flat …was…unbearable. The 'Man of Steel' was unfathomable. The Soviet side, claiming to have moved into a new era, was silent too.

'You could compare the *psykhushki* with the Gulag.'

'Absolutely right, Gels.'

'THEY've cut the article on Stalin out of their encyclopaedia.'

'Good God I didn't know that.'

'He's no longer a term of reference. Not for discussion. A non-person. Funny really. Give him a taste of his own medicine now he's dead.'

'They cut the actual pages out of the encyclopaedia?'

'All across the country. Every library.'

'But that's so crude.'

'I don't know how else you disappear someone who's already dead.'

'That's how they do things here.'

'Wormy even interviewed the woman library director—'

'Makharova. No. Makarenko. I went down to the Lenin Library and asked her why they cut Stalin out and she blew up. Head red as beetroot.' Gels pictured Wormy with his fluffy microphone, probably no hat indoors, confronting a fat woman with a face like the wind god Aeolus.

'THEY can't cope with free inquiry, let's put it that way. THEY don't think they're lying. It's just you being rude. Making trouble with your questions. Behaving like a hooligan.'

'It certainly enrages them.'

'Important to remember though,' said Howard, 'it's a good thing to be a *foreign* hooligan like Patrick or me or Arthur or nothing would get reported. The hooligans we must worry about are those wicked people, the Razumovskys.'

'To the Razumovskys!'

They resumed eating their superb dinner. It was true that little plates of black-and-white bread, offered cut side by side into half-slices, in the Soviet fashion, and with the white slices already curling, were, on the white side, not the best, because white bread was not a Russian strength. But the black bread was always wonderful. The room was festive too, *à l'anglaise*, with paperchains and holly.

'This Tsinandali's really not bad. Non-person, but he knew his wine,' said Patrick.

Catching sight of Gels's amusement, Howard for a moment was jealous. 'So, Harriet, tell us how you're getting on making friends with your car park guard,' called Howard across the table.

'I have the time, Howard. It's not his fault he has orders not to speak to us.'

'Ask him why he doesn't stop Russian passers-by stealing Western windscreen wipers,' asked Gels. 'He must see it happening.'

'He doesn't speak, Gels, that's the point.'

'Any Russian talking to a Westerner has to report the conversation to the secret police. Why would he risk that?'

'He might want to change things here. He might have got his job guarding foreigners with that special intention in mind.'

'He won't get far if he doesn't talk to us.'

'And he'll lose his job if he does.'

'So I leave out some soup for him.'

'And wait and see, Harriet? Like leaving out a mince pie and a glass of sherry for Father Christmas?'

'That was uncalled for, Howard.'

'*Is* he secret police?'

Wormy twisted in his seat. 'I don't *think* so. The secret bastards don't wear uniforms. He's just a soldier-type watching Russians don't get into our compound.'

'And ask for help?'

'It wouldn't be the first time.'

'And then what?'

'We don't know what to do with them. We just hand them back.'

'Ooh...'

'Sometimes the secret police dress up as firemen, didn't someone say?'

'Oh, Gels, I suppose it has to come to the night our US embassy nearly burnt down with every newcomer here. That frightful occasion has been reduced to cheap gossip.'

'Arthur didn't believe they were firemen. He thought the brand-new uniforms they were wearing gave the game away.'

'Maybe they just wanted to look smart, in the eyes of the world. Russians are very proud.'

'All I can say is those firemen weren't much good at putting fires out.'

'I just don't believe that.'

Arthur insisted. 'You're wrong, Howard. It was a disaster and a fantastic chance for THEM to gather information about us. THEY had low-flying aircraft up within the hour, taking pictures, while down on the ground their so-called firefighters slowed everything down and their spooks tried to get into our building.'

'So why not do just that?'

'Because they're just not *that* quick off the mark.'

'Either they're quick or not.'

'That's rubbish and you know it. It depends on the department. It depends who's in charge.'

'What caused it?' asked Gels. 'I heard...' The risk was that it would be cheap gossip again, but she wanted to know.

'The jury's still out on that, Angela. Gels. We say the Soviets did it.'

'With microwave beams,' added Harriet.

'Well, you would,' said Howard. Whereupon the company fell silent and Harriet signalled to Dusya to clear the plates.

'I guess the ambassador remaining in Moscow means you didn't lose anything important.' There was a real edge to the conversation now between Howard and Arthur.

'Ambassador Heffernan's old school. He does a great job.'

'But he doesn't see eye to eye with Carter, right?'

'Howard!' whispered Gels. 'Let it go!'

'You give your guard *soup*, Harriet?' asked Mary, who only visited her husband in Moscow part of the year. Mostly she was in England with the children, Gels was sorry to hear.

Arthur said proudly: 'That's my wife for you!'

'I leave it out in a thermos.'

'But that's ridiculous!' Howard was back on the offensive again. 'He's not homeless, Harriet. Of all the two hundred million people living in the Soviet Union who deserve your sympathy, you chose him!'

It was one of those slightly crazy stories life in Moscow pulled out of its hat. In truth everyone found Harriet's little *habitude* ridiculous.

But at least she's doing *something*, reflected Gels, who was then quite sympathetic to Arthur's protest.

He said: 'We all have our ways of dealing with Moscow, Howard.' Except Howard would not let go, agitating the loose tooth.

'Howard, really.'

'No, let's go down and ask Dmitry direct. Which does he prefer: New England chowder or Moscow Region cabbage soup? *Chto vam vkusnneya, tovarishch?*' He feigned sounding drunk.

'I leave out a thermos for the cold nights. That way he can take it or leave it. He doesn't have to compromise himself by speaking.'

Perhaps the point of the drama was that Howard had for a while upstaged Patrick Wormold.

'Won't someone tell me about this beast Korsakov?' But when Gels interjected no one took her up. The conversations fragmented as the plates were cleared. People got up from the table and formed little groups.

'…You speak and you can't help lying because all the truth has been used up.'

Gels found that view beautiful and desperate, and vowed to remember it.

'Starting with the way they talk about "the peace-loving Soviet Union".'

Fuck them. As you say Patrick, the peace-loving USSR has tested four nuclear weapons in as many weeks.'

'Semipalatinsk,' mouthed Gels, to remember the name.

'And THEY talk about the military psychosis of the Americans,' said Arthur defiantly.

'Ah now that! Perhaps there's some truth in *that*,' said Howard. 'You guys do have something in common.'

'Howard, no, that's unfair.'

'Will the world never forgive us Vietnam?' cried Harriet. 'And before that Korea? No I don't think they will.'

'But Communism is a threat to all our lives—'

'People don't care about it as much as you think, Arthur. Maybe it's just a word.'

'I just think that Russian art—'

Harriet tried to take hold of the reins of her unruly party.

Howard, revelling in the apple pie and ice cream he was eating standing up, spoke with his mouthful, 'You know what the problem is. The *nomklats* want to be you. They want to be America. Move over, Washington, Moscow's coming.'

'There can only be one America.'

'So *that*'s the problem.'

'And as for language back home…' Howard drifted sideways.

'Don't get me started.'

'But then you have this sympathy for them, Howard,' said Harriet.

'He does,' echoed Patrick.

'You're sympathetic too, Harriet, or you wouldn't bother with the guard. Or is it just some behaviourist experiment?'

'I feel for another human being. But Howard feels for the system, somehow, don't you, Howard?'

Gels heard it in her head. 'The dream, my dear, the dream!'

Howard announced: 'It's simple. I'd prefer to see this country reformed than witness it come to an end.'

'That's Razumovsky's point of view—'

'Yes, and he's right.'

'Shall we drink to *that*?' Harriet raised her glass. 'Happy Christmas, everyone.'

It was midnight and someone turned on the baton-twirling BBC World Service, with its tune for fife, whistle and drum.

'I can't get that tune out of my head,' said Gels.

'It's the Bandalera. Written by the great patriotic Henry Purcell to summon soldiers…' said Wormy, with a writhing misgiving. 'We want to get rid of it at the BBC but people won't let us. It's *tradition*.'

Unembarrassed hands darted forwards over the heavenly melt-in-the-mouth Belgian chocolates Mary had brought from London. Harriet served coffee.

'Moscow makes us all fat.'

'Speak for yourself!'

'You Brits are such hypocrites.'

'It's true, Harriet. We're socialists at heart. But we've lost our way.'

'Like the Russians.'

'You two, you're quite a double act.' This to Howard and Gels.

Arthur topped up the brandy glasses—the Gastro had excellent Napoleon Brandy for a pittance—'But, Jesus, and this was the real story, Gels…' for they had reverted to talking about the fire. 'The guy in the Mercedes came back in the early hours. And it was as if he was a different person. They'd evacuated the building. Quite a few diplomatic families were staying there. And when the guy came back he saw the Lawrences standing on the pavement. I play squash with Brad Lawrence. Their car was laid up and they needed to get to the ambassador's residence. Yeah sure it's another palace that once belonged to Prince Yusupov and his friends. We've taken over as many as they'll give us for a fat fee.'

'I understand. You can't have your ambassador live just anywhere.'

'Put him in a tower block on the edge of town!'

'Thank you, Mary.'

'So this guy wound down his window and offered, in English, to take them there. Brad immediately said no way, but his wife Laura said sure.'

'That's the difference between men and women.'

'You mean between seeking conflict and resolving it.'

'And so in they jumped. Two kids, three suitcases, two U.S. embassy personnel and a Russian kid at the wheel.'

'But that's amazing,' said Gels. (She had known she *must* find that driver.)

'Across the political divide. It shows it *is* possible.'

'It sure was a strange thing.'

'Did you report it?'

'I didn't report it, no. I'm telling you about it now.'

'Did you, did your friends, get a name?' asked Gels.

'You're kidding. That boy was destined for big trouble if anyone found out.'

'Golly, is that the time?' Mercifully Howard accepted that they should join the Wormolds in finally taking their leave.

Gels found her head was spinning as they left, but she had enjoyed herself.

So, in his way, had Howard. He drove them home in a friendly silence. 'No music?' she asked.

'Money Money Money,' he began, and she joined in.

> I work all night, I work all day to pay the bills I have to pay
> Ain't it sad?
> And still there never seems to be a single penny left for me.

'Abba, after Karl Marx.'

'That's not what it's about here.'

Seven

When Gels came down to the office on Christmas morning Howard wasn't there but Grisha, whom she hadn't expected to see, was at his desk. 'Oh, my! You can't put a bet on a White Christmas because there's snow so often here.' It had snowed overnight and cars that hadn't moved since the snowfall had been reduced to vague incidents on the white landscape. The MG wasn't visible, but then coming home after midnight they had once more been forced to park outside. There was no Howard in the office but wasn't that Mary Wormold coming out from her staircase? A lithe figure in a duffel coat and whiteish fur hat and brown fur gloves, and brown leather boots, she began sweeping the windscreen of the BBC Volvo with a hand brush. Gels wanted to call out but the office windows didn't open in winter. The Russian management—The Directorate for the Maintenance of Domestic Apartments (DIMDA)—came in and taped them up and Howard acquiesced, to save heat. So she just tapped and waved. Mary didn't see her.

'*Ego net*,' said Grisha, catching Gels at a low moment. 'He's not here.'

'Oh right, yes, he probably told me he was going out. What should I do, since I'm free? He said something about filing, if I was in the mood for it.'

Grisha stood for a moment in the doorway. He was like a grandfather clock about to strike the hour. 'Whatever.'

'So did you get me that list?'

'I got it, *gospozha*. *Vot*.'

Vot was a nice useful word. Like the French *voilà*. A 'here you are', though sometimes it came with an overtone of resignation. *Vot tak*. That's just how things are.

The big man handed her an envelope with her name on it. It was about to make her day.

For inside was a handwritten—presumably hand-copied—list of Mercedes cars imported to Moscow owners since 1973. If she did any filing it would only be while thinking about those names, or just celebrating having them to hand.

'Will that do?' the office assistant asked, without aggression, without any expression, really.

'Fabulous. Believe me, it's in a good cause.'

One of his little noises escaped him. It was hard to imagine Grisha was normally acting on orders; carrying out a subversive mission in his capacity as Howard's paid assistant. But you never knew.

The news wires reported that the events of Christmas Day round the world were just beginning. The Pope would be addressing the faithful in St Peter's Square. The Queen would have a message for Britain and the Commonwealth. The Archbishop of Canterbury, between carols, would remind people to love their neighbour and care less about money.

'*Italianskaya*,' Grisha said.

'What's that?'

'The Italian woman.' Meaning where Howard had gone to spend Christmas Day. Yes of course it hurt, and Grisha knew it. It was a tiny act of retaliation, for the situation she had placed him in.

'I hear she's beautiful.'

'Oh yes.'

It was Christmas in the West, and the whole world seemed obliged to conform; to stop fighting; cease trading. If you like. The day was grey, the snow in the courtyard turning to slush where now the BBC Volvo, now Mrs Fujimori's Toyota had departed through the old coaching arch, under the red and white *shlagboym* operated by the guard. He was on duty, of course.

(Our compound, not a prison, abutted some of the finest streets of central Moscow, nestling within the protective and historic Garden Ring Road. It was something of a Soviet trick, once again, that they treated us to a good standard of living.)

All the office's dim yellow lights were on. The 40 watt bulbs created a miserable atmosphere and hardly allowed for reading. Gels stayed close to the window and attempted the crossword in *Nedelya*.

Capital of Peru. Four letters.

Symbol of Power on the Head. Five letters.

Person in charge of an institute. Eight letters. Direktor. Like the director of VIRILE.

Suvorov's Fortress. Six letters. 'Grisha?'

'Izmail, in the time of Catherine.'

'Thanks.'

The elegant British-manufactured clock on the wall showed midday.

Howard's predecessor but four had installed it. 'Tea?'

'Nice.'

'*Vam vsego dobrogo.*' All the best to her.

'You too.'

He was a soul. He knew he had hurt her.

Pushing aside the crossword she stuffed, one by one, a huge pile of unsorted recent stories into labelled folders hanging in the already bulging cabinets. Filing, it was called, and the big metal drawers slid open with a faint roar.

'And thank you again for—'

He raised a finger and pointed at the light socket.

'Did you ever hear of Shopengauer?'

'*Net.*'

'He thought we all want too much.'

'Yes.'

'Go on.'

'That's all. *Vsyo.*'

The big man surely agreed with Schopenhauer saying we all talk too much and want too much and are too full of hope. On the other hand you can't tell people what they should wish for.

The clock had moved on barely half an hour when she decided to go out in the snow. Back in the flat she put on rubber boots, two pairs of socks, the parka and the Canadian fur hat from Harrod's that was a gift from her father. Gloves of course, and a black wool scarf wound round her neck.

The Georgian market close to the office was open. Not their Christmas. She bought a loaf of black bread, some of that salty-creamy brynza cheese that Mary had so successfully paired with sweet herring—and tomatoes. Russians could shop in the Gruzinsky Rynok, of course, but the prices were vast, so there was no crowd. Just Gels Maybey, who hardly spoke and was an alien on this earth.

'Summer food,' Grisha said, declining what she offered on her return. As she entered, bringing the smell of snow and a cold wind with her, or so she hoped, wanting to share her discomfort, she found Howard's assistant scraping at his bowl of soup, heated up on the hotplate in the back room. Now the whole office smelt of cabbage.

Oh Lord how they both missed him, and it was only a few hours.

'What about a glass of vodka? The boss left it for us. *Dubrovka.*' He waved a finger advisedly. 'The best.'

She'd drunk a lot the night before but what had that to do with it. The *Dubrovka* had a gold and green label to mark its distinctive 'Bison' brand. Jobs in vodka must be in demand she commented. I mean what perks! Almost as good as working for Westerners.

He made only the tiniest sound.

(Would you get a job in vodka, if you were Russian, Gels? No, surely not. I'd go for the foreigners. In contact with foreigners, even spying on them, you might help make things better. Choose the vodka job if you want oblivion. Choose the *assistyent* job if you reckon you're canny, or, in the end, you don't care who finds out. They think it anyway.)

She poured a tiny amount into two tumblers from the back office and replaced the cap.

'No, dear lady. No, no. Not like that.'

'You pour then.'

'I *will* pour.' He filled the glasses half-full, and tossed the cap into the bin.

The stupor that followed gave her a crick in her neck. So what did Grisha report, if he must report something. Everyone knew DIMDA reported higher. But Grisha loved Howard. So maybe he didn't report. Not everything anyway.

She slept for two hours on what Howard had assigned to her as a desk.

When she woke up she phoned Harriet to thank her for the party.

'I've been learning from our office man about the Gensec's car collection.'

'You said it, girl. He actually asked Nixon for that Cadillac.'

Arthur who turned out to be close by, even if he was technically 'working', called out animatedly: 'Tell her that Cadillac was made as a special order in three days flat and flown to Moscow by a US Air Force transport plane.'

'Bribes, I suppose, in the hope they don't NUKE us.'

He took the phone. 'As for the Mercedes 300 SL German Chancellor Willy Brandt—'

'I don't know Willy Brandt—'

'West German Chancellor who hoped to see an end to the Cold War in his lifetime. In 1973 he gave Brezhnev a Mercedes Coupé SL300 with a star on top.'

'Germany's rather frighteningly near Russia.'

'Not to be outdone, you Brits gave him a Rolls Royce Silver Cloud. What's a bet your Prime Minister Edward Heath told your Queen Elizabeth to do that. In the interests of world peace.'

'And to think people back home admire the Russians for not being "materialistic!" They seem to like the best of everything, if they're given half a chance.'

'Pass me back to Harriet, Arthur? I wanted a quick word. Harriet you know what I found out? The name of that boy driving the Mercedes. I think it was Korsakov.'

'What, Korsakov as in Arthur and Howard's Russian boss?'

'Yes. His name was on the list of recently imported German cars.'

'What's that about Korsakov, Harriet?'

'Gels thinks…I'll just pass you back to Arthur.'

'Gels, Korsakov is a man of forty-five.'

'Exactly. So it must have been his son.'

'Heh, good work that woman!'

'Thanks. Pass me back to Harriet?'

'Harriet. Where does Korsakov's family hide? Let's find him.' Gels was almost choking. She could feel tears coming, like that moment under the Christmas tree, staring at the painting.

'You mean drive out there?'

'Yes. Yes. Wherever it is.'

'Okay hon, let's do that. It's a deal.'

She put the phone down. Still no Howard.

(So I left the office and cleaned my flat for the first time since my arrival. Then, pulling the contraband books out from the suitcase I started *Moskva Petushki* – Moscow to the End of the Line – because it was about a man drinking himself to death. The metaphor was the map of the metro. Petushki was the last station. Bvaaaa. Harriet rang me back in the flat. 'Arthur's trying to get some pictures of the Korsakov boy. End of the school year. Ice-hockey team. Things like that.'

But there was nothing I myself could do in the meantime. So I phoned the Wormolds and was pleased to get Mary.

'How are you fixed, Mary? Now I mean?'

'I'm reaching for my hat and coat.' We took the tram, two foreigners in our smart clothes—smart whatever we wore—and our leather, not plastic, boots. It was a short ride—not, in reality to Petushki, not yet—from Mayakovsky to Revolution Square. We walked across the bleak cobbles of Red Square, where I nearly lost a heel in the space in between, and went to a cinema annexe of the Rossiya Hotel. It wasn't the main auditorium but a basement which specialised in art films. 'Like chez nous,' said Mary. 'They've copied the fashion.' Except that the film was far superior. We saw Tarkovsky's *Andrei Rublev.* You know that opening scene? I'll never forget it. How a bird-man with dreams crashes to earth.)

*

Howard was at his desk, and Grisha sat opposite, when Gels appeared next morning after eleven to inspect him for signs of passion spent. He seemed just the same.

'I think I know the name of the driver who helped the Americans get away from the fire. His name is Korsakov.'

'That's rubbish, Gels. Korsakov is a man of forty-five.' Hell! Why were men so condescending?

'Korsakov senior owns a Mercedes but clearly he wasn't driving it.'

'Could have been someone else.'

'I went through the list. I couldn't find any other likely candidates. Howard! I want to know where THEY live. I want to know *how* THEY live. This is going to be my way.'

He looked at her. Who was he to stop her?

'Wasn't Korsakov the one who smashed up the artists' exhibition? Didn't someone say that the other night?'

'I'm afraid so.'

Howard tipped back in his chair. 'He lives out on the Mozhaisk Road. It's where all the *nomklats* try to have a base. As to how you're going to get inside there, though, Gels, I have no idea.'

'I can do that. It's something I can do.'

'Show me on the map, Grisha? Mozhaisk?'

129

'I'll show you.' Last week Kamchatka. Yesterday Semipalatinsk. Today Mozhaisk. But the scale was tiny. All that was clear was that the direction was southwest.

The teleprinter clattered with some incoming message. Howard cursed. 'Stupid stuff from London about Russian Boxing Day. They don't HAVE a buggery Boxing Day. Greetings.' He went back into the office and returned to where she was still standing. 'Here. You need the CIA map.'

It was a spiral-bound CIA satellite map of Moscow. A Moscow A-Z, with a list of streets, and grid references, in terms that made sense to a Londoner.

'Whatever you think of the Americans, they produced *this*.'

'I won't lose it.'

'Gels, whatever you do beware of GAI!'

'That policeman just wanted to stroke your car, you told me.'

'So long as he doesn't want to stroke you.'

She struggled. 'There's always that. But there'll be two of us. I'm going with Harriet.'

Meanwhile if Howard and Apollinaria Montenari loved each other she didn't think she could bear it.

*

Howard, in that respect, was indeed spoken for. Polly Montenari, who lived in a different district of Moscow, was his lover and the person he admired most. That Christmas morning the familiar mosaic of labourers at work over the entrance to her block greeted him as he pressed her bell. He was always running his eyes over it. A positive religion of work had gripped the good world not so long ago. Late 1920s, was it built? He always wondered, without bothering to look it up somewhere. The Russian revolution is still part of all of us, he was wont to say, every time he gazed on that mosaic. It was when workmen digging with shovels replaced Jesus Christ as our deliverance. He approved of that. He was an atheist with a heart. His lover buzzed him up from the ground floor of her building.

'Ciao, amico. Stai bene?' There was something magical about Polly, in her immaculate jeans, her white shirt and her navy sweater. It cast an aura over potato-coloured Moscow and was a tonic to a modest depressive from post-war England. Howard belonged to that era which, as people said, along with its empire had lost its purpose. Many many Italian women dressed like Polly. She wore her clothes like a uniform. But you wouldn't know it because no one could have modelled them better. Polly was always flawless and always prepared. She had strong beliefs from an early age, and they helped her narrow her choices and focus her life. She lived a freer life in Moscow than Howard did, because she was an official sympathiser.

Brown-eyed, olive-skinned Polly believed Communism was the great humane hope of this country, and only crass people from a land of shopkeepers or capitalists across the Atlantic couldn't see it.

'How long has it been?'

'A month. And even then—' said Howard, doing his best not to complain. 'No! Non è vero!' She was cooking and her right hand was caught in their embrace, landing a wooden spoon close to his left ear.

A little like her, he wore the densely textured cotton shirt, thin wool jumper and corduroy sports jacket that was the hallmark of his English class. Grammar school-educated, and middle class, that was.

He removed the jacket, threw himself on to the navy sofa and loosened his tie. 'Why aren't I here more often? It's nice here. More like home than anywhere in Moscow.' Polly's furnishings were the same as her wardrobe: navy, and more navy, and white. Elegant, neat, rational.

'Sit with me. The food won't burn, will it?'

'Un attimo.' He heard a switch click in the kitchenette. The design of the flat was plain enough, but if you left doors open you had a continuous, very pleasant, white-walled space.

'You're lucky to lead an ordinary Russian life.'

'I don't know how ordinary it is but it's nice to have a balcony.'

'You're lucky as a person and privileged as a foreigner.'

'It's true. I should feel ashamed. All I can say is it's not Italy.'

'Be glad you don't have to live in a Westerners' compound.' He couldn't help feeling that life was squandering him, what with the absence of the loved one and the difficulty of the task, besides which everything else was just marking time.

'Unlike you I am not an enemy of the Soviet state.'

'No you Italians admire them so much you're going to make the whole of Italy Communist.'

They had had this ritual conversation many times. It was one reason why they resorted to irony and teasing.

Howard cast his eyes in the direction of the usual installations. 'I've said it before. Even you need to take care. Not all of your neighbours will be ordinary, by any means.'

'Sasha across the corridor plays in the interschool ice-hockey team every Saturday morning. Igor upstairs is an opera singer with the Bolshoi chorus.'

'Sasha's parents then. They know I'm here for a start.'

'You Westerners are ridiculous!'

'You're a Westerner too. You've just got a political kink.'

'I am the Moscow correspondent of *L'Unita*. I represent the Communist Party of Italy and THEY are very pleased to have my support.'

'I love the way you say that. You mean it too.'

She did, and together with her beauty—the customary Italian colouring which a white shirt seemed designed to flatter—in a way it was all too much.

'What's the latest?'

'Well, that Party conference just before Christmas…'

'I read the report. I thought they were just copying the Chinese.'

'I was there and I can say there are certain indications—'

He interrupted, 'Near-bankruptcy is one of them. Well, isn't it, Poll? They can't even feed themselves.'

'Which is another reason why they need to change their line.'

'So you think it's happening.'

'I do.'

He made a sudden faint lunge for her but very delicately. She kept him at such a distance and now she was teasing him about the job too, when she was his great hope of the second revolution.

'Shall we eat?' Sometimes she abruptly switched off like that, and it was not his desire to be ungracious. Not here.

Moreover, approaching the table it was somehow a mark of his ambivalent existence that if he'd eaten copiously twelve hours before he didn't show it. Moreover he had the taste of her lips on his.

He watched her collect the dishes from the serving hatch. His job as she set them on the table was to pour the Chianti.

'Polly darling—'

'Here's to a better future for this country. And let's not speak about the rest of the vast USSR which you and I have hardly seen.'

'I'd go, Poll. Anywhere and everywhere to find out about it and bring you back a report.' He thought of the map that fixated Gels Maybey and to which Grisha with his secondary school Soviet geography was their only guide. 'But I'm not allowed to visit. Not freely. I have to ask Korsakov months in advance and he can always refuse, or find some excuse. There's too much they don't want us to see.'

'A little hardship...' she began, aware of the irony of the topic in that moment when they sipped their wine and dug into a plate of gleaming antipasti. 'People in the West—'

'I know. They're self-indulgent consumers who've lost their souls. They're lazy and soft, like me. But what about the prisons here? What about the way people inform on each other? And what, in the end, my dear, about the *psykhushki*?'

She shrugged, and while he helped himself to more of the delicious preserved mushrooms and dressed shredded carrot, and took a slice of a Soviet baguette which she had managed to turn into garlic and olive oil bruschetta, he added that she didn't look hard enough at the boastful militaristic antics which were politically primitive and belonged to another era.

'But Howard you know how it is. They feel so threatened, as if the second world war never ended. As if the West were always about to invade.'

'That's complete nonsense, and you know it.' He rested his knife and fork. 'By the way, Poll, this is...' She had prepared for him a magnificent spread. 'And even if you could forgive the suspicion that it's more than just a cold war,' Howard insisted. 'Even if you accept that they feel they have to fight for the right to be different from the West, how can they treat their own people so cruelly?'

She called from the kitchen where she was draining the pasta. 'You have to understand their position in history, *amico*.'

Along with every other hurdle she presented to him that made him furious. He got to his feet intending to help, but all he could do was gesticulate. 'You think I don't try? I've got a whole shelf of books back in the office. One of them tells me Solzhenitsyn's lucky to be alive at all. They poisoned him but he was such an ox he survived. Then they let him leave. A very Soviet gradation of mercy. And then there's Mundt, and some philosophy professor Reikhman. All kicked out when they'd rather be here to serve their people. They'd be dead otherwise. But then they're dead anyway if they can't practise their art. Can't dispense their wisdom.'

She set down the steaming bowl of spaghetti and gave it a toss. His grievances stacked up because he didn't see her often enough, he cried.

'Well, you're here now, *caro*.'

'So what do you say? Are you with them, getting rid of every last soul who dares disagree with them? That's a dictionary-proof definition of repression. Or can't you ever bring yourself to criticise them, Poll?'

'You know my position, Howard. They will achieve their goals, one day. It's just a great struggle for them to get rid of the bourgeois heritage.'

'I don't think that's an argument, Pol. The truth is that you're an idealist. You're willing to take this place on trust. In truth you know as well as I do that this great country might grind to a halt any day.'

'The *psykhushki* worry me. Of course they do.'

'I'm glad to hear it.' He couldn't keep the sharpness out of his voice. She pleaded. 'Can we be friends?'

'That's all I ask. You torture me.'

They sat and consoled each other for a moment.

'But now a toast to your culinary genius!' Gallantly he raised his glass. The dishes before him were a delight.

How did she do it? The pea-shooter spaghetti anyone could buy from a Soviet grocer's. Take your pick of shops that were all the same. Add tinned tomatoes, brynza and Soviet green cheese to sprinkle. Brynza came from the Georgian market. Green cheese in packets from God knew where. It was only the tomatoes came from Italy. But then the combination was magnificent.

'The Soviets need you, my darling. If they could arrange their affairs like you arrange your cooking they would get there, in the end, as you say. Happy Christmas.'

'Buon Natale! Caro!' She still believed in the dream, just.

The question was when to find the time to tell him, for the gorgeousness of their shared meal was soon followed by the gorgeousness of their shared bed, in another navy and white room. Happy, he felt sorry for Russian lovers with nowhere to go.

'Their flats are too crowded. How can they make love like this.'

'They find a way.' Her head was buried in his chest. 'Or are you suggesting Russians are about to die out because they never have the time and place to make love?'

'Another possible ending to the great experiment! But then they're often drunk, so it happens anyway. Either that or wait for summer. I've seen them in the parks, when the weather's mild. And beside the Moscow River. It's Sodom on one bank and Gomorrah on the other.'

She giggled, and licked round his neck, where she liked him most. 'And when it's cold are they *celibatari*?'

'Like me. All through December.'

Her kissing aroused him again and they were lost in each other for far longer than they imagined.

'What do you find to report, Poll? No seriously, if you can't touch the dissidents and the bad news.'

'Actually, Howard, they do know they're in some kind of crisis.'

'What's your source for that?'

'Che cazzo!' She sat up, their legs still intertwined, swore at him and covered herself with the duvet. 'You want me to be *your* source? Well, I'll tell you. Because they come to me for advice. In Italy you do Communism better, they say. People vote for you. Of their own free will.'

'They worship at your shrine.'

'No, I'm serious. They want our help.' She didn't laugh, though her mouth crinkled into a faint smile. 'Because we know how to do Communism. We're their last chance. I've been out to see them.'

'Them?'

'Korsakov's Progress Group that's what he calls it. I'm happy to give them advice.'

'Jesus, that bastard! It would have to be him.' Howard was so dumbstruck it was as if he were talking to himself. 'He's got a Progress Group, has he? Would you believe it? My Italian girlfriend is keeping the Soviet Communist Party afloat with new ideas. As long as she doesn't have to get into his bed.'

Not that Howard could do anything about that either.

'I don't mince my words, Howard. I tell them the truth.'

'Well, that's a relief!' They reclaimed their legs, one pair each. And with that he got up, naked, made for his jacket which he had left on the sofa next door, and returned with his notebook and a parcel. Opening it to a clean page, he wrote: 'Can you help?'

'It's something I haven't been able to ignore,' she wrote.

'So here.' She had put on a robe and walked over to the wardrobe, taking the parcel with her. He watched her, as he settled himself back against the pillows. 'Come back?' He lifted the duvet, tugged at her hand, kissed it.

'It's been a lovely Christmas, Howard.' She struggled out of his arms as he threatened to leave her no option. 'But now I must work.'

'*Today*?'

'Perché no? You're a journalist too. The Party Congress on The Way Forward…'

Yes, they were both journalists, but also not, because their profession wasn't the same, and the world was cut in two. Except they had this feeling for Russia, which united them.

'I was going back to Italy anyway for a few days. You've just caught me.'

'Aah, the home country calls. I know how much you miss Italy. I miss it myself, for your sake.'

'Come and live with me there. One day.'

'It's a deal.' He was almost overcome. 'When are you going?'

'I've booked a flight on Friday.'

'You want me to leave now? But it's so early.'

But he was glad, all the same, that the package was on its way to becoming one of the publishing hits of spring 1979 in Italy.

*

'THEY' re weak. We're weak. What are we going to do?' Gels burst out. 'I mean the U.S. embassy in Moscow setting fire to itself and then the Russians spearing an artist and his canvas on a bulldozer in full sight of the whole world.'

'I remember,' said Mary. 'They *bulldozed* an art exhibition. Moldy was there. The picture went round the world.'

'Speared an *artist* on a bulldozer?'

'He hung on to the digger.'

'Goodness what courage! As for those stupid *nomklats*, even the Nazis only burned books. They realised paintings were worth stealing to make huge amounts of money on the world market.'

'But then you're lying, aren't you?' Mary countered, as they left the cinema, still in the grip of Tarkovsky's God-filled icon painter. 'The photograph's been doctored. It's all fake. That's just what happens in *other* countries, that artists are persecuted. Here we venerate them.'

'Hell.' That feeling of being tied up in knots, one fake argument after another, made Gels feel her own face was twisting horribly.

'That's the first rule here. Deny it happened,' said Mary. 'It's amazing how far you can get by lying. It's the enemies of Russia are to blame. It's a Western trick, to accuse Russia of the West's own wickedness. You Western bastards, don't single Russia out! Don't accuse us of your sins! Don't lie!'

'Isn't that so, Grisha? The way they reason here is a maze. You can't get out.' Gels had been telling the story of *her* Christmas Day to Howard, after he finally put in an appearance.

The big man nodded.

'So you know what I mean?' He nodded again.

'Right I'd better get on,' said Howard. He hated to admit it, but Polly had insisted he analyse the Plenary Session of the Central Committee of the Communist Party from 23 December.

'Good stuff?' Gels jeered.

'Why didn't you tell me sooner, Grisha?'

'You were busy, boss.'

The Plenary Session was now its own dossier, spread out beside Howard's typewriter.

'Damn Kremlinologist,' muttered Gels.

'Damned certainly.'

'I'll be off then.'

'Going anywhere special?'

'A run and then drinks with Mary and Wormy. It *is* Boxing Day.'

Eight

Gels was out running on a Thursday in March, when Moscow's finest bookshop came into view. She had emerged from a side road on to Gorky Street. It was a lovely building, three storeys high and with a vertical column that jutted out into the street as proud as a ship's prow. The sign, read downwards, said DOM KNIGI. The House of the Book, the name lit up in red.

Here was the ultimate home of The Book, and a refuge for the People of the Book which Russians became when all other decencies in life failed them. With their fabulous cultural resources, the Russians had taken over the world's written wisdom shortly before the first revolution, and hopeful people, like Howard and Gels, loved them for it.

She'd explored the building, with its naked plank floors, twice before and been taken aback by the almost complete absence of actual books.

Another joke? Well, yes, depending how you saw it.

Patrick Wormold had compared buying a volume of Tolstoy in Moscow with buying a bottle of wine in Finland. It made an amusing TV news feature. You had to queue in a shop where what you so passionately lusted after was stored out of sight. Women in white coats reluctantly served you from closed counters, deplored your appetites and demanded a huge price for their passing satisfaction. Or, in the Moscow version the book was not stocked at all, except in a smart Western-style shop where only foreigners and *nomklats* could make purchases, while the people remained in ignorance.

You would think Russia was the land of self-parody. Deserving of a Pulitzer prize for self-ridicule.

The ground floor sold the speeches of the present leader. Did they contain hidden references to cars? Had he written the speeches himself? Had anyone ever read them all through? You couldn't help wondering. The texts were displayed open in a glass case as if they were already museum pieces. They could be forgotten while not appearing neglected.

The second floor had children's books, for children were highly regarded in this uncanny post-revolutionary state devoted to a future that would never come.

And then you came to the floor with the posters directed against anti-social behaviour.

Gels this time was only jogging past, but she could see, extraordinarily, that morning in March, that a long queue snaked out from beneath the red neon sign and back down the Gorky Street pavement. She joined it. On other days she'd queued ninety minutes for a lemon, and more than an hour for a kilo of tomatoes. She'd felt guilty buying these rare commodities. But how better to grasp this people than to share their daily frustrations? So she joined the bookshop line, behind two women in coats and identical printed headscarves. The scarves were the kind of pink and green and red and yellow design on black that was standard for the women's clothing industry, and they looked reminiscent of a traditional lacquered box. Quite distinct from them she was wearing a blue nylon tracksuit with a white stripe down the legs, and running shoes, and a bobble hat. Behind her stood a pudgy-faced middle-aged man carrying a briefcase and altogether reminiscent of the director of VIRILE in Vilnius. No one spoke to her and as she stood in their midst their conversations also dried up.

'What are we queueing for?'

'Isn't that obvious?'

'Not to me.'

'If you don't know what you're waiting for why are you doing it?'

'I'd like to wait. It must be something important, to stand in a queue like this,' she said, striving to be inoffensive. 'I suppose it will take a while.'

No answer.

A tall thin man with a chiselled face like that of the writer Boris Pasternak, also with a briefcase, now stood behind the would-be director of VIRILE.

Beyond him the queue kept growing, even as the doors opened. 'Wipe your feet, comrades!' a middle-aged woman in a white overall tried to stamp her authority on the situation, as the public streamed in, but she was far too kindly by nature to command much attention. 'Wipe your feet! The bookshop deserves your respect.'

It was neither raining nor snowing that morning, but there was still muddy slush piled up at the side of the pavement, and perhaps some visitors had come in from the country. Variously steaming and wheezing the comrades—who would have preferred Gels Maybey, foreigner, not to be in their midst—made for a counter where two young women were handing out tokens. The drill was to take this nibbled plastic disk—as if a dog had chewed each one, but in fact because they were so worn, from hand to hand, meanwhile some had been used to open bottles—and hand that disk to a cashier who sat in an enclosed box, a little raised above the normal floor level. Had this cashier spoken, from her pulpit, in a land where money had lost its prestige, customers all around her, in the pit beneath her, might have stopped and listened in desperation. For they were so hungry to use money, in small quantities, now and again. In fact on production of that worn bit of plastic she asked for fifteen roubles. Only then was the customer allowed to queue again for the actual book.

That day they queued for an essay by Professor Alexander Razumovsky called *Living Souls*, published as a supplement to *New Literature* in spring 1979. It was the same text as was about to appear in Italian, published by a house in Milan.

Here each pamphlet was already wrapped in brown paper, as if it were pornography.

'What's it called again?'

'Find out for yourself!' said an angry woman in response to Gels and her disingenuous question: 'You can read, can't you? My God, the younger generation!'

'*Dead Souls*,' said an old man. 'Why can't our Soviet writers can't come up with titles of their own? They just have to ransack the bourgeois past.'

'*Living Souls*, Comrade Citizen. *Zhivye Dushi*.' Gels couldn't resist. 'The author is telling you you're still alive.'

'Dead Souls, Living Souls, it's all the same.' He turned away. Other people would criticise him for engaging with a foreigner, but what did he care, at his age.

As for Gels, the queueing customers couldn't avoid her, if they wanted their copy of the Razumovsky essay, but they had to pretend she wasn't there; as if she and they occupied different, only apparently adjacent, realms of space; but she'd already raised suspicion by speaking out too boldly.

As she took out her notebook and scribbled a few details: the number of purchasers, the length of the queue, the antiquated system of purchase, the white-coated manageress, a plump little creature with a large hairy mole on her white face, and thin-framed purplish spectacles, whose main problem hitherto had been to get customers to wipe their feet, now sensed a great trouble.

'Comrade Janitor, please close the shop!'

'What was that, Comrade Manager?'

'I said clear the shop, as quickly as you can. The House of the Book is under repair.'

'But we've just had the roof done.'

'So now it's the windows. Off you go!'

The flustered little woman clapped her hands. 'Comrade citizens, attention please! You are asked to evacuate the building promptly. The building is under repair.'

Remarkably, not a single voice sounded in protest. There was just a vibration in the air. Lips tightened. Hands tensed. Every man for himself, no chance of a lifeboat, whatever is coming next.

Comrade Manager gestured as if shooing away vermin. The girls behind the counter should put away their stock. No problem there. Indeed, what a prospect! It looked like no more work today.

Comrade Cashier meanwhile was only too happy to close the till and disappear.

'Heh, that's my fifteen roubles you've got!'

'What value is a mingy piece of plastic to me?'

'Comrades, a little decorum please.' The little woman summoned to take responsibility and not liking it at all looked up from where she had been scribbling a note to place in the front window. She had written in large letters, in biro, on a piece of squared paper: NA REMONT. The tiny notice would have done better on the very door of the bookshop, but the Soviet Union was not an easy place to get hold of Sellotape, with *skotch defitsitny*.

The flow of silent, disappointed, but also frightened, book-buyers carried Gels with them out on to the street. As the eyes avoided her and the hats and the headscarves became just part of the sea of human bundles flowing down the wide street, each and every person only wanted for this to revert to an ordinary, normal, morning in central Moscow.

She insisted, and that was so cruel of her: 'Excuse me, citizen, why is this pamphlet so valuable?'

She asked, running after this person and that: 'Dear Lady, won't you tell me...'

The sound of her foreign voice terrified them still more, though it was their hastening bodies, not their dulled, obscured faces that showed it.

The joy was that by now everyone knew Alexander Razumovsky had written *Living Souls*. They knew that he and his wife had also published, in Russian, their findings on the *psykhushki* in the early spring issue of the *Novosibirsk Journal of Sociology*. There was even a Soviet word, *obshcheizvestnost'*, which meant that everyone knew. Everyone knew and yet they also did not, and so they hovered in a kind of political purgatory, cherishing facts that waited to be admitted, or not, to official reality, in March 1979.

For if the facts were true, who was responsible for them? How had that fat typescript reached Novosibirsk? And how in particular had its attached essay *Living Souls* come to roll off the presses of the esteemed government newspaper *Izvestiya* in the middle of a Friday night so that at least a few people managed to buy it as a special supplement that day?

The happy fate of that magnificent essay first.

'Heh! Is it you? Heh! After so long!' Galya Obolenskaya leant over and kissed her old friend Irina Bové. She smelt of some French perfume, made by the Paris parfumier Worth.

'So how have you been after all these years?'

'You too, how have you been?'

They both shrugged, and laughed. 'Normal,' said Irina.

'Normal, me too.'

Normal'no of course meant its complete opposite. Normal meant tied to this particular reality which wasn't normal at all. And yet in another sense if people led lives which didn't change much from day to day, surely it was entirely appropriate. Roughly it meant, 'I'm managing.'

Where they bumped into each other after so long was at a show in the Manezh Gallery, the place Korsakov and his bride to be in his younger days knew well. That venue might be still be considered the very heart of creative Moscow since it was an officially tolerated, *indoor* exhibition space, thus covered by the constitution (as Korsakov remembered fatefully when those lunatics staged their outdoor show and nearly wrecked his career). The Manezh Gallery was the heart of the cultural city, in the absence of any other vital organ. Of course visitors there, crowding in, were constantly jostled. But it was an almost congenial place to meet, among people of possibly similar interests, and the risk of being overheard was slight.

There was so much to say between Irina and Galya as fellow graduates of the class of '61. For they had rarely met since.

'How?

'So-so.' Irina licked her thumb as some passer-by slopped her drink. The idiot grinned and made a lascivious comment. He got one back. Irina was so gorgeous.

'You look well,' she said to Galya and meant it, for although her friend had grown plump, she still had that dazzling red hair and those fabulous green eyes. 'You too you look fabulous. Out of a fairy tale.' Out of a fairy tale of the West, that meant, for Irina was wearing her favourite boucle two-piece with leather boots and, over one arm, a giant, ultra-stylish carpet bag. Hers was a glamorous presence, and she knew it. She did *nomklat* glamour so effortlessly it could pass for elegance anywhere in the world.

'I'm so hungry. They never have anything to eat.' It's always the slim women who are hungry. The rest of us are too, but then we are greedy. Irina directed her angry, hungry gaze instead at the paintings on the wall. 'New Visions for Our Time,' was the heading.

'That'll be the day.'

The titles were flaccid but the merit of the evening was that it was a public gathering, and who knew for certain what might happen in public, some hint of change perhaps, and anyway she was there, not hiding at home.

The paintings were decorative and empty, a stupid sop and a substitute for where something in the past, now removed, had left an emptiness in the Russian soul. Those who had the memory craved art and tried to keep the spark alive, but an occasion like this, *bozhe moi*, was bound to disappoint. On the other hand young people came too, so perhaps the truth of art wasn't only a question of memory. People still hoped to find it, to witness it, and secretly take it home with them as an imprint on heart and mind.

'No Mundts on show tonight, I see,' Galya remarked, knowing that Irina's own husband had been to blame for the assault on that open-air artist. It was how she tested the political water.

Irina shrugged under the weight of her marriage. 'The day that happens we'll be out from under this sixty-year blight.'

'My dear.'

The shows at the Manezh were what remained when the artistic voice of the city was smothered. The only real point of the gallery was to offer artists and art-lovers a place to meet and cram in the free nibbles and sozzle themselves over the free drinks.

'Irina, darling, if you feel that way why do you hide away?' Galya grabbed her arm. 'Don't hide away. We need your help.' Of course she'd heard of trouble in the Korsakov marriage. That was why their boy was so unhappy.

Irina's face tensed but she didn't pull away. 'I knew our meeting wasn't a coincidence.' She scowled.

'Nothing in our Russian lives is a coincidence. You know that. Everything has a point.'

Irina shrugged and turned. She pulled a face at an innocuous composition of blue, white and orange on the wall. 'There's nothing there. *What* do they want to say?'

'It's some national flag. You must recognise it. It's some neighbouring country we're repressing. Just not art. Irina we need your support. Look how much attention the world paid us when …our friend was caught on camera hanging on to the end of a bulldozer. Trying to save his work. For God's sake, how did your Volodya survive that?'

Irina scowled. 'He knows people.'

They walked on slowly and looked at a row of drawings. The draughtsmanship was impressive. But it was obviously hard to choose a subject that wouldn't arouse suspicion or cause offence. The censors were always on the lookout for art that claimed to be 'about art itself.' Art about art was simply dissident code for concealing a hostile political message.

An elegant waiter in a white jacket refreshed their glasses of *shampanskoe.* Up to a point the manners in the room were faux-western, though beyond it not at all. People were terribly hungry and thirsty.

'Mundt told the world we were still alive.' Irina had already emptied her glass. She was all hunger and need that night. 'I know that because Volodya bought one of his paintings—one he didn't bulldoze, that is.'

Galya gasped. 'How could anyone—'

'He could. Apparently they're worth a lot now.'

'And I thought I was unshockable.'

'That's our system for you. Don't believe a word of it.'

'Irina, I hear they want to republish your father's essays. That's another good sign that better things may be happening.'

'Maybe.'

The truth was Irina's father Nikolai Mikhailovich Bové was a great anomaly in Soviet history. There were a few. In his case he had achieved such eminence in art history that the Party did not know what to do with him other than shower him with awards, and rewards, and medals. He was an honest man and had been wary of letting the system buy him. But in exchange for his worldwide eminence, which reflected so unusually well on his country, he had accepted the rare gift of a house. A house in fact of the same vintage as the Manezh Gallery beside the Kremlin Wall where they were standing now. It needed restoring, of course, but it appeased someone's conscience to gift it to a decent man.

'My father felt that there was a quantity of good in the world, to which, by chance and according to opportunity, a human being could add. Whether he was a painter or a bricklayer. Whether she was a translator or a housekeeper. And the last thing he did was put that good into refurbishing the house.'

'And leave it to you.'

'It is my life.'

'So you'll help us then.'

But there was no response, so for the moment Galya let it pass.

'Will you write the introduction to the new edition of your father's work? Remind our people what a good man he was?'

'Edvard Vasilievich will write it.'

'Edvard…?'

'My old colleague from *New Literature*.' But Galya knew exactly who he was.

Irina said: 'He's a better writer than I am and a proper art historian. Look, is that food? I wish there were something to eat.'

So many people were now forcing their way into the room that the evening no longer felt so exquisite. Yet no one with a purpose begrudged a crowd to hide among.

'Edvard Vasilievich loved you, didn't he?'

'That was ages ago.'

Edvard did lose his head and heart to her, and it was quite unrequited.

'Love doesn't die, Irina! How cynical you are! Actually what I mean is love's always good for something. What with Edvard Vasilievich being a publisher.'

'Ah! I see. That's what you want.'

Galya slipped a package into Irina's vast bag. 'A present.' She added: 'Love's always good for something. You'll see.'

'Just in case you met me, eh? Is that food over there I see?' Tucking the package away Irina persisted in her bodily mission, the blood hammering at her temples. But it was just empty plates. All the little biscuits spread with white cream cheese and garnished with a feather of dill had vanished in the first few minutes of the show that otherwise offered Western style for those first minutes but otherwise such feeble nourishment and such a chance for renewed alcoholism and continuing conspiracy.

'God knows what they put in this bubbly of ours. France says we're not allowed to call it champagne. Quite right. That would be a travesty. It doesn't come from a region in northeast France. It comes from a Soviet factory, in a country that doesn't love its people, so its output is poisonous muck. But I don't see who's going to stop us putting a fancy name on it and pretending we love it.'

Still, 'I don't feel well,' Irina moaned. 'These awful things on the wall don't help. When you long for a baby and what comes out is still-born there's this huge feeling of loss and it feels like your whole life amounts to nothing and when I see this given the name of art I feel the same.'

It was a metaphor but Galya took it literally. 'But you have a son?'

'I adopted Matvei. He's sixteen now and he hates his father.' She looked again at the flaccid paintings of flowers, and at some sci-fi nonsense. 'It's not that I mean. I want a rebirth. For all of us.'

She asked after her friend. 'And you, Galya? Do you have children? What great plans for the future?'

'Oh, me I'm a coward. I haven't married. I didn't want children. Life is complicated enough. Another few books though. Dickens isn't finished yet.'

The whole of Dickens! Did Galya mean that? Irina was nauseous from the drink and flushed and sad to the point of tears.

'Let's get our coats. After all you've accomplished your mission. Why should we stay longer?'

'It was good to see you, Irina, truly. I hope you like your present. Let me know.'

From the art gallery named after an old riding school, Galya made for the metro station *Ploshchad Revolyutsii*. Revolution Square. Irina meanwhile found her driver in a Mercedes waiting outside. It was a fifteen mile journey, in the dark, and they quickly left the city behind. Galya was home first, and listened to Schubert's Trout quintet on the gramophone in triumph.

The two women met again on a stunning blue morning three weeks later to go ice-skating in Gorky Park, and, indeed, so that Irina could 'let Galya know'. The municipal authorities flooded the asphalt paths every winter to create canals of ice, and they were packed at weekends, free for anyone to use. Every Russian owned a pair of skates. People didn't turn up on weekdays, though, either because they were genuinely at work, or because if they enjoyed conspicuous leisure midweek they might be slated as social parasites. Parasitism was a criminal offence. So it was that that Tuesday morning, back in February, that Irina and Galya, were almost alone as they glided side by side through the trees. It was an inspiriting occasion when two old friends from university found each other again after more than fifteen years.

They skated with such vigour they were beginning to feel out of breath when they stopped to rest on a bench. Backpacks weren't the thing then, but you could twist a straw shopping bag with long handles round your shoulders, so it lay flat on your back. In one such basket Galya had mulled wine in a painted thermos flask.

'Oh that's pretty.' She had a brightly dyed seersucker cotton tablecloth, too, from India, which she spread on the wooden bench. 'A picnic! Just like old times!'

'A winter picnic. Here, I brought something too.' Irina unwrapped a packet of sponge fingers from Czechoslovakia she'd had in her pocket. 'They're nice and light. Not like our fat peasant biscuits like doorsteps. We can dip them in the wine.'

Irina sipped appreciatively at the wine spiced with cinnamon and a clove and few strips of lemon peel steeped in sugar. She picked up the flask.

'It's Chinese. From the Time of Friendship. When we were students, don't you remember? They were everywhere in the shops.'

'They're short now because of what? Are we not getting on with the Chinese so well?'

'Haven't you heard? The Chinese are reforming. They're embarking on "the Great Opening Up". Our old men are having to invent a whole new anti-Chinese vocabulary.'

'Why can't we "reform and open up"?'

'That's exactly why I asked you for your help. Our old men are so slow to get round to it.' Galya laughed. 'So what do you think? Not about the wine, or the flask…'

147

'Extraordinary.'

'So, will you ask Edvard to publish the essay?'

New Literature was routinely printed on the government newspaper press at a slack time. The challenge was to slip an unexpected supplement into the mix and bind it separately. 'I will, though it's a huge risk for him.'

'But he loves you.'

Irina raised her eyes to the sky. What fool believed in love?

'Besides, you never quite know, do you?' said Galya, possibly in an effort to placate her. 'Our country's not always predictable.' When no response came she repeated: 'You can never be sure what will happen in our country, Irina. In my view it's a good time. People abroad are following what's going on.'

'So they know we're not just sitting here in our prison.'

So the answer was yes, though Irina never uttered it. She would pass on the task to Edvard Vasilievich and he would risk his career to please her.

*

Next must come the even more momentous story that reflected Galya Obolenskaya's heroism, when she took the entire *psykhushki* report to Novosibirsk, so that the facts assembled by the Razumovskys could be published in minutely curated detail. That they had achieved so much meant some change was afoot, had to be, and believing that gave her the courage she needed to make that journey. Like water seeping across dry ground, some willingness to speak out in their otherwise silenced Russia was spreading. Just as the global sea level was rising, so Soviet ground was cracking and shifting, and what for so long was blocked began to emerge, trickle by trickle. The thirsty people were ready for it.

There was 1968 in the West, Galya used to say, their year of 'All You Need is Love.' Too bad we invaded another country that year, and didn't go through the same, That wasn't an act of love at all. But scholars thinking about *us* in '68 forget we had a fresh faint glimpse of love a decade earlier in Russia. Not a revolution, but an easing up and a chance to grow. A 'thaw', they called it. Historians wrote about it. But did they know how it felt? Galya thought not, because that uniquely hot and happy summer of '61, when she and Anna and their mutual friend Irina Bové graduated from Moscow University, was a party to which future historians were not invited. It was when a new generation felt free.

Beside the Moscow River any old meat roasted and charred over burning logs and downed with factory brandy tasted fabulous. You drank the spirits freely and finally zipped yourselves into a double sleeping bag under the open sky. Two of you next to each other, frenzied now and frenzied in the early morning, and an infinite sky overhead. Petya, he was called. Petya something.

The weather was very warm for that short, intense, dusty summer season of '61 and the city was full of those downy white fibres the poet called summer's homage to snow. *Pukh* drifted off the poplar trees and fell prolifically so it coated the ground.

Galina was her full name and she was a linguist. All Russians had their dreams and hers were rather grand, for through foreign languages it was possible to build castles in the sky and call them Paris and London. Later as a professional translator London became Galya's most charmingly imagined destination, in an old-fashioned, no longer true way, because her constant companion was Dickens. Charles Dickens was a marvellous choice of partner, superior to any husband. Now after twenty years of superb craftsmanship she was surely in line for a Lenin Prize. The Dickensian pleasures she had given to hundreds of thousands of readers, already into a new generation, earned her that many times over. She had still not visited England, but Russian children adored her versions of *David Copperfield* and *Martin Chuzzlewit.* Families grew up reading the *Chezlvit* aloud.

The Red and the Green by Iris Murdoch was a bolder choice to add to her repertoire. It was a romance of Irish independence from the British. The Soviet newspapers said British Imperialism was to blame and with that Airis Merdok became a Russian household name. Thousands of Russians were free to read a good book, not about London, not this time, but about being torn between being Irish and being English. And because Merdok was approved of, Galya could also translate her novels about modern love.

If you were a clever person in Russia, by the way, then when you graduated, you had three options: martyr yourself, throw in the towel and hope you were secretly saving your soul, or take certain actions while being careful what you said. Galya belonged to this last group but she respected the other possible choices. Instead of a translator she might even have become a censor herself. With her sensitivity to literature she would have let things through like *A Severed Head—Otrublennaya Golova*—and hoped THEY were too unsophisticated to notice. But in the end she had joined *World Events, Languages and Literature (WELL).*

149

The WELL office had on its wall a large portrait of the moustachioed writer Maxim Gorky, alongside the requisite Lenin. Gorky had helped writers survive the Revolution and the Civil War and no one forgot that. Galya nodded to his photograph every working day. On the windowsills cactuses, mostly not in good health, just scraped a living. The occasional empty kefir bottle aspired to poetry with a stuffing of wild flowers. Meanwhile a host of engaging foreign books piled up on her desk.

Contemporary English fiction was so sought-after that it was difficult to stop colleagues helping themselves. I NEED THESE BOOKS, she wrote on a scrap of paper tucked into the topmost hardcover, which was to say ask me first. I can probably get you a copy. The office, full of polyglots and their dictionaries, had a happy atmosphere, on account of plural vocabularies being pass-keys to other worlds.

Galya, who like most Russians was adept at stepping through the hoops of unofficial irony every day of her life, had beautiful red hair, green eyes and a trained, subtle mind which, though she sometimes resisted, cramming her soul with delicious fictions about other lives, brought her back to the truths of her university days in the end. Now she was working on duplicating the Razumovsky dossier at home. Fortunately her neighbours—vigilant, nosy, some intensely dislikeable, like all neighbours everywhere, these half a dozen households above, below and alongside her included some who disliked her above all because they didn't understand her work. But for all that they were used to her typing at home. So there was nothing special about the clatter of keys and the ping of the carriage return at ten o'clock at night, even if Katya Mikhailovna, a hospital matron and an early riser, wished her neighbour would terminate her services to culture an hour earlier. Galya sat in a symphony of orange and brown, which is how she had decorated her generously allotted three rooms and typed the Razumovskys' findings and played Mahler's 1st symphony, or Tchaikovsky's 4th, or the Schubert again. When she needed a break she looked out over her balcony in the direction of the Sparrow Hills, now Lenin Hills, adjacent to the university. Where she lived assured others that she was a person of standing.

From the master copy she made six more. Six sheets of onionskin paper so thin that if of an evening at home you held them up to the yellow light reality was transformed. Onionskin paper reassembled the fragments of life like a Cubist painting. Onionskin paper functioned like water, so that what you saw was not the Soviet Union but Atlantis. She sandwiched these magical flimsies together with sheets of carbon and rolled the richness of ages into the machine. The typewriter keys hit the top copy and five more emerged, freshly inked, beneath. The sheets were as thin as a fly's wings. You wanted to read through a precious report and a draught from the window carried them across the room. But of course they were numbered. Galya typed into the night and on her brown *divan* with the crudely varnished wooden legs the number of copies grew.

The sandwich was so thick she hit the keys like in Beethoven's Hammerklavier. Fate be on our side! she thundered with Beethoven who dreamt of opening the gates of the Bastille. Galya lodged five copies in different places in Moscow. Then she set off northeast with the new master copy and a duplicate.

Her nephew's friend Boris Marlinsky told her the idea of delivering the typescript to Novosibirsk was a brainwave. The city was a very useful 3,500 kilometres from Moscow and its university still had a heartbeat. The name meant 'New Siberia'. Meanwhile real work went on in that exceptionally chilly, economically lagging city because it was too far away for anyone to properly watch and the police had long since been bribed.

'It's nothing, Boris Mikhailovich. It's just I know people there.'

It was true though. Galya knew someone of importance and influence in Novosibirsk who was willing to take the risk. He, that nameless man, call him Petya, Professor Pyotr Petrovich, maybe, belonged to the same tiny, scattered sector of workers-in-the-intellectual-guidance-of-the-people that she did. *Filruks*, they were called. Under various names the *Filruk* sector had persisted with and despite the Revolution, and it existed to stop the Russian people going off the rails. They had of course gone off the rails, but not all of them, and not all the time. The sector did its work, through teaching, and books; and if a second revolution came the *filruks* would be there to guide it.

There was a train from Moscow to Novosibirsk every other day, starting on the second day of the calendar month, and—in one of those features of Soviet life that pleasantly surprised foreigners—it travelled due east in style. It had a grand name, The Siberian. When locomotives became the great nineteenth-century symbol of progress, when they started bringing all sorts of people together, from all sorts of places, they earned those heroic names. The Russians, who learnt their stylish train interiors from the British, nevertheless called their railway the Iron Way, after the French *chemin de fer* and the German *Eisenbahn*. How the locomotives became such great heroes in Russian, such Iron *Men*, had perhaps to do with the vastness of the project. The *zheleznaya doroga* pushed back tens of thousands of kilometres and conquered innumerable hectares of mountain and steppe. Iron Men pioneered a different human future. Only now, because of how this country had configured that future, Galya Obolenskaya had to smuggle on board the routine service from Moscow to Novosibirsk the truth about how they punished alternative Russian thinkers as madmen; as they had always done and even now; and how the latest treatment for alleged insanity was shockingly cruel. The Razumovskys had left their report untitled but Galya had called Alexander Nikolaevich's accompanying essay 'Living Souls', on behalf of all those like the poet Shaginyan, who were tortured alive. It was also a tribute to Gogol, who so long ago with his *Dead Souls* had made fun of the living dead without a conscience in the world.

Heaving herself up the tall step, following her two-handled bag—she was at around forty the fit if plump figure that her friend Irina had recently acknowledged—she embarked that precious typescript and kept it company like the silent stowaway it was. It lay amidst the layers of fresh linen of which her student son was in dire need, if anyone asked. It wasn't normal to search people's bags on a train that was not crossing international borders, but if somehow she had been betrayed she might need answers.

As the translator of Dickens and Murdoch, as the kilometres rolled by and the little stations fell back into oblivion, she sat patiently matching a real mind in one language to a hypothetical mind in another. The result wasn't hers. It also wasn't the author's. Who owned it? She liked to think the act of translation added to whatever goodness there was in the universe, which couldn't be measured, but was a truth many people felt. You could choose, as a person, to add to the goodness, or the harm, though since for every person only limited possibilities applied, the choice was not easy. What she felt was that this, now, was something she could do. She sat for two days on the train, and because what she was doing could have momentous consequences, the long journey seemed fitting.

Where did she get her devotion from? Had anyone asked, any foreigner, she would almost have snapped, or more likely condescended: from our great nineteenth-century writers, of course! Our writer-legislators. The answer was obvious.

Her bag contained not only a dissident typescript and underwear for a fictitious son, but bread, cucumbers, sausage, cheese and chocolate, for as everyone knew, in Russia, away from home, you couldn't be sure when you would eat next. She had water too, just in case.

The hero-trains that steamed their way to Siberia had lovely old restaurant cars, and if that car had soup on the menu it was rich and wonderful, as if at every stop some granny came on board and was willing to make it for everybody. *Sol'yanka* was best, a meat and vegetable soup, or it could be made with fish, with all the usual ingredients, but then with a unique dash of cucumber pickling juices. When the old aristocrats sent to France to hire chefs, those experts were astonished to come across this Russian recipe which used pickle juices like the French used wine, to lift the flavour, to bring out the nuances—and to find it worked magnificently. They found that the Russian was its own cuisine: unique; like their own but pickled and different.

At nine in the evening a woman attendant in a dark blue serge uniform brought citizen Obolenskaya a duvet, a starched white sheet and pillowcase. They assessed each other, as women do. They were roughly the same age though not of the same education. What would the one woman have thought of what the other was carrying? Probably, because she had been trained to be obedient, and suspicious of dissent, fear would have prevailed. She wouldn't want to know what the report said. Who the still Living Souls were that her country was persecuting. She might hope, for the sake of her own soul, that she didn't belong to the living dead who were way beyond discrimination and protest. She would still have brought fresh bedding and served bedtime tea to a woman who looked like Galya.

'You got lucky having the compartment to yourself!'

'I won't half enjoy it.'

'Going far?'

'My son. In Novosibirsk.'

'I like that city. It's not nearly as bad as people say.'

'You know what our people are like. Always negative. Our culture doesn't deserve that. What did we have a revolution for?'

'Exactly my view.'

'Goodnight, Comrade.'

'Goodnight to you.' On examination Galya found she had received an extra packet of wafer biscuits, *vafli*, which were actually rather tasty. She had made a good impression. Did it matter? Surely not but why not count it as a blessing. She wasn't a criminal. Although technically she was. Doing exactly what she had just averred the culture did not deserve.

Having put some energy into extending the bottom bunk, wrenching it into the centre of the carriage, she laid her cotton-covered feather bed upon it with quiet ceremony. The whiteness and the freshness caught her off-guard and so reminded her there were simple things this old-fashioned country did well that she almost felt dishonest in her present mission. Taking off her top clothes, and shoes and tights, she slipped not quite naked between the sheet and the covered duvet. As the train raced on, she felt excited to be underway. Or was it that its very motion made her feel desire for the male company of Alyosha Gerasimov? Nothing to be done about that, even if he was her nephew.

At seven am the same woman couchette attendant, with dyed red hair, not a natural auburn like Galya's but a kindly enough face emerging as if from a child's orange crayon, brought fresh tea and buns. She slid open the compartment door and called: *Dobroe utro!*

'Here. Please.' Galya pointed smiling to the little table under the window, as if the little table too deserved praise.

The attendant liked her job and she liked Galya, so there were two buns.

'Do you have family?'

'A grown-up daughter. *He* left ages ago.'

Galya snorted sympathetically. 'It's like that with us. If this country were led by women, then they'd see, those lazy drinkers.'

Laughter. 'Now you're an outspoken one! Eat the buns quickly. They really are fresh.'

I will. I'm talking too much. With the compartment door shut again, Galya twisted her long loose hair into a bun. Glancing at her reflection in the window, she fixed the bun in place with enough clips to make a pin cushion. It was wonderful hair, the colour of the hidden side of pine bark. Outside in the winter sunshine the flat landscape was mostly white, mostly empty, but some drops of melted snow sparkled at the corner of the window.

She thought again, this time without lust, of her dear nephew Alyosha, who was considering a career in psychology. Because the poor state of that profession in Russia had to change. He said he hoped to make it better. You had to be brave in Russia, to feel your life was worth something, but then lots of people were brave. Or they started out brave. Alyosha had told her he openly preferred the bourgeois Freud to the behaviourist Pavlov and he didn't care who knew. He would write it, and people would object, and he would stop them then to say neither guru was the right one for Russia. Freud was like a naughty frothy writer for the bourgeois stage. As for Pavlov, he should stay in the lab with his rats. Human beings were more complicated than rats. Worth more too. There was a Russian, Luria, whose work Alyosha wanted to get hold of, with an interest in child psychology. There was promise there he sensed; something to build on. But first he had to get himself admitted to the faculty.

Borya Marlinsky meanwhile was a mathematician. That was a good foundational qualification. It could see anyone through. But he saw himself as a writer. Literature interested him most. Of course she encouraged that. What did Galya think was the main difference between Dostoevsky and Dickens, he asked, and proceeded to tell her. Dickens was psychologically the healthier man, more loving and always amusing, but perhaps superficial in the end, whereas 'our Fyodor Mikhailovich struggles with nasty and negative feelings within himself. I try to avoid national schools of psychology but the complexes of these two great men do seem to have deep roots in their own countries.' Marlinsky talked of his own ambitions, that he would like to find some third path that was neither Dostoevsky nor Tolstoy, neither the nasty bile from deep inside a man, nor the more forgivable sentiment on the surface that still in the end insisted on some sameness, some simple-minded community. 'I believe in the uniqueness of every person and their right to be themselves. I might even end as a poet.'

Both boys were gifted, and did well at school. But in the background to all growing lives in Russia was the challenge of conformity; the moment they were asked to join the Party. Galya's country cruelly meddled with young people's lives if they did not conform. The medical diagnosis of insanity was a last resort to stop people daring to step out of line. The Razumovskys had catalogued the cases where medicine was used to punish, where no 'cure' was available. Mundt the artist was lucky to get abroad, well, in a way, though he lost his inspiration there. But Shaginyan the poet, a minor poet, was the present regime's victim, as was the funny girl Prishvina who was a contemporary of Marlinsky's at university who had become religious and objected to the atheism all around her. My God, *Bozhe moi*! These were not criminals and they were not mad. Let them live! Let us live!

Report on the State of our Psychiatric Hospitals would appear in *The Novosibirsk Journal of Psychology* of Spring 1979, with a modest print-run of 100,000. From Novosibirsk it would, with luck, make its way into libraries and bookshops and even the occasional street kiosk across the entire USSR.

Meanwhile Academician Razumovsky had also written that separate essay,

Living Souls, which contained these wonderful lines:

> Our country is built upon scientific progress, which is a fine thing. But science must not become the enemy of humanity. Science, I mean our human sciences above all, must not become a prison. Complex human feeling must unfold freely, or it may die off. Our vision of the future should not kill off what is best in us, that we are living souls.

Galya sighed as she read them over again, back to Moscow, in the copy of the essay she had retained for herself.

*

All the while Korsakov had known he must take action. Even the Major had hinted his position was precarious.

'I mean, Comrade, first that art show, and now those scum protesters attracting so much attention.'

Wincing at the word scum, because he was sure he didn't feel like that, that he was a better man than to silence *all* protest, that he had a little love for humanity after all, he produced a bottle from the deeper of his two desk drawers. It was Dubrovka, the superior green and gold label brand, colourless and almost odourless, but with a certain taste of the bison, or so people said.

Govoryat. Russia was a country full of rumours, and his future was now one of them.

The Major's men were heavy-handed, They spread a reputation of Russian brutishness abroad. Someone had to intervene.

'Major, my job is smoothing out the contradictions. What must the world think when it sees works of art smashed?' Korsakov groaned now as he had groaned then. 'You remember…' He had bought his own Mundt painting in memoriam, to support the poor man. Or so he told himself.

'I do.' The Major recalled with relish the best day of political sport he'd had for a long time.

'The drunken sot you hired just ploughed on.'

'But that was his job!' The Major really didn't get it.

'A day later every newspaper in the world has a picture of our Esteemed Artist Comrade Mundt dangling from a bulldozer. That's how you make my job difficult.'

'You let that foreigner intervene. He was lucky not to be ploughed up himself.'

Korsakov imagined the diplomatic frenzy that would have greeted the Major's men harming Arthur Zimmerman.

The Major frowned over his empty glass. 'It's really too bad. Now we can't even deal with the old couple. The President of the United States protects our trash.' The Major, not in uniform, almost never in uniform, paused for deep thought. 'I can tell you, Comrade, the Amis and us becoming pals is all very well but my Colonel won't accept being nice to those traitors.'

Korsakov winced again. And when he didn't wince he sighed. He wasn't the enemy of that old couple. He wasn't the enemy of artists. Besides, Russian art was revered all over the world. That was essential to the image. *Gospodi pomilui.* The Lord have mercy. Anyway if you roughed up old people there was always the risk they might die on you. And then what. He replied: 'Quite. We must tread carefully.'

'Meaning?'

Korsakov couldn't remember what he actually meant, only that there must be no more adverse foreign headlines.

'So we'll watch the situation and review our strategy in a month, hmm?' He stood up without offering the Major one for the road. 'My view is that the US embassy fire was well handled, unlike the art show, and that has helped us, overall, in the past year. Good morning Major.'

'God speed, Comrade Korsakov.'

'God with you, Comrade Major.'

Bastard, he thought, as he sat back at his desk. As for that reference to God, much like his own, well God was just a speech habit in Russia. Otherwise he'd have to chase after the military man and accuse him of being provocative.

Time for a glass of tea. He went to press the intercom and thought better of it, popping his head round the door. 'What do you think of the Major?'

'Normal,' said his secretary Katya, meaning she wasn't offering a view.

Normal meant you know how things are so don't ask me.

'There's no one you can be but you can be yourself in time,' sang Korsakov in his head, remembering a Beatles refrain. Because everyone is stupid and vulgar it all comes back to me. But who am I, actually?

One of the Westerners in a newspaper report had described his appearance as 'a rather solid, pugnacious-looking man with a Beatle fringe.' Unsure what to make of that, he'd cut out the article and saved it.

With his tea—NO SUGAR, WOMAN!—he pushed it off the saucer—he moved from his desk to one of the pair of easy chairs. It was a very spacious office he occupied, admittedly dark, but a lovely old Moscow room, saved by some fluke from being turned into a collective pigsty. The easy chairs fronted a coffee table displaying, besides the recently shed sugar crystals, relatively interesting magazines. The international *Revue hongroise*, with a couple of pretty girls in folkloric costumes on the cover. No one read it, still no one should doubt Korsakov was a cultivated man. *New Literature*, of course, which one always had to keep an eye on, in alas every sense.

When the foreign journalists came to see him they recognised his sophistication. His telephone was made of something other than cheap plastic, for a start. It was fashioned out of onyx. The cigarette lighter was onyx to match, with the actual mechanism in gold. He would offer guests his box of silky black Balkan Sobranie cigarettes and a light, quite upsetting their prejudice that Russians smoked cardboard tubes stuffed with dung.

The Daumier prints from his time in Paris hung on the far wall, lit from above. Boring, said his wife. What do you want the foreigners to think of you, that you are so obsessed with political caricature that you don't know what art is? So now beside them hung a non-figurative study in oils by Menassier, which was often noticed. Korsakov gloried in the story, told for instance to Wormy Wormold, that the famous French artist's father actually was a worker. That we Russians are not alone in our aspiration towards equality. All glory to the proletariat, condemned by the capitalists to lead downtrodden, miserable, penned-in existences as if they were hardly human at all. The BBC man's camera had swept his lens across those very walls. All glory to our dreams!

Katya smelt of some cheap foreign perfume. Chanel *nomer pyat'*. The heavy *pyatka* hung in the air. He might have preferred No 4. No 1 even. Women did overdo it.

For God's sake, who would want my job? Mostly the contradictions he had to reconcile concerned women and madmen. The Great Opening Up! My arse! Copying from the Chinese again. Better to copy from the Italians. At least they were Europeans.

'Comrade Signorina! What can I say? It is all so complicated—complex even…' Korsakov these days wore a pair of fashionable black spectacles, which he took off, twirled, sucked on and replaced at intervals. He'd been absolutely delighted when Apollinaria Montenari had accepted his invitation to help his now, it was true, occasionally struggling country make progress.

'Some things, as you say, Comrade Signorina, are not quite right with us.' He twirled the spectacles and sucked on each arm in turn. 'So we have to correct them, with your help.'

Was Polly flattered? Of course she was, though she disliked being delivered out beyond the Mozhaisk Road by a chauffeur at the wheel of a Mercedes instead of making her own way in her Fiat. The grand house out of a forgotten history impressed her: paintings and grand furniture everywhere, like a museum except someone was trying to keep it alive, on some terms or other. Though it was meant to be a home it resembled a hotel, comfortable and yet alien to those who gathered there.

'My tink-tank colleagues, Signorina…' (Think-tank came out in Russian as tink-tank and sounded like the hilarious parody it was, but when Polly's face collapsed involuntarily into a grin Korsakov was quite put out.)

The colleagues were a huge besuited man, his upper body unctuously bent forward to meet and greet, a stick-like intellectual with desperate eyes behind his plastic spectacles and a generally downtrodden look, and a solid, fat-cheeked middle-aged woman with her grey hair in a deliberately messy, flirtatious bun. She had forgotten she was not twenty. The three of them lined up behind Korsakov like staff, as Polly entered at the grand front door. They waited to be presented; waited for the visitor to shake their hands as if she were royalty and they were loyal retainers, while a tense, elegant woman in her thirties lingered to one side. Had this been grand opera hers would have been the revelatory aria.

'So good of you to come.' That's the sort of thing they said in the West, so Korsakov echoed it.

In that unexpectedly grand house out in the middle of nowhere there was a library, always an impressive sight, and in that room a large mahogany table where they took their places for Polly's seminar on Gramsci.

'You see, Signorina, our Communism…' The very word made them all nod. They automatically owned it, though the intellectual's face seemed in that moment to blur entirely. 'Our Communism, the system of our country, has alas fallen into the hands of bumpkins. I don't mince my words. I look at your dear country and I wonder how we can learn to make our Communism *chic* again.'

Who were these nomklat Russians, with dachas in the countryside and foreign cars? Polly struggled not to see them as grotesque, but it was difficult in their actual midst. From the library huge windows opened out on to a terrace with a balustrade with sculptures, and a park beyond.

'Chic?' Polly queried.

'Oui, oui. Même très chic! If communism is to continue our people have to like it. To be impressed.'

'Impossible!' scoffed a woman's voice.

'Professor?' queried Korsakov of the desperate intellectual who had briefly made eye contact with Korsakov's wife.

'Quite so. Everyone intelligent should be impressed,' said Professor Balabin distractedly.

'If we can make it fashionable, you seem to imply,' began the woman with the deliberately untidy grey bun. 'But that seems quite wrong to me.'

'But that's reactionary, Anna. I won't mince my words, comrades. We need a revolution in the spirit of '68, a mixture of politics and fashion, and, well, love,' smiled Korsakov, spreading his arms as if he felt that bond towards all of those gathered at the table. 'Love for each other and love for our country.'

'Pfff!' scoffed a voice.

But Polly had prepared her talk, and speaking perfect Russian, with only a light accent, nodded and went ahead. They could take from Gramsci what they wanted and it wouldn't be a mistake, because he had been a guiding light in that very era of love.

'Gram-shee,' someone repeated after her, because it was difficult otherwise, in Russian, to give equal stress to the second syllable.

Polly paused now and again, and, fixing her eyes on the garden outside where there appeared to be a number of classical statues, the equivalent of the half-dozen classical paintings she had noticed on the wall inside, wondered at how her hosts lived. 'So,' she continued, 'if you want Communism to thrive you must let the people embody it on every level of society.'

'Thrive' and 'embody' seemed like good words to hang on to. The thin professor however was still stuck on 'if'.

'You get rid of all that is negative and dictatorial about the Party and let the people organise themselves from below.'

'Is that so!' escaped on the astonished breath of the fat man who was in fact vice-president of the Academy of Sciences.

'Well, now you call me reactionary but I've always been wary of gimmicks,' pronounced the woman with the bun.

'Gramsci's not a gimmick, you can't say that, Anna Mikhailovna,' opined the professor.

'Gram-shee,' Korsakov savoured the word like a tasty morsel on his tongue. 'Gram-shee!' With, following Polly, the stress on the second syllable (where no Russian would otherwise put it, for that would be like pinning the donkey's tail to its ears.)

'In your Italy everything is so beautiful,' sighed Irina Korsakov, for the first time out loud. 'I wish Russia could be Italy.'

'With respect, Comrade, we have very great difficulties at present. Bloody violence in the streets, because, even in my country there are people afraid of Communism.'

Irina waved that sentiment away as if it were mere cigarette smoke.

'As I always say, it's what you need a Party like ours for. To guard against people in the streets.' The Vice-President chuckled, though Polly didn't suppose it was a joke.

Korsakov chewed and twirled the spectacles that made him look very much of the decade in question. A cinéaste perhaps.

'Yes, well, we've got troublemakers of our own. He's a student of yours, isn't he, Professor, this Marlinsky?' Korsakov addressed Professor Balabin. Marlinsky, having attended the December 14 protest, had just come to his attention; his name contained in a report that passed over his desk.

Balabin shuddered inwardly. 'Brilliant lad though we don't have much contact.'

Polly asked: 'Is he a dissident? Gramsci's line on protest is that it's healthy.'

'I see. Oh dear.'

'That kind of health would certainly transform us. It would be the death of us.'

'Whereabouts in Italy do you come from, Signorina?' The Vice-President liked to travel, if only in his mind. But Polly fended off that overture and insisted that the assembled company tell her more about their 'Progress Group'. 'The Great Opening Up,' they voiced as one, leaving Korsakov feeling embarrassed.

Russians were idiots sometimes. No, like a set of monkeys, all trained to say the same thing at the same time.

'So, I'll say it for all of us,' he began. 'The West thinks Russia is a gloomy place where troglodytic people stinking of alcohol and sausage trundle past empty shops—'

'I'd say that's right.' Irina recalled the shock of seeing Paris for the first time, and then Moscow again.

'Well, I wouldn't. Our best Russia is a cultivated place where Communist men and women discuss art and beauty and philosophy—while still caring for the working class, of course.'

'Because they are at heart workers themselves, presumably,' added the professor.

'Yes and no,' chipped in the Vice-President.

'To be honest...' and here Polly took a deep breath, 'you would need to rejoin the people yourselves for that to happen. There can't be class division, according to Gramsci. There can't be wealth like this, enshrined in a ruling class.'

'Of course not.'

'Gramsci was telling them to mend their ways in the West. And he would be telling you the same...'

'Indeed. *Tak tochno*. Exactly so. But what stands in our way, Signorina Polly...' And this was now Irina Korsakov speaking. '...is that we don't actually like our people.'

'Irina, I don't think...' said her husband.

'So, you must learn all over again how to live together,' said Polly. 'There must be a second revolution.'

The mathematician, worrying about his connection to Marlinsky, grumbled: 'All our country needs is money. With money it can stay as it is.'

Korsakov smiled and shrugged. He thanked Polly for coming, and then invited her to pass with him into the dining room. There the assembled company enjoyed a splendid traditional Russian late lunch, with fish from Karelia and wine from Georgia.

Nine

Western lives in Moscow meanwhile continued, not only Polly's but that of the whole other world community that lived in a different district. With the exception of Howard and Gels—as we shall see—they preferred not to socialise with Polly, although in what was pending, they would be, through Howard, grateful for her insights.

By mid-March the Westerners generally were feeling the weather had slightly improved. It was still winter, but there were a few clear, longer days, which inspired that repressed desire to get out and about which Gels felt so acutely. Of course, you couldn't just get out and about. Journeys of any length beyond Moscow needed a permit that had to be applied for six weeks in advance, just so it could lie on some bureaucrat's desk and cause you anxiety and force you into last-minute plans and, ideally, from THEIR viewpoint, cancel your ambitions altogether. Yet there was no exact mileage limit for shorter, unlicensed journeys, Harriet claimed, and Gels was by nature oblivious to limitations until physically she ran up against them. So, they persisted in their plan. 'I mean if we want to go out for the day then we'll go!'

And so, on a Wednesday, which they chose a few days in advance, and which was happily dry, Harriet and Gels went for an excursion in the Zimmermans' conspicuous Chevrolet to build on what the Drivers' Club had made known when it tracked the Mercedes to Korsakov's ownership.

'"Out Mozhaisk way," Grisha, what's the best way to get there?'

'"Out Mozhaisk way?" Aha.'

Howard's former driver could sometimes behave as if information itself were *defitsitny*. But then Howard himself had given Gels the CIA map, and, as an inspired Christmas gift, that sixty-five-year-old German guidebook, so she would manage without his further help. God save him.

Meanwhile they were going in the Chevvy.

'Isn't it ridiculous? We'll be driving out there in a great chromium-plated winged monster made in Detroit.'

'Well, Miss Gels—Howard adopted the way Grisha addressed her—we're all tracked by our number plates in Moscow, so even if you went on your adventure in a beige Russian Fiat they'd still know where and who you were. Besides, Korsakov won't mind. If people don't already think the West is decadent, they will when they see you two cruising along.'

'It could make them envious.'

'But that's not what you want, is it? To make people so *envious* as to start another revolution? I don't think so. That's not what any of us wants. As for your trip, it's a gamble. Everything here is a gamble. Will people be loyal to the Communist Party vision, or will they just want to leave the country and get a car like that for themselves when they see you pass by. If they are envious what can we do?'

'Stop it! You're just confusing me.'

Howard almost smiled, perhaps not entirely kindly; perhaps thinking they were a silly pair indeed. 'Anyway, you know what I like here, as a driver, I like the empty roads. You and Harriet will enjoy that.'

'He speeds,' said Grisha.

Gels grinned obligingly. 'At least he doesn't drink.'

'Anyway, have a good time you two and if they pick you up and put you in the Lubyanka we'll come down and try to get you out before they turn your minds into mush and your bones into gristle. Promise.'

Finally having enough of his teasing Gels raised her hands in supplication, got her coat, the usual parka, and Howard watched her go from the window.

Harriet was waiting to pick her up outside the arch. Having nodded to the guard and received no response, she complained: 'They're all the same. Under instructions not to make contact. What do you call him again?'

Gels had given her guard a name to please Harriet. 'Osip. Let's just leave him be.'

They pulled out on to the Inner, so-called 'Garden' Ring Road, where a few Fiats, properly called Ladas in their Soviet version, were to be spotted. Two sprayed bright orange passed. 'Paint of the month. All they had left.'

'Little orange boats drifting on the grey tide.' *Lada* meant boat.

Gels and Harriet blended with a steady stream of yellow Volga taxis. Otherwise, it was mostly green military-looking vehicles, or heavy goods lorries.

Then a middle-distance bus pulled up beside them at traffic lights. Those buses named after Icarus came from Hungary. They were supposed to give travellers the dreamlike impression of flying away from this grim world forever.

'I know those buses. They had them when I was a student in Lithuania.'

'So that's why your Russian's so good.'

Harriet always wondered whether her young friend Gels was a spy. And Gels didn't quite know about her older friend Harriet either.

But now Harriet was distracted. She had to get something off her chest. 'Gels, I have to tell you this. The last time I saw Dmitry, not only did he speak but he turned on me. "Why you give me soup, lady? I not homeless. You total American. Total capitalist. You have no sense of my dignity."'

'Ooh, did he say that? You must have been shaken.'

'Shaken? I was—'

'I mean when someone is silent and then suddenly talks. And attacks you like that.'

'I was devastated. Then I wondered if he was right.'

Gels thought it but kept it to herself. 'It's probably that bastard Korsakov. He just wants you to feel bad—revenge because your husband treats him as a fool. He told your Dmitry what to say.'

'I guess that could be it.'

That was Korsakov's work: smoothing out the contradictions, sowing doubt.

Soon enough they reached the so-called Outer Ring Road. Almost exclusively lorries—trucks to Harriet—trundled around it. The lorries were without exception old and dirty, and pumped out filthy exhaust fumes.

Harriet quoted statistics for factory and farm deliveries. 'Apparently they rarely reach their destination.'

'You mean they break down.'

'Or they just go round and round until the petrol runs out and then people can help themselves.'

'Goodness! They let themselves be hijacked! Can't be true, can it!'

Gels spoke to the windscreen. 'Everything's a joke here. Well, we know that. How can they ever get it right?'

'Another revolution, honey. Isn't that what they say?'

'I've lost faith in that word completely.'

The Chevrolet meanwhile drove them under a gantry across the broad carriageway. Harriet glanced in her rear-view mirror. It was the moment, twenty kilometres into their drive, when a police car should have raced up behind and stopped them.

'Where is the monstrous GAI then? Why haven't we been blitzed from the air? Why aren't flashing lights racing up behind us? It's so eerily quiet,' cried Gels.

'Korsakov is giving us an easy time.'

'What? You mean he knows about our trip?'

'He must do. We haven't tried to keep it secret.'

'But you're saying something else, aren't you? You're saying he's giving us an easy time because of what we know about his son. Am I right?'

'That's very smart of you Gels.'

'Wow. And you knew that when you accepted to make this trip with me?'

'I suppose I did.' Harriet smiled. 'I wanted us to get there.'

Harriet confessed she hadn't wanted to scare Gels, but one way THEY did intervene on trips like this was that the cars of foreigners unexpectedly broke down, or were involved in collisions. It was hard to believe. But it happened. They would soon see whether, and how much, much Korsakov minded. Best to put it out of their minds now.

Harriet was a good driver, but the open space did not invite her to put her foot down. In fact, she seemed nervous, her intelligent eyes fixed on the road, the skin around them crinkled, and they travelled at a slow and stately pace. As they proceeded it seemed to Gels that this 'outside the city' was near-wilderness. It was Howard's view that dictators needed cities, but they didn't care much for countryside where there were hardly any people anyway. They left the countryside to run wild because it had no political value. This 'not-the-city', where nature ruled, was the place to shoot bears and for *nomklats* to lead their idyllic secret lives.

Harriet was mildly interested. But she no longer thought of Gels as a spy. She talked too much. Unless it was the perfect cover.

'So this is what it's like driving to Nowhere.'

On the Outer Ring Road, the wilderness did now and again relent. Driving south—presumably no force could doctor the truth of the compass – oh but Gels you know that's not true—they passed settlements that looked more like state farms, a mixture of prefabricated barns and grain silos and some kind of urban-looking accommodation blocks. If they were looking for the glamorous hideaway of a reclusive *nomklat* family it was unlikely to be here.

One of the farms had a great metal arch announcing its entrance, which reminded Gels of a picture she'd seen of the concentration camp at Auschwitz. There was something strange about Soviet moral taste. That even with the door to the West half-open they didn't bother to look out and see what was done, and not, and what a decent country ought to respect. 'You can see what they don't share with us. They're living in a different time. That's another reason why it's so frightening here.'

'*Are* you frightened, Gels?'

Gels was somehow caught off-guard but perhaps she was. It sometimes seemed to her, in the middle of the night, as if she were exploring the outer reaches of her own psyche. Here was what could happen to a human life if it went astray.

'I hate that sense of being caught up in a bundle of lies I can't get out of.'

'So, you came here to explore it.'

'Whatever I intended being here has turned into that.'

'That's true of all us. Everyone is changed by being in Moscow.'

This was candour but Gels was still hiding something. Harriet was too. But no one can plumb their own depths. Or confess everything.

Gels looked to the windscreen for inspiration. Many little insects died there, swept into a sludge by the strong Chevvy wipers, which presumably didn't get stolen even though Dmitry didn't protect them. She said, to the windscreen and the road ahead: 'Right now my friend Harriet Zimmerman and I are driving through the outskirts of Moscow, in a region called Podmoskovye. There's a *nomklat* by the name of Korsakov who intrigues us and we know he lives out here with a big house and a Mercedes 300 SL. We've formed this crazy idea that if we drive around we might find him at home. And if we can find him at home we'll understand more about this crazy country.'

'Gels, whatever you are doing here all I can say is you take it *very* seriously.'

'I think you do too.' In fact I think it's *your* job, she decided, and all that nonsense with Dmitry is just to distract us.

'What I can say is I look to Russian literature to tell me what to do and who to believe.'

'Go on.' Harriet glanced in her mirror, as if there was always the chance they were being followed.

'Well, Tolstoy, Dostoevsky, it's all about saving your soul, isn't it? But here it's just cruelty and lies. Russian literature is not a place though so you can retreat there.'

Harriet slowed the flashy car even more. Honestly it was as if a moon probe had landed on a barren planet, the way they were moving through the deserted un-countryside.

'But why *you*? Is it that you…?'

'I studied Russian at university. So then Russia got under my skin. Next thing I knew, it was my job to sort this place out.'

'Crazy. I feel the same.'

Harriet switched on the car radio. Gels was surprised to find it tuned to Radio Moscow. The radio station had a nice call sign which could be heard on the hour. Radio Mayak, Radio Lighthouse: This is Moscow Speaking! The hour ticked up as they passed more open, indeterminate land, with here and there a few ethereal birch trees.

'*Govorit Moskva*! You can imagine people right across the Soviet Union listening to it and wanting it to give them guidance. It's a pity they don't play good music.'

'Listening to it makes me feel I'm actually *here*, whatever they're saying. Do you want some better music?' Harriet asked. 'Have a look at the tapes in the glove box.'

Gels enjoyed the chance to switch off from a tense few minutes. But still she listened. The radio news, skewed in the Soviet way, was full of heroic economic achievements which left no trace in reality, and what did you do with that if you didn't ridicule it. But she listened.

She rummaged with childish glee among the plastic music boxes but didn't choose one to play, because she had to concentrate.

Apart from the state farm that had relieved the second half-hour of the trip the land they passed was just this open countryside, mostly flat, not appealing, but with the occasional patch of woods that might hide a dacha. Dachas were holiday homes, mostly wooden, more like bungalows, though surely they were looking for something grander. But there weren't any stone buildings at all, just the occasional wooden shack.

'What about you, Harriet? You seem to have good Russian.' Indeed she was better than people said.

'I did a course when Arthur found out about his posting.'

'You must have picked it up quickly. I suppose you're a linguist.'

'French at Wellesley. A bit of Italian because every civilised person has that—and we Yanks do try to be civilised, whatever Europeans say.'

Gels smiled. 'Isn't Wellesley where Nabokov taught?'

'Cornell. Now there's a Russian for you!'

'Of a completely different kind. Even in his lifetime there weren't any people like him left. It must have been terrifying. But the new people put a wall around themselves and said we're going to create a new race of people and to try to live differently.'

'And what do you think about that?'

'Well—' And now she came out with it. It was the way in which she agreed with Howard. 'Truth be told, Harriet, I admire it…'

'You *admire* it? And yet you wake up in the night terrified?'

'Everyone needs the chance to start again. Countries too.'

'Countries aren't like individuals. That's a myth.'

'I think Russia wants us to think it's this unique living organism that's got to develop in a certain way.'

'That's the myth, Gels, sure. But they just hide behind it.'

'Some do. Some believe it.'

'And you?'

'I feel I can't judge.'

'That's just what they want you to feel.'

Did Gels admire a country that had driven out all the rich people because she wanted to get back at her father? Harriet asked afresh.

You might think that, Gels answered. 'But I hope it's more. To the best of my self-knowledge I hope the reason for my time in Russia, my imposing on Howard, my taking advantage of every privilege I have, is to know what I want to live for. I mean, why don't we all kill ourselves? Why don't they? Heh, didn't Baedeker mention a river? Can you pull over?' And with that they finally stopped probing Gels's psyche.

The 1914 Baedecker was so valuable to historians and curious tourists because it was the last record of what could be found by way of historic buildings in pre-revolutionary Russian streets, in towns and on outlying grand estates, before October 1917 turned the grand houses into children's homes, orphanages, trade union rest homes, pigsties and cowsheds.

'Look! Heh, I think we should turn back and take the last turning we passed.' A signpost had indicated 'Zarechye'—the area beyond the river.

'Looks like a plan at last.' And with that they were off the main road, which was almost the only road there was. The sirens should have come screaming, but they didn't. Harriet sat a little forward over the wheel, and the way her lips pulled back gave her a determined look. Gels admired her.

About fifteen minutes down the narrow, deserted road a weatherboarded cottage hove into view. By some miracle it was even populated. Two figures stood in what might be called the garden. They were sawing logs with a huge double-handed saw. A Darby and Joan picture.

'A devoted old couple. Comes from a painting I think. English.'

'Must be!'

It was tempting, in retrospect, to think the scene had been curated to catch them out in their Western sentimentality. For any Westerner in that moment had to be thinking, no one does manual work like this anymore, not in our world, and yet, look at this: an old couple sharing a saw! It was almost as good as seeing a woman harnessed to a plough (a news photograph from Siberia that had done the global rounds and also passed across Korsakov's desk some five years before.) A Russian Darby and his Joan! *Derbi s ego Dzhonoi*! The visitors would feel they'd discovered the real Russia. They'd stop. Which they did. Their tyres crunched on the gravel at the side of the road and Harriet cut the engine.

Like two startled animals, the man and woman lifted their heads and stared. First one foreign woman then the other opened her car door. A beguiling smell of resin scented the air, and the ground was scattered with wood shavings. The logs were large for firewood, Harriet observed, knowledgeable from her holidays on Fire Island. They would need to cut them again.

'Good day to you, comrades. Be so kind—*budte dobry*…' Gels had the better Russian even so and, having closed the car door behind her, walked up and did the talking. She forgot all about being so evidently a young Western woman, in an army surplus long green jacket, and jeans and leather boots, and an expensive fur hat from Canada, via Harrods, who had just emerged from the passenger door of a Chevrolet.

'Dear friends, they say—' she began. '*Govoryat*.' The point was Russia was a land of rumours. Everyone would understand she was speaking the truth if she talked about rumours. Vague information that might be right or wrong or just irrelevant. 'They say there's a *shato* round here, a kind of castle. We've come to see it.' The word *Shato* didn't actually exist in Russian, hence the blank faces, but she thought it ought to have done. '*Usad'ba.*' The right word finally came.

The natives stood expressionless, the man still holding one end of the giant-toothed saw, which rested on the ground, like a harp. He wore work clothes of blue serge and a hat with ear flaps. In her coat and leggings and stout boots his wife could have been almost any age and any Russian woman still leading a rural life.

'Good day to you, my friends.' Harriet emerged alongside Gels. 'Possibly we're looking for a church.' The old manor houses had their own chapels, it says here.' She had Gels's Baedeker in her hand. To look for a chapel, she had intelligently decided, might give them an extra clue.

The face of the bundled woman froze at the word church. Or maybe something else frightened or annoyed her. She just looked cross.

'She remembers the church was against the Revolution.'

'She's not so old.'

'Folk memory then.'

The man stepped forward, perhaps to protect his wife. 'Let me answer your question!'

'That would be very kind.'

'Now, you see this road? You continue. *Prodolzhaite, prodolzhaite*, until you come to a crossroads. *Perekrest.* Then you turn right, and right again, and then just keep going. *Pryamo, pryamo.* Straight ahead.'

Both women felt a similar thrill at the prospect of finally arriving where they wanted to go. 'Thank you so much, kind sir. Comrade. And to your wife. We wish you all the best.'

Back in the car, which seemed stuffy after the fresh air, they settled themselves, waved, and drove off.

'Amazing.'

'Life is good.'

Harriet drove and Gels stretched out her legs.

'Is it fifteen minutes? Didn't he say fifteen minutes?'

'I missed that.'

'We could easily get lost out here. There's no one about.'

'Here, look, turn right, and yes…there's the second turning.'

'Heh, isn't this—'

'I thought I recognised it.'

171

'It's the 'Zarechye' turning.'

'We're back on the main road.'

'Unless we turn back to their cottage.'

'Ah, hell, they've done for us.' Harriet stopped and rubbed her face. 'They've got us.'

They had. It was Korsakov one, Gels and Harriet zero. Gels was so astonished she couldn't speak. 'You mean—'

'Maybe it's a coincidence that we met them. But I don't believe it. Shall we have lunch?' And they both laughed out loud.

Korsakov's point of view was simply that his authority had to be respected.

'Have lunch at that charming English pub with a garden we passed just now? Let's do that. Mine's a ploughman's and half a cider.' Harriet said she'd have a ploughman's too, whatever that was. And they laughed and laughed.

Harriet parked in a rough space in front of a gate beside the road. Gels retrieved a basket from the back seat of the stationary Chevrolet. Beneath a linen cloth were slices of buttered black bread and German smoked ham from the Gastro, and sweet wafer biscuits from Czechoslovakia and apples from Georgia. She also had tea in a flask.

'Good food!'

'We deserve it.'

'Heh, that flask's so pretty. Where did you get that? I haven't been able to find anything like that here. I have to import mine from Finland.'

'Howard's assistant gave it to me.'

'I haven't had the pleasure.'

'His name's Grisha. He's extraordinary. Howard—'

'The basket too, it's beautifully made.'

'I got it from the Georgian market.' It was a stoutly woven, handsome little basket with a solid handle. The foreigners couldn't help it. They were also tourists, and they had money to spend. Condemned to stay in a country that didn't believe in money, they spent where they could.

'So does Korsakov live out this way or not?'

'I imagine he does but we haven't found him.'

'I know it sounds trivial but it does matter what the people have in their shops.'

'It never sounded trivial to me, honey. I'm an American consumer.'

'What's in their shops, and what isn't, that's a national humiliation, it shows the regime doesn't care for them when they're supposed to be building socialism *together*.'

Gels sounded naive even to herself. 'But instead of socialism they're full of tricks. Hell. That old couple really tricked us there. You remember Potyemkin Villages from Russian history? How the local authorities faked whole villages to make the Empress think Russia was flourishing. It was like a Potyemkin scenario just now. In the eighteenth century for the Empress, in the twentieth century for us Westerners. Aaah! And we fell for it. That bastard Korsakov tricked us with that cottage back there, with the contented peasants working in the garden.'

'Instead of socialism they're full of tricks, that's it, you said it, Gels.' We should be honoured Korsakov thinks we're worth bothering about.'

'We're the West, aren't we?'

'We have the power to write about him.'

'And he has the power to kick us out.'

They resumed their drive. They hadn't achieved anything, thanks to Korsakov's cunning. Now they would just drive home.

'Still you want to believe something good about them, Gels.'

'Because Russia is this great moral place. Yes.'

They fell into silence.

Gels remembered the tapes in the glove compartment. 'Is there a different way home? Let's just listen to something.'

'No chance of a different way home. There's only one road.'

'That's how he knew which way we'd go.'

'But I can drive slowly.'

Suddenly weary, Gels wanted a rest from talking, and so she slotted that little plastic package with the two tape wheels into the cassette player and sat back. It was a famous piece by Mussorgsky for piano, barely half an hour long. It was dazzling. Some critics said it was the most difficult and unrewarding piano music ever written; others that it was the finest work in the repertoire. To bring out the contrasts, to make that claim to greatness, the pianist dipped into passages so quiet you thought this was how the world began. Flashes of light and tenderness and adventure darted up and down the keyboard. When he hammered at that grand piano Mussorgsky was trying to outdo a whole tower of bells.

'It's too much. In the car. Stop.'

'I'll pull over.'

The visitors had to park again, this time seduced not by a Potyemkin village, but by musical sublimity. And then they drove the rest of the way home in silence.

Part 2

Ten

Russia fashioned itself according to the West, but the competition had to be disguised, in order not to be humiliating. To formulate the disguise had been Korsakov's job for twelve years now, and so it's worth looking back to see how he became what he was—and why he admired the Beatles.

In the summer of 1967, at a recording studio in north-west London, those four British musicians broadcast a song that excited the world. Korsakov felt he was born, as an adult and as a diplomat, that day, on June 25th that year. The Beatles performed live from the Abbey Road Studios, and a satellite relayed their message: All you Need is Love.

The United Nations should have adopted it as an anthem. Had the lads been from Murmansk, Moscow would have proposed *Nuzhna tol'ko lyubov'* as a signature tune for world peace. The idea was fabulous and only a lugubrious isolationist – everyone had a colleague like that – instantly objected. 'The West would reject any proposal from *us*.'

'*Their* loss. We will show them, my friends, believe me.'

In Paris, where he had been posted as cultural attaché, and with an informality that took his colleagues by surprise, he had watched the Love Love Love broadcast perched on the edge of his desk. His uncomfortable colleagues looked at each other nervously. Did they too have permission to listen? Might they too refer to the broadcast so informally, as if to *welcome* it? For it wasn't often that Vladimir Korsakov, all of twenty-eight years old that year, precociously talented, let himself be carried away by everyday 'stuff'. But yes a new permissiveness seemed in order. 'All you neet is luff,' the diplomat crooned, as a ray of white light fell on Soviet diplomacy.

Ignaty Petrovich, boldest among the colleagues, compared the moment with the karaoke phenomenon that had impressed him on a posting to Japan.

'So that's what you got up to, Comrade, when you weren't protecting our Kuril Islands from those thieves in Tokyo.'

'I won't deny it, Vladimir Arkadevich.'

Laughter, a surprising amount of it, lightened the usually sombre atmosphere of the embassy in the rue Daru.

Every diplomat knew that reference, by the way. All round the world were territories that Russia had added to its empire by finding some way of calling them its own.

'Singing makes everyone happy.'

'Indeed. A sound collective principle known to religions all across the world.'

'Even to ours, though not a religion of course.'

'Of course not.'

'Even if certain songs are not allowed in our country, *ne pravda li*?' added the lady counsellor, Maria Ivanovna.

'Well, now that goes without saying. Obscenity, blasphemy, crudity…complete lack of musicality… Why should we allow *that* into our country? Hmm? Why follow the West downhill? But *this* is something different.' Everyone nodded.

It wasn't easy to be a Soviet diplomat abroad, because foreign postings were badly paid. You can defect with nothing in the bank, but it's harder. With western prices so high most Russians temporarily officially planted in the West hardly went out. They hardly knew obscene, blasphemous, crude, singsong Paris, much to their chagrin. But the previous winter they had clubbed together to buy the latest Phillips cathode-ray TV which they were presently watching.

The defence attaché by the name of Yurenko had peered at the Western invention when it arrived in the office. 'We have to consider whether this *televisiya* may also contain a listening device and a camera to watch us.'

'Oh my God! *Bozhe moi!* Comrade Yurenko, what shall we do?' (The women mostly thought they'd wear their best outfits and makeup.)

In the event the *filipsa* was a chance to watch the decaying West from the safety of the office, so espionage fears were soon forgotten.

In Moscow London's defence attaché, a friend of Howard Wilde's predecessor but two, had once examined a Soviet 'Sputnik' TV set in the same Cold War spirit. Faced with a goggle box loudly referencing the space race with America, he had muttered derisively: 'Stupid clods! Ghastly-looking thing! Who would want that in their living room?'

That was the two worlds for you, into which East and West were divided. Back in Paris in the spring of 1967, the Phillips' screen was definitely more welcome. It wasn't large, the picture was black and white, but Korsakov and the team had a fantastic experience that afternoon. They heard Dzon Lyenon live, with his little wire-rimmed glasses and his sexy drawl.

'He looks just like an old-fashioned Russian *intelligent*!'

'He looks a lot better than any Russian I've ever met,' observed Masha, who was the ambassador's secretary.

The boyish figure of Paul Macartney leaned into the microphone. 'Look at him! Sweet as a lamb.'

'I prefer the *intelligent*.'

Momentarily everyone chose between John and Paul: between gravelly-voiced rebel or charming choir boy.

Korsakov, neither of those, though intelligent and educated, sat on the desk, grinning and waving his small foot in the air. 'Rump a diddle der. Great, wasn't it?'

'*Zdorovo*. Just great.'

'*Vachement bien*.' The lady counsellor had good French.

'*Suteki*!' The diplomat who had been in Japan looked around for praise.

Korsakov so much liked the mouth organ descending the melodic scale he decided to celebrate: 'Maria Andreyevna, *shampanskoe* est'?'

'Maybe.' Masha hated him. So false. He felt the same about her. She just wanted to make Russia a clone of the West.

'Do try to find some.'

'I'm afraid there's quite a bit left over from last May 1st,' said Ivanovna. 'Unfortunately, Monsieur le President couldn't make it.'

'Headache, wasn't it, if I recall?' sighed the ambassador's secretary.

'Too bad!' cried Korsakov. 'All the more for us.' Anyway, it's not our Soviet Union making de Gaulle's froggy head ache now, Korsakov amused himself with the thought. It's freedom on the streets of Paris. Monsieur le *Maréchal* should take a leaf out of our book. We wouldn't let a whole lot of students tell us they want to change the constitution! Huh!'

In one of the embassy's high-ceilinged baroque rooms, the only other benefit of being abroad, since they couldn't afford to go out, a cork popped. In a room now blue with the smoke of Gauloises and no prospect of its being requisitioned for its use as a communal flat any time soon the Moscow diplomats raised their glasses.

'*Prekrasno*! *Otlichno*! Fit for a French president!'

'Even if he ignores us.'

'*Suteki! Kanpai!*'

Three bottles soon drained away. Moreover, it was right not to try to replace a cork in a bottle. Please! We may have turfed out all the aristocrats but we know how to behave.

'Why don't we make champagne like that in Crimea?'

'We haven't stolen the recipe yet. Ha ha ha.'

'*Na zdorovie*! Your health!'

His fantasy ignited by the champagne, Korsakov imagined 'All You Need is Love', if not as a new anthem for the UN, then as a propaganda slogan for the next Revolution Parade. How the girls would blush to carry the banner! How the lads would march proudly (and with a great deal of new hope, since nice Russian girls were rather conservative.) In *Pravda* the love message from Liverpool would top the list of new slogans for the next half-year. For in his native country there could never be enough exhortations to be good and kind and work hard and build for the future.

His report finished, however, Korsakov was more thoughtful. Who dared tell the Russians about love. After all, they had the unmatchable Pushkin. And people say, *govoryat*, we should be less uptight about owning Pasternak too.'

'It's true that *Dr Zhivago* is inspired by the poetry of love.'

Korsakov nodded, his huge eyes suddenly full of a strange, dog-like melancholy. 'Sad to say that great novel got smuggled out just as I was finishing school. They published it in Italy and it won him the Nobel prize.'

'How do you mean "sad"?' asked Maria Ivanovna.

'I kept telling them in Tokyo Russian literature is the greatest in the world.'

'I'm sure that went down well in such an ancient civilised land.'

'I mean sad that we behaved in such a confused fashion in those days.'

'Anything changed? What will we do when Solzhenitsyn gets the Nobel?'

'Murder him before he can get to Stockholm.'

Korsakov frowned.

'Sorry, Comrade, I mis-spoke.'

'Pasternak didn't dare go and collect his prize in case we didn't let him back,' Maria Ivanovna moaned.

'Fuck,' muttered Masha, coming off her high horse. 'That's how it is with us. What we're good at we ruin.'

'These are the contradictions of our existence.'

'"Effree man destroys the think he luffs."'

'Aaooden?' queried the lady counsellor. 'I don't think he meant it like that.'

'Whatever *he* meant. This is what *I* mean.'

No one who met Korsakov thought of him as subtle. Ivanovna thought of him as downright two-faced. One moment he was a humanist aesthete and the next a foul-mouthed pig. What character did that amount to? Though no one could deny he was intelligent and hard-working.

To justify to Moscow the afternoon spent in front of French television, meanwhile, he would report that the Californian religion of love had now spread to France, and Great Britain and indeed the entire West, and that was serious, because it was a *kind of* revolution. 'Not every social change is political, though it may have huge political consequences.' Not having a clue which way the free-love revolution would go, he aimed to sound both enthusiastic and critical. Something fresh from a West in decline. Something we could do with in Russia too, now that our Communism is sufficiently advanced and we can relax a bit. No need to be so ruthless, after all. Maybe all you *do* need is love. Maybe we can make this one work.

'I need the whole text, our man-in-Tokyo.'

'Here you have it, Comrade Cultural Attaché.' Ignaty Petrovich had taken the lyrics down in English shorthand.

'Really? But that's remarkable.'

'My pleasure, Comrade Cultural Attaché. I was afraid I would never hear it again.'

There's nothing you can do But you can learn how to be you in time/ It's easy/ All you need is love.

'There's nothing you can do that can't be done.' Korsakov sang it in a whisper. But then finding his confidence he sang it louder. 'The *Beatl-sy* are philosophers, don't you think?'

Masha, Mariya Andreevna, as he addressed her, put down her pen and pursed her lips. 'This is a consideration, Vladimir Arkadevich.'

She had a face…he was of a stature… She had made a note of what had been said that afternoon, in case any questions were asked about the unusually relaxed atmosphere it brought about. Any chance of seeing VAK removed from his post lifted her spirits.

Meanwhile he watched how, that day as on other days, when, leaving the office in which the junior staff and the ambassador's secretary worked together, as she went off to make tea, she smoothed her little skirt. He reflected how fashionable she had become in Paris and watched her rump. He'd never desired her. He didn't like her backside and as for that face like a crumpled bun… But ought he to court her, the ambassador's secretary?

A man with such tiny feet! She loathed him. But she should suppress it and be friendly, for he was clearly going places.

As he went down the murky corridor to relieve himself, squeals of some other feminine joy escaped the broom cupboard, followed by a deep masculine shudder, and he wasn't even envious. The power of champagne is the power of love and it's there for all of us and we can all learn from it.

All this in the Russian embassy in Paris, rue Daru, which was a mirror of Russian politics in stalemate.

Back in Moscow Irina Bové in her little flat in the Arbat had also tuned into the Beatles' broadcast with her two girlfriends Galya and Anna. Galya was, then, already, an editor at WELL, while Anna Lunina had thatcoveted job at the Tretyakov Gallery. That was the generation of '61 for you. Hunched over the little screen, how they admired those handsome lads who looked so Western and free.

Irina, with her magnificent golden hair and mysterious slanting eyes that seemed to melt whatever they touched, was a great beauty by any standards. She had a tall, slender figure and her lilting voice made men quiver. Her superiors, underestimating her other great quality, her intelligence, chose her to work for the resident foreign community as a translator. She arrived in their midst to their great delight and torment. Especially the bureau chief of the New York Report desired her with real high-class Ivy League lust. It couldn't happen. It would end careers on both sides. But it didn't stop that reporter gazing at her as she scanned the Soviet provincial press. An agonised moment caused him to stand up against the window and scream. This beastly Moscow, imprisoning my soul in a cage!

To appease his soul he made unnecessary detours around the office furniture, and bought her presents.

'Irina Matveyevna just a little something.'

'Reelly you shouldn't have. Reelly.' Her fabulous English only occasionally sounded peculiar.

'In view of your excellent work for us.' Because it was true. She read the newspapers of an entire empire for the Amis (as the Russians called them, and that was ironic for anyone who knew French). Irina Matveyevna not only detected tiny signs of shifts of allegiance in the Kremlin, passing them on without comment, almost as a test of the Western reporters, to see if they would really take note of what she left out. She also dug out the real-life stories the foreign reporters would never find, from across the steppes and inside the closed cities; from inside the collective farm and among the sun-kissed rice-growing fields of the Kuban beside the Black Sea. Through her diligence news tucked within the dim and frozen urban precincts of Novosibirsk came to light, and events and facts from Lake Baikal to Vladivostok, from the tundra to the Pacific Ocean, had their significance. Not just the statistics churned out by the Moscow ministries but something of the truth emerged through her endeavours. Oh, vast country! Oh, imperfect ideal land of air crashes, failed harvests and serial murderers. The regional newspapers arrived in the offices of the Amis every day. Every town that was a half-civilised outpost of Moscow, and townships known to the world beyond only because they boasted labour camps paved with human bones, they too sent their local newspapers to the capital. A revelation! *Ce n'est pas vrai! Höchst unwahrscheinlich!* As the Germans said. Almost pretty places existed where Russians went on holiday.

Irina Matveyevna knew what she was allowed to point up, to give her country a presence in the world, and what she should pass over. Seth and Hank might catch her out over her omissions. They had good Russian. But their time was limited. They had to rely on her.

This gorgeous Russian blonde, skilled beyond any wooden set of instructions, smiled as she undid the gift-wrapped package Hank had just presented her with, and then blushed and raised a finger to her lips. Her American boss ('*moy shef*', she called him) had chosen gold paper, and was proud of it. Her slim fingers teased the sealed edge. He waited. He never knew, was she, when she talked in that friendly way with him, when she urged him to keep his voice down, when she flirted outrageously with the packaging of his present, turning it into a displaced striptease, was she afraid of the ministry, or was that all part of the game? All you need is love! He couldn't be sure.

The gift, in view of Irina Matveyevna's continuing excellent service to the American press, was a recording of that famous song on 7" vinyl, one of a million copies released on July 7th, 1967. An inspired NYR manager had ordered copies to be sent to bureaux worldwide, each correspondent to inscribe the paper slip cover with a personal message for a local contact. In this case the Russian bureau chief wrote: 'Dear and respected Irina Matveyevna with cordial greetings from your American colleagues.' In Hank's case he really meant it: all the respect and wonder and recognition of her talents and her beauty that would have made him her humble servant between the sheets. Or on the desk. (In fact in the NYR's cramped office a casual encounter with *lerv*, not to speak of a gesture of true love, was not easy. The back of the door had coat hooks and all the walls were fronted by metal bookcases.) Hank would still have joined himself to her anywhere and anyhow, except—and this was the penultimate hurdle—evidently the office was bugged. That was yet another factor to bear in mind. Cameras were the ultimate threat. Whenever there was sex the Russians always got photographs. Murky shots of entangled limbs, of the woman's head tilted back and the man riding supreme, dropped out of blank envelopes. They claimed it was your body, and. hell, if you were even half-guilty, if it only happened in your mind, you weren't quite sure. Thus the Cold War kept bodies, as well as east and west, apart, while bringing them dangerously close together. That moment when he scraped his fingernails against the office's sealed windows often haunted him.

'Wanna play it?'

He'd never asked her up to the flat above the office before. Fortunately his wife was out. They sat on opposite sofas and he watched her with a terrible fixation. '*Zdorovo*!' she breathed. She called him Khenk. 'Who was it said, Khenk, that life without music would be a mistake?'

'I really don't know.'

'You don't? Nietzsche I think.' She made him feel a fool and, with that, his lust died down.

Of course she noticed; but she was professional. Her job as a secretary to the foreign press corps was the best thing that happened to her and she wanted to keep it. She liked the presents too. She had black winged sunglasses from Finland and French moisturiser for her impeccable skin, and a stack of copies of *Time Magazine* which she kept under the mattress. She liked being allowed to keep all these good things in the one room flat in the Arbat that she was lucky to have, and where she slept alone, for the moment, biding her time.

Later the NYR bureau chief played his own copy of the song and wondered what it actually meant. Once you got away from Love Love Love, it was a deep philosophical puzzle. 'There's nothing you can say but you can learn how to play the game.' What? Did the distrust of language go so far with those British guys that they thought words could *never* really mean what people wanted them to mean? Was language no more than a social game? All I can say is it's one helluva political game here in Moscow.

Korsakov had met Irina Bové in Moscow where everyone who was anyone met, he thought, namely at an art exhibition. The show was for an unusual French painter. His own embassy had begun the negotiations which made it happen. Moscow promised to lend a couple of Matisses in exchange. The French lapped up the deal and both sides benefited.

Alfred Manessier had risen from a working-class family to create these magnificent modernist works of colour and texture and humanity. Of that fact Korsakov was subsequently so proud, when he became the owner of a Manessier, the one the foreign press community subsequently admired on his wall, that he told everyone. The Frenchman's father was a stonemason, his grandfather a fisherman. If only Soviet art history were like that! Or, rather, if only they didn't insist that *only* working-class artists could be shown.

'It's not quite like that,' said Anna Lunina, from her sanctuary in the Tretyakov.

'You know what I mean, Anushka! They always want to force art into a mould. The artist whatever his social origins needs to be free.'

But that was a year or so later, by which time he had come to know his future wife's friends well enough to use their cosier names. As for now…

'Vous parlez francais?'

'Yes of course,' she answered sharply. 'But I'm Russian. You can see that.'

'But you're so beautiful. Only French women are so beautiful.'

'As it turns out that's not true. But you must have travelled, Comrade.'

'Indeed.'

Not a bumpkin then. Promising.

So that's how they got to know each other. In the encouraging company of really remarkable paintings, some of them like stained-glass windows and some like pick-a-stick heaps of colour, they entered into that tangle of shared illusions which, if human beings are lucky, resolves itself into the beautiful fabric of love. Perhaps only art can give you that gift of seriousness and joy at the same time, that might end in marriage. Vladimir Arkadevich Korsakov—extending a hand—and with his huge eyes moist with interest and his smooth cheeks hanging appealingly, not because he was old but because there was something of the Kalmyk in him—confessed he retained the habits of three years in Paris where possible, though he was now back in Moscow.

'Three years! That's a long time.'

'I miss it. I shouldn't say so but I do. But then France comes to us in these paintings—'

'The France of a religious man, I think. I feel for his art but I strain to understand his religious sentiments.'

'How subtle is your experience of life, Irina Matveyevna.'

Indeed. Before an abstract painting representing a mother condemned to death Irina felt a deep fear stir inside her. Another, an imposing splatter, 'Blood and Water', was not normally a painting anyone would dare show in Russia, out of fear it would be taken to allude to terrible things in the past.

'So you loved your time in Paris.' She brought him back to it, to find out more of what he truly cared for.

'I did, for you see, I like the possibility of free human exchange. Something more exciting than a closed-in, fenced-off world. And I felt it there.' His exchanges now, with her, a woman he had only just met, were very bold. 'Look at this. "Tumult." If he'd been a sculptor Manessier would have been Giacometti. Then all this blood red. Red is his colour. And black, and all the blues in between.'

Paris must be wonderful, she said. Still her dream was to go to Rome.

Tumult reminded her of a Gallery in Milan.

'Apparently Monsieur Manessier lived with monks for a while.' A label from the show quoted him: "I felt profoundly the cosmic link between sacred chanting and the truth of human beings…the world of nature all around."'

A Soviet show which included such sentiments was not totally rare, but it had to be organised carefully, with just a touch of alternative sentiment here and there.

'If I could get a posting to Rome I'd take you there. I'd take you anywhere in the world. Would you come with me to Rome? I could apply for visas.'

'So you know someone?'

'Someone, surely.'

'Sounds fantastic.' She got a lot of offers, but this one was worth real consideration. She believed he did know someone.

He was rather a small man for her taste, but he had lived somewhere other than a collective farm or a communal flat. Moreover, those eyes promised a depth of feeling, not unchastened by melancholy, which was fine. It was the condition Russians wanted to get out of, but it was also an essential factor of their humanity. His hair was thick and dark brown, and cut straight in a way that looked really up to date. Also you could take him to a gallery and he didn't make a fool of himself. 'Do you speak Italian?' she teased.

'Spaghetti. Mussolini,' he replied. 'But I could learn.' He looked at her long and with sympathy, unafraid of intimacy. Shared secrets was how any relationship began. He was prepared to share.

She noticed his strong hands and wondered whether they were capable of a tenderness to match those Kalmyk eyes.

'So how is it that you too come to be so interested in foreign parts?' he asked.

'My father.' Women have to confess their fathers, and many fathers are a hurdle to their love of other men.

He didn't know that. She didn't. Soviet psychology didn't teach that sort of thing. He would have needed a Western education to understand what he was getting himself into. She was oblivious.

Irina's father was of course Matvei Bové, who had enjoyed before and after the war that unique privilege of being a feted Renaissance scholar. He was that marvellous, educated, subtle, successful man who bequeathed her a palace, and Irina in her soul was heir to her father.

A superior soul, she was, as her father had been, and Korsakov intimated it and loved it. What he had hated in Mariya Andreyevna at the Paris embassy he now loved in Irina Matveyevna. Was he up to it? It's not easy to marry a woman with a grand inheritance. Perhaps even Volodya Korsakov from the Russian foreign ministry should have known the dangers that awaited him in choosing an evidently remarkable woman. Her unusual heritage was not quite foreign but it was not a Soviet world that had inspired her father.

'My father taught me Italian. Mi insegnava la lingua italiana.' She let that gem sparkle. 'He gave me a taste for foreign languages.'

'And what do you do now?'

'You must know that. Which ministry did you say you worked for?'

'You know our efficiency.'

187

They were laughing happily, slandering their country. 'I'm a secretary to the Amis.'

'So you have English too.'

'That's right.' In an impeccable intonation he could appreciate, if not imitate.

He understood that she was very bright. Yes, she acknowledged. She'd studied her English at Moscow University.

'Year of graduation?' He demanded, as if he were all too familiar with the faculty.

''61.'

'Aha!' As if the date meant something special to him. 'And now you make phone calls and arrange interviews for the American spies who can't speak our language, so they can write reports on our country that aren't true.'

'You shouldn't be so negative, Vladimir Arkadevich. Some of the Amis are nice.' (She had warmed to Seth, tolerated Khenk.) 'Besides, I make them believe that in some mysterious core of its being our country actually works. We must build our reputation. I know how to do this.'

Oh my! He let that sink in. He agreed propaganda was his own work too. The right information put to the right use to allow our country to flourish. What they had in common, these two interesting souls: a certain patriotism.

A patriotism which nevertheless meant that with every word he spoke she remembered her debt to her father, and with every word she spoke his brain revisited Paris: the smell of coffee and croissants and the rich meaty sauces of fine bourgeois cuisine; and a Gauloise to finish. He'd met a woman who equalled 'Paris'. She'd met a man who knew what the Renaissance was, and why, sadly, its spirit in art had not reached Russia.

'The French are great sensualists—' She began afresh.

'But also very superficial,' he warned.

'The Americans often smile and laugh.'

'They sound stupid to me. A lot of imbeciles.'

'They have a lot of sex.'

'The French do it even better, from what I've heard.'

All this in implicit comparison with Soviet life, which never had the liberty to be frivolous, and where almost every citizen would have preferred a little more privacy, and too many women craved tenderness, and the men drank too much.

'Do you know why the French enjoy sex so much? They have this contraceptive pill. Imagine, women don't have to worry anymore.'

'Our Party considers the *tabletka* decadent. Quite rightly so, don't you think?'

'Oh no! Don't pretend, Vladimir Arkadevich! You're not a Catholic like our painter here!' (This aspect of Manessier's work she specially admired, for her father had taught her Christian iconography too.)

'The pill is just too expensive for us to produce. That's why they disapprove. Also we need our people to make babies. Socialism needs labour.'

He laughed, defeated. He imagined. He speculated. He imagined she could winkle the pill out of the Leader himself. That her own personal supply arrived monthly from Sweden. That a store posted it to her from West Germany, in confidence.

Irina found Volodya Korsakov politically a bit timid; but he looked unusual and she liked the fact he promised a certain tenderness and worldliness combined, and had good prospects in the ministry.

He touched her arm as they rested in front of another blood red and passionately black painting, *Les Tenèbres*. The Darkness. That was not darkness but the flames of Hell. She enjoyed these passionate paintings in Korsakov's company.

So then, not long after, having in his office inspected the satirical Daumier prints he kept on the wall there, to be admired by the foreign correspondents who came to see him from time to time (and which said very little to Irina, for the power of Daumier was not aesthetic, and Korsakov seemed to have lost interest in them too, only that they were part of his official credentials, as a diplomat); having drunk some real champagne, she consented to take him back to the Arbat and test the pleasure-enhancing power of that handy little *tabletka*. (All you need is love and you can have it.) He was surprisingly keen and long-lasting and that would do fine. They got married in 1969.

Only when his own career in the foreign ministry began to soar he couldn't have a wife so close to the foreign community.

'But Volodya, I must have a job!'

He chucked her under the chin. She hated that. But there was no way out and so with regret she moved back to the Russian side of things. Galina arranged an interview at WELL.

Irina wore a severe grey homemade skirt to attend. The grey colour, reminiscent of the uniforms so widely worn in their country, was intended to confirm that she was a serious person capable of ideological commitment. But it was rather tightly cut, so you could see the exact curve of her slim hips and her slender thighs. She wore it with high heels and fine Parisian nylons.

The five board members lost their heads to their nether regions as soon as she walked in. It was true that in all but the case of a lustful grandfather on his third marriage those regions had long since been pickled in alcohol and were only suitable for display in a glass bottle in the laboratory. Still the memory remembers limbs, and other parts, even when they aren't in service anymore. When the interviewers recovered their wits, and judge number two had set his awkward toupée straight, and number four fumbled the badge of Lenin on his lapel like a rosary, praying for guidance, they remembered collectively that after recent unfortunate deviations the board of their journal had to take GREAT care with whomsoever they admitted to their circle and what they chose to publish. *Ostorozhno, molodtsy!* Careful how you go, lads. The scandal of '62 still rang in their ears: how could you, comrades, possibly *print* and *bind,* between your *revered* blue covers, that *obscene* fantasising so-called work of literature about how we help our citizens remaster their life goals by sending them on long holidays to the east?

(Solzhenitsyn's *One Day in the Life of Ivan Denisovich* was meant.)

Yeah, how could they. How shameful of them. Still, *why* refuse her? She was gorgeous and clever and her literary taste was not bad either. Jean-Paul Sartre, Iris Murdoch, Alberto Moravia, she confessed. Heh now that's something. And of our own writers? Andrei Bitov? Oh yes, but above all the miraculous Bulat Okudzhava, heir in Soviet prose to Pushkin, she replied.

Edvard Edvardovich, number five on the panel, and quite normal-looking, gazed at her and swooned out of real literary passion. She loves Okudzhava! Then she's the one for us.

But Irina missed the foreigners.

Marrying Korsakov had meanwhile also distanced her from her university friends Galya and Anushka. ('Fancy taking up with that toad!') They couldn't bear him. What was he after? Well, wasn't that obvious? But was it? Not all men are driven by desire. Desire is pure. It's all the rest that galls. Cold, uninspired, clammy handed men who pretend to woo; reptilian kissers without the faintest grasp of true jouissance. Galya Obolenskaya and Anna Lunina had their suspicions about what Volodya Korsakov was, or would turn into.

Yet this was the point where Irina's paternal inheritance saved her. She was in a very un-Soviet sense not just a wife and mother and a worker, but also an heiress. When someone somewhere high up had decided the Renaissance was, next to American wheat and industrial secrets, what Russia most needed after the Great Patriotic War, and that Professor Matvei Bové through his deep learning was its embodiment, as a reward for his lifetime's work they gave him that house which he was still restoring to its eighteenth-century glory when he died, aged only 68.(Even eminent and thoughtful Russian men smoke and eat too much pork fat.) That house in the Podmoskovye environs, Moscow's Green Belt, then passed to his daughter and her new husband, whose address became somewhere unnumbered, somewhere not far from the Mozhaisk Road.

The house, oh the house! She loved the house and she loved the memory of her father and that almost made up for being married to Korsakov, while he for his part was delighted to have a beautiful worldly wife whose father had taught her Italian and who knew French and English.

And so they settled to bringing up their only child, Volodya's son by a previous marriage while he was still only a student. Matvei, born in 1960, became *their* son. She liked the boy from the start.

By 1972 Korsakov had important work to get on with. As he rose in the foreign ministry he kept somewhere in his bull-necked, Beatle-fringed head, atop his brown-suited, small-footed body, the idea that 'There's nothing you can do but you can learn how to be you in time/It's easy/All you need is love.' Derda diddle der.

Well, Russia, my country, why not? Become what you are with *lerv*. It couldn't be worse than the game we've settled for now.

Eleven

The student Marlinsky came of age in a Russia confused and subcutaneously in ferment. As he prepared to see in a great change, in which he would play his part, his debut at the 14 December protest was enough to alert Korsakov and alarm his Major, but perhaps Korsakov also welcomed him.

In the West it was early 1979, but because of the vagaries of the calendar Russia still lingered in the last days of 1978. New Year approached, and the two families who were close, the Marlinskys and the Gerasimovs, arranged to meet out at the Marlinsky family dacha. They had been close since the boys palled up at school, and that was now a matter of fifteen years. The young boys were opposites. Marlinsky liked to wear the uniform of the Pioneers — that was the earliest schooling of young Communists. Teachers and envious parents of less promising children thought that with his sweet good looks, when he wore that white shirt and red neckerchief, he embodied the dream. He recited the pledges of the nation with intense conviction.

Gerasimov tackled him in the playground. They were twelve years old. 'This place isn't heaven, you know. You haven't been sent by God.'

'Not by God, no. Of course not.'

'You sound like it, boy.' With his physical power it was natural for strapping Alyosha to challenge authority. Something animal about that. But Marlinsky came from somewhere else and the animal in Alyosha was humbled.

'Are you accusing me of being a bourgeois idealist?' Little Marlinsky's eyes blazed with indignation. Not a note of humour there.

'You talk like one. You idealise everything. It's time to be a realist.'

Marlinsky swallowed. He admired his friend. He learnt at the earliest age that a good Russia depended on friendship. 'Perhaps you will teach me then.'

Gerasimov, with his natural confidence had no need to profit from that plea. He simply answered honestly. 'You need to be realistic, that's all I'm saying.' And probably from that moment he pledged himself to Marlinsky's support.

To reach the dacha that pending New Year the women and younger children travelled by car while the men, because they liked being men together, citing lack of space, resorted to the hourly bus service from central Moscow. It passed within a couple of miles of their village.

Their greeting at the Bus Station—*privet!*—was a brief hug. Each carried a backpack as if he were going on a hike, and were an independent soul roaming the cosmos. Every man needed that.

The modern architecture of the *avtovoksal* always gave Marlinsky a boyish thrill. Revolutionary history, the national epic, unfolded around its walls. Here the tale was of shovels and pickaxes, but also of buses and trains and space rockets to stand at the service of the people's vision. So much imagination went into the everyday routine that it was a pity that, over the decades, fewer and fewer people noticed the works of art that stood shoulder to shoulder with them and adjacent to their daily labours. Some of them already minded that there was no Western-style advertising. The bus station reflected the original, severe, single-minded, uncommercial Soviet way of living.

Gerasimov joked and recited a Mandelstam poem they knew from their earliest years. It concerned two trams:

> And Tram finds Klik on the square. And one tram is telling the other:
> – I'm missing you, Klik, I'm really glad to hear
> The sound of your bells.

Evidently, he and Marlinsky were Tram and Klik. 'So, Borya, what will I do when you steer off the rails?'

Marlinsky smiled shyly as if they had just made friends yesterday. When Klik went missing, Tram was frantic.

> 'I will be frantic when I can't find you.'

Tram asked all the buildings in the street:

> 'Have you seen my friend Klik?
> He usually carries a pinkish light ahead of him.'

> 'The houses won't help. They won't even speak my name. Who do you want, you stupid tram?'

> 'I mean my dear Klik.'

> – There are lots of them who passed this place. The horses said: 'We know nothing.'

'38, wasn't it? When they did for Mandelstam.'

'The right paperwork didn't arrive.'

'He fell ill and died. Terrible.'

They stood for a while in silence. People could overhear them, but they couldn't easily follow the discussion of a poem.

The women had gone on ahead to the dacha, because, as Ella Gerasimova declared, 'after all *somebody* needs to prepare the New Year food.' The Gerasimovs had a car and Ella Gerasimova drove. They seated their younger children in the back, piled the car around them high with tins and boxes and bags, and commanded the dog to sit on top.

'Niki! Niki!' The dog thumped his stubby tail. '*Poyekhali*!' We're off!

'*Poyekhali*!'

Like the icing on the cake, the tiny canine, His Highness Nikolai, lay spreadeagled, only looking up when someone spoke, smacking his tail hopefully against a cardboard box. Now and again his nose quivered at the half-metre long salami buried in the mountain beneath him. Ella couldn't see out of the back window and kept checking her wing mirrors. She didn't want to damage the car or its contents.

Her husband was proud of the car. It rewarded the valuable job he did. But the women tended to chatter and nag. So he too took the bus, just like his son, who had inherited his view that Soviet women were very feminine and manipulative. A Soviet man had to learn how to resist them. Thus Dr Igor Gerasimov joined the bus that left Moscow on the hour at a later stop, outside his hospital on the outskirts.

When he boarded, after nodding to the lads engrossed in their talking, he took a seat on the opposite side a few rows back. As he made his way down the aisle crowded with legs and bags, he knew everyone in the bus would recognise his son, and his friend Marlinsky, as intellectuals. Even if they said nothing you could just tell. 'We've got a couple of brainy boys on board. Perhaps they can sort out this country!' The boys knew it too and were proud of the badge society pinned on them. If you felt something was good in Russia, why not celebrate it. Nowhere else in the world did intellectuals have such stature. Still, boys, this is Russia, and I would advise being a little cautious. Be proud, but be careful. Our country exists half in light, half in darkness. (He was quoting Dostoevsky, of course.)

Gerasimov senior took out a book.

For Alyosha Gerasimov, who had heard this warning many times, one trick was to talk academic jargon. Thank you, dear university, for having given us the means to confuse everyone. Not just our stupid censors. That sounded arrogant, but you had to arm yourself.

Only remember, Dr Gerasimov warned, people get irritated with hearing a lot of stuff they don't get, and if they suspect you're laughing at them with your spiky words and your complicated sentences they'll hate you. They'll denounce you if they can.

'Dad! The hard times of Stalin are gone.'

'Still in the memory though, son.'

'Still in the poetry,' volunteered Marlinsky. 'I mean—'

> It's nice to chat, but still, it isn't done.
>
> Never forget your enemy, - the snitch, the creep.
>
> The wise man doesn't chat. He will discuss,
>
> and only with one other he can see.

Marlinsky smiled hopefully, and they passed to talk about the university. With the semester half-over now, interrupted by the holiday, what stuck in the mind from before Christmas was a minor scandal that had happened in their weekly seminar with the maths professor, Balabin. No one mentioned it again but Marlinsky remembered. 'Balabin cracked up over *diamat*. Some girl asked about the perfect future and why it was so long coming and why things seemed actually to be getting worse and what was the philosophy behind that.'

'Prof Balabin fell apart. Said he'd forgotten a book and fled the room.'

'Our official philosophy is nonsense. Why didn't he say?'

But then Marlinsky felt hurt for his old professor. 'Hold on, my friend. We can't all be tough guys like you.' It was a strange inversion of not caring for his own safety that he made huge concessions to the weakness of others.

'Ought to be tough, boy, if we're going to build socialism.' Gerasimov laughed.

Marlinsky raised a finger. 'Listen now! You'll forget what socialism is if you don't keep the weaklings and the poets on board.'

'And the disingenuous, cowardly professors?'

'Yes. Them too.'

Gerasimov said nothing.

'Balabin steadied himself and came back after a bit. But then he just took a seat at the table with the rest of us instead of standing up out front. "So, my friends, where were we?"

'"With the historical process," I said.

'"Ah yes, thank you, Boris Mikhailovich, exactly that."'

'You gave voice to that bollocks!'

'I wanted to help him. I couldn't help liking him in that moment. For God's sake, aren't we all tortured?'

'But he's a teacher!'

'I'll tell you how it went on.' Balabin started up: 'To master the, er, historical process, er thank you, Boris Mikhailovich, most grateful for that reminder, well here's what I suggest. A career in Sanskrit would best suit the philologists among you.'

'Hasn't Sanskrit only got 500 words?'

The professor inclined his head. 'Indeed. It's easily learnt. Or you may care try with a mixture of languages to decipher the Voynich Manuscript and bring glory to the motherland.'

'Do you get travel as part of the deal?'

'"No chance. Don't do that. You'll be sitting in the library for the rest of your days." But one of us said that.'

'Libraries are better than other places I could think of.'

'Or if you are numerically inclined, I suggest solving Fermet's last theorem.'

'"Before they do it in the West," said our sharpest brain. Samsonov. You know him.'

'Yeah, Samsonov.'

'Forget about the philosophy. Cultivate your friendships. Work on the deep past if you can. Avoid trouble.'

' Balabin said that!'

That Wednesday afternoon ought to have ruined the professor's career.

'He likes you, Borya. That advice was meant for you. "Become a mathematician like me." But then you declined.'

'I told him: "Thank you, Comrade, but I know how the university works".' He sat there in silence, pursing his lips.

Gerasimov shook his head. 'Now look, my friend, I even agree with your prof. You must take on *some* disguise. I've been telling you that since you were twelve years old. Why don't you become a doctor like me? They need doctors and then you can get on with …other things.'

'Don't worry about me. You know that other Slutsky poem?'

 Just think of that:

 a nation

one and one half million strong,

and all of them have taken a short course

(and lots of them a longer course as well)

instructing them about a Theory

that not a single one of them,

not once in their whole life,

has tried in practice!

'Shshshsh!' Alyosha put a finger to his lips.

'In the end I said it outright, that afternoon, "Professor, our society *is* about a lot of theorems and mysterious signs and quantities. It's hocus-pocus, not science. Is it worth spending a lifetime deciphering a lie? I want to live. No one can live in Algebra."

'"We can," he replied.'

Gerasimov sighed. 'See that pretty girl two rows in front of Papa? She's the reason I'm not going to live in Algebra.'

'What about Raisa?'

'It's over.'

Marlinsky sighed with relief. He shook his head. 'Anyway I'm fed up trying to grasp what's wrong with our *country*. What can we *do*?'

'You're like Raisa. You think truth comes through confrontation.'

'Whatever.'

'Raisa's mother was our trouble.'

Marlinsky was silent.

It was also unspoken between them that both had been afraid in that windowless van on the night of the 14th.

Gerasimov said: 'Our friends from that evening—'

'Great people.'

'They try to do something and you will live up to them and I will help you.'

Silence again, with Alyosha stealing a backward glance at the pretty girl. 'Heh, have you heard this one? What's wrong with the idea that a Marxist changes things from the inside?'

'I don't know. What's wrong with the idea that etc., etc.'

'That poor Marxist never wanted to change anything. He was just signalling he couldn't get out.'

They laughed till it hurt.

The Icarus bus was from the fifties, a sign if anymore were needed that Russian history moved very slowly on. It had rounded bodywork and sleek flashes of chrome.

(Russian culture collected doomed heroes, by the way: Icarus, Rublev, Don Quixote.)

Marlinsky could feel a spring protruding under him. 'How did Icarus die?'

'He flew too close to the sun.'

'Was Kirov poisoned?'

'I don't know, Comrade.'

'Was Stalin poisoned?'

'I don't know, Comrade. There was a rumour.'

'Do they still poison people?'

'I don't think so. Poison's short.'

'Are car crashes short?'

'No, no. They still happen. When they're needed. Car crashes are cheap and plentiful.'

Now they'd turned off the high road deep country snow lay everywhere around them but more like a blanket of deadness than that mantle of pure holiness you sometimes read about in visionary poems, where snow falls fast and plunges Mother Russia into a winter epiphany. No, no, *no*. There was *no* life everlasting into which Russia might be transformed. Just deadness. Here and now there's just bareness, nothing happening, apart from a few noble telegraph poles showing the people the way into the future. Just a few loitering crows who when the moment comes will trust their own sense of direction and fly off.

'Heh! Look, it's mama and Katya and your mum and Sasha!' Gerasimov waved frantically at a beige Lada they overtook.

'All Ladas are beige, my friend. Don't get so excited!'

'I tell you it was them. A stuffed sardine can, with half my family and half yours and the dog on top.'

Marlinsky growled: 'What does your sister see in that cutesy-cutesy canine?'

He's a pedigree! He's an aristocrat.'

'He'd better watch out then.'

That he'd seen the family car, or might have done, cheered Gerasimov no end. 'No worries!' he slapped his thigh. 'The dog will be ok. Blue blood will come round again. Perhaps he's Prince Yusupov. Or the tsar! D'you believe in reincarnation?'

'I'd like to,' Marlinsky grinned. 'On the other hand if I were a Russian prince I wouldn't want to come back as that pathetic pooch. It's a Western fashion anyway.'

'And so?'

'It's rubbish.'

Marlinsky turned and stared out, as if hoping to catch his own cheering glance of the Lada, token of the festivities ahead. One shouldn't be negative. 'They're surely there by now.'

'Must be. Someone has to make the lunch.' Gerasimov imitated his mother.

'I like your mother. She's such a good driver too.'

'Just how our Soviet women should be. Just how…Eh, Dad,' Gerasimov turned his shoulder and called out boisterously: 'Mum's a good driver, Borya says. Always cheerful too.'

The doctor looked up from the small print and huge intensity of the Okudzhava novel he was drinking in. Everyone was reading Okudzhava's latest, and greatest, in the journal *Friendship of Peoples.* The pretty girl looked up too and smiled.

A woman raised her voice: 'Citizens, please, sit still and don't shout! Show better manners in the bus.'

Shameful of us, muttered Alyosha. Marlinsky sniggered.

Dr Gerasimov went back to his reading.

To be well-mannered in Russia meant being silent. So now they stared at the road again. The muddy slush piled up at the side, and the frequent bumps suggested roads too found it hard to live under Communism.

'Not many people have cars.'

'Cars are short.'

'Just as well. We don't want to encourage private motoring.'

'Western decadence. I quite agree.'

Finally Gerasimov tugged the cord above his head. They were reaching the turning called Turning in a country called Algebra.

'It'll soon be New Year.'

'Wo-heh. Happy New Year, Comrade citizens!' To the whole bus, who decided the intellectuals were drunk.

'Bye, Comrade Driver! Happy New Year!'

The two friends stepped down on to the pebbly compacted snow, stretched their legs and sniffed the fresh air.

Dr Gerasimov looked worried.

'What's the problem, Dad?'

The doctor glanced back at the driver and the big open steering wheel on its stripped-down shaft, and the bobble-topped gear shift jitterbugging on a nervous stalk beside. Once with a clatter of its folding doors and a farty puff of exhaust the bus moved on, he shook his head. 'A man with a beetrooty face like that, and hands like parsley roots making an octopus grab for the steering mechanism…'

'You mean the driver? But that's poetry, Igor Petrovich. You should join our group.'

'I only mean to ask, Boris Mikhailovich: how many years has our state been abusing a creature like that?'

'We were just talking about changing things from the inside, and, well…'

The doctor harrumphed. 'We'd need a whole new medical programme and countrywide education.'

'And why shouldn't we?'

'It's just not *possible*. *Sovsem nevozmozhno*. THEY haven't got the money and they've lost the will. It's not working.'

'Mmm. Smell the air of the forest!'

'Don't look away from true concerns, my son! How is it we've brought you up that you're so selfish?'

Alyosha put a hand on his father's arm. 'You can't be responsible for everyone, Papa.'

'But our comrade driver couldn't have been more than forty.'

'You'll be calling him one of God's creatures next.' Gerasimov flashed a look at Marlinsky, whose own aspirations to God Gerasimov had nipped in the bud so many years earlier.

'That too. It's all my responsibility.'

'Well, keep quiet about it, Dad. They could do you for religious propaganda.'

Marlinsky laughed quietly. Emerged from his reverie he realised, once again, how much he liked his friends. Dr Gerasimov had a huge body that might itself have been faulted on medical grounds, but his mind could still discriminate between the good life and something less. As for his strapping son Alyosha, the friend on whom Marlinsky could absolutely depend…

'We're none of us fainthearts here.'

'Even so.'

The clean air, despite the foulness the Icarus bus left in its wake— Hell, it was so exhausting to be Russian.

'What do we want to import those crappy charabancs for?'

'The Hungarians are our friends.'

'You mean they let us have them cheap.'

'They haven't got any money either. That's the way the system works.'

'To do without money's good, isn't it? People dream of a world without money.'

'Ever the idealist, Borya. If it's not dollars it's roubles and if it's not roubles it's vodka. There's always money.'

'Of course it's right to dream,' said the doctor.

But Marlinsky was enjoying the sound of their boots crunching on the snow, and he so much wanted to be in a celebratory mood. Call yourself a writer! If you're a writer you can't be so negative. He cried: 'We've arrived for the holidays, we've arrived!' And hoped he wasn't being irresponsible and selfish, reverting to the pleasure of being alive.

He would think in retrospect that pledging himself to Razumovsky was even a sensuous decision on his part. New Year 1978 stole up on him like a lover and wrapped her arms around his waist. He turned in delight and embraced her.

As a boy going to the dacha he used to picture himself on a pilgrimage to some great Ice Palace in a fairy tale. Some years the path through the fields was just like a tunnel. Yet this year was modest.

'That no-good apology for a dog could have made it after all.'

'Why are you so anti-dog?'

To which the true answer was Russian lives were full of deflected loves and hatreds.

They rammed down their hats. The greasy ear muffs tickled their ears red and kept those susceptible organs alive. The choice when it came to ears was between blood red and bloodless white.

Now here's a thought, as it occurred to Marlinsky. 'The first revolutionaries—and I mean the first, the activists of February 1917, half a year before Lenin came from abroad—changed our calendar from Julian to Gregorian. But now, because of the terrible stagnation of our lives, we've taken action of our own and changed our calendar to Dionysian.'

'What?'

'We drink or we die. Every day is a feast or a hangover. With extra drinking on high feasts. Like New Year.'

Alyosha was shadow-boxing, shaking off the cramped space of the bus. 'Race you to that tree.'

'You're in good shape.'

'I am.'

'How can that be? Not our Russian diet.'

'The way of Dionysus!'

'He was fat.'

Igor Petrovich had once again tactfully fallen behind, and all they knew of him was the acrid smell of his Russian cigarette drifting over their heads. They lit their own.

'How's work?'

'Now I've got my bachelor's I'll specialise in psychiatry.' Alyosha was following his father into medicine.

Marlinsky bumped into him hard. 'Psychiatry in our country? How can you even think of it?' It was the new, deadly way to get people to behave.

'I want to try to change our attitude to psychiatry. Explain the role of compassion.'

'You're mad. It's a tool of the Inquisition here. That girl Prishvina...Our friend Shaginyan. I wouldn't be...'

'There you see, you want to do something about it too.'

'I just don't believe *I* can do it "from the inside"' Marlinsky avowed. 'It has to be...something else.'

'They accused that poor girl of *klikushestvo*. I had to look it up. "A type of mental illness caused by religious beliefs and prejudices,"' Alyosha recited.

'"A woman possessed by the devil." They must have dug it out of the Inquisition. It was barbaric.'

The story was of a fellow student who took a love affair too seriously and then had a breakdown when it went wrong. Gerasimov said she was a bit odd but Marlinsky felt there was something of himself mixed up in there, something that made him sympathetic to feelings other people called weird.

'She was odd because we are an atheist state. She was odd because flirting with divine love is a criminal waste of human energy. Meanwhile all she actually did was to fall in love!'

'She distributed Bibles, didn't they say?'

'She joined some underground sect because she needed to talk about yearnings and longings. She couldn't manage on her own after her man left her. But, well, who cares?' Marlinsky retorted angrily. 'They'll soon be trying their psychiatric voodoo on me too. Soon there will be two of us to bring into line.'

Gerasimov sighed. He was the one, at school, who was far naughtier than Marlinsky but Marlinsky now was adamant.

'I may not be able to help you, my friend, where you're headed. I won't get there soon enough.'

'I know that, old friend.'

'I'll just remind you that speaking the truth about this country means straps and a needle. A straitjacket on conscious days. They don't hang about.'

'You wouldn't be trying to frighten me?'

Gerasimov sighed again and stopped and offered Marlinsky another cigarette and took one himself. Holding a glove in his teeth, he cupped his huge hand and lit them both. They leant on a tree and smoked for a moment. Desert orchids came to mind as Gerasimov blew smoky budgerigars out into the country air. He set them free to fly wherever they wished. Smoking was bad for his lungs but he couldn't see why he should stop, all things considered.

As Marlinsky threw his cigarette away he watched the snow snuff out the fire. The glow that had lately been his pleasure hardly survived its short passage through the freezing air, and now lay there lifeless. He thought: 'I may be the only man in my whole country who dislikes litter as much as he dislikes the evil old men in charge of my fate so instead of dwelling on my potentially terrifying future I'll just tidy up after me.' He picked up the fag end, pressed the dead tip with his thumb and stowed it in his pocket.

'In any case I don't have a choice.'

'That just means you've made your choice already.'

'True.'

'Nobody really understands decision-making. It just happens.'

'Part of the human enigma, as you say, doc.'

'Funny country we live in, where to find humanity enigmatic is a crime.'

'Any kind of generosity would be the end of them.'

'It would mean freedom.'

They did talk in those grand terms, those two young Russians, with the father of one carefully maintaining a distance behind, desperate to keep out of earshot.

As the party of three walked from Turning to New Village the knife of rural cold slashed away at any bare skin it could find. It found a way in somewhere between the rim of Marlinsky's hat and the top of his collar. His feet were cold too. He ran for a bit, banging them on the ground and wumping his gloved hands together. If you got the right technique you could produce a sound like a shot in the woods and make it reverberate for miles.

Alyosha zigzagged and woowooed like a boy in the playground.

'I sometimes wonder whether you're Russian, my friend. We Russians compromise, you know. We're not Protestants.'

'Me?' He gestured.

'Yes you. Maybe your mother had a fling with a German. No, I take it back. I like your mum and dad. I mean them no disrespect.'

Marlinsky loved his parents too: his father Misha who had come out to the village a day early to warm the place for their arrival; and his mother, Maria, so long, perhaps for too long, his teacher.

The sky was darkening now, and the sun was isolated on a long thin island of red and gold. There must have been ice on his long eyelashes, because it seemed to Marlinsky as if some forest god were lighting matches beside his cheeks.

He was a bit mystical and sensitive as a teenage boy, but only a team of psychoanalysts, political scientists, philosophers and friends could try to tell him why he felt he didn't have a choice in life, when it came to this moment. Why he was ready to put himself at the mercy of unfriendly ways.

'Heh, you two, come on! We have a lot of feasting to do.' Igor Petrovich suddenly overtook them. 'We don't want to turn into iced tree stumps before we get there.'

'No we don't. Dionysus wants us for a spark in the dark night.'

Dr Gerasimov didn't pry. Only he was freezing, hanging back for so long, as the lads got slower and slower, talking.

So now he had them march like soldiers, which, remembering their military service, Marlinsky's albeit foreshortened service, because he had replaced it with teaching, they were perfectly able to do.

The few lights of the 'main street' where the Marlinskys had their dacha glowed white. From their poles slack wires hung down like abandoned reins. For a moment he imagined a horse splayed on that tall pike. Only the bridle and one white porcelain eye was left. All our villages will be lit, under Communism, our founding leader said; only don't ask how.

'Greetings!' Two neighbours, young men of Marlinsky's own age, were sitting in a car with the doors open and the engine running. They wore track suit bottoms and plastic trainers and huge padded jackets. 'Cheers!' Already drunk, they were luxuriating in the continuous blast of hot air that ran up their legs, until the fuel ran out.

'Greetings to you!' Alyosha and Borya tried to see the positive side. Everyone is equal. But then they positively ran down the bank, as if they were running away, and were mercifully soon out of their neighbours' sight. There the cottage sat in the quiet lee of the hill, in front of the now deeply frozen pond behind its picket fence.

Some people are outwardly orderly, and some people need to put their inner affairs in order and some people are both the same inside and out. Everyone is equal. All of us mind the monotony of our lives.

So, the clock ticks on and the calendar pages turn.

The festivities began that evening. Russians were all in the same boat and there was plenty to discuss about how to keep afloat. When even that topic got boring they kept on about it anyway, drinking themselves silly meanwhile. The trinkfest that began on January 6 was strictly speaking the Festival of Epiphany, but no one went to church, or missed it, and no one needed a religious excuse to drink. Perhaps it was a religion in itself. Perfectly useless. But comforting and even ecstatic if you took it far enough.

'Oh, it's little Katya's piddly-widdly little doggy! He could have come with us instead of dripping saliva on the seat covers.'

'He can't walk so far.'

'Oh, lazy doggy! How was your luxury journey, doggy? No public transport for you.'

'Nikolai, not doggy!'

Oh, forgive me, how shameful of me. It's His Royal Highness Nikolai the Second!' Marlinsky scraped a bow and got a lick on his face.

'I want one. Kiss me, kiss me!' cried ten-year-old Sasha Marlinsky.

'He doesn't want to kiss you. You're rotten.'

'No, I'm not. I rescued the sausage. You'll thank me when you're hungry, boring little Katy-Weighty!'

Marlinsky bent down again. 'Did you want to eat the New Year salami, doggy? I'm not surprised.'

'Nothing is surprising in our country,' observed Igor Petrovich, passing by.

The atmosphere at these times was always jolly, thanks to general expectation.

'How big is the sausage? When are we going to start on it?'

'This,' Katya measured.

'No, this, stupid.' Sasha spread his hands.

'Oh, wow, a metre long. And the very best of its kind, so this poor doggy nose must have quivered all the way from Moscow, halfway round the Outer Ring Road, through the microregions. I make that forty kilometres. You were supposed to sleep, Napoleon.'

'Nikolai!'

'I prefer Napoleon.'

'But he was an enemy of Russia.'

'He set fire to Moscow.'

'No, no, children, we set fire to our own city, to drive the invader away. To drive him back into the snow. Napoleon's men succumbed there. But we destroyed our capital city in the meantime.'

'What's succumbed?'

'Sounds like suck your thumb. You still do it, Sasha. You're a baby.'

'I do NOT!'

'It means they died. It was too cold. They didn't have food.'

'So, Moscow burned and the Frenchmen died.'

'But we've got food, haven't we? We're still alive?' Marlinsky felt he had almost gone too far. 'You know what's good about Nikolai the Second? It's positively good that he never sleeps. He's an example to all of us.'

Sasha came close to his brother. He wanted to sit on his knee but thought better of it in front of Katy-Weighty. 'It's true. He doesn't sleep. He's either lying there, thinking about something, or sort of twitching, and wondering. If you so much as look at him he jumps up.'

'He's the last Soviet citizen who is fully awake and wondering,' said Marlinsky. 'Remember that!'

'Cheers to that!' Gerasimov poured a fresh shot of vodka. 'Salutations, children, Nikolai. Your health.'

'Borya, I really like it when Niki walks over me,' confided Sasha.

'Nothing to be ashamed of. I do too. Come on, doggy.' He lay back on the floor, his brother with him, as they waited for the dog's little feet to prod them.

There's only so much you can say about eating and drinking in quantity. At some point the children went to bed and the two young men went out to smoke before bed.

'Take the dog with you!' cried Ella Gerasimova, from the sink.

'Will do.'

They had not gone far, only five minutes or so, when the two village lads jumped out on them up the narrow path to where the telegraph lines had fallen. The lads had run out of petrol but not of alcohol and they were shouting into the startled night: 'Take that! Intellectual scum!'

Marlinsky managed to dislodge the smaller of the two from his shoulders. The two were yelling a barrage of insults. 'You dumb creatives with your *inostranshchina*!'

'Oh, so we've got foreign ways, have we?'

'Got it in one. Fucking silly head games you play!'

The larger one headbutted Alyosha, who, however, had not been in the army for nothing, and, grabbing the other's hair, crashed his knee up into his face.

Yelling, Marlinsky landed a punch on the second lad's nose.

'Fantasists! Left Fascists!' The attackers yelled, and finally ran away.

'Christ, the dog!'

It lay there on the snowy path, immaculate but immobile, not much more than the size of a six-month-old baby. One kick from a boot, whether under the orders of the Major, or Korsakov himself, had ended its existence.

'Ohwaaah.' Marlinsky, weeping, carried it back to the house and covered the body with a tarpaulin. 'Bvaaaa!'

In the morning they buried the body in a weepy ceremony, after which no one spoke. The death hit them all differently. Sasha wept on his mother's knee. Otherwise he did everything to be kind to Katy-Weighty who was white and silent. She meanwhile locked herself in the bathroom, the only room where she could be alone.

After a couple of days Igor Petrovich ended his holiday early. 'I should get back to saving lives at the hospital, At least I can do that.' Petitioners at death's door rolled up in large numbers after any festivity. He saw them in his mind as a great queue painted by Breughel. 'Not a Russian painter, we were only painting icons then, but in a different history we would have a painter like that.' Dr

Gerasimov worried for the future of his son and daughter, and their friends, in a pointlessly cruel world. Marlinsky reminded himself that what offset the cruelty was friendship.

Marlinsky senior meanwhile fell into depression. He attacked the very turn of the calendar as the cause of all their Soviet woes. Why did the annual digit *have* to move on one? It was as if THEY had inflicted a relentlessly unkind numerical system on the people too. 'New Year means they can demand from us another 365 days of hard work for no obvious goal, except the sacrifice of any *real* human needs. I agree with Igor that New Year presages only more of the same exhausted pointlessness.'

'Forget you said any of that, husband,' came a whisper. Misha Marlinsky shrugged.

Addressing all present company and who knew what hidden ears his wife Maria now declared it was a good job we're living in easier times than years ago, otherwise who knew.

'Well, that's another thing,' said her husband, taking her warning.

The older Gerasimov asked: 'What's the difference between a car and a medal? Owning four wheels is more useful. They will get you all safely back into town.'

It made him feel good to leave behind the car for the use of the holiday party. The older couple, driven by Ella Gerasimova in the sturdy, dusty, much treasured Russian Fiat, actually returned to Moscow on January 15, as the GAI traffic police registered. Katya, once emerged from the bathroom, allowed herself to be so much reconciled to Sasha that he became her new best friend, as they shared the back seat and faced the same return to school.

Marlinsky saw his mother off alone from the kitchen. 'I'm so sorry. But I have to do it, mother.'

No one blamed him. But the holiday was ruined and there were tears in Maria Marlinsky's eyes.

'I have to do it and there's always the chance it can do some good.'

'Alyosha will help you but you know what it means. As for your father…'

Perhaps Boris Marlinsky did know what it meant, but the rational processes had long since been overtaken. He was following an image of himself, enacting the person he'd wanted to be since he was twelve years old.

Twelve

Back in Moscow Marlinsky turned up at the faculty. The place was buzzing after the vacation and the infectious excitement stirred him. He would write to Okudzhava. He would get up at six am to work on his novel. But ambition was everywhere that morning; not just his own. At the faculty entrance, someone had put a chair to stop one of the two great doors closing. The doors were heavy, twice the height of a man, padded with wool and some new-fangled material imitating leather that kept out the cold. But it was an effort to keep pushing them open and the students voted with a chair. Buildings, even Russian buildings, have to adapt to the needs of impatient, eager people looking for short-cuts. That day, for some reason, the spontaneous gesture was allowed.

Familiar faces were standing exchanging views, wanting to be liked, and to impose themselves, and to be admired, and loved by their friends, while they kept an eye out for newcomers with promising looks. They stood with their plastic briefcases and flowery fabric bags loosely anchored between their feet. A dark-haired girl waved and gestured towards the refreshments area—the *bufet*. A wide solid staircase led obscurely down from the back corner of the aula into the basement. Unlike the promise held out by the Western word this 'buffet'— from the French, why not, Tolstoy used French—was a dingy social space, with raspberry cordial for 5 kopeks from the automat. But it was what was on offer, and some thirsty people even enjoyed it. That day, as it happened, a day-duty lady, a *dezhurnaya,* was selling thick-cut, nourishing biscuits named after the Roman goddess Ceres, exchangeable for the same 5-kopek coin, from the customary little table that held her knitting. She who generally kept an eye on that floor of the building had branched out into snack-selling in a rare act of free enterprise.

'Misha, over here!'

'I'm wanted,' Marlinsky called apologetically to the voice appealing to him. He mimed being dragged in an adverse direction, reluctant to go. 'Maybe later.'

'*Tak*, see you, Misha. *Forza!*' A bit of student slang borrowed from the Italians. 'All power to you!' *Bon courage*, as the French said. What a mess the Russian language was, with so many social visions commandeering it, and all but one of them suppressed.

Marlinsky strode along the dark corridor—the university was a dreary nineteenth-century institutional building, a dark leftover from times that were never talked about but were surely no more sordid than the present—and tapped on the familiar plywood door. The door had nothing to identify it but a number, 52. Grocery number 84, professor number 52. That's our world: no personal identities at all. Ours is a scientific vision for the future of mankind and in it everything is clearly and correctly labelled and numbered. We're not citizens. We're automatons in white coats, patients and prisoners, underneath our shabby clothes.

'You wanted to see me?'

Balabin was sitting at his desk with his back to the window, wearing his usual brown suit and yellowing nylon shirt. His office was tall and thin and plain, and scuffed, just like him. Marlinsky didn't mind the battered environment. Learning actually went on in the university, practised by real people, despite the threat of theory. Truth was an impalpable mixture of the surfaces and the substance of things; of the way human beings used them, and the limits of the human substance itself. Only theory was simple and immaculate, theory as taught by the dreaded, ridiculous 'Short Course' and not true at all.

'Oh er yes, come in and sit down. Good holidays?'

In fact Marlinsky loved the university and was happy to be back. To be a worker in ink had been his goal since he was even younger than twelve—ten maybe. One of the great revolutionary poets—quite which he had forgotten—had styled intellectuals as workers in ink—*rabochie v chernilakh*. The ridiculous combination of words was fresh and poignant, witty even, and touched the soul. Although no one talked like that now, people of Marlinsky's generation still felt it as a responsibility, and a calling, to imagine themselves as labourers in the general cause. Education! Education! Education!

Rabochie, by the way, not robots, which was how they preferred people to behave now.

Had the holidays been good? Did anyone ever answer a question like that seriously? Marlinsky wanted to say 'There was an incident over the New Year', but sidestepped into stating he'd enjoyed 'time with the family'. He added: 'You know how it is' and wondered if certain political offices linked to the police had kept the professor up to date.

'I don't actually.' Balabin meant he didn't know family life. He wasn't married and had few friends. Still he might have heard of events concerning Marlinsky.

'I imagine *you* were caught up in your work, professor. It must have been a blessing, all that time to yourself.'

'Well, yes. I do enjoy my work, although,'—a slight smile here—'The *physis* makes its demands. I go walking.'

'I like to ski. I need to move. We all eat and drink far too much.'

By skiing Marlinsky meant gliding on waxed wooden skis through the forest: an experience of solitude and inspiration, to the sound of a whisper unique to the slide of wood over deep snow. Three little letters like s-k-i, attached to an -ing, couldn't do it justice. He had skied after the family left, before his own return to the city, by bus. Alyosha had gone earlier. Marlinsky needed to be alone.

'Marvellous. I haven't been out on cross-country skis for a very long time. Do, er, take that other chair. It's more stable.' Another faint smile issued from Balabin, as Marlinsky set his black briefcase aside and exchanged one seat for another. He set the favoured seat on the near side of the desk, but slightly to the left, the angle he preferred at interviews, if he had the choice, because then he could turn his left shoulder to the right, and properly engage with another human being.

Professor no 52 seemed embarrassed. He had a file on his desk which he opened and closed; pulled towards him and pushed away again.

Marlinsky felt confident. All power to you, Comrade, as the students said amongst themselves. Strength and resolve! *Forza! Bon courage*!

'What on earth have you been up to?'

'I've been doing what *I* think is right, Sergei Mikhailovich. You know my weaknesses.' Keep it personal, if possible.

Balabin slammed the desk. 'Well, and all of a sudden you can't keep yourself to yourself. Is that it? An attack of incontinence, is that it?' The question *ne pradva li?*—is that not true?—spat itself out.

'There are things about our society just plain wrong—'

'About our *society*!' The older man repeated scornfully. 'And so you've been protesting. That's what it says here.' He laid a hand on the awkward buff file on the desk.

Marlinsky really did love the university. The knowledge it taught—once you had navigated the Short Course—ennobled the humanity he believed in. Education gave people real tools to grasp the life around them—and change it.

He looked around the barren room, where those values were hard to discern. Worse, the space seemed under a curse, just like the shabby man whose number was on the door.

'Bad things have been happening in our very midst. How can the Party allow that?'

'The Party!' Balabin moved a pot of pencils that seemed to obscure his view of his student.

'Yes, I mean how can the Party tolerate the decline in our standards? To treat our people unjustly and without respect brings shame on our state. It's inhuman to lock people away just because they disagree with the vision of a man who died fifty years ago.'

There was a Lenin on the wall to whose steely gaze no one had responded in decades.

Balabin cast his eyes vaguely upwards now and shrugged. 'We're still struggling to fulfil that vision, surely. It's a matter of faith.'

'I don't like that word faith.'

'My advice is just call it what you want to and shut up.'

Balabin's crudeness caused Marlinsky a hiccup. He resumed emphatically: 'No! No one believes in that ideal future any longer. The Party no longer understands itself.'

'All that may be true…' The professor snorted. 'Look,' he tilted his head as if in fondness and genuine puzzlement, 'I'd like to help you. I mean, there are things, as you get older, you just have to accept.'

'Hope to change them from the inside, you mean? Hah!'

'What's wrong with that?'

'It's just that's what they all say. They don't mean it. It's just a trick to trap people. You suck them into the system and then they can't get out.'

Balabin clapped his palms together, as if Marlinsky had made a good point.

But it was rather that his own arguments had run dry. He tried love instead.

'So you are prepared to give up everything here? I just don't understand. You could have a career, some satisfaction. The chance to travel abroad occasionally. It's more than most people have. You have intelligence, integrity. You are hard-working. You lack very little, Boris Mikhailovich, very little in my eyes. All you have to show is—loyalty. Love your country.'

Marlinsky didn't reject those things. It was just… 'I must live a true life, professor. To the best of my ability. I can't live a lie.'

'And you think I can live a lie?' the professor shouted, getting to his feet and staring out of the window. 'Bah! For God's sake!'

'I know you struggle. All our best people do.'

Professor no 52 sat down again, frowning at the pencils. He cursed the shortage of biros, and the need to write in lead that was too soft. From there he moved to hating the porridge-coloured, bland, hateful file confronting him. 'What someone will ask is how you got like this. Then there'll be a bloody inquest and it will all be my fault—'

'Strange as it may seem, you did help me, professor. You remember the day we were talking about *diamat*—'

Balabin held up a hand. 'Say no more!'

'Tripe I know, but—'

'Damn it, just shut up, will you? I just can't believe I've had a hand in the making of a sociopathic lout.'

The condemnation was so strong Marlinsky could only grin. 'I *can* pretend you didn't.'

Balabin shook his head.

Marlinsky turned the tables. 'I could help *you*, professor, maybe.' But that was a little mischievous, in the presence of a cowed man.

His teacher continued uncomprehendingly, as if the facts about Marlinsky defied the laws of the universe. 'How can *you* be so uncouth as to criticise your country in public?'

Marlinsky clearly wasn't uncouth. He still looked like an angel. He shrugged. 'Drink?'

'Please.'

A vodka would have been the thing. On the other hand Professor no 52 was a genuine puritan and only had vodka's semantic distant relative, plain water, to hand. (*Vodichka*, a nice wee dram, you see, as opposed to *vodochka*, a nice glass of water.) He flipped off the metal cap. The university supplied every staff desk with a couple of dark green half-litre bottles of mineral water, and a pair of slightly murky tumblers. Sometimes the brand was sulphurous to the point of undrinkable, but today it was elegant Borzomi from Georgia.

'Oh, that's good.' Marlinsky hadn't seen, or tasted, Borzomi in a long time. 'I thought it was short.'

'They commandeered it from our colleagues in Tbilisi. They have their ways. *Ne pravda li?*' Balabin laughed openly. 'Come on, boy, please! We blame Reikhman. He's abroad now anyway. There's no difficulty.'

Marlinsky didn't have a desk to slam and anyway he wasn't that kind of man. But the proposal made him furious. They would blame Marlinsky's former philosophy teacher who was abroad for leading him astray! Of course he was abroad. Anatoly Reikhman was in Switzerland because THEY took his citizenship away when he was attending a conference.

'I have an idea of the good life which is not theirs.'

Balabin smacked the offending file so hard that his hand hurt. 'Rubbish! Bilge and filth! You fell into Reikhman's clutches.'

Marlinsky sat back in the uncomfortable chair the professor had assigned him. 'That's nonsense and you know it.'

'Reikhman was anti-Soviet.'

'He cared for the people of this country. Every last man and woman. So do I.'

'Bah, who are these people! Good, intelligent folk or scum? I suspect they're scum.' Balabin shrieked.

The professor was under extreme strain. He was reacting to propaganda words like one of Pavlov's dogs! A story to tell Gerasimov! The student replied: 'Please show respect. professor. I'm just a man with a mind of his own and there are millions of people like me.'

'Hmm.'

They sat in silence.

'What's in that briefcase of yours you keep fiddling with?'

'A tape recorder, you mean? No I don't have one of those. I leave that to the Western spies.' Marlinsky slid back the catches and drew out a sheaf of handwritten sheets of paper. 'I owed you some work.'

'Give it to me! Hmm. So you prefer the West.'

'Not at all.'

The paper concerned the social consequences of the theory of relativity. It stated that Russia had struggled with them, and Marlinsky, who was capable of ridiculously huge projects, had wanted to understand why.

His professor was really annoying him now. He went on the attack. 'Why are you all so paranoid, Professor Balabin? If anyone criticises Russia people like you just freak out and put them in prison. I love my country.'

'This…' But Balabin, visibly sweating in his nylon shirt, was so touched by mention of love he went feeble. 'This is not the right way to go about it.'

'And what would be? There isn't any other way.'

The 52nd professor on the payroll of Moscow University steepled his fingers thoughtfully, elbows on the desk. Love was such a difficult thing. He tried a different tone. 'You think of yourself as a writer, isn't that so?'

'I do but I haven't published anything.'

Of course it was hard to publish in Russia because you had to say the expected thing, or catch the rare unexpected wave. 'Whom do you admire?'

'Pushkin. Tolstoy…'

'Yeah, yeah,' Balabin tapped impatiently. 'You know what I mean.'

'Slutsky. But I'm not a poet. Okudzhava—'

'Okudzhava! Now look what he's been getting away with! A disquisition on our slave Russian soul.'

'The way we can't help grovelling. Indeed!'

'Can't you take him as a model?'

'Well,' Marlinsky thought, yes I could, and I do. 'But that might take years and I might never achieve…his greatness. So I go with what I can do. I can inspire people with my actions.'

'We call it distributing anti-Soviet propaganda.'

'I can't help what you call it.'

Balabin held his lips together to stop himself laughing. Fair enough. Fair enough! But as an official educator, professor no 52, he had to keep trying.

'So, tell me, Boris Mikhailovich, what's so wrong about being born in a state devoted to peace? Isn't the Soviet Union the greatest peace-loving state in the world?'

It sounded like one of Marlinsky and Gerasimov's jokes. Isn't the Soviet Union…? I don't know. You tell me. Isn't the Soviet Union etc., etc. 'I've nothing *against* peace. It's just how YOU make it happen. YOU stick a needle in people who don't agree with you. YOU ban their books. YOU stop them talking in public. The great Soviet pacification project is a war on peoples' brains. Peace itself is a noble thing.'

Balabin winced. And then he started up from nowhere, a torrent of sarcasm. 'Ah, woe is me, how the soppy suffering people do go on. They whinge to pathetic outsiders like you and your friends. They blab to foreigners who conspire against us! You screech about how these people suffer. Are the shoddy people really worth it? You have your little love-in in Pushkin Square with each other more like, and then it ends, because we don't much like you and your friends, boy, in a midnight trip out into the sticks. Call it a peaceful demonstration? It was a Christmas party for anti-Soviet conspirators. All those foreign ambassadors who turned up to watch, too. Why did you choose those friends? What made you organise that?'

'I didn't invite the ambassadors.'

'Nonsense. You knew they would come. Your Razumovsky knew it too. That was gross. Crude and disloyal. A whole lot of lies all wrapped up in festive paper to appeal to the Westerners who think they're Christians.'

Balabin retreated again into examining his long, slim fingers. A set of reactions had been forced upon him as the correct way to behave. Still he didn't know how to go on.

Marlinsky seized the moment. 'YOUR peace is just a fantasy. YOU think nothing of human beings and how they actually are. YOU just want to silence them. But it's gone on too long. Everyone knows here and everyone knows in the West that it's over. YOU just have to give people freedom.'

'I am not THEY!'

'You are. You don't have the strength to be anything else. At any rate you can't be like me.' Meaning, as it seemed, I can't love you. The corrected professor yelped inwardly.

Dear God, I'd love to be you. That's what love's about. So much not wanting to be me, not wanting to be alone anymore. With this burdensome train of thought Balabin made a move to suggest he would like a break in the proceedings. He went and stood looking out of the metal-framed window.

Not much of a view, Marlinsky thought, arrogant and malicious, now he had the advantage. A few brown stalks where weeds had lived on through the winter were picked out against the grey sky. Some chairs more broken than the utilitarian pieces they were presently sitting on clogged the wasted space.

Balabin wheeled round. 'Freedom you talk about! That's ten times more nonsensical than my love of peace—which is quite genuine. I'll have you know, Boris Mikhailovich, that yes, I do like to think of myself as a gentle man—'

Poor chap.

'I mean to say, how can you justify imposing your freedom on others? Soon you would have one man telling all the rest how to be free. Americans do that. They alone know how to be free. Isn't that so? *Ne pravda li?*'

Heh-ho, America! America was a weakness in anyone's argument. Marlinsky leant forward and did his best to look into the darting, nervous, lonely little eyes behind the steel spectacles.

'Freedom's not something you define, Sergei Mikhailovich. You live freedom. A good society would teach the generosity and tolerance that surrounds it. I *will* be a writer and a teacher of such things and nothing THEY can do will stop me.'

'Well, then I can't help you because we both know THEY can.'

Balabin had slipped into calling Marlinsky *ty*. It was an appeal to a friend. He glanced at the file. 'I've just one more thing to say. Will you hear me out?'

'I will. Of course.'

'We Russians are inherently corrupt. You know that. Okudzhava knows that. That is why we must have—our system. You know what I'm saying. There can't be politics in Russia. The difficulty has been the very remedy you have put forward today. The vision of freedom. We do not have the level of education to meet it. Vision on the part of troublemakers like you brings us chaos.'

'But we're people before we're Russians!'

'I wish that were true.'

'Well, then send me away, like Reikhman, so I can remain a real person!'

The professor shook his head. 'I'm afraid THEY will.'

Marlinsky walked over to that same window which just now had given Balabin some respite. The professor turned in his seat and followed the boy—he thought of him as a boy—with his eyes. Not only frostbitten weeds and limping chairs but broken electrical appliances and discarded palettes offended the earth and all were signs of the kind of people who offended the earth, everywhere. He turned. 'I do not respect, or love, this Russia you choose, Sergei Viktorovich. Your country has no vitality. Your discipline doesn't work. You are forced to declare so many of your opponents mad or criminal that soon you will live in fear of the hospital doors bursting open and the prison walls crumbling.'

If it sounded like a warning to Louis XVI Marlinsky meant it.

Balabin shook his head. 'Dear boy, you're utterly condemning yourself. Please don't.'

All the conversation was now *na ty*, from both sides.

'It's you who are condemning me. This country is a shambles. A fake. A ruin.'

'You'd better go. Er, thanks for coming.'

'So you'll let me know what you think of my paper?'

'Whatever.' Balabin raised his eyes to the ceiling.

Thirteen

No one likes being put on trial. When Marlinsky entered fifty wooden chairs stood ready, arranged in five rows of ten, and again, or as usual, none of them seemed designed for him. Where should he sit? Should he sit at all? Roman Timofeyich, janitor to the building, was finessing the back row when Marlinsky came in early to confront this problem. He leant into what had happened so far and what was to come. This private meditation on his personal history made him calm and gave him perspective.

'Ah, Boris Mikhailovich, *privet*. You don't know where I can get my watch fixed, by any chance?' The man who greeted him they called Comrade Repair. He had decided that university students, because of their status in life, were in the know. Because of their intellectual gifts they easily mastered the basic problems in life. Roman Timofeyich considered these learned young folk a race apart and was determined to benefit from his proximity to them. Yet it was possible that deep inside himself he didn't like them at all. He would have needed to belong to a different culture to excavate that disgraceful contradiction and purge himself of it.

'Greetings to you!' Marlinsky almost called him Tovarishch Remont to his face. They laughed. 'I don't know but maybe I can find out. By the way, how was that cobbler?'

'Brilliant, Boris Mikhailovich. I should have thanked you.' On the last occasion they met the janitor had needed a good leather stitcher for his boots. 'I got them from my grandfather, when boots were still made of leather.'

'Right. Very fine.' Last autumn Marlinsky had been given the very product to examine: dusty, wrinkled, battered, like its owner. 'Repair Shop No 172 should do it,' he'd advised. 'My mother has her winter boots done there.'

'Your mother! It will be an honour to follow in her footsteps. I mean…'

Marlinsky, while they both chuckled at the unintended pun, suspected Comrade Repair was a fantasist. Next it would be where to buy cockroach powder, or ether, or paint in a shade other than orange.

'Anything special happening today?'

'Not that I know of.'

'Tsh tsh! All this work putting out the chairs. You students are always having meetings!'

'We do spend a lot of time talking about nothing. But, no, look I'm fibbing. I can tell you there's definitely something on the agenda.'

'Give me a clue.'

'We have to repair *someone*.'

'Someone!' Comrade Repair blinked. 'Whatever you say, Boris Mikhailovich.'

'Do stay around for the fun. There are people here who can spot a misdirected person as quickly as you can detect a wonky chair. Or, rather, how would you describe the skill you have?'

'Oh well, I—' the janitor was close to blushing—whenever the chairs come out I look for the ones coming loose at the joints, or something written on them. You know, graffiti,' he whispered, 'Sometimes obscene. There *are* warped minds like that, and I sand all the filth away and make them useable again.'

'So it is with our people. We strip out the filth and make them useable again.'

Roman Timofeyich stood there now, stroking his chin. He was a thin dusty figure in his brown janitor's overall. He was probably already too ill to drink, for he looked more dried out than pickled. 'Well, that must be to the good.' Or else the student talking in riddles was making fun of him.

Marlinsky ran that danger. But when you live in a world of fools…

'Heh, greetings!' Gerasimov came in with a stream of others, as the clock ticked nearer the hour. 'You look spruce.'

'In case they accuse me of being a parasite.'

'A clean shirt and shaven chin won't deter them.'

'It will remind me of who I am.'

'I'll tell them who you are. Disciple of A. P. Reikhman who introduced you to the writings of that ancient Greek pervert Aristotle three years ago. Defender of a silly Soviet girl in her first year who became a religious fanatic when she got dumped by her waster of a Polish boyfriend. Admirer of Academician no 14 Alexander Nikolaevich Razumovsky, who despite warnings continues to wash

Russia's dirty linen in public. Likely inheritor of that sacred role and all-round good fellow.'

'Don't say that. And especially don't say the bit about Razumovsky.' For a moment Marlinsky looked fearful. His eyes narrowed and flickered like those of a trapped animal.

Gerasimov took his friend by the shoulder. 'I'm with you. I'll shut up now. Whatever it takes.'

'Please. Go easy, dear friend. I need you,' Marlinsky sighed. 'Someone has to survive to work on the inside. I mean it.'

'Didn't I promise you?'

'You did.'

But then Marlinsky went off and sat down alone. He needed one of those meditative moments. He might even have felt tears coming into his eyes.

Somewhere still in earshot Roman Timofeyich was expressing his views on the malfunctioning cucumber harvest. 'Someone grows them all right but then some fool doesn't harvest them and they rot. Another anti-social fool puts in too little salt because he's hoarding it. Then the bloody van driver sells the whole lot off cheap before they even get to the shops. So what if he turns up with a depleted order! Take it or leave it, *comrades*! he says. So obviously the shop people take the few remaining jars for themselves and feel happy in their jobs. It's all right for them. Life is good. They get paid. They get fed. It's only you and me, eh, who just want to buy something tasty in the shops…Now if you young boffins could solve that…'

The janitor had missed a useful vocation as a campaigning journalist on a Soviet newspaper. A newspaper that defended the citizens and their need for everything from cucumbers to justice, while remaining obedient to the Party. *Komsomol Truth*, *Evening Moscow*…he could have worked for them and once a year Grisha would have spotted a report that Howard Wilde could turn into a story of the Soviet economy in meltdown.

'*Akh, chto eto*?' What's that? cried Marlinsky, startled. He was meditating when he felt a physical attack. Some Lusya he vaguely knew sat down tight beside him just as proceedings were beginning.

He smelt her Soviet perfume. No self-respecting woman would wear that sweet chemical concoction called Lady Cosmonaut.

The pressure ran the length of his thigh. 'A love story, eh, Boris Mikhailovich, isn't that what happened to that girl you tried to help. It's all we have, the pleasures of love.'

Marlinsky moved himself away as far as he could but the chairs were close together. 'We also have the pleasures of collective action, Lusya Aleksandrovna.'

'Sounds like the same thing to me.' She pressed against him. 'Come on now! Who are you kidding? By the way Alekseeva is my name. You can't have forgotten.'

'I had forgotten.'

'Nonsense. Over there they've got this philosopher Fred who says people don't forget anything.'

'Freyd.'

'Freyd then. Freyd says it's thwarted sexual desire that represses memories.'

'Hah!' He shuddered. 'So they've got a crude school of psychiatry in the West too.'

'For myself I can't say.'

'Well, I can. The whole discipline of psychology needs overhauling, everywhere.'

'Ooh, you're so clever, Boris Mikhailovich. I don't know what we'd do without you.'

'We meaning?'

'Us here in the student branch. I decided to come and see you today because I heard they wanted to elect you secretary. Apparently you can write.'

'You may be in for a surprise.' Maybe they'd put out that lie to make sure people came.

'Mmm, sounds good. I like surprises.'

Meanwhile at that moment the branch chairman, one Sasha Vladimirovich, came forward. It was a moment like the lights going down in the cinema.

'Sasha's a nice fellow, don't you think? I think he's free too,' Marlinsky whispered.

'You're too modest, my darling. You're really so much more cute than he is. Like an angel. It's you I've come to be near.'

'So, I think we can begin…' Sasha Vladimirovich was a clean-cut lad, with short hair and an open face that held no secrets from the world. He was a boy from the country, Marlinsky mused, who moved as if he had been born in waders to surmount marshy terrain, and so now he moved through intellectual Moscow. It was with thoughts like that—elitist and totally permissible, under the circumstances—that he also defended himself.

'We have before us a most curious case…of a comrade…who used to be our friend, but who has turned against us.'

'Is she here, that silly girl?' The Alekseyevna woman craned her neck. 'Neurotic, they call people like her over there, making so much fuss about *lerv*. If he turns out to be a jerk do it with someone else, I say.'

'No. And it's not about her.'

All of a sudden Marlinsky stood up and recited, even he with a touch of the automatic response because after all he'd gone through the school system and the army. 'My name is Boris Mikhailovich Marlinsky. I am twenty-five and an advanced student of mathematics and philosophy.'

Everyone turned. Lusya repositioned herself in her chair.

'Not anymore you're not studying anything, you anti-Soviet scum,' a male voice cried.

'Blimey, you might have said,' Lusya muttered.

The chairman evidently felt the same, and tolerated the intervention. Roman Timofeyich was standing beside the door and his jaw fell open.

'Boris Mikhailovich, you of all people!' A tiny bit of disobedience mesmerised him. He was that kind of ordinary man, in whom certain reflexes occurred, and no self-knowledge had ever been built up to quieten them down. Disobedience in others excited him. A truly horrible inner life.

Gerasimov suddenly stood up and, thanks to his commanding physical presence, got the floor. 'Mr Chairman, I don't really know what we're doing here. So far as I know being an admirer of Aristotle isn't a crime. I for one have shopping to do.'

People laughed. The point about Saturday mornings in term time was that in the park nearest the faculty there was always a market for second-hand stuff. That mostly meant covertly imported records and tapes and jeans, aspirin, Benzedrine and condoms.

'You're always so subtle, Aleksei Igorevich.'

'I just need a few things for the weekend, like anybody else. Life is good.' The meeting kept laughing.

Marlinsky, grateful for the breathing space, reflected on the way the little market, consisting of a lot of people gathering purposefully, all of them with shopping bags, in a place where there were no shops, only benches and trees and ducks and little children and grannies, was *allowed* to happen. Someone somewhere understood the function of pressure valves. Besides, whichever *nomklat* came up with the idea of a Saturday market for foreign goods smuggled into the country was himself trading a great deal more. He was buying luxuries direct from Finland and West Germany. Perhaps he had a conscience and therefore—even out of a kind of suppressed fear of being confronted—he allowed the citizenry a few casual perks in the park.

'Thank you for your contribution, Comrade Gerasimov. However I'm afraid we can't be "subtle" about your friend. He's made himself our enemy.'

Whereupon Gerasimov, far from backing off, offered the meeting a disquisition on the meaning of the term "enemy". 'Oh no, I won't have that! What is that thing "our enemy"? The person we don't know, the person whose tongue we don't understand. What we Russians used to call the Germans—before we realised we could learn a great deal from them! How to make decent condoms, for a start. How not to ruin our love lives with pieces of Soviet garden hose.'

'Oooh!' A few people tittered. Lusya looked horrified and Comrade Repair as if his bluff had been called. Especially that bit about condoms.

'So I'm just saying, before you label this good man an enemy, you might try understanding what he has to say.'

So then Marlinsky told them he wasn't really a bad Communist. Only that he really believed in a rational, scientifically-minded, open, charitable and peaceable society and he found that there were too many instances when the present leadership was getting it wrong.

'They were wrong to banish my professor, Anatoly Pavlovich Reikhman, for instance. They had no right to take away his home. They needn't have sentenced poor little Anna Prishvina to a couple of years in a so-called reform camp. And the things they do to so-called dissidents—people who, after all, are only 'those who think differently from us'—the things they practise in the *psykhushki*, in the name of the health of our society, are vile. They are crimes against the human soul.'

Roman Timofeyich mopped his brow. Phew! Say what you liked, but these young boffins had a way with words.

The chair brought the meeting back to attention by saying that the event of the 14th of December couldn't be overlooked.

'He's a bloody Decembrist!' another male voice shouted.

'And so?' responded Gerasimov, back on his feet. 'Shouldn't you get your history right before you speak?'

The so-called Decembrists were actually Russia's first revolutionaries. They had called for a constitution—and rule of law!—and that in 1825!

'I make that one hundred and eighty-three years and still counting that we've been kept waiting.'

'That's what we call a specious, pseudo-historical argument,' said the chairman. 'Overruled.'

'Boris Mikhailovich, personally I don't know what caused you to become an enemy of the motherland—'

'He thinks for himself!' shouted Gerasimov.

'I don't know what caused you to throw in your lot with a disenchanted professor and his scheming Jewish wife...'

Gerasimov wanted to speak but found himself gasping instead.

'As for this terrible individualism with which you allowed yourself to become blighted, the result is the complete abandonment of your patriotic and filial duties.'

A shiver ran through Marlinsky as he wondered what they planned to do to his parents. A distanced Lusya continued to stare. As a potential friend of the culprit she'd had a close shave.

'Egoism and quite frankly, what it amounts to in our collective state, treachery...'

'That's ridiculous. Boris Mikhailovich wants to save this country. Not betray it.'

'The way to serve Russia is to keep her problems within her own four walls.'

'Where have I heard that before!' Gerasimov sat down miserably. 'All he has made clear is that humanity itself in this country is *defitsitny*. Humanity itself is short. Something a bit more important than cucumbers, Comrade Repair, when you get round to writing your report on this occasion.'

The chairman resumed: 'To sum up, I propose expelling Boris Mikhailovich Marlinsky from our Students' Union. We'll take a vote. The documentation supporting the charge will be in my office until Wednesday.

That about wraps things up. Thanks for coming, comrades, and have a good weekend.' He even winked. Condoms and Benzedrine, the privilege of the country boy who'd taken off his waders and come into the city to serve the Party.

'You and your friend there, you're right kinky ones,' hissed Lusya, horrified, as she was the first to leave.

Marlinsky and Gerasimov left together. 'I'm with you, my friend. All the way.'

Roman Timofeyich, his eyes down, began dismantling the rows and stacking the chairs.

Fourteen

Marlinsky met Razumovsky for the first time alone in April.

The two men met in a pretty little park, not local to either of them, and which, with its winding paths and gentle slopes created a striking artificial charm for those who strolled there. The atmosphere was a little bit theatrical, and park visitors became part of the idyll. Howard Wilde's Italian girlfriend Polly, who lived just ten minutes away, loved it. It was there she took Gels Maybey for a run, when they finally met and of course liked each other—what had they been afraid of?

The weather was slowly warming up, although the children still wore gloves and woolly hats. An American sociologist said that not only swaddling babies but the way Soviet mothers overdressed their children was a sign of their future social conformity. The children couldn't move freely. But wasn't it rather that those young mothers, in a newly made society, cared for their children all too carefully? The book of the new life after the Revolution said little heads should be protected well into the month of May. Now it wasn't even Easter.

The sturdy metal-framed wooden benches seemed made expressly for women to sit down and go on sitting, along with the old men who had nothing better to do. We all sit down far too much, thought Marlinsky, as he made his way to the designated bench.

The same sociologist who had commented on the habit of clothing children too warmly and tightly had also noticed the close surveillance under which children were kept in the playground. That too surely made them compliant adults.

Or it stopped the little ones coming to harm, thought Gels, enchanted that afternoon.

The mothers watched their offspring totter, clutching leaves and grass in their tiny hands. The Presnensky Children's Park, with its magical mystery tour paths and sympathetic trees was quite Moscow's answer to the Jardin du Luxembourg. What poetic soul would not want to sit there? The vistas skimmed tamed patches of silvery water—a boating pond, in season—and ventured through freedom-loving trees. Moody and unbounded skies, silver, blue, pink and grey, bowed low to salute park-goers in winter or arced high to bathe them in full sun in summer.

In the would-be Parisian quarter of Moscow where Polly the Italian Communist was allowed to live, this new-old city was a much nicer place to live than in a tower block in a *mikrorayon*. The bristling, hostile propaganda of the city was hardly imaginable. The fumes from cheap-grade petrol dissipated in the abundant fresh air. The park itself was dedicated to the child's imagination. 'This park is not some money-making Disneyland,' Polly scoffed. 'In America they turn innocent souls into passive and sensationalist consumers by the time they are ten years old. Whereas here, who could deny we live in paradise.'

Gels nodded. Once you felt the presence of that anti-capitalist inspiration, so many details of the Soviet dream fell into place and did not seem odd or corrupt or desperately imitative at all. Even the anonymous, all-the-same, microregions had a certain appeal, from what she experienced going to the Baikonur cinema, a marriage of space rocket design and modernist film. The new housing blocks were a bold and rational solution to the housing problem. Or maybe she felt all this because she so admired tall, brown-eyed Polly, who believed in the dream.

As they jogged, both in blue tracksuits—though Polly's was far more elegant—the mothers and grannies surreptitiously eyed them. Toddlers stretched out a hand in curiosity before being hauled back to the prison of maternal knees.

'Lovely. Thanks for bringing me here.'

'It's—well you see how it is. I only wish they wouldn't stare at us so.'

'The children want to talk.'

'They want chewing gum,' Polly admitted. 'But it's nice, isn't it? The Grand Designer of this utopia actually wanted them to grow up rich in imagination.'

Magical creatures especially friendly to children dwelt in the bushes. They were chess pieces the size of a five-year-old child and they seemed to be alive. You would be walking along and suddenly a fairy-tale character would peer out. Heh there, little Sonechka, little Vanya, do you want to play?

Oh yes! Out of the hedgerows of enchantment the Rook and the Bishop and the King often took a walk down through the sloping flowerbeds to the asphalt path. And look, here comes the Queen! She's abandoned the chess board because it's so much more fun to join in with you and me, in this happy Soviet life.

'Fantastic! By the way, you're fit.' They took the rises and falls in the path in their stride. Gels was fit too, but she wanted to pay her new friend a compliment.

'You need to keep fit here. It's a difficult place. The difficulty goes with the idyll.'

'How do you manage?'

'You mean living alone? I'm not lonely. It's just when a new person arrives from outside we all want to get to know her.'

'I'm glad of that.'

Polly glanced at her watch. 'I do half an hour then I go back and eat a huge lunch.'

'Sounds just the thing.'

Nor did Marlinsky want to disappoint Razumovsky as they sat together with a view of the duck pond. Anyone passing—even two foreign joggers, who were a rare sight—would have noticed they looked just like a professor and his student. Their tieless shirts, the unofficial uniform of Workers in Ink, poked out of the thick winter jackets they no longer wore so tightly buttoned.

Marlinsky had his usual briefcase between his feet, as if he could go nowhere in town without an essay in preparation, or intended for delivery.

'Will we be all right here? They're surely watching us.'

'You'll have to get used to that, Boris Mikhailovich. You're about to become famous!'

The old man, who seemed to have aged a couple of years in the last four months, with—now he took his hat off, for it was warmer than he had anticipated—his grey hair and his soft sunken pink cheeks, had a nice mild manner about him, the irony and detachment of his words making him sound as if he were about to tell a joke.

'My wife is always on at me to take greater care. It's a burden. Have you got an other half? You'll need one. On the other hand—'

'Frankly, sir, I didn't feel I was much of a prospect for a woman, the way I've organised my life.'

'Well, that's a pity. Bit late now. Sown your wild oats, I hope. A man must...'

'Oh yes,' Marlinsky lied.

'So the Komsomol chucked you out. I'm afraid that's only the first stage.'

'I only worry about my family. They're already in difficulty.'

'Tell me. I'm listening.'

'My father is agronomist. But they "retired" him a couple of weeks ago and it devastated him. My mother is a kindergarten teacher—' He waved a hand. 'She's part of—all this. She's also been told not to come back. So now they will look after each other and my brother Sasha. But as for him, when he gets to university age ... It's terrible.'

'Ah yes. They blackmail whole generations. The parents must conform or the children will suffer. The grown-up children must conform or THEY will punish the parents.'

The women close by wondered what two men were doing in the park during the working day. All the legitimate men, all those who were not parasites, were employed. So they watched them for what made them peculiar.

'I always say I'm not even a dissident. I just think more freely, the way a scientist should.'

'We writers think freely too.'

Razumovsky looked into the distance and his smile faded sadly. 'To be honest the choice you're making means you'll squander your talent.'

'Then the fate of my country will be written on my body.'

'Heh! Heh! I can't bear to hear it. Young man, won't you change your mind?'

They took refuge in a moment's silence, with Marlinsky shaking his head. 'Alexander Nikolaevich, why have all the good things in our world gone wrong?'

'The West has conspired against us.'

'Whaa-t?'

'Only joking.'

'Oh, you're only joking. *Bozhe moi.*'

The jokiness was disconcerting. But there, *nu vot*, that was the way *his* soul survived.

'I got a letter from the faculty. I'm no longer a student of Moscow University.'

'I'm not surprised.'

'My old professor tried to persuade me to give up. Like you just now—'

'We probably didn't mean it in the same way.'

'Agreed, Sir. Agreed! But I must tell you even he and I sat for hours talking about Truth—and he worried about us being spied upon and afterwards I realised he was right. You can't do or say anything decent in our society but someone will use it against you. Anyone can betray you. State your beliefs and someone else will be listening in, to see how he can manipulate and betray you.'

'It sounds as if you were afraid for him.'

'He's not a happy man. But what is it Okudzhava says? How can we live as we do?' Marlinsky took the novel from his briefcase and read out a passage he had marked.

> From early childhood we sharpen our weapons against one another, each of us hoping secretly he will be the lucky one and that fate will bring him to power over everyone else. And that trifling microbe, eating away at our insides, forces us to be hypocrites and to lie, wheedle and finesse until we can get close enough to stick the knife into our enemy's soft back…

'That's very fine.'

'I wish I could write like that. My friend Gerasimov—'

'I met Gerasimov. Fine fellow.'

'He says we must be strong. That *we* have to show people a decent life is possible. That's our task.'

Razumovsky twisted his lower lip between finger and thumb. 'Not an easy task. If everyone is compromised then no one can be good. No one need even try. But shall we have tea?' From the Academicians' briefcase he produced a flask. 'My wife never lets me go anywhere without provisions. That's what we need. Provisions. Haha. Not scientific papers.'

Not moral courage either. Marlinsky completed the joke.

They unwrapped a packet each of wafer biscuits, in which the surrounding pigeons and children took such an intent interest that a little arm in a bulky crimson jacket stretched out—

'Vanya! *Nel'zya!*'

Absolutely forbidden. Not from that man!

Marlinsky, who had welcomed the child with a smile and a promise, was outraged to be viewed as a pariah. He hurled the offending biscuit away. Wings fluttered. One pigeon alone flew off with the prize.

'You can step out, boy. It's still possible. Don't do it! Don't surrender your life—by which I mean your future happiness!'

'Don't do as you have done, Sir? Why in heaven's name not? You, you of all people, must not tell me that. I beg you.'

'But I am so much older. I've had a career. I have a wife. Work for us from *outside* Russia! Don't sacrifice yourself!'

'Oh no!' Marlinsky felt wounded. As if Razumovsky didn't believe he had it in him. 'I'm not going abroad. I'm staying here. To breathe *Russian* air. Look at what they did to Anatoly Pavlovich. He can't settle over there. He's no one in the West. Whereas here, with us, he might still play a valuable role.'

'You could settle abroad as a someone.'

'And end up teaching Russian?'

'You could teach good Russian, not our mangled Sovietspeak. What a contribution to civilisation that would be!'

Marlinsky beseeched the latest and most important of his advisers. 'No! It's one thing to teach, and another to do. The English saying is right. I want to take action. I want the history of my country to be written on *my* body.'

The old man raised his hands in defeat. 'So goddam it, Boris Mikhailovich, you will be my heir. Natasha will help you.'

'I'll be grateful for that.'

After their run Polly and Gels went back to Polly's flat. The river was nearby, a calm and salutary presence. Countries, and cities within those countries, claim to possess their rivers but rivers belong to the earth. To live beside a great river is rich good fortune. Rivers mean calm in change. You never step into the same river twice. Only false pride appropriates rivers for the nation that resists change. Turns them into landscape decorations and wish-you-were-here postcards.

In fact the nearer the two women approached the bridge, as heavy with traffic as anywhere in inner Moscow, the less they could see of the water. Off to the left the Kremlin loomed.

'You know where you are? That's the Arbat.'

'A smart street.'

'Once upon a time.'

So proud of itself, because to reach for pride is natural, Moscow was sadly run down, as if it had no earthly gifts at all. She had love to give to that city. They all did.

Now walking elatedly, slightly sweaty from their exertions, on the far side of the Moskva, on Kutuzovsky, Gels and Polly bought bread in Bakery no 26. It was a tiny, dark shop, a relic of a food dispensary all made of wood, with a row of self-service shelves, tongs dangling. The manager, a thin-lipped man in his forties standing beside his abacus, in the familiar brown overalls of an operative, appeared to acknowledge his frequent customer. But you could never have pinned down the gesture to mean this or that. There was a Soviet art to cultivating a look of complete expressionlessness and anonymity.

'It's because I'm here. I'm intimidating him.'

'They do have to be careful about foreigners.'

The baker wasn't worth thinking about. But Gels cared about that fateful morning at Dom Knigi. 'A few weeks ago a whole bookshop closed because of me.'

'So you learnt something.'

'That the culture here is so fearful of threats from outside. I prayed I didn't make things worse. It's so sad that those threats are imagined.'

'There I'm not sure, Gels. We are a threat to their way of life. Given the chance we'd abolish it. In the name of freedom and democracy. *Spasibo*,' said Polly to the baker, and then back to her new friend. 'Do you know *Borodinsky khleb*?' She was picking the coriander seeds off the top and popping them in her mouth.

'But Polly! Where can any friend of Russia stand? The system here is unbearable.'

'It's a choice.'

'Impossible.'

'Try!'

'Fabulous!'

The coriander seeds, that was.

They clattered in through the front door to Polly's block, still exuding energy and warmth. Gels felt hungrier than she'd felt in months. Perhaps it was the effect of the open air and the spring coming, albeit very slowly. 'Is this where you live? And you don't have a militiaman guarding you?'

The block was set back from the main road and had that colourful mosaic mural of men with pickaxes hewing out a decent, kindly and beautiful environment for coming generations. The same message as in the park.

'That's what I believe in, Gels. That it's possible to live that, with effort, and goodwill.'

Climbing the stairs Gels choked off tears, and once indoors steadied herself staring at Polly's leather keyfold now lying on the hall stand.

'What do you think would have happened to the bookshop manager then? The one I made panic.'

'She will have been punished.'

'Oh Lord. How?'

'Her life messed up. That's what they do. If she came from the provinces they'll send her back there.'

'Hell.' The state here was cruel on a vast scale. It was also so poisonous in the minutiae that you could only feel an evil spirit had entered its bloodstream. That poison was a threat to every last person who lived in Russia, whether as a carrier or a victim.

'So, please, this is *chez moi.* In Italian we say *da me*.' Gels felt a strange relief on entering a private space without any political messages or warnings attached to it. The small modern living room was painted white and had a navy sofa—the two colours which were also the colours Polly wore. There was an Italian Futurist painting on the wall. A reproduction of the fire in the Milan galleria. By Severini, wasn't it?'

'Boccioni.'

'Of course it is. I get my Futurists mixed up. It's a favourite of mine. Did you get it framed here, for a bottle of vodka?'

'I did.'

'I hate paying them in vodka.'

'Everything's a compromise.'

'Poor Russia.' She'd done the same with her kitchen posters. Grisha had taken them somewhere and thus the precious colourless, almost odourless 40% spirit paid for those crude, violent pleas for sobriety.

They took turns in the shower. Gels went first. The flat didn't come with a shower but Polly had fitted a rubber hose to the bath taps. Gels stood up in the tub and let the powerful stream of hot water massage her shoulders and trickle amiably down her back. She washed away the sweat from under each breast, soaped between her legs and stretched out each lower leg in turn.

The hose popped off the hot tap as she did her left leg. 'Damn.'

'*Cosa che? Posso*?' Polly entered, laughing. 'It tends to happen. Take this!' Polly's long brown back wrestled with the rubber hose. Of course she was Howard's lover. Why would he settle for less?

Gels wrapped herself in the white cotton robe and retreated to the sitting room. The phone rang when Polly was still showering. She called through the open door, from across the corridor. 'Leave it, he'll ring back.'

'My God, life is good! Running, showering, being hungry.'

'I second that.' There were many auto-pleasures in life. That too had once been part of the revolution. Gels had something in common with Polly that mattered deeply to her. She hadn't found it elsewhere. It was the sheer chic-ness of being a woman free to enjoy her body; and to work; and to be part of the most important things.

Wrapped in a white towel anchored above her breasts, and which left her silky brown arms and long lower legs uncovered, Polly took the phone when it rang again. 'Pronto!' A trail of wet footprints stretched across the wooden parquet floor back out into the corridor.

'Enzo, *ciao*. How are you? *Come stai?*' It was the news desk of her newspaper in Rome, where they read the global news agency wires with a mixture of professional avidness and scepticism. *L'Unita* was a Communist newspaper. The editorial team in Rome needed *her* take on the most recent events, not the usual spew of anti-Sovietism.

Polly spoke Italian at the embassy, on Italian TV, and when Italian radio asked her for an interview.

Did she speak it with Howard, owner of a poster that reminded him every day of his love of Italy, Gels wondered enviously.

Polly disappeared and re-emerged dressed in jeans, a white shirt and a navy pullover. *Mi dispiace*, but they want something from me.' She clipped a handsome man's watch, big clear face, steel bracelet, on to her left wrist. 'I've got time for lunch though, *cara amica*, if you have.'

There was a rudimentary dining table beside a hatch that led into the kitchen. Polly set out the Borodinsky on a board there and pulling up chairs they hacked into it greedily, topping it with brynza cheese and the sliced tomatoes mixed with sunflower oil and black pepper and fresh dill that Polly had prepared for her guest. 'You can eat well here. You just have to know what to choose.'

'So what will you say?' Gels helped herself to a paper napkin. 'Proper size too, not one of those useless things cut into quarters that you get in the restaurants—'

'—but they're short of paper, Gels, have a heart!'

'But they've got excuses for everything!' Gels poured them both a glass of sparkling Borzomi.

'You mean how will I get round just cataloguing one awfulness about this place after another? How do I?'

'The *psykhushki* for a start. The victims we hear about from Razumovsky. And Howard says they've starting piling the pressure on Marlinsky.'

'Dear Howard!'

Was Gels in love with him? Surely she was. Did she think Howard was in love with Polly, and she with him? Surely he was. They didn't talk about it.

Polly wiped her mouth and drank that Georgian mineral water which, however it reached Moscow, by what coerced and unfair trading, served perfectly as a substitute for Sanpellegrino. 'First thing to understand is my paper. You remember "Workers of the World, Unite!". This is what I tell the kids in school in Italy, when they invite me to come in and talk. We are that 'unity'. We encourage it. We see Russia as a positive example.'

The cheap plastic phone plugged with its two pins into the wall with little more strength than a hair clip, it seemed to Gels, rang a third time. 'Ah no *basta*. I can ignore it for a while. Where were we? We have a huge circulation. Italians are the world's happiest Communists. They are voluntary Communists! Perhaps that's all I need say.' She collected the attractive plates—a creamy white pottery with swirls of cerulean blue—she must have brought from Italy. You had to be in Moscow with its crude factory output of utilitarian goods and near-empty shops to realise how much the art of the everyday mattered.

'Howard said you'd been out there. To the house on the Mozhaisk Road.'

'I suppose so. They took me there blindfold.'

'In a Mercedes?'

'That I saw. I met them at the metro station in Mayakovsky Square.'

'The journey lasted about 45 minutes and then it was this huge old house *Ottocento* we'd say in my country. Apparently Korsakov's wife inherited it from her father. Even though this country doesn't do private ownership of property.'

'Except in special cases.'

'You're right there, Gels. They'd change the constitution for special cases.'

'Or not have one.'

'They pretend they do. I went three times. He, Korsakov, wanted me to talk to his Progress Group. So I told them about Gramsci. You know Gramsci?'

'I don't Polly, I'm sorry.'

'It's about involving all the people in the decisions of the state. Not just the Party. Let the Party wither away.'

'How did they take it?'

'Hah! You can't imagine, Gels, they were such strange people. There was a fat old woman, the Director of the Lenin Library, apparently. But her main claim to fame is as a science-fiction writer. Makarenko. She sells millions. Then there was someone high up in the Academy of Sciences, another huge man, with cheeks blown out as if the wind had got stuck in there. He was not so old, at a guess. Fifty, maybe? He kept telling me how much he loved art and Italy and that the two belonged together and he hoped to live in my country one day. Then there was a skinny maths professor from the university who hardly spoke. I thought he must be ill. Korsakov's wife joined us I think just because she was curious. But you know Korsakov surrounds himself with mediocrities out there. It makes him feel he has built a world and that he is in charge of it and can make it better. Strange psychology but it might even make him feel he's a good man. One who feels he's thwarted by being surrounded by fools but that there's always another chance.'

'And did you think they were serious about whatever they call "progress"? We Westerners, well you know what I mean, we really hope there's a second revolution in the offing. This country can't go on like this.'

'I think that's why they asked me to talk to them. But what they'll do with it heaven knows. The truth is, Gels, my own country is not in a happy state these days. Some of us believe in Communism but quite a few sincerely do not. There are deep feelings that go back to before the war, and there is much violence. We have blood on our streets. I'm not sure how much longer I can stay here. I haven't told Howard.'

'He'd be sorry to lose you.'

'Yes.'

'Polly...' With her tongue, Polly was chasing some remnant of tomato between her teeth.

'Wait, I'll make coffee.'

Polly must have disposed of the remnant of tomato core, because her tongue wasn't searching for it when she came back with two squat thick white cups on a tray.

'Polly, you see everything from the inside. Tell me. The U.S. Embassy fire. I heard about the Russian lad who came and offered a lift to the stranded Amis in his Mercedes.'

'It was the strangest of nights. The office rang from Rome and I drove down there.'

'I so much wanted to know more about that boy. Harriet Zimmerman and I—you know the Zimmermans—We tried to find out where he lived.'

'The Zimmermans give me a wide berth.'

'I'm sorry. They're not bad people.'

'Idiots in my book.'

'They're afraid of Communism. That's what you have to be to be a good American. But tell me…'

So Polly told the story of that August night. The car windows were open, it was still summer, and as she approached along the Garden Ring she could smell the smoke. As she parked and got out, it hit her, hot and acrid, mingling with the cooler air of the dawn. The upper windows of the building were black.

She counted. Seventh, eighth, ninth floors, all gutted. How had they saved the roof? She asked two Marines, smart in their navy and white, rifles shouldered, guarding the site. She spoke English, albeit in singsong Italian, and asked them and this is what they answered.

'Call themselves firefighters! Our Soviet colleagues couldn't extinguish a barbecue.'

'Those Marines were stupid brainwashed pricks, you see, Gels. *Stronzi*! *Cazzi*! I was sorry they were the only witnesses I could ask. I don't like the Russians maligned on no evidence.'

'Howard says sometimes you have to be against the anti-Communists. Sometimes that's the decent thing.'

Polly's lips parted a fraction. 'That's right.'

'So go on.'

'So I asked, "Who did put the fire out then? When did it start raining?"' In fact, it had been raining lightly since midnight.

'We did, Ma'am.' The speaker was a young white man, his pudgy features emphasised by the tight-fitting cap and no hair visible beneath it.

'I didn't like the look of him. He was so proud, standing there to attention, saluting the achievements of his side in this stupid Cold War.'

'We put the fire out but with the Russkies' help, to be fair,' admitted the other.

'How much help?'

The black man had serious eyes. 'We couldn't do it alone, Ma'am. We don't have the equipment.'

The second marine continued: 'Still I swear by the time the rain came you couldn't see no more flames.'

'So let me sum up. This is how I saw it, Gels. The Amis called the Russian fire brigade because their Moscow embassy was burning down. The *pozharnaya brigada* arrived late and were inefficient. Who knows whether there was any *Schadenfreude* into the bargain.' The Italian-German had a lovely melismatic lilt. 'Anyway the Russians would have panicked, with their meagre resources and suddenly their performance under the world spotlight.'

The black marine, more articulate, keener to pin down the truth, went on: 'They sure set us up to look like fools. The fire burned on and on because of them. The ambassador got furious with the firefighters. The fire chief wanted to go up to the top floor. The ambassador wouldn't let him.'

'The Russian brigade told *me*—' here Polly was confidential.

'Of course you were able to talk to them.'

'They said the Amis caused the fire themselves with all their spying equipment. Not deliberately of course. But they'd overloaded the circuit.' Sirquit, Polly said, in a rare lapse.

'They said the Amis didn't want the Russians to see what they were up to. So that's what I wrote.'

'What a farce!'

'The whole Cold War's a farce.'

'Except for what it does to people's lives. The dissidents. The people thrown into a lunatic asylum for their views. This Marlinsky, what's going to happen to him?'

Polly bit her lip. 'It's just one side trying to get the better of the other.'

'It's only better than actual fighting, this stupid Cold War.'

Gels began again: 'And what about the young Russian? Wasn't his name Korsakov? We tried to find him.'

'I didn't know who he was, then. But yes, he's a Korsakov. He parked down below when the fire was raging. He played a song called "Burn Baby Burn" on his tape deck. You know it?' Polly sang the Trammps' hit with so much gusto.

'Heh, wait!' She had it on a cassette tape and clicked it into a recorder on her coffee table. They started dancing, either side of the table. 'You like disco music?'

> Satisfaction came in a chain reaction (Burnin') I couldn't get enough, so I had to self-destruct The heat was on, rising to the top Everybody going strong, and that is when my spark got hot I heard somebody say disco inferno (Burn baby burn) burn that mother down y'all (Burn baby burn) disco inferno (Burn baby burn) burn that mother down.

'God, with music like that! You can't choose. It just grabs you.'

'Made the Russian lad happy too, I guess.' The excitement of dancing made it hard to talk without reaching for breath. 'But then he drove away, and when he came back he wanted to help. I heard him drive up to the Ami diplomats who were standing on the pavement with their bags packed. There was a family. "Ken I pleess give you ride?"'

'He had some kind of crisis of conscience.'

'He probably believed he'd get away with it because of who his father was. Anyway the next day there was a press conference and the ambassador said the Russian side attacked the top floor of the embassy with radiation beams and *that*'s how it caught fire. Mama mia! I wanted to laugh. I reported that with a great deal of scepticism.'

'As you say, pride and idiocy on both sides.'

'The Amis are imperialist bullies. They pretend to be moral but they tell lies as readily as the next country.'

'But America, for us, they *can't* be the enemy! We share a language. We share attitudes—'

'You share intelligence! At least the Russians have a vision.'

'But Polly how can you be on the side of a country that tortures its own people?'

Polly marched on: 'Your American correspondent Arthur Zimmerman and I avoid each other. We always quarrel. That morning he insisted at least half the firefighters' uniforms had been new.'

'Which meant?'

'That they were KGB agents, kitted out at the last minute.'

'I've heard that before. But I thought we said the Russians were inefficient and slow? How could they have done that so quickly?'

'Howard told Arthur Zimmerman his view was ridiculous. But Zimmerman felt hurt for America. He had to win the clash of theories.'

'It cut deep. They were still talking about it at Christmas.' Which seemed much longer ago than a mere four months.

Gels glanced at her watch. 'It's been wonderful, Polly,' she breathed. 'But I'd better let you get on. By the way, don't they listen—' Her eyes roamed the otherwise pleasant room. Polly shrugged.

'I'll see you out.'

They stood on the front paving, beneath the lovely mosaic, Polly in her stylish jeans, white shirt and navy sweater, and Gels in her familiar parka, carrying her running clothes in an army surplus kitbag. They hugged, kitbag and all. 'You'll find your way to the metro ok?'

'I got here ok!'

Polly clutched her leather key fold. 'Gels, just so you know if we are to be friends, I can't support the dissidents. That's not my…well, I just can't. It's not my role in life. Unity you see. L'Unita!' She paused. 'But I did help Razumovsky's dossier on its way. I can tell you that out here.'

'Oh Polly! I'm so happy to hear it.' They exchanged a second hug.

Razumovsky returned home by taking the metro at Krasnopresnenskaya and alighting at Pervomayaskaya. The narrative bas reliefs adorning the white walls of Krasnopresnenskaya gave him a dose of the story of the successive revolutions, 1905, 1917 February, 1917 October, which he never minded rehearing. He even remembered when life-sized statues of Lenin and Stalin standing beside each other marked the culmination of the display, and, as travellers rushed for their trains, these two men who changed the country forever seemed also to be among them. The statues disappeared, when was it, well some time after Khrushchev's speech denouncing Stalin. It wasn't a good thing, to keep rewriting history. But Russia seemed to need it. To keep reinterpreting herself and trying to move on. Well, put it like that and that's only what the whole world is doing. It's just that we in Russia do it so abruptly, and with such violence, and we don't think, we rush, and then we have to change our minds, and people get hurt. *Bozhe moi.*

When he rounded the corner to home Natasha was in the forecourt shooing away a cat. *Idi von! Von s toboi! Ubiets takoi!'* The cat was a murderer! She was in her slippers and the overall she wore for housework, and was brandishing something in her right hand.

The two snitches in the yellow Volga didn't know which way to look and of course both looked in the same direction at the same time. 'He's back!'

'She's got a gun!'

'They're making fools of us.'

'Dear one!' Razumovsky greeted his wife. Her weapon was a blue plastic water pistol.

'My God, where did you get that?'

He'd just caught sight of her firing it with some glee at a bundle of tabby fur.

'At the *kommissiony*, the one where they do kids' things.' The *kommissiony* were second-hand shops, though there weren't many of them and they seemed like a relic from another system. Still they could be useful.

'Heeee.' He wheezed. 'Give me a go!' To get the gun away from her.

One policeman said to the other: 'They frolic about like little kids. Think he's still got the hots for her?'

'You're disgusting.'

'But has he? They look like they're dancing.'

Natasha was explaining herself, as they walked up the stairs. 'Sash, I'm sure the people on the top floor got that monster deliberately. "That's nature," they'll say, to arrange to kill something I love, and to which I will reply "and the way we ought to live, comrades, is culture. Make friends with the birds and keep the cats away".'

Razumovsky smiled his tortured smile. 'I suppose the cat can still climb down from upstairs. Cats are amazing. That would be nature.' Razumovsky could feel the sharp little claws digging into the pockmarks in the concrete as if it were his own skin.

'He'll have me to reckon with if he does.' She squirted a last jet of water for good measure, which fell on the concrete staircase. Razumovsky pictured Tom the big unlovable kitty catapulting through the air. He didn't want anything to die. All the same…

'Dear one.'

'Just jettisoning my unspent armaments. You know what I'll tell them upstairs? "It's just because you're bored with each other at night that you've bought a cat to stroke. Look to yourselves and put your marriage right. If you're not too old. *Comrade* neighbours."'

As they entered the flat:

'You're not wheezing so much. Just once downstairs.'

'I had a restful afternoon. Good too. I even had some thoughts…'

He took off his outdoor clothes and exchanged his boots for slippers. He washed his face and hands. He wasn't looking so bad. All that fresh air, and a hint of spring. She made him tea and set it down on the baize table. He began the number puzzle on the folded newspaper where he left off. One puzzle every week, in the periodical *Nedelya*.

'Have a biscuit, Sasha. You need to keep up your strength.'

She watched him and found that despite his protestations he did seem tired. 'No food! I'm not hungry. I'm just old.' He pushed the plate away, cross to have to acknowledge the fact. His head nodded on his chest.

'So just drink your tea and I'll play you some music, sweetheart.'

She stroked his balding head where the once thick hair had thinned to just a few stray threads on a red scalp. He took her hand and kissed it.

It wasn't everyone's good fortune to have a concert pianist for a wife. But amongst the people they knew, among the intelligentsia, many played an instrument and almost all read music. And if they didn't play an instrument they knew languages and were numerate too. Marlinsky's younger brother was already an expert in Pushkin's poetry, and could recite whole poems. The Gerasimovs' daughter Katya had a Grade 6 on the violin, and was starting on the Tchaikovsky concerto. As for Marlinsky's auntie Galya—you know she's made these Dickens translations that people are queueing up for—Myshy asked me if I could get a subscription for his granddaughter, me being an Academician and I said I'd try, though the Academy isn't doing me any favours these days. As for Galya Sergeyevna her role in getting Razumovsky's essay published in Novosibirsk—she took it there by train, yes, personally—now this I have to tell you, my dear, and it's not good news. Please to sit down.

'Listen carefully. Anna Lunina sent word that our friend Galya Sergeyevna nearly died last week.'

'Oh! Oh, *Bozhe*!'

'Somehow or other, *koe-kak*, she contracted acute food poisoning. But *only* food poisoning. They didn't want to lose out on a brilliant new version of *Martin Chezlevit*.'

The news about Galya never made a newspaper.

But it was shocking. And was it Korsakov's doing again? Or the Major's? 'They like *Chezlevit* because it's against American capitalism. That's why they kept her alive.'

'Galya didn't die because she was rescued by the hospital matron upstairs and taken to hospital in time.'

'Lucky for dear Galya that the plan worked for once.'

'They coerced the medical lady.'

'I'm sure they did. Either do it our way or you retire tomorrow, comrade matron. We're going to not quite murder your neighbour and your role will be to rescue her.'

'Oh, Sasha, it makes me weep. I think I know every bad thing about this country and still I'm caught out.'

'Marlinsky told me Okudzhava has described all these things. Isn't that amazing? He just set them in the nineteenth century so the censors wouldn't notice.'

'Our censors are idiots.'

'Maybe. But, you know, my darling, maybe not. There are tricks to keep our country alive that we still have to learn, even us. For instance, if a novel is set in the early nineteenth century that gives them an excuse not to notice that it's also a description of today.'

'We must get a copy of the Okudzhava. I'd like to read it.' But she was looking through the music she kept in the piano stool for that was more to her taste.

'*Tebe nravitsya Shuman*, Sasha? Shall I play that Schumann again, Sasha?'—He seemed so sleepy after his afternoon out, and now all that excited talking.

'Please, my dear. Play Schubert. Play The Trout. He survived after all.'

Marlinsky after his meeting with Razumovsky reflected that there was this strange dichotomy in the Russian soul. 'If you're Russian one half of you is in the light and the other in the dark. Maybe that's the truth. Maybe you are to blame. Maybe it's just how you are. Not just Russians. All of us. "Every man kills the things he loves."'

'So we know what our job is, Sir.'

'I don't know, boy, I really don't know. My best thought is it can be very clever, the way the two halves of our society, and maybe the two halves of our own souls, work. Take the cooperation between writers and censors. My theory says that every force, every passion, every love we feel has its counterweight. Everyone knows good cop and bad cop, but they don't always think of censor and reader, friend and foe, teacher and pupil, father and son, and so on and so on, each pair of souls inspiring energy or inertia, each arranged so that good counteracts evil. It's true that we are all suspended between innocence and corruption. It's true that in Russia the corruption goes so deep that only a theology of good and evil can account for it.'

Marlinsky jumped in. '"We are merciless liars, informers, snitchers, traitors..." I can quote again from Okudzhava... "We live in a state of venal sin."'

'Yet we are all caught up in this condition. We are one people, after all.' Razumovsky was growing tired, still sitting on the park bench.

'All I have to say, boy, if you have through your reading acquired the least capacity in yourself to reject the corrupt side of things and withdraw from it, then you are to be congratulated. But you mustn't make it easy for THEM. You mustn't live in isolation. It's not hard to live secluded from a world that doesn't tempt you. Love our world! But don't give in!'

As Marlinsky struggled to take in this weighty advice Razumovsky chuckled. Marlinsky feared another joke, as a terrible let-down. What he heard was simply amusing. 'Currently half the governments in the world are offering me their help. As they will offer it to you. You could take it. You could teach at the university of Aloe Vera.'

'Alexander Nikolaevich, please. I live here. I am Russian. I will take on the darkness and the light.'

Fifteen

In the nineteenth century, before the October Revolution, the Russian authorities had a tool they called administrative exile. They would arrest, and banish to some faraway place, anyone who seemed likely to excite disorder. On a whim they plucked politically suspect individuals from the city streets and transported them to Siberia. But any faraway destination would do, for the chief condition was that the unwanted should not find themselves close to a railway line and a city. That is why, if you are a Russian, you love trains. Indeed, you love all forms of transport, which, though they may sometimes move in the wrong direction, ultimately lead to the city, and to the chance to be a citizen. Against that *ssylka* still continues.

Marlinsky was not yet exiled, as he expected. Would they really let him take over from Razumovsky? Perhaps. Meanwhile his days hung in limbo. No one could tell him where his life was headed. I'm no longer a student. But you still have a brain, Boris Mikhailovich. Of course I have. I'm a writer. But, be honest, you haven't written anything! True. Can I begin now? How can I? They've relegated me to stay at home, but I want to make something happen. What exactly do you want, Boris Mikhailovich?

In a way it was an unfair question to put to such a young man so willing to sacrifice himself. Was he waiting for Razumovsky to die? Of course not. The old man was a marvellous, wise fellow. Despite his jokes. Besides he was right. We are one people. I hope I can help us become one people.

Gerasimov was less complimentary. He felt the Razumovskys had set Marlinsky up, as a decoy to buy themselves some respite from the constant onslaught on their days. Marlinsky should take over the movement now and give it fresh impetus.

'If they've chosen me to block the path of that bloody archimandrite I'm honoured. What a legacy that would be, to swap the Razumovskys for a *pop*!'

cried Marlinsky from the sofa bed. 'An old man with a long beard who models himself on God!'

Gerasimov stood leaning on the bookcase which he almost equalled in height.

'I don't know why the Party puts up with Dargomyshsky either.'

'Because he's a fly in our ointment. He's found a nice role for himself.'

The movement associated with Razumovsky was in fact not properly a movement. It was more of what in the West had the name of a pressure group. As a citizen you saw injustice at work and you brought it to public attention, and shamed the politicians into action. Yet in Russia you couldn't be a citizen. The old men in the Kremlin viewed such action as treachery. The system was not to be criticised in public.

'It's the system that's one people. It's just a different way of achieving the same goal.'

'You'll be telling me next that the Party and Sasha Nikolaevich make up one of his famous dyads.'

'I'm afraid they do. Our job is to make the better half prevail. The system is us, Alyosha, one people.'

Gerasimov disliked the dyad theory. He thought it was a trap. But for Marlinsky it was a way of saying he wouldn't go abroad. All families have their problems. He wouldn't abandon the greater family either.

Caught as he was, neither a leader nor a follower, neither an acceptable Russian nor a person living somewhere else, Marlinsky experienced the condition of stalemate, when no piece on the chessboard can move. He experienced what sailors know when no wind blows to fill their sails. A lull descends. They have no momentum and can choose no direction. 'I once knew a pianist who couldn't get out of the circle of keys, and just had to play on and on, with no end in sight.' Who told him that story, long ago? His music teacher in school.

Now, was anyone listening to the conversation Gerasimov and Marlinsky had just had?

'Greetings, boys, I've brought some tea. Sit down, Alexei Igorevich.'

Gerasimov stopped propping up the bookcase. 'Let me take that.' An uncharacteristically lethargic Marlinsky sat forward and tried to show interest.

'Terrible what happened to Galya Andreyevna.' The hallmark of Marlinsky's mother's mind was that she never forgot a thing.

'She did recover.'

'She half-recovered, without her hair.'

Marlinsky reflected, God knows what they'll do to me.

'The question is how they found out.'

'Someone didn't like her.'

But the compartment supervisor had liked her. Even so.

'They would have asked questions at the university. You know what universities are like. Like ideological sieves. Full of people ready to make themselves small enough to fall through the tiniest mesh.'

'And someone from the university would have put them on to the Dickens specialist in the English department at WELL, who was seen to take a great deal of plain paper home with her in the evening?'

'At WELL, where a junior colleague wanted her job? It may just be a question of luck that they found out,' said Marlinsky.

'I'd prefer it that way.'

'We'd all prefer a universe in which God was on our side.'

They were sitting over their tea in the sitting room of the Marlinsky family home, whose chief distinction was that it was not a flat. It was an old-fashioned, wooden, one-storey cottage, along an unmade-up street. Tower blocks surrounded it in the middle distance on every side. It was as if their street, consisting of about ten similar buildings, had been forgotten. They couldn't be removed so the Party just built around them. Or they could have been removed but the will to cruelty was slack on that occasion.

'I heard the poison made her lovely red hair fall out.'

'It'll grow back. That's what hair does.' Gerasimov had a way of sounding confident, as if he could master any situation, which sometimes unnerved Maria.

'Where is that hellhole of a place anyway?' Marlinsky meant Novosibirsk. His mother was outraged.

'Don't talk like that, Misha. That's terribly rude.'

She got up and pulled an atlas from the ugly plywood glass-fronted bookcase which stood in every Soviet home. In the matter of bookcases, by the way, you took what was on offer or you didn't have one. The odd thing though was they weren't short. Bookcases were much needed; every self-respecting family had books; and the state accepted that state of affairs and supplied them.

'You should be ashamed of yourselves, not knowing your geography. You too, Alexei Igorevich.'

Grinning, Gerasimov opened the gazetteer and read backwards. 'Novosibirsk, Novorossisk, Novopetrovsk, Novomalinsk—heh, nearly a Novomarlinsky—'

'That's what they want to do to me. Make me a new Marlinsky.' He really was depressed.

'In the West they pay money for "makeovers". Here in our USSR, U-Boat Russia, you can get one free.' Maria didn't follow.

Marlinsky cried: 'Keep reading, my friend!'

'Novocherkassk. Novobelinsk. Novoarkhangelsk.'

'All these new places. Why can't we have some old places.'

'Ah now you weren't paying attention at school. The future's the thing. History's not allowed.'

'Quite right too. History's the story of how we got it wrong.'

'Except the Revolution, boys,' Maria finally interjected. 'I won't hear you say that was a mistake.'

Gerasimov smiled. 'Of course, Maria Borisovna. Of course you're right.' To malign the Revolution was the last taboo, and, indeed, none of them wanted to. Not even the suave Gerasimov. You had to go abroad, to the last relics of the emigration, to find impossible types who wanted to bring back the tsar. Unless, just supposing, the archimandrite held that view, and was just waiting for the moment to spring it on the world and call it dissent, when Razumovsky died. That, it seemed to Marlinsky, would be the ultimate betrayal of a new Russia. A family full of potential, which wanted to become its own best ancestors. It was true that many of them preferred to live in the West, or lead a Western life, if they could. But that was a mistake and he would teach people and show them it needn't happen again.

'That Myshy thinks the Revolution was a mistake. He wants the tsar back.'

'Myshy? The Mousey One?' Maria laughed. Marlinsky realised it was a long time since he'd seen his mother laugh.

'We call him that.'

'Or we call him the archimandrite—'

'But that's a holy man.'

'He's not holy. If Boris Mikhailovich can do anything for Razumovsky it will be to keep that bastard at bay for as long as—'

'As long as I can. Right.'

'Language, boys, language!'

In her wake, Gerasimov commented: 'Your mother wouldn't even denounce the devil, for fear of naming him rudely.'

'Leave my mother out of it. She's the last good woman on earth.'

Marlinsky went back out to the dacha to be alone and think about his life. He was still depressed but knew the countryside would help him. Easter had just passed, and with the misfortune that had befallen the family, and the memory of that cruel night in January, the second festivity of the year had been short and muted.

For Easter the women had painted eggs. One had to admire their painstaking work. On the other hand fine decoration was a women's thing, like embroidery. He personally wouldn't have the patience for it.

'A women's thing except when that Frenchman turned it into a jewellery business.'

'He made millions out of exporting a Russian folk art to the world beyond. Why didn't we get that idea?'

'You're asking me? Was he French?'

'*Faberzhe* got stuck here. Like Lenin's mistress. Made the best of it. He did get out in the end but he nearly didn't. The Bolsheviks nearly killed the bloody Fabergés off. They stole their business instead.'

'So that ruins Easter, when you think about it.'

Katya had a new interest in learning to make her own clothes, which Sasha refrained from ridiculing. 'How else can we manage in this country, Sashenko? A woman likes to make beautiful things. And to wear them. Besides, patchwork is an art.' She had begun to talk like her mother. She sounded twenty years older than she was.

Dr Gerasimov, Igor, reflected that there were women revolutionaries but his daughter was not shaping up to be one of them. On the other hand it took all sorts.

'Now who's heard about the latest extraordinary development in medicine called a heart transplant?'

'Can you buy it in a shop?'

'How do you get it inside you?'

'What do they do with the old ones?'

'I know. Sell them off cheaply to Czechoslovakia! Crappy Soviet hearts that don't work properly anymore.'

'Now, now!' The kindly doctor kept them entertained with his recent reading of the medical journals. In fact the first successful operation in the West had happened more than ten years earlier. 'But we don't publicise the achievements of Western science before we are poised to catch up.'

'So they'll be doing that in our hospitals now?'

'*Mnye kazhetsya, da.*' The newly published papers, remarkable in themselves, were also a signal.

'God, the thought of it happening in Moscow!'

'Heart transplants!' The term unfortunately reminded the younger Gerasimov of a classic story by Bulgakov.

'I've read it!' cried Sasha, ticking off a mental list of required reading.

'I've read it!' cried Katya.

Marlinsky grinned. *Heart of Dog* served as a reminder why no one in Russia should risk such an operation, for it might be used to perform an act of reincarnation. That finally was how the Party would make its new people. His spirits plunged. 'That's what I can expect. A makeover, forced upon me. How does the phrase go, they'd like me to have a change of heart. They'll turn me into a lapdog with some surgical procedure.'

'Borya! *Nel'zya!*' He shouldn't make sport with such a serious subject as his own life. Sometimes already even Gerasimov had had enough.

Our Russian fate! declared Sasha, sitting on the floor, trying to work some puzzle where two wires were tangled up and you had to find the way to release them. 'I don't know why Borya shouldn't wonder what they'll do to him.'

'Sasha, really!' said his father.

'He's such a clever boy.' Maria patted his head. Marlinsky made a face at him.

On the low coffee table, to which Sasha was conveniently the nearest, the remnants of Easter cake lay in the form of sweet, yellowy ruin strewing its crumbs about. None of the men could resist venturing a moistened finger in its direction, just to neaten up the display.

'But I had such a small piece!'

Sasha, followed by the adults who though they had no space left definitely weren't going to say no, had a second helping. With each slice came a spoonful of the customary sweetened cream cheese, full of raisins and lemon peel, and which the women had made in advance.

'I helped to stir it.' Katya looked up from her sewing.

251

Maria lifted the kettle and topped up the samovar.

'What a specimen!' Marlinsky gestured as the magnificent silver urn. 'I forgot. Where did you get it, Maria Borisovna?'

Misha's grandmother.'

'We managed to keep it in the family.' But Marlinsky senior was still thinking about what his younger son had said. 'Our Russian fate you say, young Sasha! What do you know about it?'

'I know Pushkin. And guess what, Dad, he told us even love wouldn't help us.'

'But you don't know love. You can't at your age.'

'I know great poetry.

> You left foreign parts
> For the distant shores of your heart;
> In the hour unforgotten, in the hour uncomforted
> While you were still there I wept and wept.'

'Who taught you that?' his father asked tenderly.

'School.'

'But who, your father asked.'

'A teacher.'

'A teacher who knows that the very idea of "abroad" causes us heartache,' said Marlinsky.

Gerasimov chipped in. 'Schoolteachers too have their alternative ways.'

Dr Gerasimov nodded. 'Pushkin's one of our alternative ways, I see. But it's such raw stuff.'

'So we train our young people, father. We teach them that they won't survive the torment of our society without Pushkin to console them.'

'God in heaven!'

Alone in Maria Easter invited some religious feeling, whether out of conviction or the comfort of habit. To her son, occasionally affected by scepticism though he resisted it, those two possibilities were probably one and the same. But wait! Would he say that of his own beliefs? If they were just habits why was this threat hanging over him? That would mean THEY were right and he just needed to change his habits, which weren't beliefs at all. But they were!

His mother crossed herself.

Khristos Voskres! Christ is Risen! The cherished refrain made Gerasimov and Marlinsky think rather grimly of that Russian God-Man of some new era that suddenly threatened them from a new direction. If they failed he would step in. They set themselves determinedly against the archimandrite, for he would not flood their parched human country with humanity but bring some new Inquisition.

Long live Alexander Razumovsky! Gerasimov raised his glass, containing some homemade apple and ginger vodka. He held it up to the window. Maria followed his gaze.

'Only drink what is homemade, nothing from the factory!' their neighbour Kurakina had warned. Make everything yourself if you want to survive!'

'Eh,' sighed Maria, 'but what a work.'

Sixteen

The Westerners spent Easter in a similarly disjointed way. The foreign ministry offered the reporters a trip to Lithuania. That a Polish priest—a *pop* of the highest order—from just across the border had been elected Pope was potentially an extraordinary story, for what journalist could resist speculating that also on the Soviet side of the frontier the Catholic faith was poised to challenge the atheist USSR. Yet why draw attention to what might hurt the motherland? Mindful of an age-old rivalry between Poland and Russia, Howard felt that he was being manipulated within a deep-rooted quarrel. There was no likelihood that Popism would sweep away Kremlinism, and THEY knew it. THEY just want me out of Moscow.

'But you're nostalgic, Gels. You'd like to go.'

'Vilnius was where I got the idea of coming here.'

'Those Lithuanians have something to answer for.'

These days, with tender feelings for him, she felt embarrassed.

'Just teasing. Honest, I'm happy you're here.' He felt the same.

But the memory turned urgent. She was back in her unfinished thesis. Such appetites we human beings have! Such dreams! Should we reject life? That's what set Tolstoy off, reading such a great German pessimist as Schopenhauer. Once you have the suspicion that life isn't worth living you have to find…well…other goals. Art. Music especially. Not difficult for a man who loved Schubert. But not everyone can love music. For other people it's their role in life…that's what saves them. They find some meaning to …being here. I'm asking myself what's mine.

Howard said: 'It *is* the way we *all* are. We're all a bit of both. Happy birds and hopeless pessimists.'

'What's extraordinary here…' and with that she reverted to the present moment—'is that the Razumovskys and the Marlinskys have to be so brave.

You're not getting anywhere with words, so you take action. You risk your own life. That's not suicide. It's martyrdom.'

'It *is* depressing to even think about.'

'I realised you were a depressive type. I thought it was about England. No purpose left.'

'That too.'

Grisha stood for a moment in the doorway. He was like a grandfather clock about to strike the hour. Then he grunted. He had these little noises, mostly the equivalent of '*nu ladno*': whatever it takes.

Still it was Easter, and Gels was still in Russia, and there was music.

The invitation to Howard came from the Patriarchy via Father Sergei. It was to a church officially long closed, but surviving, just, deep in the recesses of the Tretyakov Gallery. 'An accident of our crazy Moscow topography, or how do you say?'

'*Bezumnyi sluchai nashei topografii*. I'll remember that phrase, Sergei.'

He didn't trust the priest but he liked him. Besides, they did try to lure the Westerners in with stories like that, Howard felt. Parts of Moscow conceivably forgotten in the great makeover; treasures from before the Revolution that still survived, locked in cupboards and forgotten; faith enduring in the atheist darkness: every Westerner was susceptible. For Westerners were sentimental about memory. Memory reached across many minds, and you couldn't stamp on them all and sweep them all away as bone shards and gristle. Memory survived. It was sacred. Perhaps the terrible change that the first Russian Revolution brought could be reversed. Many implicitly hoped that, because what had followed was evil.

Howard only resisted being manipulated by the priest because of his susceptibility to that very belief that memory endured. He didn't want to reverse the revolution. But he wanted old good things to endure.

The confrontation with Father Sergei made him think. Think of memory as resurrection, no less. The layers of history that make us Westerners nostalgic for the past do live on. That is our culture, to delay, if not deny, the death of all things material. Here they think we're weak and it's something they can exploit. But I won't give in. Call it my spiritual side! Hah!

All this by way of saying Howard disbelieved any story spun about a forgotten church. Yet because his information came from Sergei, and he thought

Gels might enjoy the occasion, he was prepared to go along with the hellish fairy tale.

He found two streets adjacent on the CIA map where perhaps the remains of a church could have hidden. 'With no bell towers to give it away it *might* have disguised itself.'

'As just another palace. Then the Amis could rent it. Which makes one ask, why don't the Soviets *rent out* the churches they do still have? Make themselves a few more dollars.'

Now, now, Gels. The poison's getting to you. But she always got in an anti-American dig if she could. She replied she felt perfectly justified because it was gross for the Amis to buy their way into history.

'Spoken like a true Brit.'

'As for the Soviets, short of hard currency, they don't care about history at all. If they've got any left they want to sell it.'

'You're just disappointed you haven't found paradise.'

'That's true of you too.'

Grisha grunted.

'Don't mind us. We've got our own battles to fight back home,' she cried gaily.

'It seems, to me, Miss Gels, that you have a problem with capitalism,' he said solemnly.

'She has. I don't think that's true of me.'

Grisha grunted and muttered something followed by '*gospodin* Howard!'

'You mask it, Howard. That's what Grisha means.'

Things had so developed these days she rarely let anyone else have the last word.

Meanwhile as the night before Easter approached Howard was so wary of the priest's invitation that the hair stood up on the back of his neck at the thought of it. The Moscow Synod was pretending to offer him privileged access to the mysteries of Russian Faith. But *why?*

'Easter?'

'Not enough.'

'Dargomyshsky?'

'Now that's a better idea. To counter his influence? To encourage us not to take the church at face value? But would they be so devious?'

'You've taught me the answer is they just are. They don't like Razumovsky.

But they don't like Dargomyshsky either.'

Father Sergei had no doubt of his noble and important mission. When he phoned he insisted: 'I will only speak to *gospodin* Howard. Not to some lackey.'

Holding the plastic receiver away from his body as if the whole damn apparatus stank, Grisha had an answer to that. He called out to Howard—*govorit etot proklyatyi pop*—which made Gels look up and grin. 'It's that blasted churchman on the phone.'

Pop. The word was Greek, then Russian, and provided a nice historical-philological theme to toy with in Holy Week.

'Howard Wilde speaking. How are you, father? Saturday? Oh well that would be a distinct possibility if you could accommodate two of us.'

A weighty silence, as if a huge concession were being demanded. Then 'Ladno.'

The price that trickster had to pay. And to think he once liked him! He didn't even like him anymore. He wouldn't get Howard Wilde to himself. Gels and a faintly smirking Grisha were satisfied.

Replacing the toytown bit of engineering that *Sovtelekom* called a handset, Howard replayed the conversation in his head. 'Just for you, Gowart, I know the ways in which you do indeed love our country. I would like to remind you of them.'

'No garlicky fish this time.'

'Excuse me?'

'Just reminiscing about our last meeting.'

'Our great composer Sergei Rachmaninoff will feature.'

'Ah, yes. The composer your esteemed predecessors forced to go and live in Paris.'

'The crimes of my countrymen lie heavy on my soul.'

'I'm sure they do, father.' They must weigh heavily on someone's. Errors too. For you need your Russian culture to define you for better for worse, don't you? The excuse of your great literature and your great music come in handy, eh? 'Eight o'clock, right?'

'Agreed.' Reverting to a tone that suggested the whole outing was a conspiracy on the side of the goodness that would eventually prevail.

It was an easy journey, down to the Tretyakov Gallery, itself just a few streets on from the British Embassy, crossing the river and driving south. They parked close to the embassy as agreed, for surely that was a good cover for where they were headed. Gels could smell the river when she got out of the MG. Not a benign presence but an independent force. One THEY couldn't tame. But that was ridiculous and sentimental. Of course THEY could. THEY could block it off and poison it as readily as THEY trapped and poisoned their human enemies. They'd done it to the river Volga and they'd done it to poor, poor Galya Obolenskaya who came within an inch of her life.

Father Sergei, not tall, waited in the deep and heroic black marble entrance of a block of flats on Lavrushinsky Lane. Moscow had these old, quiet streets which the pre-revolutionary merchants called home and where they showed off their wealth. No one could deny the power of that stone which, even with its human history hollowed out, stood there defiant on its own terms. Still it could be bulldozed. Everything could be destroyed. That evening the old merchant streets sheltered a priest in long black robes, under a shabby black overcoat.

'*Vsyo v poryadke*?' Howard grasped the priest's elbow, asking if everything was in order. Gels, with whom the priest made no eye contact, decided her friend was humouring his Russian 'source', to make him think he was a source, and not just a con man they'd seen through before they set out.

She studied the priest while he talked in the dim street light. Father Sergei had large disconcerting eyes—as if his mind was on God, or full of some terrible fear—picked out by these weak, picturesque lamps like in Pushkin Square. He had too, flowing out from under his priestly hat, long dark unkempt hair: a *pop* just as Westerners might imagine him and just as the satirists of *Krokodil* used to lampoon his kind when the Revolution's victory over the priesthood was still recent. *Krokodil* stuck cigars in the mouths of every capitalist and made all priests look like lascivious gluttons, by comparison with the clean-living, athletic young Communists, with their utopian social vision. She knew where her sympathies lay.

'We go this way. *Tuda.*' Which was round the corner and a few doors on into the narrower and even quieter Little Tolmashevsky Lane.

The priest buzzed for entry into a plain brown wooden door. It opened on to an unexpectedly grand staircase with a great curving mahogany rail.

'That looks amazing!'

'Not that way!' Father Sergei barked a warning, but hoarsely, for who knew who was listening.

They passed either side of neglected wood panelling along a tiled corridor— 'Must have been some grand house!' she whispered—and out again into an external courtyard. Howard felt a visceral excitement emanating from his guest, now his friend, as the very sentiments he guarded against in himself pressed themselves into emotional service in her. 'You seem to feel someone stole the past and hid it somewhere.'

'Everyone needs the past as a companion. It's only human.'

'And you need the Russian past?'

'The past doesn't have a nationality. Just so long as human beings like me—not me but who I might have been—lived it.'

'*Syuda!*' whispered the priest again. 'This way.' Through an unassuming iron gate they found themselves in a second, much larger courtyard where in the entrance porch to a large rectangular building a light flickered. As her eyes settled she could see the building was in the usual neo-classical old Moscow style, its walls distempered yellow, with decorative borders of white, though of course the decor was flaked and faded.

'I'd get those squeaking hinges oiled, if I were you.' If their passage was supposed to be secret, the iron gate had surely given them away.

'Don't be afraid, my friend. God is with us.'

Howard sighed and wondered what he'd let himself in for.

But then singing greeted them as they entered the candle-lit darkness.

Greek Orthodox chant filled the dark room, where many other worshippers and onlookers milled, holding their candles. The only dim electric light, which seemed to have been rigged up for the occasion, and left trailing wires, was to allow the singers to follow their scores. Sixteen of them, men and women, and a white-haired conductor. The men wore plain black shirts and trousers, while the women resembled nineteenth-century country-women wearing their Sunday best. They wore long black dresses high to the neck, decorated in white lace.

The chant they sang was meant to bring you to your knees. To fill you with an overwhelming sadness. And it did, to Gels, who trembled a little. Howard stood beside her in silence.

The church was no longer a church. But then what is a church but the worshippers inside it. Maybe a hundred people—more, he whispered, a hundred and fifty, more like—stood listening. Listening meant yielding, as the spirit of the occasion enveloped them.

Not only the music but the alto soloist herself, half-lit, with her broad face, flat cheeks, deep nasal philtrum, eyes almond-shaped as if copied from an icon, was otherworldly. The sounds of Old Church Slavonic—the liquid 'l' sound and

259

the vowels, Gels thought, close to actual Russian but in a reserved, poetic use—created a music without parallel, a wild and urgent bliss, quite beyond the temporal world.

Gels recognised the portly figure of the Italian ambassador, to whom Howard nodded in the sacred twilight. Howard kept his professional head. 'Who else is here, I wonder?' If there was one ambassador there were likely to be others. This was a diplomatic initiative as much as it was a private treat.

'They want to tell us there's this secret, other Russia, a Russia of the spirit, living underground.'

'I'm on my guard. Who are these people?'

'Whoever they are some of them are here to show off. Or it's a wager. Maybe God exists. Maybe he doesn't. Better be on the safe side, seeing what this country has become without him.'

'The language does it for me. It's full of beautiful Slavonic Greek.'

Father Sergei disliked what Gels was wearing. Besides, with the coat open he could easily discern the outline of her body. The priest also wanted Howard's whole attention, and grew bolder in the information he disclosed.

'So you notice who is here.'

'You mean…' Through the exalted tenor solo Howard had fixed on two faces that seemed familiar from his office wall. Grisha had cut press photographs of the country's leaders and stuck them on the plain white back of a poster (one discouraging drunkenness in the workplace).

'Indeed. *Tak tochno*. One is probably our next leader.'

'Why? Is the present leader weakening?' interrupted Gels. 'Is he ill? Has he crashed one of his cars? That would explain a lot.'

'Or it could be the other one, you know, the tall thin one with glasses who likes jazz. In which case we're in for an insider struggle.' Howard shook himself as if out of a trance and wondered how he would report on that. 'There must also be policemen here tonight.'

Father Sergei, he of the blazing eyes and sober intelligence, smiled a smile of astonishing falsehood with his full, fat, girlish lips. 'They too want to save their souls. Who would deprive them of that?'

'Is Korsakov here?'

'Who is that? I don't know what he looks like.'

'Squat, pugnacious little chap with a Beatle fringe.'

No one looked like that in the devout, candle-lit darkness.

'Maybe that big guy could be the military type Korsakov works with. He's sometimes around at the foreign ministry.'

'The bastard who ploughed up the art show!'

'That would be the one.'

'I think I don't like Russian churches after all.'

'I hate all churches. All the sweet excuses they give people for doing evil.'

Oh, but the music! Howard would have wished the music to fall silent—and for someone to turn on the non-existent lights—so he could take in the facts. God give me facts was the only prayer this church would hear from him.

Call it a church? It was full of packing cases pushed aside, as if the building itself were temporary and might be packed up and made to vanish any moment. And here they stood partaking of a Potyemkin church service, convened to fool foreigners. That he could imagine.

But then, beside the packing cases, and the crude wiring, there were also what looked like canvasses stacked on the ground, turned to face the wall, and an unmistakeable smell of turpentine led him, as in a confusion of aims he sought the WC, past, in an ante-room, a paint-stained desk with a jar of brushes. How would it be if the artists of the city had at last found a studio where they could work! They would have to share and the light wasn't good. But again, oh no, oh no, that was just what Westerners were primed to discover in 'old Moscow': the survival of the human spirit. So that could have been arranged, or 'tolerated' too.

Meanwhile you had to worry for the paintings. A good number of frames no longer contained the works they were made to display.

'Let's get out!'

'But Howard!'

'Don't fall for it! The great Russian soul in which all Russians are one! What rubbish! What pretence! Just don't fall for it!'

And with that they were back in the red car, speeding home, though she forbade him to play a tape, which had been his angry, sacrilegious instinct.

Seventeen

Easter fell on the 22nd and the Marlinskys and the Gerasimovs returned to the town on April 25th, leaving only Marlinsky himself behind. He counted them out of the door one by one, part of his preparations.

'Now at last you're rid of us.' His mother pressed her cheek against his and whispered. 'The leftovers should keep you going for a while and Mrs Kurakina (maker of the surprisingly good apple and ginger vodka they had been drinking for a while now) has eggs.'

'See you, dear friend.'

'I don't have a choice.'

'Nobody really understands decision-making. It just happens.'

'Part of the human enigma, as you say, doc.'

'Funny country we live in, where the human enigma is a crime.'

'Any kind of generosity would be the end of them. It would mean freedom to be something other than THEY imagine us to be. *Bon courage* and all that. *Forza*!'

'And don't forget to come back to meet the foreign press. You have to prepare for that too. They're gagging for interviews with the next Razumovsky. You're the new Jesus.'

'Jesus, ME! Sorry, Mother.'

'*Poka,*' he said then. Not a formal 'until we meet again' but a friendly, casual, 'whatever happens in the meantime.' *Poka.*

Marlinsky had a desk upstairs under the eaves, on the landing between the two bedrooms. There was no window but it was comfortable to sit at the core of the little old house. Of his pile of three empty school exercise books he opened the first and gazed at the blank page. The light overhead was more like a flask filled with urine than a tool of illumination. He screwed up his eyes and wanted so much to write.

Now stop letting your thoughts wander! Any fool can spin metaphors. He went down and made tea. Urine-coloured reddish tea, like the issue of a man who has eaten too much beetroot soup.

Once he had established the right tea regime, not more than a weak glass every two hours—maiden's water more like—some words flowed. Still he wondered whether he was a writer at all. THEY don't think I'm a writer either. Just a troublemaker.

'Write that!'

'Write *why have I got no future?*'

'I'm twenty-five and I have no future.'

The thoughts came in a staccato rhythm, some of them long spaced out. 'Well, first let me just say that in our country writing, joking and loving get people into trouble, and since that's normal human activity we're all stuck. Every day we hope THEY won't sooner or later insist on changing our hearts for us. Because of what we are.'

As the house dried out for spring it creaked. Writing! Huh! He hadn't done much loving either. He paused. What did Sasha say about Pushkin and love? Ai, Boris Mikhailovich, cribbing from your little brother now.

Amazing though he should quote that poem about unfulfilled, desperate love, so much more desperate for being endured in a Russia isolated from the world; in a Russia so dark that a quite ordinary teacher wanted to warn ten-year-olds to be prepared.

'I was a bit mystical and sensitive as a teenage boy. I guess that's why I supported that girl Anna.

'When I had my first girl, when I did that bit of teaching instead of military service, the whole physical thing just woke me up to…well it made me notice our untrue ways. Love prepares us for the truth and that's a terrifying fact if you live in an untrue world.'

'Boris Mikhailovich, at last you've dug yourself out of your books!' Nadya Kurakina turned her soft, plump Russian face towards him. Mothers liked him. He was a charming young man to have as a son. 'Ooh, red eyes. So much reading is not good for you.' His lips puckered and hovered over a spongy layer of collagenated, hydrogenated powdered flesh. One mother was enough, close up.

She unwrapped her plump arms from his skinny torso. 'Kolya!' she ordered her husband. 'Set to! We'll make this a feast.' Marlinsky's mouth watered. He hadn't eaten properly since the family left.

(To add to his notebook: 'I would say we are a very theatrical people, routinely staging the whole range of human ways of self-destruction as we proceed through the calendar each year, and that helps us.')

He was already drooling when a terrible high-pitched scream carried through the double windows. Russian windows were tightly sealed against pain but even so. The Colonel had not wasted a minute taking himself out through the kitchen and into the back yard, where Nadya housed the rabbits.

'Does it suffer?' he began, but his mother's friend, their village neighbour, shot him such a complicated look he dropped the query. There is so much *else* wrong with our country, she seemed to say, *complications* that befall human beings, that to start discussing the ethics of a carnivorous diet would be frivolous. Certainly futile, he thought, in a country that depends on the deepfreeze lorry and the half-efficient collective farm and the alcohol factory to nourish its people.

Nadia was in fact a prize-winning domestic science teacher. Name a true Russian dish and she could prepare it. And apple and ginger vodka to boot.

'Fancy that!' he whistled, the first time he heard of her great expertise. Mushrooms in sour cream came to mind, but also his favourite solyanka soup, soured with the liquid used to preserve cucumbers. If she would kindly oblige him some time.

'I should make my own but alas these days it's easier to import cucumbers from Poland,' she said, wiping her hands on her apron and pushing back strands of grey hair. She straightened up and faced him. 'What can you do, Boris Mikhailovich? That's what I ask.'

So she had heard of his present difficulty, he felt.

'Our Soviet meat patties could do with some spice, don't you think, Nadya Mikhailovna. We learn from the West in medicine so why not in catering. Our meat patties are just not hamburgers. At least, that's what people say. I've never eaten a hamburger.'

'Well, *people* would say that, Boris Mikhailovich, but how can *people* know? They don't know any better than you. Besides, isn't patriotism taught in our schools anymore?'

Their eyes met and they both laughed. To her he was a good type, Russian too, and he returned the compliment to her as a Russian woman.

She was seconded to cooking from teaching in 1965, she had once explained, when in a push for modernisation and a better image in the West, THEY had thought public catering needed an overhaul. To feed the Western tourists in a way that would impress them. Also to feed our own people better. ('Always in second place, our own people, but still.'). So Nadya's job became to test and develop national recipes. But in secret.

'Why secret? Dear God, do they think other countries will get hold of our high-quality cooking and lay claim to it? THEY are ridiculous.'

She only replied that hers had been a very serious task, for it also concerned the nation's health, which could be sabotaged, by the American capitalists, for instance, for they had ruined the health of generations of their own people, all for profit, by addicting them to salt and sugar. God forbid that that should happen here.

Marlinsky knew that in America they were all very fat. 'Hell no, disgusting. I read that in Wisconsin, have I got that right, there is such a place, there was this woman so enormous she couldn't get out the door of her house. They had to lift her with a crane through the window, and then she complained because the local council charged her for closing the street.'

The Russians fell about laughing.

'I would have fined her,' said Nadya, shaking her head in an effort to be serious.

'With us they would have put her in jail for not working.'

'But there wouldn't have been a cell big enough.'

Guffaws of laughter. Tears in Nadya Kurakina's eyes, which she wiped away with her pinny.

It was fun to joke. It was wrong of Marlinsky to reproach Razumovsky for his jokes. It was just in Razumovsky's case the humour was so dry it disoriented his young disciple. He needed to focus, only for the moment not too carefully on how his mother's friend was expertly butchering the carcass for the evening.

(For his notebook:. Because, you see, our idea for a special Russian twentieth century was often good, tasty even, only something went wrong in the practice. There was always some goodwill. But then someone forgot to slaughter the bunnies until they were old and tough, and someone else threw them with fur still stuck to the carcass into the deepfreeze, and a third chancer sold them off cheaply on their journey to the city's butchers. We couldn't trust the farmers, nor the storemen nor the drivers; but we had the occasional good cook and we are a hospitable people. That's how we lived.)

The aroma from the sizzling pan brought Nikolai Ivanovich Kurakin for the first time properly into their midst. 'Ah, the joys of life! What have you two been laughing about?' He sat down opposite his young neighbour Marlinsky. With two glasses down and many more to come, in an early evening prelude to the feast his wife was preparing, Colonel Kurakin felt very satisfied. Now they settled back in their chairs, self-consciously as men did, and waited for their dinner.

Marlinsky remembered the scream of the rabbit.

The Kurakins had heard he'd lost his place at the university. Why else would he be out there now. His mother may even have let slip he had taken on a special task.

When Marlinsky finally owned up where his career was headed—his career, could he call it that—Nikolai Ivanovich stiffened. He was at that moment on his feet, twisting the neck of another clear-filled bottle with a green and gold label. At the whiff of Marlinsky's disloyalty to his country the Colonel stood to attention. He couldn't help it. Next thing the Colonel would arrest him. It was a striking, frightening moment.

'I'm sorry if I've shocked you. I wanted to be truthful. I want the best for our country.'

Kurakin was a fine man in his mid-fifties, with clear blue eyes. His thick grey hair was no longer shorn to military standards, but he was tall and broad-shouldered, and retained an upright bearing. He could wring any neck.

'Forgive me, Colonel, our people are defenceless, someone must speak for them. Terrible cruelties are practised by our state…' Marlinsky searched for something like a tiny broken vein in the Colonel's cheeks: any sign that he might have a human weakness.

Though, for God's sake, we don't need any more alcoholics.

In the end the tall man flinched, or shrugged, neither of them knew which, but it was enough, and it allowed the evening to continue.

(For his notebook: 'It has never been easy for men of my country to be always and invariably loyal soldiers; but also not disloyal either. And that applies to all of us.')

266

Colonel Kurakin didn't name Marlinsky's crime—or what would have been the obese American woman's crime too—. They both knew it was parasitism. He was out here not working. Living off the state without contributing. Punishable by up to ten years enforcing the very thing that parasites don't do. HE WOULD HAVE TO WORK!

The Colonel silently acknowledged his young neighbour's difficult future, as their eyes met over the rim of their shot glasses.

Marlinsky was, most likely, destined to be sent, officially that was, to wherever building socialism was understaffed. He would tax his spine and break his fingernails, learning his lesson. Meanwhile other prisoners, themselves so deeply harmed, would harm him too. To bring him down, or up, to their level of pain.

'Plenty of others have gone before me. There's this poet named Kolya Shaginyan…We have to be allowed to protest at the injustices of our society! We can't live in this cruelty and untruth!'

Nadya, setting plates on the table, raised her eyebrows.

Marlinsky didn't see Colonel Kurakin snapping shut a ball and chain round his ankle, to stop him escaping in transit to where builders of socialism were needed; but he knew he would have done, if the order came. A Russian life is a fine balance.

The Colonel pressed his lips together in a grimace. 'What I don't understand, Boris Mikhailovich, is why you had to defend a mad woman. I forget her name.'

'"Our Moscow Ophelia!" they called her. But you know Prishvina wasn't mad. She had personal troubles. People can get like that.'

The case had been in the Moscow papers where, indeed, some wag had come up with the Shakespearean headline.

'Who are you then in this story, Boris Mikhailovich? Hamlet?' ('Gamlet', he said, the way Russians do.)

'Not Hamlet, Colonel. Laertes I'd have to be. Ophelia's brother.' But just as the Colonel now failed to do, THEY didn't follow through on the headline. THEY just liked the comparison.

(For his notebook: Our journalists wrote like this because it made us seem like cultivated people and put us on the world map. Look, look! We've read Shakespeare too. Our journalists were never newshounds, but they had this talent for naming and shaming. They invented Our Moscow Ophelia as a character. Then they assassinated that character over and over again. One day they denounced her as promiscuous. Another time they mentioned her "latent schizophrenia". Readers were hooked. How will they tell *my* story, when the time comes. No country was ever so good at character assassination, as a prelude to real assassination. Oh, malign power!)

Nadya appeared again, wiping her reddened hands on the floral print of her overall, this time to target her husband.

'Of course you don't understand the case of a young woman like that, Kolya, because you're too rigid. When they taught you to drive a tank they also taught you to think like a tank. Poor young woman.'

The daughter she never had. But then she laughed, to give them all a way out.

'We all know things can be improved here.'

'That's true.'

'We can eat now.'

'At last!'

'I know it will be superb! Did we thank you for the apple and ginger vodka?'

'Nothing to thank.'

And so they approached Nadya Kurakina's rich table, with the Colonel only once backtracking in the conversation to insist that it was just not done for Russians to wash their dirty linen in public.

'Not even in our own country?' Marlinsky asked.

'Well, now you're never going to confine it to this country, are you?' the Colonel said crossly, and Marlinsky was left defending the existence of the international press.

(For the notebook: Which I will have to learn both to value and to ignore.)

But now the high tide of appetite flowed. The same the world over. The oohs and aahs and slurps, and the clink of cutlery, the gorgeous sight of it lying there sharp and silver beside the plate, waiting to tackle the feast, albeit laid out on Soviet factory porcelain, drowned out all else. The browned rabbit, spatchcocked on a white plate, tasted heavenly.

'Nadya has pickling to perfection,' her husband said, enthusiastically helping himself to baby tomatoes preserved in a brine made pungent with cloves. Nadya's dear Kolya, enjoying himself, feeding his muscular body and his good habits in life. They ate silently. Nadya's cucumbers were indeed superb, crunchy, salty with a hint of sweetness, and they partnered boiled potatoes straight out of the soil. A third bottle of vodka—plain to go with the meal, of course—still full but already de-capped stood at the ready.

'No girlfriend at the moment, Boris Mikhailovich?' Nadya ventured.

'Right now I'm glad I haven't.'

The older woman looked bashful on his behalf, as if what he was saying wasn't quite right. His mother thought he was slow too, unlike his friend Gerasimov, who'd already lived with a woman, as man and wife, though it didn't last. 'He's just a boy, in a way,' she said, and Nadya had nodded understandingly.

'Why do people think sex is the norm?' He retaliated in his mind, knowing full well what was insinuated. Why do even good people like Nadya and my mother long to see evidence of *lerv* in my private life? Keep out!'

Still Marlinsky enjoyed that whole evening, including the moment when he and the Colonel stood in the porch and smoked under the stars, under the electric moon over the threshold, and nothing else moved, seemingly, for this was indeed the countryside.

'How will you manage out there?' Nikolai Kurakin asked finally, with a great many more words unspoken. And he didn't mean building the new Baikal-Amur railway line.

'Yoga. Self-discipline. The hope of a little kindness.' Ai, life is fragile!

'*Bog s vami*, Boris Mikhailovich,' the Colonel concluded, with a squeeze of Marlinsky's arm. 'God be with you. Yes, yoga's good. Something for the body.' (For his notebook: None of us believed in God, but we used His language hungrily. Even a Colonel in the Red Army did. Such was our situation. God be with you, he said. Well, if there was a chance God would be with me perhaps that's what I meant by the unexpected kindness I would look out for, in the course of my cast-out existence. I have some faith in my fellow human beings. I am not lost.)

Eighteen

Howard had two sets of bilateral meetings to cover and a curtain-raiser to write for Senator Kennedy's visit.

'Oh, my, is a *Kennedy* coming?'

'That's just what he'd like you to think. He's another shyster.'

Grisha smirked.

Gels grinned. 'I can't help that. He's interesting.'

'As I say he's a bastard. Don't get your hopes up.'

'A bastard among bastards then.'

'The two countries do have certain traits in common.'

She shook her head, standing in front of him. 'What can we do, then?'

'That is the question: What is to be Done?' As Hamlet and Lenin said.

'Tea?' offered Grisha.

'*Spasibo* but no. Look, spring is here!' Beyond the little double window over the ring road the sky was intermittently blue. Enough to cut a sailor's pair of trousers, her mother used to say. At least she noticed. Her papa never would have cared. The next thing would be to unseal the window taped up for winter and actually open it. Aah, fresh air! Did no one else crave it? When would DIMDA say the word? She ran down the stone stairs, ducked under the arch, glanced at the *militsioner* and was gone.

Magnificent wrought iron gates announced the entrance to the Red Army Park. Sometimes, at the weekend and on holidays, as she snaked her way up the path to the bandstand at the far end a brass ensemble would play and every last sympathy she had for leading a life amongst her fellow human beings, for all their faults, for all the misery, would pour out of her in a stream of emotion. A boating lake and a chess pavilion seemed to be standard for Soviet parks, and lovely they were too, conjuring up a very thoughtful idea of leisure, and what made it different from work. Work building socialism. The burden did sometimes lie heavy. But it gave meaning. For time off then there was a firing range, one of those stalls you usually saw in a fairground and where, if you had a good eye, you could win a doll, or a rubber duck. TIR, it said, Russian borrowed from French. A lot of the modern language was borrowed from somewhere, disguised in Russian letters. Stand on your own two feet, Russia, will you?

(I'm learning to stand on mine.)

Marlinsky and Gerasimov called their own press conference for the first time. Gels and Howard arrived in the red MG. Gels demanded the roof down.

'Gels it's still April and freezing.'

'Please.'

They had to park in the street.

Arthur drew up in the Chevrolet. Howard said: 'This district will be awarded the Order of Lenin next. People will be wondering what's going on.'

Arthur gave a kick to a huge iron wastewater pipe laid on the surface of the unmade-up street. 'The Soviet Union was built too quickly. No time to bury the plumbing.'

The Westerners poured into that old wooden house where Marlinsky and Gerasimov had recently ridiculed all the place names in the Soviet gazetteer beginning with 'New'. To Maria Marlinsky their tread was too heavy, and as for the clothes the woman wore, what was she supposed to be? Refugee, soldier, nun or tart? Gels had just removed both the parka and a sweater to reveal a tight black body—the garment called a body—underneath.

Marlinsky apologised for his English. But it was crisp, formal and efficient, learnt from the BBC. A family room with an open door led to a small kitchen. Another door led to a yard with what looked like a small garden.

'Mr Marlinsky, do you want Russia to be a Western country?' A hush fell.

'The West is not all good. But it is a better way for us.'

Misha Marlinsky walked in from the back door in stockinged feet, with Sasha.

'This is my other son, Sasha.'

'Hi Sasha, how old are you?'

He'd recently become eleven. The journalists made a note.

'Sasha will recite Pushkin to you, if you're not careful. About our cruel Russian state,' Marlinsky jested. Everyone, thought Gels, seemed to be fond of jokes these days. He did recite some lines too.

'It's better to have dreamt a thousand dreams that never were/ than never to have dreamt at all...'

'Submit to your grief! /Your time will come, believe me!'

The Western press applauded politely.

'Sit, sit everyone!' Maria set down hard-boiled eggs, salt fish and pickled vegetables on the crisp tablecloth.

'Oh now this! Dear Mrs Marlinsky, we weren't expecting to eat.'

'This is a Russian house, Sir.' Marlinsky's mother replied so sternly that Howard had no further comment.

'So you are going to make our son famous? Asked Marlinsky senior. 'Will they understand our Russian problems?'

'That's our job,' said Wormy consolingly. 'We'll do our best.'

'What about your own dissidents?' Maria asked.

'Anyone can say what they think in our countries.'

'But they murdered the President of the USA in the street.'

'Yes,' replied Arthur. 'But that shooter wasn't a dissident.' He was about to start on certain psychological problems under certain social conditions but the initiative faded.

Were all Russian families so well-informed? So high-powered? Gels wondered in admiration. Polly would say their brains were not addled by Western media, although Maria Marlinsky's question had been peculiar.

Marlinsky came to the Westerners' rescue: 'The freedom of the West is not true freedom, mother. It's just they come closer to it than we do.'

Gerasimov insisted: 'It's important to add that in the West they have their ideals too and mainly they don't punish people for pursuing them.'

'Well said, Sir,' enthused Arthur.

'So what is this true freedom, Borenko?'

'Freedom is the space in which the individual defines himself in commitment and action, Mama. Here we are not allowed that space.'

Heavens! Howard made a few notes while Wormy produced his fluffy microphone and interviewed Marlinsky directly. Maria replenished the table with cakes and stewed fruit and brought tea.

'Many people want to get out of Russia, don't they? What do you say to them?'

'When the plague comes, or the rivers dry up, the ships no longer call...' recited Sasha.

The other interviewers took turns.

Marlinsky to Howard Wilde, *London Global News*. 'I understand but I still say it's not the best way, to go abroad. This country can be reformed. We can discover the medicine, dig out the silt, forge new bonds.'

Marlinsky to Patrick Wormold, BBC: 'I'm not a hero. I just believe people should be allowed to criticise the authorities without being thrown into a lunatic asylum. They shouldn't be made to conform in their lives to some ridiculous vision drawn from a philosophy no one cares about.'

Marlinsky to Howard Wilde, 'It's an outrage that my family should be made to suffer.'

'How do you deal with the threat of prison? Many people would say you're very brave.'

Marlinsky, smiling, to Patrick Wormold, 'Well now—you've heard about our Russian jails, I suppose. And our camps. I'll keep up my spirits with yoga.'

'Yoga!'

Marlinsky asked them if they had a better idea. 'We practise here. When my friends come.'

'Who are your friends? Can you trust them?' Visitors had started arriving, in ones and twos, since he was blacklisted. Best was to space the visits out and pose as friends and family. Some of them he was sure he'd never met.

'God knows who they are. But it's a chance to talk.'

'There will always be a spy,' said Gerasimov.

'That's how we live. Reikhman told me that. He said when he read Plato's *Symposium* it seemed to him that in Russia that book would need to be called "Symposium with Spies". Because in Russia whatever you say, whatever you think, however noble the thought, someone's always listening, seeing if they can take advantage. But can that be a reason not to pursue the truth?'

'A great dialogue about truth and love and our Soviet mentality corrupts that too. Huh! That's us.'

Gerasimov reflected out loud. 'Do you think the spy is Lusya, Borya?'

'Let's not talk about that here,' said Marlinsky. 'I've no intention of washing my dirty linen in public. Isn't that what you say, in the West?'

The girl who'd been so keen on him at the Komsomol hearing, and then shocked at what she heard, had indeed reappeared in his life.

'Please. Let me be here. As Sonya's friend.' Sonya was a religious friend of Anna Prishvina. Giving her the benefit of the doubt Marlinsky learnt that Lusya's elastic body excelled at yoga, to which she brought a certain unexpected discipline. She took over as instructor of a whole new group that now formed around Marlinsky. The reconciliation made him happy. But who were the others? Afanasy? Efrast?

'No, I don't think it's Lusya. She means well.'

'You've changed your mind.'

'She learnt something from us.'

Moral arrogance had a place in Marlinsky's life.

'So yes, ladies and gentlemen of the Western press, we do yoga.'

The journalists reshaped that theme for a Western audience. 'Gymnastics for Anti-Totalitarians'. Or maybe 'The Gymnasium of Protest'.

'Second one would tell a story. Your editor will prefer the first. It's a headline.'

'So you're an expert now, Gels.'

(I was. At watching how the reporters worked, and making a quite different set of notes myself.)

Marlinsky to Arthur Zimmerman, *Washington Globe:* 'I look at my country and I wonder what happened to all those things the USSR once stood for: enlightenment, internationalism, the rational progress of humankind.'

Arthur to Marlinsky: 'I wish you well, Sir, and thank you for talking to me.'

The Russian had hoped for a hint of mutuality from the American, but he didn't get it. Merely professional politeness.

Gerasimov, talking unofficially to Howard, in Russian. 'You've got this philosopher too, Layng—'

'R.D. Laing, yes. He says we shouldn't separate sanity and insanity the way we do.'

'Sounds like what we believe.'

'We don't have *psykhushki.*'

'He thinks you do.'

Howard in a moment of diminished self-control, bellowed in frustration. Everyone heard but pretended not to, for the two men had drawn aside and were standing by a far window. 'Look, I know what you mean, but it's not the same. Believe me. It's not the same because it's not a political conspiracy. We are *not* a totalitarian country.'

'But some people are mad and others are not.'

'Well, yes. What can you do?'

Gerasimov shrugged.

Howard said: 'Excuse me. I must check a few things with Boris Mikhailovich before we finish.'

(He felt dissent could go too far.)

Maria Marlinsky meanwhile addressed the whole company in Russian, focussing on Gels in particular. 'In our country we don't have justice, Madame. *Net pravdy.*' Gels was preparing an answer when she found herself under personal attack. 'And you, young lady, the way you dress! Are you married to that man?' She gestured at Howard and pointed out that there was no ring on Gels's finger.

Gels only smiled. 'We are good people, Mrs Marlinsky. Don't doubt that.' The dissident's mother shrugged.

Arthur caught the drift and smiled supportively at Gels on his way out. Howard drove the two of them home. They both felt exhausted.

'Marlinsky said it was a group but it's a kind of seminar he has. They talk big ideas all the time. He said: "We're trying to be conduits for something…something decent…something good." I'm quoting him: "We read together. Our Russian literature helps us."

'Marlinsky said: "Our true Party is a great network of friends and lovers…that's how it started out and that's how we are, we Russians. You can't make an institution of us. We are the people we are."'

Marlinsky to Patrick Wormold, BBC: 'The untrue Party as THEY've made it is like a nineteenth-century family with an authoritarian father at its head, That's why they are so hard on their prodigal sons.'

Wormy: 'I can't use that on TV. It's not an interview. It's a sociological thesis.'

Marlinsky to Arthur Zimmerman, *Washington Globe*: 'Our country is decadent. Our ideals are rotting.'

Howard to Arthur: 'Sounds like your country too.'

'Fuck you Howard Wilde. You guys are so fucking anti-American. It really gets me.'

'Nothing personal, Arthur.'

But it could so easily become that.

Nineteen

'So, Progress Group colleagues, What to do. That is the question.' The Group peered at Korsakov from round the empty dining table. 'He stopped cooperating at the university.'

'I warned him.'

'Of course, professor. You were there.'

'So now he's technically a parasite.'

'I loathe parasites,' said the woman with her grey hair in a bun.

'Except, Anna Ivanovna, how can we go on—'

'Did he have a hand in getting out all those lies about our hospitals? Of course he's another scoundrel in the making.'

'In view of that dossier we need complete revision of our powers of oversight.'

'We did punish some woman—'

'Now that's just it. About punishment…' Korsakov removed, wiped clean and replaced those glasses that these days made him resemble a 1960's French intellectual. Yves Montand, perhaps. Except that he was a Soviet Russian. 'Comrades, colleagues, listen to me! One thing matters. We need to change our thinking. We need to stop wasting our good people.' Korsakov paused. 'We waste our talent. Now, if we could give our brilliant men and women a *chance*. Russia could become great again.'

The Progress Group listened warily.

'Some new way of making them do what we want?'

'*Without* coercion.' Korsakov's own wife and son were in his mind.

'Hmm.'

'Before I die I would like to see arise a generation that truly loves its country.'

'Truly? Good Lord!'

'To love it of its own free will? *Gospodi*!' (It meant 'heavens!' and was another appeal to the Lord.)

'Impossible.'

'Like it happens in Italy.'

'Ah well la bella Italia, where the weather's better!'

'And the women look like Signorina Montenari.'

'I propose not to arrest him but to invite this Marlinsky here to join us for a weekend. Make a date in your diaries, please!'

The two artists lingering ex officio at the table perked up at that. They liked an audience. They were not part of The Group but on vague undefined terms members of the household where the Progress Group meetings took place.

Irina, who liked the company of Zorin and Zolodei, and wished them an audience, re-entered the room with a bottle and glasses on a tray. 'I'm Lisa this evening. Lisa's gone to bed.' Lisa was the maid. 'Brandy, anyone?'

'Is it a good one?' the Vice-President was peering rudely at the label.

'Courvoisier but I can fetch you Kursk if you want.'

'Boss, that bookshop lady. This seems to be about her.' Grisha had underlined the key words which included immature, ideologically under-educated and socially irresponsible. She's been sent back to Dzerzhinsk where she came from.

'Where's that?'

'On the Volga.'

'Show me on the map!' Gels dashed into the back room. She would have travelled there to repent.

'Boss, they're saying she, er, had intimate relations with her Komsomol manager to get the posting in the *Moscow* bookshop in the first place.'

'Bugger it bugger it! They always say that. Even here, it turns out. Achieve something and it's because you've slept with a certain man. It's just sad.'

'Heh, Gels…' Howard grinned.

'How do you get on in a country like this anyway?' Gels cried angrily. 'There must be worse ways.'

Grisha rolled his eyes to the ceiling. 'Anyway, this article, Mr Howard, Miss Gels. This is also how we punish people.'

On another evening it was Korsakov's turn to dole out the cognac, this time from Maison Prunier. Again there was a tray with small glasses, which he handed round. Irina didn't say no. A second glass caused her to observe what she always felt on these occasions: Our factories make a *konyak* too. But people aren't idiots. They know it's not the real thing. *Konyak*'s just a word.'

'Superb, is it not?'

For once she agreed with her husband. This liquor contained a depth of flavour in which she could disappear. Drink enough of it and she wouldn't regret her departure from the world one bit.

'We mustn't encourage our people to drink alcohol,' said Anna Makarenko: the Mack, the woman with the grey bun on whose Lenin Library watch the encyclopaedia article on Stalin was excised with a razor blade, though she was only obeying orders.

'Oh please!' Irina came back at her. Our people drink themselves silly because they can't bear too much reality. Just like you write your science-fiction stories. Our everyday life is cruel.'

'Irina, darling…'

'You didn't have to banish that bookshop woman either, Volodya,' Irina began anew, targeting her husband. 'She was just a scapegoat.' Possibly Irina was on her third glass. Nor did she eat much. 'Where has the poor woman been sent? My friends, this can't be right. If you want a better country you can't just move people about as if they were chess pieces. You can't just remove them from the board altogether if the desire takes you.'

'Why not?' asked Naumov, who was the vice-president of the Academy of Sciences.

'Volodya, sweetheart…' always a bad sign when Irina went so far as to throw in a term of endearment. 'Think of the headlines the Western press will come up with. MOSCOW BOOKSELLER BANISHED FOR SELLING WRONG BOOK. BOOKBURNING NEXT? You'll open *The US World Report* and there'll be a headline REDS ADOPT NAZI BOOK POLICY.'

'Comrade Colonel, your wife has a diseased imagination. I can't hear such things.'

'That's why you write science-fiction, Miss Makarenko. Anything to shield you from the truth.'

'All this abuse!'

Korsakov shrugged. 'I would say we're having a free discussion. Just what our country needs. 'In my view that bookshop manager lacked education and doing some revision won't hurt.'

'But it's all so *trivial!*'

'She allowed the sale of literature against the state. She was acting out of vengeance. Is that trivial?'

'You can't possibly know what her motive was if she had one at all. Anyway vengeance isn't a crime.'

'Maybe it was just a mistake. Maybe she didn't know what tripe she was selling,' said the lugubrious professor. 'Many of our people are stupid. Gut instinct or lack of brains. Either way they get things wrong.'

'That's no good for Anna Ivanovna, Mr Balabin. Our Makarenko here wants to punish people.'

'Nothing wrong with that,' said the Vice-President of the Academy.

The lady added: 'Besides our law *does have* a way of dealing with vengeance. The desire for vengeance against society is a symptom of schizophrenia.'

Irina cried: 'What an outrageous and ignorant thing to say!'

'Unfortunately Anna Ivanovna is not alone in her view, my dear. As a result of recent publications the whole world has now got an inkling of how we think in such matters,' said Korsakov. 'They have even discussed it at the United Nations.'

'The devil take the United Nations,' boomed Konstantin Innokentevich Naumov.

'The whole world has grasped that for us politics is either compliance or revenge. What peasants we are!'

A silence fell.

Slow to puncture it, one of the artists—the weary, handsome one in his forties, whose name was Zorin—finally felt moved to defend the United Nations. 'The United Nations can be very useful. That's why I have included Dag Hammerskold in my collage of the twentieth century.'

'Collage? Hmmm.'

'What do you mean hmm?' he addressed the other artist.

'Well, it's not very up to date as a practice, is it?'

Irina wasn't in a mood to hold back. 'Are you suggesting the bookseller was schizophrenic, Miss Makarenko? Is that the wisdom on Mars, or something? Here's another headline for you. SCI-FIT SPINSTER BACKS LOBOTOMIES FOR ANTI-SOVIET BEHAVIOUR. You do know English, don't you?'

Makarenko didn't. But everyone else understood.

'*Znachit*,' began Balabin, 'Which means…'

'It means we are the most boorish and the cruellest nation in the world.'

'I don't know who's going to measure that.'

'Damned Western press, peddling lies about Russia.'

Irina got to her feet. 'I'm just asking you to imagine, comrades, that we might do better.'

Korsakov, completely against his expectations, was delighted at what he took to be his wife's support. 'My wife is right. We *can* do better. Which is why I want to bring that boy out here and show him how he could…join us. Help us find the shared path.'

Balabin woke with a start. Korsakov wanted to invite Marlinsky out here to talk to the Progress Group. *Bozhe*! He had to defend him against that. 'Anna Ivanovna's right. Such an overture would be a waste of time. The boy's already been sacked from the university. That's enough.'

'Enough for what, Sergei Mikhailovich? My intention is *not* to punish him. Can nobody understand that? We have to do something *other* than punish people.'

'So, what's the plan?' asked the second artist, a dancer whose name was Zolodei. He had a little bit of rebellion in his nature, and Irina liked his company because he was graceful and fun.

'The plan is to let him see how we live. Make him understand why he might join us to make a better country.'

'You mean you'll arrest him?'

'I'll invite him, Sergei Mikhailovich, and you can be useful in the matter. You can go and take him the invitation, as it were.'

'He doesn't like me.'

'Nonsense. You're too modest.'

Twenty

A black car came to the dacha. They knew Marlinsky's habits on a Friday evening. The Kurakins' two grandchildren were playing outside. Keeping watch, Nadya Kurakina saw out of the kitchen window the unwelcome arrival. 'Bedtime snack!' she cried. 'Come and get it!'

'But granny!'

'A special occasion, Vanochka. How many days is it to your birthday?'

Balabin knocked and stepped back. A tormented man, Kurakina said to herself. Skin-and-bones, not like my Nikolai!

It was about 6.30 pm, still light. The driver was a bulky unfit man whose job it was to sit on Marlinsky's face if he gave trouble. Waiting behind the wheel he looked up when the quarry appeared, then returned to one of those plastic children's puzzles which in the West you could buy for a penny or get free in a Christmas cracker. Hopelessly he moved the disordered pieces around in a grid in which there was a single manoeuvring space. The task was to get the digits in order. But how could that one space be enough? You went up, you went down, you went sideways...

'Professor, why—'

'Pack a few things, Boris Mikhailovich, if you please.' Balabin sounded as dispirited as he looked.

'Well, that's abrupt! Let's have some tea first.'

But Balabin had stepped back so far from the threshold as deliberately to station himself in the front garden. Marlinsky said: 'Surely you have time to sit with us for a few moments, professor, as a good Russian, before a journey?'

'I can offer you tea with homemade jam.'

'Alas, good lady, we must be off.'

Marlinsky, as he went off to 'pack a few things', looked down from an upstairs window and saw that the professor was a stick and his companion a brutish fatso; that together they made up the number 10, one thin stroke and one round; that the number 10 was calling Marlinsky in like a rowing boat that had overstayed its time on the lake. For the first time his situation amused him.

What does 'a few things' mean? He put some clean linen, a couple of shirts, a pullover, a toothbrush, a razor, soap, toilet paper, a candle and matches into a sports' bag, Never go anywhere without a toothbrush, etc., Natalya Razumovsky had advised him. He added Okudzhava's novel, because, as for so many, for all its savagery and despair, it had become his companion. So someone else not only knew but could write what things were like. He loved to read and it was because he loved to read that he was taking his present course of action.

He nipped his mother a kiss. His father called out: 'Have a good trip!'

'I will, Pa. *Poka.*' Later the Kurakins popped over and Maria cried and the men downed a few vodkas.

It was an unseasonably warm evening and the car reeked like an ashtray. Marlinsky wound the window down. No one objected so they didn't think he was ready to throw himself out. The car passed the bus stop called 'Turning'. 'Nice, isn't it?' Marlinsky gestured at the mushroom-shaped concrete shelter. 'To have good architecture at a local bus stop, not just in the show-off capital, that's what I call a good country.'

No response, as they headed for the main road. 'I find it poetic.'

'What?'

The bus shelter.'

'Better you don't speak Boris Mikhailovich, if you're going to be sarcastic.'

'But no! The architecture of a dynamic modern world belongs to Russia.' He added: 'Everyone should travel.' Which was sarcastic.

'Where are we going, if I may ask? It's true I love to travel. You want me to guess?'

'You'll see. It's what you've brought on yourself.'

'For my sarcasm? Can't be!'

But it was like that when you ran into trouble with the Party. It was like being in school. You were blamed and that was that.

There was not much traffic because of all those who wanted to travel, or even just move about in their own country, even in their region, few did. He watched the road signs, deducing that in half an hour they had covered around thirty kilometres. He could still read the names of the destinations in the evening light. The name Sheremetyevo recurred. Sheremetyevo with a picture of an aeroplane.

'What the hell?'

'I told you to behave.'

'You're joking. You're fucking joking.'

'You'll see.'

The driver flicked his eyes up into his rear-view mirror.

'That can't be true. I haven't done anything.'

'You're a fool,' Balabin muttered under his breath. 'That's as good as.'

Approaching the airport the car headed for a modest spread of low grey buildings.

Recovering his spirits, Marlinsky decided that was a pity, because a flying saucer shape was the main hub and he wanted to see that.

'Oh but look! It looks like our bus stop but so much more ambitious…'

What was the scumbag on about, wondered the driver.

'For God's sake shut up,' said Balabin.

'Our architecture is all about the Space Race, don't you think, Professor? We're telling the Americans we're winning the Space Race.'

He kept talking. He reckoned he could talk his way out of this difficulty, an educated man like him. Because if you are afraid of other human beings, it's automatic you offer what you do best as a gift, so they might take pity on you and remember that you are a human being too. Only don't use long words.

But silence in response: a muddy, treacly kind of silence, that could turn into anything.

'As I said, I like travelling as much as the next man. Have you been to Kiev? Bus station No 7 is fabulous.'

'Of course I've been to Kiev. What do you take me for?' answered Balabin irritably.

Out on the forecourt Marlinsky choked with emotion. His nose prickled. He grabbed the professor by his open jacket. 'You can't mean this. It's insane. What have I done?'

A kind of smile spread across Balabin's face as he enjoyed Marlinsky's physical proximity. The boy had to pay him attention now.

But the boy was so afraid he fell into a creative trance. Those huge red letters spelling АЭРОПОРТ prompted a veritable concrete poem in his head:

А for take-off (nose up, vertical, be brave!)

Э for a reclining seat (I'll be glad of it)

Р for a solicitous air hostess (our Russian women are well-built)

O for my neighbour's mouth open in sleep (never the most flattering pose)

П for the aisle with a trolley for refreshments

O and P as before

T for our eventual descent from the heavenly horizontal.

Where would this plane descend? He'd only ever flown to Sochi before. The flying saucer building, the airport's control hub, looked modern and possibly the equipment inside it worked. But the glass-walled terminal was just a box where passengers, treated not like workers but like robots, waited for planes that sometimes took off and sometimes didn't. Marlinsky through the plate glass watched the driver pull away, his red tail lights like bee stings in the early evening.

Where were the other travellers, with only the stick-thin professor by his side on the tarmac?

'It was nice of them to send *you* to keep me company, Professor.'

'You like to torture me Boris Mikhailovich and they do too. That's what I'm made for. We'll board now.'

'But honestly you can't do this!' Marlinsky cried, and there were tears in his eyes. The professor took his arm but when he resisted let the prisoner walk alone.

There was a smallish plane parked ahead of them.

Marlinsky wasn't handcuffed, he imagined telling some Western reporter, because in our country there isn't any need for bracelets. We're not free from the day we're born. You can't escape. THEY always know where you are. So best cooperate. Live a little longer.

It was a small passenger jet, with about eighty seats, he did a quick estimate. So their seats had to be at the back of the cabin, otherwise the plane would nose-dive. Marlinsky stowed his bag and sat in front of a plastic wall with an empty magazine rack above his head.

'Handy for the facilities.'

Balabin grunted. He had just a briefcase with him, which, as they sat down, he hugged between his feet.

'I've got a spare toothbrush.'

'I'm perfectly able to equip myself, Boris Mikhailovich.'

'But they've been short for months! You must have a special supply, as a professor.'

Marlinsky could feel springs prodding his backside, just like in the Icarus bus, but there was something superior about the flossy seat covers. He knew from his mother they were made of Flyon. Flyon, with the glossy finish of silk and the durability of plastic, was a famous Soviet invention. In the age of Rayon and Orlon in the West applied chemists in the East had triumphantly come up with Flyon.

Marlinsky slid back in his Flyon seat and rested his head on the headrest.

Something like a paper towel covered it. 'How long's the flight?'

'*Keine Ahnung.*' Balabin for some reason retreated into creaky German. 'Look!' Marlinsky turned and grabbed him again. '*Frankfurt am Main oder* (since they were speaking German) *Frankfurt an der Oder*? I DON'T WANT TO GO. SOMEBODY HELP ME!'

A stewardess came to help the puny academic. She almost knocked Marlinsky out. 'You forgot your belt, Comrade. Keep your belt done up.'

'Don't joke, Boris Mikhailovich, *es gibt kein Oder.*' Finally Balabin expressed himself. He came up with a pun. The pun in German meant: 'No alternative exists.'

Marlinsky laughed heartily. We Russians have always liked jokes, especially if we can make them in clever language, he said… Balabin repeated: Ess geebt kayn oderr. 'I did warn you.'

As a few sobs crept into the laughter the woman brought a tray of boiled sweets. 'Heh, you,' she prodded him. 'Take one!' Then, with a wobble they were airborne.

The epitome of the fifteenth letter of the Russian alphabet reappeared with drinks.

'No I—'

'Drink it.' The beverage on offer was the colour of water in which you might have washed a bloodstained shirt. He sniffed (as his mother had taught him). 'Cherryade? Fortified with some alcoholic ferment? Wait, I know, it's Crimean sparkling wine. Cheers!'

The last thing a suddenly sleepy Marlinsky remembered was his seat reclining under protest, like some garden tool left out in the weather.

When he woke, they were not in either of the Frankfurts, however, but in somewhere corresponding to 'or'.

'What time is it? My God, we're on the ground!' Through the thick window glass he could see only a few lights. As they disembarked Balabin had the sports bag over the same shoulder that was carrying the briefcase, and with his left was propping Marlinsky up between his own skeletal physis and the more capacious endowment of Comrade Tray-Bearer.

'So we're in—'

'No idea. They didn't tell me.'

Remembering the carefully selected contents of his sports bag, and observing that he was wearing nothing more than a track suit and old running shoes, as they walked through an almost identical low grey building to the one where they had started out, Marlinsky speculated how his reception in the first of the two Frankfurts might have gone. Like so many émigrés over the generations, he would have thrown himself upon Western charity and, in the name of his mother, felt ashamed.

But this place was nowhere. The star-filled night was thoroughly dark. Yet it was somewhere, and in that he rejoiced, for to be alive and not in pain is the thing.

A car drew up again. It wasn't a taxi. Russian taxis are pale yellow, as if the Volga river long ago diluted the sun in the direction of pus. Our *nomklats* prefer black cars.

'My God, it's a Mertsedez!' He spluttered, and even pronounced the brand in the correct German fashion. 'Where have you brought me? It's still Russia, isn't it? Nowhere else could be so crazy.'

The air was cold, and it somehow felt like his native country. Unless it was Finland.

'Don't talk so much,' Balabin drawled.

Marlinsky could stand up unaided now. The fresh air helped. He gulped it down. Who knew when he would be in the open air again, on what soil.

'Now we'll continue our journey.'

The allegedly sarcastic young man who was being escorted somewhere bent in half and slid across the mud-hued leather. He liked the idea of a Mertsedez, who didn't, but he would have been happy with a little Russian Fiat like Dr Gerasimov's, with its quite bearable blue plastic seats. (Beige outside, blue within, because they had run out of the matching interior material. Beige seats had become *defitsitnyi*, around the time Igor Gerasimov got his car.)

'Have you got my bag?'

'In the boot. What have you got in there anyway? I know there's a book.'

'I can lend it to you.'

Balabin scoffed.

'Still at home then,' Marlinsky sniffed. Suddenly he shouted hysterically, as he insisted on opening the car window. 'You should be ashamed of yourself, professor! *Kak vam ni stydno!* We Russians allow ourselves books. Remember?'

Silence. And they were moving.

As they settled in Balabin evidently knew the driver. 'Good evening! I must say I wasn't expecting you, Matvei Vladimirovich.'

'Dad offered,' said a young, cocky voice. 'I said yes. It's a chance to drive the car. And—' he turned. 'This must be Boris Mikhailovich Marlinsky. Hi there!'

The detainee from the back seat nodded. 'Heh, what a car! I can see why you might want to drive it. Nought to a hundred in how many seconds?'

'Sixteen! Just imagine! Almost faster than that aeroflop crate you flew here in.'

'Now, now Matvei Vladimirovich…'

The reference to the national airline was not welcome but this young man didn't care about slander. 'Everyone calls it that. Not just in the West.' The driver addressed Marlinsky directly, 'Yeah, I drive it whenever I can. I did a ton on the way out.'

'The road police don't like that sort of thing, Matvei Vladimirovich,' groaned the professor.

'Goons! They won't touch me.'

'Don't say I didn't warn you.'

The *nomklat* boy had smart black leather boots and his Wranglers would have cost Marlinsky half a dozen forbidden books, twelve West German condoms and a hundred roubles in foreigners' store coupons.

'Where did you get your jeans? I've been looking everywhere for a pair.'

Shock in Marlinsky gave way now to euphoria. The chilly pine forest seemed to float on the air of a warm day slow to depart. The Russian forest lowered magically in the light of a technologically advanced pair of German headlights. There was a road, but it seemed as if the Mercedes were cutting a fresh path. From the woods came an intense fragrance. Marlinsky worshipped at the open window.

They were three men alone. Should he take the young driver in a headlock? He could have held down Balabin with one hand. But what could he have done with freedom won like that? He would need the car, he could steal it, but the car would mark him. He could lie low in the forest, but what would he do for food? No one lived out here. No man wants his rebellion to kill him unnoticed.

He was trying to piece together the journey so far. The single tarmac runway, with a two-lane road to nowhere, where only the sleek foreign car had waited, Now flying with its wings back like a crow through the night, it had a MOS number plate. (Tracking others, the idiots allowed themselves to be tracked.) It made sense to think they weren't far from their wild capital city.

'Close the window, it's cold,' insisted Balabin.

'It's always cold out here,' replied the driver, looking directly at Marlinsky in his mirror. 'I like it open. If he does.' He told Balabin: 'It keeps me awake.'

Marlinsky realised they'd embarked him on a flight not in the end to banish him but, by flying round and round, to impress a distance on him. To tell him he couldn't go back even if he was still in his native country. Slowly he turned the window chrome handle and watched the glass ascend like the end of a film. He needed his wits about him; not to be emotional.

'It is a bit chilly. How much longer?'

'About half an hour. You've something to look forward to, you know.' The Cuban-heeled Matvei wanted to be Marlinsky's friend, taking the tone he did.

The passenger intent on ordering his emotions resisted. 'I'll be the judge of that.'

'Suit yourself!'

As the car became the container into which they all of them emptied their confusions in silence, Balabin whispered to the driver; 'Vladimir Arkadcvich shouldn't have sent *you*.'

'Tell him then,' challenged the youth.

'You don't mind if I play some music? If I haven't got the fresh air it keeps me awake.' Matvei fed a recorded tape cassette into a post-box affair in the middle of the dashboard, where horizontal black plastic lips swallowed it. With a click sound eclipsed the silence. A voice that was ragged and irreverent was crooning what he felt about girls. Oh yes! Marlinsky, who had passed through several extreme emotions in the space of a few hours, shuddered a very different excitement now, belonging to a part of life he had not yet sufficiently explored.

Out of the pitch black of the surrounding fields and what seemed to be a bank of trees some house lights called. As they drew up a welcoming party waited in the open door. Marlinsky sniffed water nearby before he focused on whatever it was awaited him. For although an adult, he was being propelled into a situation of which he was entirely ignorant. He had no idea of his role.

'Welcome, Boris Mikhailovich!' The strangers in the doorway seemed somewhere between a search party and a family he was supposed to recognise but didn't. A stocky man with long hair greeted him as if he were indeed a relative, albeit one he hadn't seen for some time. Reluctantly Marlinsky gave up his hand to the alien grip. He felt the power of the man's forearms, and spied his strange haircut and the penetrating eyes that surmounted great drooping cheeks. Now this man introduced himself as Vladimir Arkadevich Korsakov.

'And this is my son and this my wife.' A slender woman, singled out, stood to one side. Truly she had a lovely figure in a slim grey skirt and a face that was alert and inquiring. In her presence instinctively Marlinsky realised he was still wearing the tracksuit he slopped about in at the dacha, and, his mother's son, felt ashamed. But Irina Korsakov didn't speak. She only faintly smiled as she surveyed his arrival. He filled in the missing words silently, that it was a great pleasure for her to meet him, and he knew that it wasn't, for she too —all of them, somehow, everyone present—were being forced into something.

Balabin, poor termite, eaten up from within, by whatever it was, ulcer or conscience, also kept his counsel as they were ushered indoors, a great deal of attention being given to Marlinsky's sports bag as the only luggage.

'Irina Matveyevna has prepared a banquet. Come, let's go through.'

At the back of the welcoming party stood a tall, thick-set older man, and a woman to whom the same description applied. They stepped forward and introduced themselves though he instantly forgot their names. Meanwhile, had Korsakov really announced that they were going to eat?

'It's the least we can do. Your prolonged journey was a little mistake on my secretary's part. I hope it didn't inconvenience you too much.'

How could anyone say anything so idiotic? It's true, some people are good at being insincere. But Marlinsky fell in with whatever was going on by simply nodding. 'The cherryade certainly made me sleep well.'

'Sparkling red wine from Crimea,' corrected Balabin.

'Ri...i...ght. Is that what it was. Yet more produce of our fine land.' Korsakov stood reflecting on the stupid subterfuge he had been forced into.

But then he too was not entirely master of his own fate. There was in Russia always another power above you, insisting your words and actions travel along deeply trodden, familiar, stupid paths. He was allowed to offer Marlinsky hospitality, but with the usual Byzantine conditions attached.

'Volodya, I'm sure our guest would like to freshen up.' Irina tried to soothe the situation. But what was the situation, other than the wish of Marlinsky, a good-looking young man kidnapped by a house party full of strangers, to go to bed? 'Let's take your bag and I'll show you the bathroom.'

It was the grandest bathroom he had ever seen, including in films. As for what he saw in the mirror, who was this scruffy intruder and what was he doing here? Under the shower his hands caressed a slippery orange ingot that bathed his senses in sandalwood. He rubbed his stubbly cheeks with it and smelt it on his dried palms. The women he knew smelt of carbolic mixed with a perfume called Lady Cosmonaut. He had to laugh, though the situation reminded him of poor Katya who had locked herself in the bathroom last new year, out at the dacha, after those brutes kicked her dog in the head. Lovely scent though. Only Galya, Alyosha's aunt, smelt of something equally exotic: roses from Bulgaria. Parts of his life lined up before his eyes.

When he found his way back downstairs Matvei lingered to show a Marlinsky still with wet hair to the dining room.

An irregular curvy chequerboard of smoked salmon and sturgeon, the lines as if distorted by a funfair mirror, the slices upon the board alternately the colour of blood orange and of the palest veal, passed from hand to hand. What a feast for the eyes that fish was! Surely Russian grannies, *babushki*, could have told the nation's future by reading those slices.

Irina was already stealing amused little glances at Marlinsky. She hoped he was both surprised and impressed. He was. Perhaps he was hallucinating.

The big man, the male half of the duo in the hall, spoke of the delights of foreign travel, much as Marlinsky had done, out of fear, as they drove from the dacha.

'Sorry, Sir, your name again?'

'Naumov, Kiril Innokentevich.'

'We call him Mr Vice-President.'

'Foreign travel, to resume…'

Marlinsky got the idea they felt foreign travel was a theme in *his* head which they would now draw out of him. He was on his guard.

'I've never been anywhere. Well, only to Sochi.'

Naumov with his brownish colouring must have been good-looking once, but now his face was so bloated that his tiny merry eyes struggled not to appear mere surface decorations. As he spoke he had the mouth of a choirboy. But perhaps that was because it could never open wide enough to appear in proportion to all that surrounding facial flesh.

'Myun-khen,' Naumov said, was his particular favourite.

'Oh yes. Professor Balabin speaks German, he was telling me.'

The Professor looked sullen. 'The Vice-President of the Academy speaks far better German than I do.'

A real high-up then, Lord!

The anecdote continued, about how that great Russian foot of his had once lingered 'several seconds already' in the devil's imprint in Munich's Frauenkirche, after which he had drunk a Bock in his shirtsleeves in a café on the Leopoldstrasse.

'Really, Kiril Innokentevich?' Irina was surely sarcastic in her turn.

That was the fantasy, Marlinsky realised. As if foreign travel were easy! As if they could tour the world at will. The fantasy they were telling themselves.

'I know who the devil is but what's a Bock?' Irina gently mocked.

'A Bock is a beer, Mama, in a tall glass.'

'We have them, if anyone would prefer beer to wine,' offered Korsakov. He couldn't remember being so happy for years. He was about to show a discerning young man just why he should give Russia another chance. Here, at a certain level, in a certain way, was a country crying out for his talents.

'I thought you preferred Italy, Vice-President,' said the Mack, whose full name was Anna Ivanovna Makarenko.

'Like the educator,' said Marlinsky recognising a famous name.

'My great uncle.'

Bastion of the early Soviet state then. Another high-up.

Naumov protested that he did love Italy. 'Only we can't always have what we want.' Others understood the reference. Recently Naumov had not been allowed to attend a conference in Florence.

'Florence is a woman. She would have seduced the Vice-President and we wouldn't have got him back.'

'Hah, that's why they didn't let him go. We need him here.' The speaker was a young man, Ivan Zolodei, who introduced himself as a dancer.

'Where do you dance?'

'I do mostly *gastroly* abroad.'

'Oh my! You must be very good. Where exactly?'

'Warsaw. Budapest. That sort of thing.' Dancing for the friends of Russia then; for the neighbouring countries THEY called 'the near abroad' and which had no choice but to be Russia's friends.

Marlinsky thought this Zolodei might not be a bad type. Here though he was confined to being one of a pair of clowns to amuse the company. His partner was an older man by the name of Zorin, and both were artists.

And where had he travelled? He asked the second artist.

Zorin had spent a week in East Berlin (where he had bought that boxy leather jacket he wore now. He had stood beside the Wall in a stupor.) In Warsaw meanwhile Zolodei had danced *Swan Lake* at the vast Palace of Culture. Balabin had also visited Warsaw and, as it happened, had made an excursion just a hundred kilometres east, to the town of Lublin, which, Mr Vice-President, since it has many of the touches of an Italian hilltop town, the exotic circumstances might well delight you.

So they needled each other.

Korsakov reminisced about the Boulevard Saint Michel and that little road leading from the metro, he forgot the name, ah yes, Sèvres Babylon, down to the Seine, where you could browse in the book barrows of the bouquinistes.

'Not Sèvres Babylon, Volodya, that's nowhere near the river. You mean rue de Berg.'

'Of course I do. Thank you, dear.'

When the conversation was not directly addressed to impressing Marlinsky—surely that was the aim—the guest's mind at 4am wandered along strange paths prompted by the sturgeon flesh. It looked like a slab of pale rock, or a tree trunk cut open. Any scientific mind must wonder where those complex patterns had come from. 'I think we are,' he made a note to himself, 'regardless of animal, vegetable or mineral, one slowly diverging species on earth, with trees mutating into stone, stone into fish, fish into human. Our existence can be stated as a mass of equations. But, just a moment: all for what? I would need my own private Darwin, my personal Einstein, or perhaps I should go back to Leibniz, and finally to Aristotle, to tell me *what for*, if not for love, for God, for freedom, for whatever we call the best we can do.'

'Mr Marlinsky?'

'As I said, I've been to Sochi.'

'Nothing wrong with the Black Sea. I sometimes go there just to eat fish,' said the Mack.

Marlinsky too had eaten the equivalent of fish and chips on the *chernoe morye*... He too had nothing to report. He even found the conversation grotesque.

'Nevertheless I am very fond of the Germans.'

'Oh, forget it, Mr Vice-President!'

'Oh yes...the charms and rigours of the intellect and at the same time...the cosiness of rural life. When I think of those little villages, Schwenningen, Schleichingen, Speichingen, dotted over the Schwabian hills, I cannot imagine a more enchanting setting for the best days of my life.'

'Does that mean we still have a chance of getting rid of you?' Matvei muttered at the opposite end of the table.

Irina put a finger to her lips.

Korsakov wondered, not for the first time, if his friend Naumov, so often impatient with Soviet crudity, would not have preferred to be a Nazi.

'Not that I do not admire Russia, but we must admit our climate is not good. I could go east, but that is not to my taste. I am a European at heart.'

That would do it. Nazis were Europeans too. He's just missed his moment in history. The Mack too. The times of Stalin would have suited her.

'And do you think Europe wants *us*?' Marlinsky suddenly wrenched off his napkin, stood up and addressed the table angrily. 'A people who can't keep their house in order without cracking the knout? You talk all this drivel and it hurts my ears. Europe is a free place.'

'Oh!' Balabin shuddered. Matvei kept his eyes on his mother.

Meanwhile Marlinsky thought: I'm glad I said that. On the other hand maybe *this* is what I'm here for. They want to see how someone behaves who's not like them at all. I'm their white mouse under the bell jar. He plunged into sudden bitterness.

'Your kind are always rude,' said the Mack, with a reproving glance at Korsakov, who should never be trying this experiment. 'You just don't know how to behave in polite society and so it starts.'

Bad behaviour, yeah, yeah, yeah.

'So you, Madame, at least realise we Russians are not wanted in Europe because of what the system you approve of has done to us,' Marlinsky insisted. 'You holiday at home and that shelters you. But even that is a lie. We Russians amuse ourselves beside a lake stolen from Finland. We ski in mountains borrowed from Georgia. And call the whole world our home, whether the world likes it or not.'

'Well, I never!' muttered Balabin.

The gross woman meanwhile was tucking into her eggs in cream, not listening. After a substantial mouthful, wiping her mouth with a napkin, she closed her eyes and clucked in disgust.

Korsakov held his glass up to the light and said something about the wine. 'Something else for which we need to go abroad, alas, albeit through no fault of our own.'

'S'right. We Soviet citizens don't have good wine. Only a factory substitute you can sometimes get at the kiosk.' Marlinsky, tired, was getting slightly drunk.

Irina began again: 'Where *I* too would like to visit is Italy.'

'It's not for the wine why she wants to go to Italy,' said Matvei. 'She's—'

'That's quite enough,' said Korsakov. 'Besides, isn't Italy in a terrible state of bloodshed and turmoil at the moment? Almost civil war with that railway station bombed and riot police in the streets of Milan. My dear, you can easily disabuse yourself of at least some of your illusions by reading a newspaper.'

'Oh yes, which one?' asked his son. 'Is there a New York Times or a Herald Tribune handy somewhere?'

'And your dreams, Mr Marlinsky?'

'I do have dreams, as it happens. I'd like to see this Russia of ours transformed—'

'Sold to the West, you mean…' That was the Mack.

'Of course not.'

There was some quarrel within the family now over what Matvei had said. But Marlinsky didn't know what they were talking about. He clung to their formality, the only fact he could discern. 'Madame, you permit me? It's very hot in here.' Was he serious, talking like that? Or was he adopting their tone, and parodying it? Probably the latter. He took off the tracksuit jacket, in which he felt like a bumpkin, and sat in his tracksuit bottoms and t-shirt, round a grand dining table, in a Soviet room furnished in antique pink and gold, with rather grand-looking nineteenth-century oil paintings on the wall, at 4am.

She smiled faintly.

'You have one advantage, Irina,' said her husband. 'You know foreign languages. You can read more than most of us and find out more about life in other countries.'

Which languages, Marlinsky asked.

She said she was more or less fluent in English, French and Italian, but not the German he evidently knew.

A young waitress in black appeared. She had a nice figure and a stylish short haircut. The more the night wore on the more Marlinsky had to wonder who these people were. Korsakov called the waitress Lisa and Matvei followed her with his eyes.

To Marlinsky's distress it was yet more food. Balabin took the occasion to slip away. He evidently had the right to do that, or wasn't afraid to disobey.

The teenaged Lisa brought in a huge side of beef, and a steaming bowl of crushed, yellowy potatoes, a Russian speciality that every non-cook the world over can imitate but not necessarily get right. Marlinsky tried to get himself in the mood by noting that the pickled tomatoes could never be as good as Nadya Kurakina's, By someone unseen two bottles of claret had meanwhile been opened and placed on the table, their corks beside them. The corks just lay there, like discarded limbs, at odd angles, on the white tablecloth, because Russians didn't know what to do with them.

'You know English too don't you, Mr Marlinsky?' It was the Greybeard, taking a rest from her grotesquely methodical treatment of the food on her plate.

'I—'

'You have some English acquaintances we're aware of. Did she bring you books?'

'Who are we talking about?'

'Your English visitor. Brought you copies of novels by writers we don't allow.'

Marlinsky denied any knowledge of any visit by any Western journalist.

'Nonsense! Tell us about the Englishwoman,' Makarenko hammered. Irina to Marlinsky's right took several large sips from her glass.

'I've nothing to say. I don't know what you're talking about.'

'These Westerners think they can come here and understand our country,' laughed Korsakov, 'Just by reading Pasternak. And Nabokov, for God's sake! They take *him* to be a Russian! He's long since become an American. Sold out on us.'

Irina stirred. 'Mr Marlinsky, we met Apollinaria Montenari. Do you know her?'

'I don't.'

Naumov chipped in: 'She's an Italian Communist who understands Gramsci.'

'You fancy her because she comes from Italy and she's stunning,' scoffed Matvei. 'Didn't you ask her for some postcards, Mr Vice-President? You're not interested in Gram-shee. Go on, admit it!'

As Marlinsky was pondering the weird nature of his adversaries, who all seemed to be at odds with each other, whatever they were instructed to feel about him, Makarenko shouted: 'And Meester Oyart *OO-eye-ld, heem* you know? *On vam pomogaet, ne pravda li?*'

She was suggesting Howard Wilde gave Marlinsky help.

'Normal human kindness,' he said. 'I like him.'

'And Meester Artur Tseemerman? *Chto s nim?*'

'Anna Ivanovna, please!'

'Comrades,' Irina stood up, 'I really think our guest must be tired.'

Of course he was, his condition aggravated by their making him travel in circles and then stuffing him like a goose at dawn. But his hostess too had had enough of their bullying, which was interfering with her dream of the graceful buildings of Florence and a stroll with her putative lover through the back streets of the Trastavere, a complex of feelings she was already inclined to transfer to the new guest.

'I'll show you to your room.'

Up a wide staircase she opened the door on an interior that he had only ever seen in a book or a museum. Though the walls were of a pale yellow, they did not draw from him the usual poisonous comparison. Though the green upholstery was faded, it was not by a chemical process that at best was part of a drive to make material life more comfortable for the Russian masses and at worst just foolish industrial showing-off. It bore the gracious mark of time. It was simply lovely.

He rested a hand on the polished surface of the chest of drawers where he might have stowed some more decent clothes, had he brought any with him.

'Walnut,' she said. The floor was also of polished wood.

'I've never tasted a walnut.'

'I'm sure I can get you some, if you'd like to try.' She smiled. 'I hear you're a writer, Mr Marlinsky. I hope you'll find the room comfortable. You might even write something while you're here.'

There was a small bureau under the window that had been laid out with writing materials. There was a packet of Swiss pencils and a steel sharpener, and beside them a stand with German ballpoint pens in four colours. A sizeable blotting pad prostrated itself before an English fountain pen, and a bottle of ink. The display was absurd. Who had researched the deep desires of the markmaker in him, he thought. It must have been that very special psychoscience of ours made them try to bribe me like this, by affirming me as what I am, in such a crude *material* way. He wanted to laugh out loud, but he saw she wanted to please him, just as her husband wanted to impress him. The top sheet of a sheaf of white paper was matte to the eye and silky to the touch. Every sheet beneath was of the same gorgeous pristine quality. He caressed them and flicked through them, and waited for her to leave, which eventually she did.

Beside the bed there was a bookshelf with, amongst lesser work, a volume of Tolstoy stories. But he was too tired to read, and the many thoughts he had in his head could wait. He'd already showered, and so, wrapped in a duvet, he lay down and slept.

Twenty-One

Irina would have liked to tell Marlinsky straight out. All of us dream of another country, Boris Mikhailovich. Volodya denies it, the Mack invents alternative planets, whereas my son and I, and our Mr Theory, Kiril Innokentevich Naumov, are more straightforward. My son Matvei wears everything American he can lay his hands on and longs to own a German car. Naumov alternates between Germany and Italy. He would take either. Italy is my love.

My other marriage is to this lovely house my father restored. Volodya used to say, when we first lived here and we were still in love, that like the gardens that run front and back of the house he thought his own temperament was poised between the classical and the romantic. An old-fashioned way to talk but it impressed me then. Nowadays I wonder whether he didn't marry me for the house, and I haven't stayed with him because of the house; though I find my temperament is embedded here too, in a quiet grandeur that gives me privacy.

Whatever is the state of grace I sometimes think I experience it here. I commune with the house when everyone is asleep. I read into the night and get up early to have it to myself. Every morning the drawing room offers itself to me as a cool and noble presence. In the company of the old civilisation, I commune with my father who introduced me to a land, and a happiness, our Russia could never match, he said. Still I never quite believed that. One day we will be a great country again, surely!

Whatever you think of me, Boris Mikhailovich, all I want is to be free of constraints. I'm not unpatriotic, but I still have certain hopes.

She wanted to open his door and wake him up as soon as she opened her eyes. But she confined herself to a tap on the outside at eight, and then her husband took over.

'Good morning, Boris Mikhailovich. Did you sleep well? Wouldn't you like some breakfast?' Korsakov was waiting at the foot of the staircase like a traffic policeman. Evidently there was no choice but for Marlinsky to head for the dining room again, this time alone. 'Just tea,' he replied. Korsakov made a gesture. Lisa brought a china cup and an English teapot.

Korsakov pushed a plate of breakfast cakes in his guest's direction. 'They're what the French called madeleines. In any case, when you've finished we'll join the others in the library.'

Marlinsky watching Lisa and Korsakov leave the room felt *embarrassed* at these people, and therefore for himself. 'We are all Russian.' They, who had taken refuge in luxury, had taken him prisoner, to some mysterious end.

Korsakov situated the interrogation in the library. That choice was a 'device', a *priyom*, or a 'mechanism', whether he was aware of it, or not. Silently Irina parsed her husband's unconscious desires: to associate the present day with the noble volumes of the past, and thus make it seem less wretched. He had something decent in him, but it was long buried.

She hoped those packed *ottocento* shelves, recently catalogued by his old professor—another refuge-seeker, for God's sake—would give Marlinsky courage.

'We can't understand why you hate your country.' Naumov began. In a cruder world Volodya and the Mack would have held Marlinsky's arms while Naumov slapped sense into him.

'It's not true. I don't hate my country,' he murmured. 'I love it more than you do.'

'You're a friend of Russia's enemies. This much we established last night.'

He shook his head. 'It's rubbish what you imagine on my behalf. You're paranoid.'

'You're pleading you don't know Meester *OO-eye-ld* and Mees Dzhels Meibi?' The middle-aged choirboy with the piggy eyes and the open-necked shirt and the plastic shoes pretended to be incredulous.

'It's Why-ld, Comrade Academician,' Irina intervened, 'Like the famous Irish writer.' She was not sitting at the table but standing to one side, as if exercising her right to be present not as a co-accuser but as the owner of the house.

'Is that so?' Naumov conceded. 'Very well! With these non-phonetic languages you never can tell!' He looked into the distance.

The Mack began; 'She's a nice woman, eh, that Dzhels Meibi? You might marry a girl like that.'

'I don't believe she has any interest in me. In my friend, perhaps. Every woman likes him.'

'The daughter of a wealthy and powerful capitalist makes you an offer you can't refuse, no?'

'She's done nothing of the kind.'

'She offers to get you out of this country.'

'Nonsense. This is my country. I'm happy here.'

'You did seem rather perturbed at leaving it,' drawled Balabin, 'though frankly a man like you would be far better off abroad.'

'Oh yes, like Reikhman?'

'He was a fool.'

'A fool for the good life. For the truth.'

The memory of Reikhman took away Marlinsky's self-control for a moment. He turned on Korsakov. 'A mistake on your secretary's part, Colonel, that fantasy trip last night? Don't condescend to me!'

'You are such a complicated fellow, Boris Mikhailovich. All we did is enact one of your wish-dreams. Your friend is a psychiatrist. Ask him what it means.'

'Leave my friends out of this.'

'Your journey last night was a prelude to the fascinating scenario of which you are now part. All of your own wishing.'

To see Russia as one country again? To see this terrible secret division exposed? For a moment he wondered.

'You're a writer, aren't you?'

'You think I'm taking notes?'

'I would, given the chance. Have you got a girlfriend?'

Marlinsky drifted off, staring from a distance at the books on the towering shelves.

'Mr Marlinsky, don't you want to answer the Colonel? He asked you about some girlfriend.'

'My private life has got nothing to do with you.'

'Ah, so you haven't.'

'I can't take on family responsibilities in my position.'

The Mack changed tack. 'You made a personal friend of our Professor Balabin here. When you were at the university.'

'No I didn't.'

'Were you obliged to reject his advances?'

'Of course not.'

Naumov interjected: 'Balabin was a friend of Professor Reikhman.'

'That's as may be. Anatoly Pavlovich had many friends.'

'You don't say, a man with a warped brain like that!'

'He was brilliant. Russia lost a good man there.'

Balabin sat silently spluttering and Korsakov took no part.

'Didn't you, Boris Mikhailovich, in fact, model yourself on Reikhman?' He hadn't thought. Perhaps he had.

Naumov read from a file: 'You were found guilty of "behaviour not conducive to responsible study." For which you were expelled from the university.'

Marlinsky banged his hand on the table quite unexpectedly. 'Reikhman taught me philosophy. He taught me the good life. Ever heard of Aristotle? You're idiots.' He reflected on what he had just heard. 'Behaviour not conducive...that's just the kind of pseudo-legal formula you would come up with.'

'Pseudo-legal, eh!' muttered Naumov. 'You'll see.'

Marlinsky stared out of the beautiful floor-to-ceiling window. Irina said the house dated back to 1810.

The Mack resumed: 'What sort of life do you lead? We'd like to know who you are. Agreed it's a nice day outside. But we'd like an answer.'

'I read. I do jobs round the house. I see my friends.'

'Would you say your life was socially useful?'

'No, but whose fault is that?'

Korsakov spoke at long last: 'You have no job.'

'You took away my research. Now I would like to teach.'

'Apparently you're not suitable. Report from SOVUCH.'

'They must know.'

'It's says here too that you're sarcastic.'

Makarenko continued: 'You're idle, Mr Marlinsky. In our country we do not find idlers useful citizens.'

'I would teach, if I were allowed to.'

'You're a young wastrel. You don't work, you don't earn, you have no idea how to serve your country. You're a parasite!' The Mack threw back her grey head.

'You've certainly set yourself on a solitary path, Boris Mikhailovich,' said the porcine Academician, as if wanting to be kind. 'I couldn't do it. I'd be too lonely. Why did you make this Robinson-Crusoe-like choice to live alone? I suppose your parents neglected your social education.'

'Leave my parents out of this!'

'Children want for nothing and still they go off the rails,' said Korsakov, despite himself, for they could all hear Matvei's music pounding somewhere in the house.

The Mack again, as if she were preparing notes for a new plot: 'How did you make contact with Western agents? Was it Reikhman? Or Razumovsky? Who took the Report on our Psychological Institutions out?'

Did they really not know? he wondered. They'd almost killed Galya Obolonskaya tracing that work's Russian career. 'You know full well.'

Irina trembled inwardly.

'In any case, our constitution says we have freedom of speech and freedom of expression.'

'Perfectly true,' said Korsakov. 'But please also note that "Exercise of rights and freedoms is inseparable from the performance of citizens' duties and obligations. Citizens are obliged to safeguard the interests of the state, and to enhance its power and prestige. Defence of the motherland is the sacred duty of every citizen. Betrayal of the motherland is the gravest crime."'

The pages, as Korsakov turned and read from one to the next, had been bookmarked in advance.

Marlinsky sat in silence.

'But what if I told you that your actions could be forgotten, what would you say?' Korsakov suddenly changed to the familiar version of 'you'.

Marlinsky didn't speak.

'Can you not speak? We're asking you whether you would like to be a free man, Boris Mikhailovich,' stated Naumov testily.

'I don't want anything you offer.'

'We'd like you to change your friends. Choose a clearer path in life.'

'No chance.'

'But you can't follow your old course. You've broken the law!'

'I'll find a course for myself.'

'You'll miss your Alyosha and your little Sasha.'

'You can't take them away from me.'

Of course they could. That outcome he couldn't begin to think.

'You're already in hiding. Look at you!'

But, even as they stared at him as one team, heh, wasn't that Matvei's favourite anti-capitalist song Marlinsky could hear in the dim distance of an upstairs room? Matvei liked 'Money Money' because it was raucous; because, whatever the words said, it stirred the visceral passions. Perhaps those would be the people who would one day stage a second revolution and destroy people like his father. And he loved Burn Baby Burn because he couldn't bear the prison he lived in.

'Through your support for Comrade Professor Razumovsky you give the impression our system is malevolent—'

'You would have to apologise publicly, of course. Write some story of how you were misled…'

You should let the whole world know how we are *trapped*, reflected Irina. 'So we'll leave it there for now.' Korsakov stood up. 'My dear boy! Good to talk to you. Thank you for being so frank.' Arseholes the lot of them, Marlinsky thought.

'Now is when your weekend begins. We like our guests to have a nice time. We can offer you almost any diversion you like.'

'Whaa-t?'

'It's how we do it,' whispered Irina.

Chess with Balabin? A walk? A Hollywood film? A Swedish film? Marilyn Monroe or Ingrid Bergman? A horse ride? A horse ride! Korsakov caught up with him on the terrace, where, finding no hindrance, he wandered out, for it truly was a lovely day. 'Brandy? Coffee? Both? On the terrace?' Marlinsky accepted a black coffee.

'You see, Mr Marlinsky, what I wish most in the world is for this country not to waste another generation of its good people. We are, frankly, in awe of your talents. We only ask that you work with us and not make fools of us, the way you have been doing.'

Marlinsky stirred his coffee and drank it with a pleasurable shudder. From Brazil? From Africa? We'll buy your coffee and even build you a train line if only you will support us against the West.

'How can I work with you, Mr Korsakov? You're all liars. I've never met so many liars. Mendacity is an illness here. The way you brought me here—'

'Look, I *am* sorry about last night. I've heard people say the lie is in our Russian genes. But sometimes there's a reason for that. A man in my position…I can't explain now.'

'But it's not sometimes, is it? It's every day. It's a great moral sickness.'

'That's very harsh.'

'And you forbid me to say it.'

'Not exactly. We need different leadership. Different laws. Honest judges. A scrupulous press. Otherwise nothing's ever going to change. So work with us. Teach us to love the good Russia. All we need is love.' Korsakov twitched. 'But I'm keeping you from Matvei. I know he's waiting for you.'

God what a house that was, with its imitation Greek statues, and aura of timeless peacefulness! Even those rich Russians from way back only stayed because they owned these great houses and had serfs to work for them.

From the terrace Marlinsky made his way to the romantic sprawl behind the house, which led to the river. He might even like to ride a horse, they said. A horse! Again he was incredulous. That might have brought him time with Irina. But with Matvei he felt he had something important to do, so he chose the quadbike option.

'Hi there! Good to see you, Boris Mikhailovich,' the son of the house called delightedly. The Wranglers suited his stocky build. Over them he wore a t-shirt and a camouflage jacket.

'What exactly is a *kvadrotsikl*?'

'It's great. You'll see.'

Together they headed towards the ivy-covered ruin of an outbuilding. As Marlinsky pushed up the sleeves and unzipped the tracksuit jacket into a deep V—for it was turning into an unseasonably hot day—he thought he caught sight of Irina at an upstairs window.

'You'll need a crash helmet here. Got a driving licence?' Matvei shouted excitedly, uncovering two giant-sized toys under tarpaulin wraps in the outhouse. 'Ha!'

Marlinsky peered at the steering and patted one of the huge tyres. 'No and you haven't got one either. But you're a great driver, Matt. Wow, last night on that quiet road! Nought to a hundred in sixteen seconds.'

'It's true. I'm such a good driver I don't need one.'

'You ought to get one, all the same.'

Matvei scowled. 'Just remember who you are and don't dare tell me off.'

Marlinsky shrugged and the volatile boy moved on. 'We won't get even sixty out of these Ami crates!' He kicked the one nearest him. 'But they're not bad.'

Unlike their description the *kvadrotsikly* had six wheels, but that made them exceptionally stable and tough. The tyres were huge, rising up to Marlinsky's elbows.

'Attex Superchief All-Terrain Vehicle...' Marlinsky had played tank-drivers and moon-landers in his time. But this Attacker, as they tugged it free of its wraps was—well, he'd never seen such a vehicle before and he was just as excited as Matt.

'Race you to the river!'

The steering was light, the suspension robust. Marlinsky got to the path beside the water first, a natural stop line. But he simply shot over...into the water!

'Eeeh, we float, we're amphibious. C'mon!'

Matvei did a U-turn, gave himself a long run in, full throttle, and not exactly soared into the water but plopped in and floated. They switched off the engines.

He turned to Matvei. 'So this is where you live. Where is it?' The lush, sheltered, lightly undulating countryside was surely reserved for *nomklats*.

'You won't have been here. It's a closed area.'

'On the road to Mozhaisk, I noticed last night.'

'Yeah.'

Marlinsky enjoyed the unseasonal sun on his face. It turned the water blue. 'Didn't Napoleon pass through?'

'When it wasn't closed, you mean?' Matvei grinned. 'The Germans came here too. That's why this place was wrecked. Still, pops loves the past and he's trying to restore it.'

Marlinsky fell into his trademark sarcasm. 'But isn't your father building socialism for the future?'

'You know what? If only you hadn't been such a swot at school they wouldn't go for you the way they do.'

'I'm not going to apologise. It's fantastic out here. But it doesn't belong to our way of life.'

Matvei shrugged. 'That's how it works.'

'Hardly fair, is it?'

'It's not for me to say.'

'You'd still leave, if you could, wouldn't you?' Matvei stared moodily as Marlinsky went on. 'Most of Russia wants to leave, and you're part of that. Your father wants to make use of me because everyone else is leaving. In the West they call it a brain drain. All the best people are finding a way to leave Russia. Don't you want that?'

'And you?'

Marlinsky stared back into the boy's eyes. 'No. I want to make things better here.'

'That's mad! *Ty s uma soshol.*' Matvei was seventeen.

'They may send me out. Stick me somewhere abroad like they did to Reikhman, and Mundt. But it's more likely they'll send me to a *psykhushka*. Will you mind seeing that happen?'

The boy turned away. He was ready to cry. 'They're cruel. They're all liars. I'll never get away.'

Marlinsky would have put a hand on his shoulder but they were in separate craft, floating on the blue water.

'Maybe you will, maybe you won't.'

'Is that all you can say? I thought you were a writer.'

'You want me to write you your life story with a happy end? All I can say is you'll need an education if ever you're to sort out where you come from and where you can go.'

The boy shook his head. 'I can't be bothered with that. Anyway an education is where they lie to us most.'

'Matt, believe me, I got through *their* education. So you can. They can fix it but not all of it. One day you will get out of here and then you'll need to know what to criticise, and what to fear, and how to lead a proper life. Don't mess it up.'

The boy blinked. 'Whatever.' He had a packet of Marlboro, which he opened and took out a cigarette.

'See?' Out from the dashboard of his supercraft emerged a magic stick that glowed red. He lit one cigarette and then the other, handing it to Marlinsky across the water.

'Magic.'

'Everything they make over there is BETTER. More efficient. More fun. More modern. Our industry is ridiculous.'

'Doesn't mean to say you can't enjoy life here.' Back and forth they went. Marlinsky liked his companion. He blew smoke rings to impress him. 'Still your plan is to live over there one day. Is that what you and Lisa dream about?'

The thought of his girlfriend bucked up the boy's spirits. 'We make fun of these awful people my mum and dad hang out with. That lady writer! What crap!' Matvei put on a high, imperious voice. '"My adventures are set in the highly developed technological society of the future. When you work in another galaxy, the chance of ever meeting the beloved again is a billion to one. Yet work, duty to the motherland call." Complete crap. Then there's that evil Comrade Academician. He'd be a Nazi if he could. He's just a bit late. Then there's the professor. My mum feels sorry for him. But he's a nasty type too.'

'I imagine there are lots of bad people in the West as well.'

'Yeah, but—here we make them like that. Over there, surely, people have more choice.'

'Study hard then. That's your best chance of getting out. Times will change. This country's already on its knees as it is.'

'If I have to do it through school it won't happen. I'm not like you.'

'Do it and don't be so damned lazy! There are some of us who are trying to make things happen here. The old men can't go on forever.'

'Plenty of younger ones to take their place. Look at my Dad.'

'No, no, it doesn't have to be like that. Read Okudzhava! Read Okudzhava on what's wrong with us. You can marvel that at least one man can see it all clearly… You'll get things clear for yourself.'

'I can't read all that.'

'Yes you can. I'll give it to you.' The boy sighed.

'Race you in and out again!'

They raced and raced again. But then because its waterborne activity was not the best part of the Attacker's repertoire, Marlinsky suddenly abandoned it, stripped off and hurled his body into the freezing water.

Was Irina still watching?

He stared back up the incline at the luxurious house and asked himself who were these people who threatened to put him in prison or deport him if he didn't join them. Who were these vicious people living in a fantasy. Truth told, they were living their own private Russian version of a rich man's 'West'.

Which showed just how bizarre it was to ask after Marlinsky's contacts in the West, when the West figured largest of all in their own perverted imagination.

Eventually he and Matt drove their vehicles back to the shed and replaced the tarpaulin.

'Thank you for a fine day, partner.'

His host's son steered him towards the buffet lunch in the dining room. 'It's just help yourself on a day like this.'

Afterwards, having carried a plate of sandwiches up to his room, Marlinsky slept for several hours. It was the room where Irina hoped he would begin writing the perverse and tortured truth of her life. But all he did, when he awoke, was stroke that luxurious paper.

'Boris Mikhailovich?' No sooner did he emerge to get himself a beer and it was Korsakov. 'I'd just like to show you something.' He led the way to yet another room which turned out to be his study. 'Excuse the mess.'

Of course the house occupied a lovely spot in nature. 'Look, look, I want to show you something.'

The painting showed a fence with a lock on it.

'It's a Rukhin. Another one I rescued from the art show.'

'You *rescued* it. But wasn't it you—'

'I can't control the people who work for me, Boris Mikhailovich. That's the truth of the matter.'

It was a work of art, and the style was not the usual socialist realism. The lock was the main feature, not enlarged, but in the centre of a canvas featuring a fence and that otherwise might have seemed empty. The flat fence dominated the picture plane. But then the paint brought it alive so you knew exactly what that fence felt like; how people lived it. The thick, uneven, whitish surface was mightily distressed. It looked old and rough, solid and yet full of weak spots, and gaps, as one paint trace faded into the next. A smear of dirt. Some surface ripped by a thorn. A line slashed by a knife.

That at last was true.

Over the meal and into the mid-evening, just as yesterday they had talked of foreign travel, so tonight there was indeed talk of art. There were those classical paintings on the walls, classical statues loomed gracefully on the terrace, art was definitely a theme out beyond the Mozhaisk Road.

Irina whispered, as they milled around the sideboard where the first course of dinner was served to them standing up, that all this talk of art was just a code in which they talked to each other. Yet the exchanges surprised Marlinsky.

'Zolodei, was it?'

The unashamedly beautiful dancer puffed up his feathers.

'So you manage to get abroad somehow. I admire your effort.'

'They'd hobble us like camels if they could.'

When they sat down the overbearing Italophile, the Nazi born too late, began, like someone who was bound to make the first move on the board. 'Art and love are what matter. Is there anyone here who would disagree with me?'

Naumov spoke of Goethe. Irina, who was enjoying the wine, chipped in with Dante.

'Italy, always Italy,' said her husband a tad sourly, holding his wine up to the light. 'Everyone here loves Italy. Is that to do with art?'

'They've got a brand of Communism that works.'

'They practise it, as they say, *con garbo*.'

'The chic way.'

'Apparently you have to consult all the people. That's what Gram-shee said.'

'But that would never do for us.'

Korsakov fascinated Marlinsky with his contradictions. He had told him: 'I do have that show on my conscience, Boris Mikhailovich. But then there were so many so-called artists there making a fool of me. So much of it wasn't art! It was children's doodling and adolescent bodging! I believe I rescued what was good. Though even this Rukhin must be imitating someone in the West. Our artists, even the real ones, are stuck with that.' Marlinsky had replied: 'I don't think Rukhin is imitating anyone. That's our world on that canvas. These still-lifes—this magnificent example you have here—are of a world drenched in concrete dust and locked up and left to die. Look how he has drawn red lines across these terrible images, as if forbidding them or deleting them from some invisible catalogue of what a good nature might once have been. Believe me, I can read a painting. Rukhin was saying these objects died for their country.'

Now though, back in company, all Korsakov could do was joke. 'Why do I have you and that dancer out here for weekends? To tell me the truth about art! Ha ha ha.'

Marlinsky said to Zorin across the table: 'Don't I know your name?'

'Oh I'm broken. Like one of those old fences.' Zorin laughed. 'You probably know my name from "Lenin descending a staircase".'

'I do. I know it well.' The work had served as a model in schools of what Soviet art should be.

'You should look up close. It's subtler than you realise. Lenin has no staircase to walk down.'

'Next time I get the chance. But now…'

'I've got this collage on the go. The faces of the twentieth century.'

'The one like the Beatles' album.'

'With the Kennedys on it. But THEY'll like it. And it buys me time.'

'And you, Boris Mikhailovich, as a writer you evidently feel that you too serve the causes of art and love, and truth,' Naumov broke into Marlinsky's reflections.

'I certainly think that from beauty and love and art we take our highest inspiration, as human beings. And that inspiration is the search for truth.' It seemed unusual for a humble student to be telling this to the vice-president of the Academy of Sciences.

Naumov pursed his fat lips. 'Never mind if the kind of art you're talking about distances us from our present social reality.'

'Never mind if it does.'

'I don't see why we *all* have to have the same taste,' said Irina, who did not want to miss the chance to speak for herself. For she was not like Marlinsky. Only keen to take advantage of his presence to say what she might not otherwise have the chance to express. A simple feeling: I am here on earth too and there is a life I would like to lead.

'In Russia we do have to be the same or else things fall apart.' Korsakov finally realised the arrival of his chosen outsider had left his circle quite disturbed.

So then Lisa, a neat and fashionable young woman, with a lively face, entered just like last night, but this time in a waitress's black-and-white uniform, with a very short skirt, and set on the table a whole roasted sucking pig, with pickled apples and kasha. As Korsakov scraped out the last of his mushrooms in cream, Irina stood up and began slicing the crisp and steaming flesh.

As they dined at the laden table, enclosed by rose-pink walls, in the presence of those old paintings, works that no one looked at anymore, but whose disposition in gilded frames was somehow friendly and welcome, Makarenko silently helped Irina distribute the generous portions. The food was rich, the vintage wine superb.

Marlinsky took stock. They wanted to make him one of the family, and even of the Progress Group, and what that involved was to inherit the insoluble problems they were discussing, along with all the passions and disappointments and dreams of escape that set the family and the Group against each other. The only condition was to say nothing about it to the West.

He became aware he was expected to make a pronouncement. Everyone was waiting. ('They thought that offering me a place in the system would redeem them. Suddenly they needed me.')

One truth was obvious, he said. 'We are, as a nation, withering and dying, because truth doesn't matter to us. Because long ago we retreated into a morass of fabrication to replace it. Fabrications to make us believe we belonged to the greatest nation on earth. The most just, the cleverest, the most artistic, the most moral, and, one day, perhaps the wealthiest too.' He wrenched off the napkin politeness had persuaded him to tuck into the collar of his t-shirt for the second night in a row, and stood up and addressed them: 'Do you know what, ladies and gentlemen, our country is dying of a disease called purely theoretical terms, and it's the fault of all of us.'

Makarenko shook her head but stayed silent. He even had the impression she was mentally taking notes.

All this while Matvei must have been plucking up his courage. 'We should listen to Boris Mikhailovich because he *can* tell us. We have to open ourselves to the West. To love the West honestly. We'll all die if we don't.'

But the conversation wasn't going the way Korsakov had planned and after a while, since they didn't know what to do or say next, it was as if he too tired of the strain of being open-minded. For it led to nothing but disputes and recriminations.

'I wish to hear no more of this mindless speculation, Matvei. We have nothing in common with the capitalist world.'

Irina said: 'But you can't just tell freedom to keep out.'

'People don't have rights here,' said Matvei. 'That's why we should all go to America where they do.'

'Artists are stifled. It's impossible to be an artist!'

'But look at Rukhin—'

'He died.'

'The universities are in a straitjacket. Ask our poor professor here!'

'I don't know the answer,' said Marlinsky. 'We can only start by being honest.'

Irina said to Matvei: 'Darling! Didn't you have something to show us? We are at least free to dance.'

Next moment her son and Lisa were setting up an enormous black sound system.

'Japanese?'

'South Korean.'

Korsakov called for *shampanskoe* and soon the necks of fat green bottles were spuming into the air as everyone helped clear the dishes. Irina appeared with fresh glasses and some bowls of wrapped chocolates that Lisa had prepared in the kitchen.

'Move the table back against the wall!'

'Who's dancing? Come on, Boris Mikhailovich!'

To Chubby Checker Irina and Marlinsky did the twist in the bright overhead light from the chandelier.

('Our ideologists considered dimmed lights decadent. So we danced in bright light.')

Oh well, said Naumov. 'Madame, this dance, if you please.' He and the Mack tried a chachacha to something upbeat by The Supremes. Incredibly Balabin asked Lisa. 'Show me how, my dear! I've still time in my life to learn.' Sitting watching the dancing Zorin and Zolodei lit their respective smokes.

After all, no one expected Zolodei to dance *here*, with them!

'Now watch!' cried Matvei, targeting the dancers on the dance floor. First the lights faded then they passed the dancers rapidly through a spectrum of colours. The spectacle fragmented like the clown suit of a Picasso Harlequin.

'Someone in the ministry got it from West Germany. Isn't it brilliant?' Matvei addressed himself specifically to Naumov, before plunging the room into near-darkness and out again, into an inferno of red. 'They're called strobe lights! Go on, everyone, dance again.'

Which they did, with Matvei beaming patterns of light on them. Now the lights flickered in silent machine-gun bursts.

'Oh, that's enough!' cried the Mack. 'My head hurts. I might fall over. Matvei Vladimirovich, is this not their latest weapon in the West, designed to undo us?'

She was possibly even joking.

Korsakov signalled to Lisa to switch the music off for a rest. Everyone smoked again. Marlinsky finding himself holding Irina, became self-conscious.

Then she, Korsakov, Naumov and Makarenko all disappeared, like the King and Queen and their courtiers, leaving the commoners to wonder what next.

Twenty-Two

We sat like nomads, spread out, arms outflung, eyes half-shut, drinking iced vodka, and the firm, fresh salted pickles cracked with a crunch on our teeth. We were silent, reliving our lives for the hundredth time, fishing from the depths the same shining splinters, now beginning to fade, covered with the weeds of forgetfulness. Once in a while we would exchange a look, and then Myatlev's sudden bewitching and slightly guilty smile would flash at me, as though we had both been thinking about the same thing and he was embarrassed by his memories.

Oh, if that miracle were only possible! But we enlightened men are not inclined to superstition and do not seem to place any hope in miracles. Yet, if you were to dig deeper in our souls, you would certainly find something borrowed from our naïve and uneducated ancestors and see hope for a possible miracle glimmering in our cold and calculating consciousness. I secretly imagined that a sudden healing of Myatlev, the crossing of his earthly path with my sister's, a benign attitude of the gods, and God's goodwill would unite their hearts and cleanse their spirits. Actually if it weren't for his eternal and incurable torment and her vow to live a solitary life, and if he were capable of loving deeply and strongly, and she could allow herself to break her vow--

—but there are no miracles.

Above us an alien, distant land spread across the entire wall, and a long-gone time completed its sad orbit, and the small cluster of doomed, high-cheeked natives was still not thinking of its imminent and inexorable end. And there, in that crowd of the condemned, stood the man with the European face, with a high brow and a gaze whose nobility hid a sense of death and powerlessness before the harshness of nature. The conquistadors with evil faces were crawling up to them from the left side of the canvas, already imagining the belated cries of the wounded, and the moans of the dying, and the dusky cold bodies. Their dirty, louse-ridden lace-collared jackets and their boots with wooden buckles gave them a sense of superiority and courage. Their bearded, unwashed faces seemed to them the epitome of perfection. Slaves in their homeland, trained to depend and beg, often beaten and mocked by the aristocrats, they dreamt of power and rushed eagerly to achieve it ...

Gentlemen, our pride and our cultivated bloodlines, refined upbringing and exquisite manners, our preference for philosophy and the noble twinkling of our eyes—all this does not guard us from the insatiable microbe of servility, which penetrates our souls by the most amazing paths. What are the preventative methods against it, and what does salvation promise us? Could it be that mankind, perfecting itself, is incapable of withstanding this absurd organism that is eating away at the tribe of man? Look around and at yourself. In our presumptuous passion we fail to notice that the contagion has touched us as well, and here in our golden age, when ships are powered by steam and we are transported by smoking, speeding locomotives instead of capricious and fragile carriages, when the thoughts of mankind are directed to the skies in the hope of giving us wings, in our golden age when literature has already reached its zenith in the line of both Alexander Pushkin and our present genius, Turgenev, whose works will never be surpassed, could it be that in our golden age, secretly hating our brothers, like our uneducated ancestors, we, too, try to establish ourselves at their expense, and that envy, hatred, and passion are the only things we have? Where is perfection then? In what? In our clothes? In our ability to tip our top hats? Our souls are empty and our eyes cold confronting another life. From early childhood we sharpen our weapons against one another, each of us hoping secretly that he will be the lucky one and that fate will bring him to power over everyone else. And that trifling microbe, eating away at our insides, forces us to be hypocrites and to lie, wheedle, and finesse until we can get close enough to stick the knife into our enemy's soft back and, after dancing on the corpse, to proclaim ourselves the only one. ...We carry an arsenal of tried and true methods: lying, calumny, toadying—all of which are more terrible than the knife. And it's always like that. What is civilisation? Why doesn't it ennoble us, cleanse us, heal us? In all ages and times there are born lone geniuses who are not concerned with the thirst for power over others and become the victims of their brothers, who in turn swear to their holiness as they gather to perform the next vile deed. History moves on, civilisation flourishes and proudly shows only its façade, behind which, in dark corners, helpless geniuses are still murdered, squeezed, and robbed of the fruits of their tormented, inspired and brief lives.

Twenty-Three

'Am I disturbing you?'

'You've been disturbing me since I first saw you.'

Unable to sleep, he had been reading the Okudzhava for the last time, before passing it on.

She stood there barefoot in a white slip and a dusky pink housecoat. The housecoat was knitted and misshapen and her toenails were painted to match. As if she had removed her mask. Alyosha said women did that, when they really loved you. Otherwise love is just a power struggle.

He took his clothes off the chair so she had somewhere to sit. 'Please.' As if he were the owner of the room. As if he were her equal. 'Irina…' He was glad she had a name.

'Did you have a hand in this strange experiment they're wreaking on me? I've been touched by your support—'

'There was always the risk you would be rude and ungrateful. My husband is trying so hard to please you.' She was close to weeping.

'He's certainly tried. I just don't see what can come of it.'

'Boris Mikhailovich I don't want them to hurt you!' It was a passionate cry and he wrapped his arms around her, really out of confusion.

'What can come of it, given the man I am. I'm not an actor looking for a part. I'm a person.'

'Yes. We—we love you for it.'

In that beautifully appointed room so strange to him they stood like planets, normally far distant from each other, surprised to find themselves in each other's orbit.

'I wouldn't want you to think….'

'Irina Matveyevna, I really don't…' he waved a hand, but neither of them moved.

'Boris Mikhailovich...' and now they were circling like dancers in slow motion. Her left hand rested on his waist. Her right hand he pressed to his shoulder. 'This can't be a secret.'

'You and I are used to nothing being secret.'

She took him by the hand; led him through that house on which her survival depended. At the centre the architects of long ago had built a balustrade, and this they now walked down.

('We Russians are a very theatrical people.')

He supposed that the grand staircase in old houses reflected the moment long ago when the gods descended to sort out human action on the stage below. 'All our houses are also stages for the gods to descend.'

So they descended the grand staircase of the well imagined life. It wasn't cold outside due to the unseasonal high pressure but the sky was clear and she was lightly dressed. Boris put the tracksuit jacket around her shoulders.

'You could transform our entire country, Irina Matveyevna, with your magic.'

'Don't think...'

'I'm not thinking. We've all done so much talking.'

'You were out here this afternoon with Matvei. I saw you from the window.'

'You were my beautiful lady at the window.' He took off his shirt. This was madness.

'Is this...?'

'How can I feel free inside that house. Only in your arms—'

'It's a refuge for all of you, but it's—'

'—a refuge for each of us separately. For as long as we can make it go on. There isn't anything else.'

'My dear.' He laid the shirt on the grass. 'At least there are no insects in April.'

He caressed her. All his instincts strained towards her. They wafted off him in a stream of animal warmth she could feel and smell. So now they were describing what they felt, and there was this 'we' that had not been there before that made them both so happy.

'Today the whole of summer has flowered in a few hours.'

It was not that she gave herself to him. She was far too proud. She straddled him. She took herself to him and he hungrily accepted. Wearing just the tracksuit top she put on an act for him. Her body told him of all the frustrations of a half-life, his too.

He loved her in that moment. He liked what she did and he wanted them to be a normal couple who were hungry and delirious, and who wouldn't care who photographed them and who would get the blame.

Only a cat was watching. The ragged, timid, curious, glass-eyed creature sat and stared.

'What does he think?'

'That you're magnificent.' Irina wept on his shoulder.

'You'll get cold.'

'Not if you hold me.'

'There's that tarpaulin in the quad bike shed. Put the shirt on while I fetch it.'

'A tarpaulin!'

He stood there naked and delicious, caught in the moonlight. 'Irina Matveyevna, this is Russia. We make do. Tsshsh!'

When he returned the heavy waterproofed canvas cover was hard and smelt of engine oil.

'Like building a hut around us.'

'We're still naked.'

'We'll always be naked in each other's presence. That's how it should be. Adam and Eve.'

'You make it sound frightening.'

'Maybe.'

They lay there, but not entirely comfortably, and to that post-coital calm which everyone knows there was an edge that excluded laughing at themselves.

'Volodya's not a bad man. He's just—'

'His plan was absurd. However did he think he would persuade me?' With her, he wondered, just for a moment. 'Persuade me to do, to be what?'

'To work for them. To be their eyes and ears wherever you go. Especially if you go abroad.'

'And ruin my life! Besides I don't want to leave. I have work to do here.'

'You may have ruined your life anyway.'

Of course it was frightening. At the same time it felt right.

'And you, Irina my darling. How will it be for you now?'

'They will interpret my…action…my commitment…my deviation…to suit themselves. Or maybe…'

He'd thought of all of that and he hoped none of it was true except this moment they were together.

'If it's useful to them they won't say a thing. What they will want is to feel that they own us both.'

They did. Of course they did.

'But they can't stop us giving away what they think they own. And that's our freedom, to be ourselves. We are living souls.'

'I love you for this.'

'I love you Irina.'

After which they both had to think of their survival.

'So we'll be in touch,' waved Korsakov, as if nothing had happened and Marlinsky prepared to leave. For Marlinsky, whose mother would have expected a 'thank you for having me', there was no honest sentiment he could express, though he managed a slight wave as the car set off.

'I'm afraid you will be disappointed with me.' Marlinsky forced himself to say it.

'That's for me to deal with. In the meantime please go on considering. My offer will not expire overnight.'

But it was an offer no good man in Russia could ever take up.

The Mercedes, with its unique elegance, saved the quality of the moment as they drove off.

'But I don't need to describe our country to you.' Marlinsky, resting against the back seat had closed his eyes. The voice was Balabin's. 'What it is to be Russian is to speak our language. If the nation is sluggish, decayed and corrupt that just can't be helped. What do you think?'

Marlinsky refused to open his eyes.

'We all of us dwell in confusion. We are actors, not persons. And yet the culture remains. We exist alongside the great characters, their passions, disappointments, the sheer tragicomedy of their existence. In their shadow we persist.'

'If you say so, Professor. If ever there was Russian greatness we exist in its evil shadow.'

The Last Toast

I sing of this house, ruined forever,
And of this blighted life of mine,
Of the loneliness we felt together,
I sing of thee and thine.
Of the lies on lips that betrayed me
Of the deadly cold of your eyes
Of a coarse life, cruel and unfree
For which no thanks. God did not save me.

Marlinsky remembered. Katya's dog had died and he believed Shaginyan dead too; and while he had tried to save his classmate Anna Prishvina he feared she was also lost. That the Party could be your conscience, and mine! Whoever made up that slogan knew this country had achieved the ultimate, diabolical parody of anything worth living for.

To accept Korsakov's 'offer' would have been ridiculous. It would have meant humiliation somewhere deep inside himself; the reduction of himself to a nobody, willingly, and he, Marlinsky, was far too proud to accept that sentence of self-destruction. He was not a leader, but he would lead if need be. He was a teacher—that had been a fulfilling interval in his life. There remained too that ambition to write, though he had written almost nothing to date.

'But I don't need to describe our country to you.' Balabin was sitting alongside him in the back of the Mertsedez, whose driver was not Matvei but resembled the chauffeur who had first ventured to the dacha to collect him, an enforcer through his very own bodily bulk, of the present order of things, was it only two evenings ago. The weather that Sunday morning had turned unsettled, with isolated raindrops hitting the windscreen like shots from a hostile army.

'I was talking about the West. What they are only beginning to know is how vast masses of people behave. We have known it since the beginning of the last century. But they are naïve sansculottists. They believe in a kind of political free-for-all. You know the results: uneven government, loss of central authority, dilution of culture and general disintegration of the old fabric of society. They only pretend to believe in their triumphant and progressive capitalism as a force for the good because they haven't got anything else. They are in as much of a mess as we are. You should take this into account before you make your final decision. You have my support of course, whatever you decide.' The little wisps of hair left on his skull were floating and falling again in the breeze. The driver had his window open a fraction.

Marlinsky scoffed: 'So, Professor, never mind what the West is like—and how can you know that—you've changed your mind about Russia, is that it?' (The language was so obscure it was hard to tell.) 'You're prepared to be critical of Russia, as any decent man must be? You'd have to reckon with that, if you want to be my supporter. If you truly love Russia you must be brave and speak out.'

'No I have not changed my mind! No I will not denounce my country to become your supporter! The very cheek of it! But I would like to see you survive, dear boy. Not let them waste your life. I tried to persuade them to let you go abroad but I failed.'

'You think you know what's best for me, Professor, but you would have done me great harm.'

'Love—'

'You may love me, Sergei Mikhailovich. But if love is so cunning, so self-interested, then perhaps it isn't the virtue we take it to be. Anyway I don't love you and I'm not grateful.' But then Marlinsky paused and half-relented. Generous in his love for Irina, he gave up attacking the desiccated pedagogue and let his mind drift off.

The car swept them along. The German tyres were of the highest quality, and cut a straight path through the dust, peppered with bullets of rain, on the Moscow periphery road.

'You might do me the honour of listening in any case!'

'Go on then.'

'I wished you to understand Russia and keep your private thoughts to yourself. Many great men have flourished and done good work that way. You could have done well, had you heeded my advice. You still can. You could perfectly well be loyal to your country without compromising your precious individuality, you fathead.'

But Marlinsky, having drifted away, only laughed distantly.

At which point the professor asked the driver: 'Have you not got something to drink for me and my friend?'

'Like what?' retorted the disobliging soul at the wheel of foreign luxury.

Marlinsky realised he objected to being called Balabin's friend, but then what did the ears of this driver matter, so he left it. The driver stretched across the empty front seat and rummaged with his right hand in the far pocket. Fortunately they were now in the city, with frequent stops at the lights keeping their speed down. He handed back a plastic bottle whose contents had a frightfully unnatural colour, somewhere between yellow, green and a chemical explosion. The professor swigged it, as the tall buildings either side of them imitated a European city.

'What is it? Nitric acid with food colouring? Is that all our soft drinks industry can manage?'

'Always so scornful, boy! You should grow up and be grateful.' The driver took a careful look at Marlinsky in his rear-view mirror.

'I'm coming to see this country is hell. Despite the love I feel.'

'A young person's problem everywhere…'

'Oh really? And how can you possibly know that? Isn't it so, driver? This country is hell for you too. You all would leave if you could. Except me and a few others, you see, because we do have the love. My friend Gerasimov for example. Our hope is to make this country better. To exercise the skills of a physician and psychologist and poet and set it on a better path.'

'Shut up! Just shut up, will you? You're just a sodding troublemaker.' The pop rattled and slithered in its prone bottle as they made a sudden U-turn.

'Whoopsie! Heading back out to Korsakov's so soon for a refresher course?' cried a euphoric Marlinsky.

'Normal driving,' said the voice in front.

'Normal, eh?

'Just shut up, boy! All you can do is scoff at everything. You're not a superior being, you know.'

'Except when you want me to be, you and Korsakov, to salve your conscience.'

'Anyway now they won't let you just leave. You've got to be punished. You know too much. Sorry. I just can't bear the waste of you.' Balabin's voice cracked and Marlinsky had the impression he touched his hand but he couldn't be sure.

'And what about the waste of *your* own soul,' Marlinsky began. 'Do you really not care what happens to this country in your heart? Do you honestly wake in the morning and think "it's all one to me."?'

'I—'

'And I'm the one who's supposed to be a traitor! You're a pathetic spectacle. You and your friends. You don't love this country at all, otherwise you would help it out of its delusion.'

'They're not my friends.'

'*Comrades*, then. You're all the same.'

He shook his head. 'We're not all the same because I…have feelings for you.'

What could Marlinsky do with that? There was no need to be cruel, so he just kept staring out of the window.

The driver stopped outside the Kursk railway station, with its immense forecourt.

'Why here? Am I going on a train journey now?' Marlinsky mocked them to the end. He had individuality, he had dignity, and he would, so far as was humanly possible, because he was a human being, be master of his fate.

Alas, Korsakov had said: 'Just don't make fools of us!' But he couldn't hold back from that.

As Balabin opened the door from outside, and Marlinsky got out, the usual stream of people carrying bundles of this and that passed by, determined not to notice the Mertsedez.

Balabin standing beside him tried again and again. 'Every intelligent Russian needs some compensation, Boris Mikhailovich, for being born of God's unchosen people. Some of us must be the rulers, some of us the subjects. We none of us have a choice.'

'God and his choices, eh? What nonsense you talk,' Marlinsky said.

There were so many ways in which Marlinsky could still save himself.

Why didn't he? Balabin renewed his appeal.

'What makes you think I'm not saving myself? I have made my choice. It's just that in Russia our choices, even when they are beautiful, even when they are noble, tend to lead to a dead end. *Poka*, Professor. See you in the eternal meanwhile.' Marlinsky walked away.

Twenty-Four

Harriet Zimmerman meanwhile had done her own reaching out to the other side. She had put on a play. Her players were the various English-speaking children who found themselves in the expatriate Moscow Anglo-American school, and a few supportive adults who were immediately the object of local curiosity. Howard tackled Arthur at the foreigners' petrol station: 'Is it true you're taking a part yourself?'

'Howard! Good to see you! Who told you?'

The row of premium petrol pumps which could only be accessed by foreigners paying dollars was a Cold War forum. No one could bug you there. Or could they? You had to laugh. *Plein air* had taken on a new meaning.

'You know how these things get around.'

Arthur did. If the secretive Russians didn't make mischief with what they overheard, the Westerners happily gossiped among themselves. 'Proud to do it for Harriet and the school. The kids are wonderful.'

Howard unhooked the heavy petrol head and slid it into the unlocked tank of the MG. The pump whirred and the numbers began to spin.

'Price of fuel's not going down.'

'Whatever game the Arabs are playing.' Moscow seemed distant from the other crisis besetting London. The West's reckoning with the rich and powerful new Middle Eastern countries threatened for a moment to move Moscow from the front page.

'Korsakov's coming too. She's invited him to come, and his wife.'

'Korsakov will be in the audience?' Howard was nonplussed.

For it was a very pointed play, about Russian ways.

Arthur advanced the black Chevrolet the few metres he needed to take his turn at the pump.

'Harriet wants to *communicate* with the Soviets. She wants us all to get together.'

'Just like your hippy president.'

'Don't you start!'

Korsakov had raised it, the last time he and Arthur met. 'Your *khip-pee* president wants us all to love each other.'

'I didn't quite get that, Korsakov. Hips? Kippers. Oh, *hippy*, right.'

'Khee-pee, yes.'

'Our president is a good man,' countered Arthur loyally, 'Just wrong in some things.' Not admitting that out loud, he added: 'Surely an end to the Cold War is what everyone wants.'

'I do think they'd like to get out of their own trap, after sixty years.'

'But what the hell then after it?' Howard couldn't imagine. Or rather he could. Chaos, rebuilding, chaos again. The second revolution couldn't work unless it was open-ended and eternal.

'Has Korsakov accepted the invitation?'

'You know his secretary Katya. She said he's coming with his wife and son.'

'The one with the perfume and the mile-high legs?'

'That's Katya.'

'He offers her to every Western journalist that walks in. And no man has ever accepted, right?'

Arthur smiled but only faintly, as was his way. 'She even rang me… *On s zhenoi i synom budyet.*'

'But that's amazing!' Howard bowed. 'Chapeau Harriet.' He opened the door to the MG.

'Off somewhere I should know about?' The same faint smile. 'I'm going for a spin to enjoy this lovely weather.'

'Another sortie into *nomklat*-land?' The women had landed a blow, though they hadn't been able to drive it home.

'Aah, now I understand. Korsakov's coming to the play to rescue his image as a family man.' But he kept that thought to himself.

In fact Howard was on his way to the Razumovskys. Natasha Razumovsky had rung. There was a shortage of Razumovsky's pills in the polyclinic. 'Those rude women told me "Ask your friends in the West to get them for you! Keep your Sasha from the brink!"'

'What are they called? I'll pick some up and come over.'

The British Embassy in those days employed a tall grey-haired doctor apparently born in the nineteenth century. He wore a three-piece suit for every appointment. But that suit was so old even a tramp would have pitied him. Gels bristled when on her sole visit he diagnosed neurasthenia. 'I feel a bit depressed, that's all.' The wife of one of the diplomats, fearing that her husband was losing interest in bed, was not consoled to hear that she had breasts like a bloodhound's ears. Once women were forty, the Embassy doctor was renowned for declaring their bodies cast-aside glove puppets. Too loose. Too open. Indeed he hated his women patients so much that they together decided he must have been struck off the medical list in England for some misdemeanour, *of that kind even*. Or sheer incompetence. Dr Mackintosh further offended by filling his large consulting room in the embassy across the river with stuffed animals—there was an eagle, and a parrot and a racoon—'pretty tail, don't you think?'—creatures once alive, now immobilised in time. Like other British institutions of the day, the Foreign Office had a weakness for eccentricity and Dr Mackintosh epitomised it.

But Howard had the medication in his pocket because the medical man was slack. Delighted, he drove back north and east across Moscow, singing all the way 'All You Need is Love. Do-da diddle do.'

'Actually I think we're getting somewhere, with love of humankind!' The flat beside Ismailovsky Park gave him a good role in life, and he wanted that so much it almost felt like driving home. To that home of homes, in the human mind.

The dancer Zolodei was even now briefing Korsakov on what Harriet Zimmerman envisaged with her version of Gogol's *Revizor*.

'About corruption, eh? Well, that's a surprise.'

Korsakov had about him a bumptious cheerfulness that Saturday morning that put the entire household beside the Mozhaisk Road on its guard. Irina had rediscovered her precious Beatles single from 1967 and was playing it through an open window.

'Nothing you can do, but you can learn how to be you in time…' But time is limited. Get out now!

The painter Zorin popped into the meeting to appear useful. People always coupled him with Zolodei, as if they were a pair of comic conspirators. They weren't exactly friends and they never saw eye to eye on art, but they shared a need to survive.

'You'd do best to laugh along with everyone else, Vladimir Arkadevich,' Zorin said. 'This play presents us Russians as…less than perfect. But the Westerners are hardly perfect themselves.'

White they chatted they dipped little sponge fingers from Czechoslovakia into their black coffee with brandy. Probably no one else in the world did that, but Korsakov thought it chic.

'That play is how Russia was then. Not now.'

'But it's possible to think nothing has changed. I mean—'

'Right.'

'Best just to laugh with the audience.'

'That's very good. Our common human plight.'

'Exactly.'

'In a civilised way we admit our faults. Without actually doing so, of course.'

'Exactly.'

But then Korsakov remembered another aspect of the universal plight. 'Will it be about my wife?'

Zolodei didn't dare snigger. 'I don't see why…'

'There's nothing in Gogol's script—'began Zorin, similarly self-disciplined.

'Well, we'll see. And and—what are *you* working on, Comrade *Khudozhnik*? You're always up to something creative.'

Zorin, Comrade Artist, delivered his usual spiel about the collage of the century.

'Will you include, er…Sta…?' Korsakov felt as if the Mack were peering over his shoulder. 'Was HE so important in the end?'

'I'm thinking more along the lines of Jack Kennedy and Marilyn Monroe. People we can share a world with.'

'Excellent.'

Zolodei broke in to remind Korsakov of a playlet the dancer himself had written and recently performed out at the house. 'With respect, Comrade Colonel, you didn't understand the play I wrote for your wife's birthday.'

What had happened was they had been sitting around the table eating one of their grand meals when Zolodei in a leotard shimmied his way in, in place of Lisa with some dish or other, and offered Irina a bird on a stick. He held the stick in one hand and produced a song on pan pipes held in the other. He looked quite the part. Like a Shakespearian fool. Idly Irina had run a delicate finger over the bright feathers that death within had not destroyed. (For the bird, of course, in order to be mounted on a stick, definitely needed to be dead.) She looked up sadly, intuiting her part. Death threatened her soul too. 'Ah, I see my gift is not enough to make you happy, princess. Maybe this will. And with that he had produced from his pocket a live songbird. He positively threw it into the midst of the room, where, while the greedier diners continued to gorge themselves – no guesses for thinking that was the Mack – for a short while the little creature sang sweetly.

'What you didn't understand, Korsakov, was that my performance explored the dialectical meaningfulness between the live bird, eternally free but full of fear, and the dead bird, eternally unfree but perfect. My play experimented with a deep longing for life which we can only begin to measure when we contemplate death. Your wife appreciated that.'

Korsakov pulled a face. How our Soviet artists talk dialectical meaningfulness, when they want to curry favour! What tosh!

'You just enjoyed scandalising Comrade Makarenko.'

'Well, there was that. Silly old biddy.'

Zorin ventured: 'Comrade Dancer's *heppeninks* are highly admired.'

'As is your cutting and pasting of Western magazines highly admired, no doubt, Comrade Zorin. The question is by whom. But all right. I accept. You artists have your language. Then you build a house with it and live in it and the rest of us can only look on baffled.'

'If it's in that house we can say something about eternal Russia,' mumbled the artists in chorus, 'then we do right to try to build some shelter of some kind. God save us otherwise.'

'Let me just remind you this is the Soviet Union. We believe in history, not eternity.'

'So there's history in my collage.' Zorin sucked on the last Czechoslovak biscuit dipped in French brandy and chased it down with a mouthful of hot coffee.

Zolodei muttered to his friend as they left the meeting: 'At least no sodding censor can tell me where I have to put my feet. By the way do you think I got through to him?'

'No chance.'

'So,' said Harriet, with the senior class of eleven-year-olds grouped round her informally. 'Here's the basic story. If you're faking it's terrifying to be found out. Everyone knows that feeling, I take it?'

None of them spoke. All of them did.

They were children but they rose to the occasion as she took them through the play. It was a great work and because of the blessings it bestowed for a moment they were their teacher's equals and they felt free and responsible. She explained there was a baffled young man called Khlestyakov who got his chance in life when he was mistaken for a government inspector. A little town in the middle of nowhere was expecting a high-up from Moscow to come and audit their books and *he* appeared. He soon seized his chance. People bowed to him and fawned and offered him money. Normally he was doing the bowing and scraping himself. Now for some reason they were terrified of him.

'In our version,' said Harriet, as she distributed the parts, 'He will be a she. Not Mr Whippet but Miss Whippet. You'll see why.'

Moldy's wife Mary, over for the Easter holidays, had agreed to play Miss Whippet. 'I think we can all have more fun if we make him a her. We also have some Russians with us to help make our production more authentic.'

Korsakov had asked Zolodei: 'I've forgotten how you know the wife of an American journalist.'

'The Mundt affair—'

'Enough said.'

Korsakov rummaged in his head to get a grip on proceedings. 'And it's a fashionable idea in the West, you say, to do *versions* of the classics?'

'So new generations can understand them.'

'But isn't Naumov always telling us art is timeless?'

'He is. But there are ways in which it is and ways in which it isn't. We were talking about this before—'

'Well, that's clear.'

Pursing his lips, moving them from side to side, as if swinging his way like a labial acrobat through an agenda, practising in front of a mirror—an absent mirror—, anticipating some unknown confrontation, Korsakov turned to the question of style. 'And it's realism, you say, more or less?'

'That's debatable even in the original. In fact Vsevolod Meyerhold...'

'I don't want to hear about the debate. What is it today?'

'Satirical fantasy.'

'Meaning they'll be laughing at us.'

'No no you'll be laughing *with* them. We'll all be laughing at human folly.'

'Hmm.'

Korsakov feared that he might be cornered. The whole crew of Westerners and their sympathisers were ganging up on him. Just as the bulldozed show had almost cost him his job, here was another 'stunt' in the offing, drawing him into their midst, daring him to be 'civilised'. Westerners always work the 'this is how *we* live' factor into their political offensives these days. Be like us, not like yourselves, you Russian bumpkins! That would be part of 'the play'. On the other hand he couldn't refuse to go. He had a place among the Westerners, as the loving husband of his wife and the proud father of his son.

'Before you go, Comrade Dancer, remind me again how you two come to play a part in this foreign community production?'

'But we've already—'

Indeed. Why had he asked again? Well, because he was obsessed. That ludicrous occasion from two years ago– the outdoor art show – constantly shoved its way back into his mind. It was like a blot on his eyesight. And on him.

'—through those channels the idea reached us…'

'Channels?'

'Through those contacts the American lady director made it known it might be a friendly thing for Russian artists to collaborate with her.'

'Collaborate can't be the word—'

'Work side by side.'

'Better.'

'And through other channels she made contact with your recent guest Marlinsky.'

Korsakov choked. He waved the smoke from Zolodei's Marlboro away from his eyes. 'Look, must you? I do hate smoking indoors. What's Marlinsky got to do with it?'

'Nothing to do with the play. But they all, well, they're all on his side, because they're afraid something bad will happen to him.'

'I suppose he'll turn up in the audience. That's all I need.'

'No doubt you could prevent that if you thought it necessary, Vladimir Arkadevich. With respect.'

But Korsakov, again off on a tangent, was worrying that in some sense Harriet Zimmerman *must* be a connoisseur—*zhenshchina-expert*—with regard to something Korsakov couldn't put his finger on. What should Korsakov know about Harriet Zimmerman, as opposed to her husband?

Zolodei exhaled thoughtfully.

'Smoke is definitely bad for the books,' interrupted Balabin, from his table in the corner of the library.

'Oh, professor, I didn't see you listening in on us.'

'Working quietly on the house archive. My task is our heritage. 1812 when Napoleon tried to invade us down the Mozhaisk Road. 1941 when the Nazis did the same.'

'Of course that's your task,' said Korsakov sarcastically. 'So what's she an expert in?'

'I don't know.'

The Anglo-American school was another of the good old Moscow buildings that the foreign community rented, and thus helped to preserve it from the end of vilified tsarist times into an uncertain future. A rich merchant had built it in the stocks and shares boom of the 1890s in an opulent neo-baroque style. Twenty years later his kind were purged and their bank accounts emptied and buildings became sober again. After the Revolution the Bolsheviks vowed to create a society reflecting the common man's *real* needs. The common man wanted a good-enough place to live in, with an efficient kitchen and bathroom, not all those gargoyles and statues and whatnots. So now, as the simple life prevailed because no other life was officially allowed, the two styles were in perpetual stand-off. These days every superfluous architectural whorl from the pre-Communist past was loathed by Soviet design and prized by Western visitors. That average Westerner looked at a Soviet street and thought: oh, Lord! How did it happen? Who invented a system to strip out the joy so brutally. Ornate bourgeois opulence wins over the plainness of Soviet functionalism any day. To which came the robust Soviet reply that only selfish idiots would construct edifices decorated like cream cakes, when too many citizens needed a place to live and money was short. Briefly, this network of feeling and counter-feeling was stored up in the walls of the building that had become the Anglo-American school, and, for once, God didn't know how to adjudicate.

The assembly hall had an elegant parquet floor and must once have been a ballroom. Now a hundred and fifty chairs filled it on Harriet's first night. The auditorium was remarkably full—of parents, who were most of them diplomats and employees at the various embassies. Danes and Germans, Italians and Americans had come to watch their children. Their friends and colleagues came along too, as did all the journalists, because not much of this kind happened in their foreigners' circles, and rumour had it, carefully orchestrated by Harriet and Gels, that this was quite an event.

Howard momentarily screened Gels out of his attention and scoured the room before the lights went down. Korsakov wore an inconspicuous Western-style lounge suit with a narrow tie while his wife looked ravishing in a dress of green silk. Wormy, who arrived late, looked anxious. Uxorious, thought Howard kindly. He's suffering from anxiety on account of his wife. He also *performs* his anxiety. He can't help it. Catching Howard's eye and, loading his characteristic rueful smile with all sorts of unspoken ironies and caveats, the BBC man waved. Correspondents from Denmark, Sweden, France and all of Arthur's American colleagues from Christian Science Monitor, The Boston Globe, even the NYR, had gathered. Chapeau, Harriet! Chapeau!

Howard ran his eye down the list of characters. The names had been changed, as had the title of the play, but if you knew the original you could see these were amusing English equivalents. The director had meanwhile added two interpreter-figures front of stage to make the sometimes obscure behaviour on stage clear to a foreign audience.

The Audit

Act 1

In front of the stage the dancer Zolodei, interpreter No 1, pattered back and forth, tilting his head, pointing, mouthing this and that, as if caught in a web of chatter with invisible others. He did this until he had everyone's attention. Then knock-knock-knock, the action started.

The scene was 'the drawing room of a nineteenth-century house, rather grand', with a chandelier and one gilded chair. The ballet dancer stood front left of stage, while a Russian artist-type in jeans, a pink shirt and a boxy black leather jacket, interpreter No 2, stood to the right. Zorin's task from the front of stage right was to cheer-lead, raising his thumb or turning it down, as the action unfolded. He might also now and again hold up a banner. Zolodei meanwhile would mime the complexity of emotion.

Miss Whippet entered a gathering of Party apparatchiks. The artist held up a banner to say they were called The Group. The doorman meanwhile announced Miss Whippet as the inspector. The apparatchiks (with enlarged badges on their lapels) froze in fear. Zolodei mimed fear. God had sent her to punish them.

The Group hummed and heaved and seethed at being caught out. They fell over themselves. They paced the room, consulted their watches, looked out of the window. Who would be the first to take Miss Whippet aside and establish his innocence? Or she?

'It's good,' Howard whispered. 'Better than I thought.'

'Thank you.'

Six children in the final year had roles in the Group. One vivacious brunette was Mrs Vroon, wife of the Town Prefect Mr Vroon, played by Arthur. This English-seeming surname was Russian for 'liar'. Good for a laugh. Mr Box was another character in code. He was obviously hiding something. And Miss Pry, perpetually wanting to know what was in the box.

Harriet took the trouser role of Mr Brainy the Schools chief. Roughly speaking a brainy man might be called a 'Naumov'. Another girl from the final year played Miss Pry. A tall thin spotty boy with a ready grin was Professor Steed. Professor Shame, the name meant, and whenever he appeared the artist in the leather jacket turned his thumb down. Everyone jeered. At which Zolodei looked sad. He mimed the drama of just another victim of the system. You mean me? What can I do? What makes me different from anyone else? He brushed his hands over his head from behind, as if pulling on a hood that would also cover his eyes.

'I heard,' said Miss Whippet primly, with raised finger, 'that this town was recently very unkind to its bookshop manager.' Howard led the laughter and noticed Korsakov join in. Good strategy. How did the king behave when Hamlet put on his playlet about murder? He got unsettled. Korsakov was more brazen. Irina sat motionless, uninterested, only with her lips curled.

Vroon offered to summon that local Party official who had 'allowed' a certain Serebryakova to Moscow in the first place. He should be punished, because it was 'a nasty business, that Party chap from the sticks quite took advantage of a sweet girl. He told her he could pull strings in Moscow if only she—. That's why she wasn't up to the job in the first place.'

Zolodei was busy miming the equivalent of Leda and the Swan and then covering his eyes in shame.

'How did he know she wasn't up to the job when he took her into the cupboard?'

'He promised her the job in Moscow no questions asked.' Thumbs down from Zorin. Jeering from the audience.

'Morals are lax in some parts of our town, Mr Vroon.'

Arthur's eyes went up into his head. 'Sadly so, dear lady.'

'I think you should give the poor lady back her job.'

'I agree,' came a female voice from the audience. Anyone who turned around at that moment would have seen Korsakov shoot a glance at his wife. They might have heard her whisper: 'So what? *Nu chto*? Doesn't make any difference now. We're all lost.'

'But she let people buy copies of that report…' protested Vroon. Korsakov twitched.

'What does it matter now? Everyone's read it the world over. They all know what we're like.' A guffaw followed the twitch.

Zolodei meanwhile mimed a madman rattling his prison bars, and followed it with worry and sadness.

'Everyone's read The Report! Everyone's read The Report! Why's she being punished?' the cast declared in chorus. Zorin held up in two hands above his head a blurred photo of the manager in question, blown up from some Bookshop Union Yearbook.

Miss Whippet, for a moment alone, shorn of the odious company of Miss Pry, grinned directly at the audience.

But then the hideous Mr Brainy approached. Jeers from the chorus. A thumbs down from Zorin. Leering, Mr Brainy insisted on sharing with Miss Whippet his admiration for the Italian painter Piero della Francesca, so much more important than some petty functionary from some god-awful place on the Volga. (More pictures held up by Zorin.)

'I think we have more urgent business to attend to, given the state of your town,' admonished the visitor from Moscow.

'But that's just it. A civilised man must save his soul. I thought we might—
'

Mis Whippet wagged her finger.' Oh no! Oh no! You can't get out of it so easily!'

Zolodei performed a little drama of conscience and self-exculpation. He pointed to himself, on behalf of Mr Brainy, and vigorously shook his head. The chorus shouted gleefully: 'Wasn't me! Wasn't me!'

Miss Pry when she at last got Miss Whippet alone, confessed on quite another matter to having excised whole pages from a set of town records in her care. Zorin held up a large picture of Stalin with a red cross drawn through it.

'He was a bad man. They told me to do it.'

'Yes! Yes! Her task was to undo the cult of personality!' shouted the children who, stepping momentarily out of their specific roles, cried: 'She cut out Stalin. But she would destroy Pushkin too, if THEY asked her to.' The children formed a chorus of accusation. Thumbs down from Zorin.

Miss Pry protested: 'What can a poor curator do? Madam, is it not true that history is always changing?'

Hellfire threatened. The ballet dancer fanned himself and swooned. 'She rewrote history! She lied!' chanted the chorus.

In all this time Miss Whippet was offered many tasty morsels to eat and drink to distract her from the terrible revelations. These choice victuals, including evil-smelling Soviet chocolate, which she sniffed and threw back down, piled up on a table beside her. Presents of lace, jewellery, a West German fountain pen, an audio tape of Some Girls and another of Saturday Night Fever also stirred her interest.

Zorin could hardly raise his thumbs fast enough.

Arthur as Mr Vroon the Town Prefect surreptitiously examined the tributes on the table.

All the while a real fire raged in the drawing room which once lit was not allowed to go out. Miss Whippet, the inspector sent by God, red-cheeked and exhausted, at one point stepped aside from her interviewees and watched as Mr Brainy, Miss Pry, Professor Shame and others threw documents and even whole books into the fire, hoping they weren't being observed.

Act 2

Miss Whippet would like to go on profiting from the mistaken identity yet she knows her trick can't last. Vroon is already suspicious.

In conversation with Mr Vroon: 'Are you sure God sent you, Madam? You see we don't believe in God in this country. We don't think He exists.'

Miss Whippet (cleverly turning the situation around): 'I represent good people. I am your conscience. Yes God did send me.'

'It's all a trick.'

'No no. It's not. You *are* afraid of being found out.'

'Everyone is.'

'How do you mean?'

Well, Madam, [the] Party....'

'Aaah, the Party!'

'The Party sees everything.'

'Like me.' (Interrupts, laughing) 'But enough of that nonsense. What you really believe in is having a good time, Mr Vroon. Isn't that what you're trying to say? Your bad English is trying to mislead me again. You Russians must learn where to put in a 'the' in English and where not. Everyone believes in having a party. It's written into the UN charter of human rights. Everyone is free to have a good time. Except your rulers want you to suffer, so that just a few of you can have parties.'

(At which point a curious expression crept across Korsakov's face, as if he felt a point had been made which was true enough, nothing to do with him.)

'Actually Mr Vroon means the Communist Party,' insisted Mr Brainy, coming to his colleague's rescue. 'The Party that is the mind, the honour and the conscience of our Soviet people.'

Miss Whippet (laughs helplessly). 'R—i—ght. Let me write that down so I don't forget. Isn't it up on a building somewhere, in red letters?'

'On the town hall. In case people forget it, Madame. Some of our people are very stupid.'

'And *The* Party is the reason for not having *a* party?'

'I think so, Madam.'

Miss Whippet: 'By the way will there be lunch?'

'Of course. We like to do things properly.'

'A French déjeuner? Three courses with wine? At twelve noon? I'd like that.'

Mr Brainy called to an invisible servant: '*Shampanskoe est'*?' Zolodei mimed opening a bottle of champagne. Zorin raised a thumb.

'Sounds like you,' said Irina to her husband.

Act 3

After lunch Miss Whippet asked: 'Is there a wireless? I'd like to listen to the BBC.'

'Boy!' a man clicks his fingers.

The boy brings a German-made transistor radio and Professor Shame, Mr Brainy, Miss Pry and others gather round. Mr Brainy fingers it admiringly and exclaims in German. 'Schön ist das! Wie schön! Schöne Musik auch.' (In which he was praising the musical quality of the famous theme tune.)

During the 1pm world news bulletin, as it is announced that 'Soviet dissidents today accused Moscow of imprisoning critics of the system in mental hospitals...' Miss Whippet suddenly holds up a finger and writes down some letters on a pad. She licks her pencil and writes some more.

'What is it, dear lady? Is God speaking to you?' (They thought she was having a séance.)

Understanding that she has been given a message in code, she reads the letters against an English copy of *The Government Inspector*.

'I've been sent a message.'

337

'A message from on high? To send us to hell? Oh no! We implore you, dear kind Madame, save our souls, we are not bad people. Only like everyone else.'

'We are both women of the world, Miss Whippet,' whispered Miss Pry. 'We know that it's rarely easy to do the right thing all the time.'

Miss Whippet (frowning over the text emerging from her decoding): 'I **am** to…show the people mercy…'

'Hurrah!'

'What a fine man is God.'

'He was invented because we needed him.'

'Except we abolished him.'

'Really I blame the Party for usurping His role.'

Miss Whippet (concentrating hard): 'Oh!'

At which all around her gasped all the more terribly.

Zorin pointed his thumb towards Hades, while the children cried out: 'Oh Oh What is it? Tell us? What is it? Are they going to Hell?'

(There was spontaneous applause from the floor for the chorus, and they clapped back in the most social moment of the evening.)

'Oh, I'm so, so sorry, but it says here that I must leave immediately. *Seychas.*'

'*Seychas.*' It went round like a whisper. '*Eto znachit bez nekakoi zaderzhki.*'

'I know what "straightaway" means,' retorted the professor to the schoolmaster. 'I'm an educated man.'

'I must leave as soon as possible. Can you arrange that?' Whisper whisper whisper. *Seychas'. Seychas'.*

Vroon sighed with relief. 'But of course. My driver will see to your every wish, Lady Whippet.'

'In which case it had better be a Mercedes. Got one of those?'

'At your service, Lady Whippet. Straight away.'

'God appreciates German technology surely,' said Mr Brainy.

'Oh yes I think so.' Miss Whippet uttered the mantra *Vorsprung durch Technik*. The chorus then whispered it repeatedly, adding: 'That would be progress! *Vorsprung durch Technik.*'

'To Moscow, Madam?' asked Vroon as he saw the visitor comfortably into the back seat.

'To Sheremetyevo airport, if you please, driver.' Miss Whippet turned a final time and waved to the party, the Party, and they joyously waved her good riddance, with the fire now dead in the grate.

'Some Russians are stupid, driver, wouldn't you say?'

'Some are stupid but not me.' He glanced at her in the rear-view mirror and drove on.

The scene in Moscow meanwhile returned to what it was at the start of the play. Nothing had changed. Vroon and his wife, Mr Brainy, Miss Pry and Professor Shame were variously running an appreciative hand over the imitation classical statues, dusting the European-style oil paintings, taking a sneak peek at a foreign film, or even just grinning, blowing bubbles, raising their glasses. But then suddenly they froze.

Zolodei shrugged and lay down in the pose of a dog on the floor. Zorin opened both hands to show them empty.

Two children walked across the stage with a placard saying THE END. No one moved.

'How long are we going to stand like this?' someone called out.

'According to the instructions "almost a minute and a half,"' said the voice of Mr Vroon.

'That's right,' confirmed the director.

But when the curtain was lowered they were still standing, frozen.

Korsakov clapped loudly. 'Brilliant! Brilliant stuff!' To Irina: 'What did you think?'

'You let them make fools of us.'

'It's like Pompeii,' said Howard. The Westerners went off for a meal.

Twenty-Five

The LGN office was more inviting now that DIMDA had unsealed the windows for spring. Howard had sent London the outline of what he would write that afternoon, designed to make an impact the following day. The Russians were forging contacts in the Middle East. Their influence was spreading in Africa. Washington disliked these developments.

Meanwhile, in the noon lull, over coffee, they chatted. 'She did it brilliantly.'

'Except he just sat there laughing and applauding. It didn't touch him.'

'That's his strategy. We can't know.'

'Satire as a mode of protest just isn't strong enough.'

'God, Howard, half of their literature is satire. What would you have them do? Or us?'

'We must assemble the facts. The incontrovertible facts. That's why I'm a journalist.'

Pompous ass, she thought. 'What are the facts? That the place is broken but they're always trying to fix it? You could say that about England.'

'It's not broken in the same way.'

She scoffed and changed the subject. 'Howard, I'm worried about Marlinsky. What will they do with him?'

Grisha, listening in, uttered a strange noise. It sounded like 'the house at Nikolskaya 23.'

Howard was quickly alert to what Grisha mumbled, as if he had been entertaining the same fears, only to deny them out loud. 'No, my friend, no bullets, not anymore.'

The big man grunted. 'Prison or poison then.' Bvaaaaaa.

'What can we do?'

The weather made possible frequent walks in the park. The buds on the trees seemed to open in real time. What was an empty space yesterday was green today. But then you remember that even as beauty enchants you your fellow human beings are dying horribly. Auden of course, and he said it better.

Gels had such a knack for destroying her own happiness. But then a country like Russia responded: you need misery? I'll take you to the brink.

The boats were back on the boating lake. She was desperate. Any cliché amounting to happiness would do. One afternoon she and Harriet took it in turns to row a boat. They were both strong women, and there was companionship in that.

'Any feedback from *The Audit*? It was a triumph.'

Harriet was deflated and sad. 'What effect could I expect it to have?'

'Hamlet didn't ask himself that. You gave Korsakov a conscience. Whether he agreed to receive it or not.'

'I don't feel it worked. It won't make any difference.'

Spring meanwhile brought new ingredients into the foreigners' shop called the Gastronom that, though hardly Mediterranean, they really presented a culinary challenge. Kohlrabi and celeriac were dug out of no longer frozen ground. Pineapples from New Guinea reappeared. Next door in the general store you could also find, for a price, cigars from Cuba. With the unusual vegetables Gels adapted recipes from a cookbook that had recently hit the headlines in France. If you thought the winter had left you heavier by a few pounds, here, with *Cuisine minceur*, was a way of producing spectacular meals full of air.

Alone in the park she lingered to watch the giant chess being played outdoors. Marlinsky admired chess because it was about the freedom of the imagination. She wished that respite, and that glimpse of happiness, on the twenty or so older men gathered here in the company of colossal castles and knee-high knights.

The shooting range meanwhile had some targets to shoot at, after a long wait for tins. The plastic dolls that rewarded an accurate shot, back in production again, had also been delivered. The TIR beckoned.

'I invite you for tea in the park.'

'I only ever go to the park when I need to talk to a contact.'

'Think of me as a contact then. Please come. A meeting *en plein air*.' He agreed to a Saturday afternoon, because there was no Sunday edition.

She took a flask—the most popular contribution of Mao's China to the economy of stagnant 1970s Russia—and filled it with superb Russian tea; amber perfection. If Russian tea amounted to Russia itself then the country would always have friends and admirers. But you could say that of Italy too. If Italy equalled pasta Rome would have changed the world by now and we would all love each other.

She was gloomy but, vaguely remembering Dr Mackintosh's diagnosis tried to snap out of it. The hardly sweet oat biscuits from the Gastro were dry and thick as door wedges. You couldn't fault them on health grounds. Indeed, to buy such old-fashioned biscuits you would have to patronise a health food shop in London, and risk being seen as a crank, for food in the West had become dangerously refined. The West consisted of consumers who no longer knew how to consume.

A slender, strongly-built woman in jeans, boots and a lemon-coloured sweatshirt laced with a silk scarf, of mustard and white and red and blue, knotted at her neck, and wearing sunglasses, and a slender man of medium height, in jeans and a navy sweater, over a white cotton shirt with a thin grey stripe, his sandy hair already a little receding, sat on a bench beside the water. No one seemed to take notice of them. She carried a basket which she set on the bench between them. Good tea, he said. But that comes from the habit of drinking it black. The actual tea comes from China.

'Nothing's what it seems.'

'This is the life.' He tilted his face to the sun. 'Can you imagine actually living here?'

'If I could have a *dacha*.' A wooden house in the country with a kitchen garden was almost a Russian birth-right. You lived in a little flat. There were constant food shortages in the shops. But out in the country you grew your own.

'I'd like to be a native of somewhere.'

'Not London?'

'Yes and no. You can be anything you like in that city.' There was a pause as they enjoyed being alive.

'So the Kennedys disgusted you.'

With the attention briefly away from Razumovsky and, sadly, even Marlinsky, the talk of foreigners' Moscow had been the visit to the Kremlin of Senator Edward Kennedy. Edward was the younger brother of President John F. and of Senator Robert, former Attorney-General, who had both been assassinated in their native streets. These were the actions Mrs Maria Marlinsky couldn't fathom, if America was such an ideal country.

'Do you ever run "America" past Harriet and Arthur? They're quite patriotic.'

'You know what they say. To which my answer is Americans are from Mars and Europeans from Venus.'

'That's it.'

The Kennedy visit had brought about a valuable trade in freedom. Some Russians were being allowed to leave. Still the political compromise on both sides hurt.

'The Russians make fools of the Amis, and get paid for it.'

The deal was that every Soviet citizen released to Israel would bring a stash of US dollars into the Kremlin treasury.

'The Cold War at its grubbiest. It's desperate.'

'Still it shows they can't survive here much longer. They're selling their unwanted people in order not to go bankrupt.'

'In Lithuania, the whole VIRILE institute existed in order to bring in hard currency. They were nearly bankrupt then too.'

'The best thing about the Kennedys is that it was a visit from royalty. The senator and his wife were THE WEST, if people here could catch a glimpse of them. If they could touch them.'

'Celebrity culture comes to Soviet Moscow. First Sophia Loren. Now Edward Kennedy.'

'The Kremlin put them in the Rossiya Hotel.'

'So they could listen to them in bed.'

'Porn in politics, porn in private lives.'

Well, Dr Mackintosh, who wouldn't show signs of neurasthenia.

The toddlers in the park were enjoying the sunshine, though their mothers still dressed them in those bulky layers, topped with woolly hats, in Moscow's interminable not quite spring.

'Ne'r cast a clout…'

'Mary Wormold and I saw *Andrei Rublev* in the cinema at the Rossiya. Aah, Howard, the intensity, and the beauty! Who else can do that, today?'

'But didn't that great artist crash to earth right at the beginning?'

'We tried not to think about it.'

'Intelligence bugs *and* bed bugs in the same hotel!' The Rossiya Hotel was a convenient monster to attack. 'In the capital city! Why did they agree to stay there?'

'They could take a whole floor for their security people. 'Besides, they weren't given a choice.'

'Yet they were invited.'

Yes, what a strange game was the Cold War!

In fact the cortège that drove from Sheremetyevo airport, led by the presidential candidate's Lincoln Continental, was a controlled invasion, permitted and not, of freedom-loving, individualistic America into Communist, collectivist Russia. Possibly it was a trial run for something extraordinary. Because you couldn't forget the opposite moment, when the Russian tsar arrived at the head of the Holy Alliance in Paris in 1815. Note for future historians, including Professor Balabin: 1815 when Russia triumphed over the West; 1979, when the West triumphed over Russia.

The senator was pudgy. He struggled with his weight and was obviously a drinker. He had escaped a prison sentence because of the family name. Any other man who'd picked up a woman for sex, crashed his car into water and left the woman to drown would be behind bars, in a civilised country.

The journalists baited him on his unappeased wrongdoing.

At the ambassador's residence (where once American families had sheltered after US diplomats had set their own embassy on fire), he first bowed to the requirements of the press, by holding a press conference. They grudgingly acknowledged what they and he needed from each other. The Stars and Stripes prevailed like the colours on the mast of a battleship. There was only Coca-Cola on the table, where the Russians would have served Borzomi. A young black boy acted as a waiter. Two Marines in full dress uniform stood guard.

'What happened, senator? What was the truth of that night?'

He eyeballed them, still handsome somewhere inside the pudginess. He spoke slowly, laying his hands palms up on the table and inclining his head to each reporter in the room in turn. 'It was a tragedy. You all heard about it.' With his slow speech, he forced them into a gesture of respect, so it was an effort for Arthur to ask: 'Were you drunk, Senator? Is that what happened?' His heart was hammering, but it was a question any decent American had to ask.

A familiar figure, superbly suited, stepped in. 'I'd like to remind you, ladies and gentlemen of the press, that the Senator is in Moscow to talk about arms limitation—'

'Arms limitation!' Gels refilled their enamel tea mugs on the park bench beside the boating lake. In the arms race Moscow was playing a grimy game, threatening to put guns into the whole of Africa.

'They're a great power. They have to show off.'

Back at the press conference Howard had intervened. 'I believe the Senator is in Moscow as part of his campaign to stand for president.' An election was due the following year.

'As I said—'

Kennedy himself spoke up. 'I'll take their questions, Mr Ambassador.' He had a lumbering dignity.

'It must have been hard for him to decide which line of our inquiry was more risky.'

'He's a gifted man, no doubt.'

The tea had cooled, but it was still smoky and soothing, a rich amber-brown as she poured it, in the soft April afternoon, on the park bench.

'I, Edward Moore Kennedy, made the decision to continue in public life after the tragedy and I'm now a different person.'

'A different person, Senator?'

'In my view of life, my view of people, and my faith in God.'

'Is that what he said! An outrage! Since when has God become the refuge of scoundrels?'

'Since forever, you know that.'

'I'll be talking to President Brezhnev about relations between our two great countries. I'm also in Moscow to save lives. Certain individuals have asked for special dispensation to leave this country and I have come to plead their cause.'

Howard had felt queasy.

'Drew?' motioned the senator.

An aide read out names. A Mr Stern wishes to leave with his elderly mother. The Zilberberg family has a sick baby.

'The deal was, let these people out and we'll pay you. Both sides win.'

'President Brezhnev and I will be looking at ways to bring our two great countries closer.'

'He's found a way to upstage Carter. It's all politics.'

The journalists didn't give up easily. Kennedy was grilled again about the horror of that night when his car overturned in water. 'I wanted to protect the young lady.' He enunciated very slowly, one word then the next, and you almost believed him.

'You didn't protect her, senator, you ran away. You set off alone to find a hotel and when you got there the staff said you were drunk.'

Kennedy sat with his palms open on the table, as if inviting the nails of the stigmata. He had nothing to hide.

'I made the decision to continue in public life after the tragedy in Chappaquiddick and I'm now a different person. Like some of you have been transformed by coming to know Russia—this difficult, tragic country—It's like that, the tragedy I've been through.'

It was a masterstroke.

'The way in which I'm a different person is reflected in my view of life, my view of people, my faith in God...I'm a different person.'

The journalists sat mesmerised.

He was a pious American, only here to do good in the world. 'As you know I'm in Moscow to save lives.'

'Senator, there are many, many men women and children trying to get out of here. Not only Jews.' There was that one big problem about this huge gesture of compassion, and Moldy braced himself to state it plainly. It was possible to get out of Russia if you were Jewish. The Americans would buy out Soviet Jews. But what of the others.

To that there was no answer.

Later, after the senator had been received in the Kremlin, in various cars both sides drove to the US embassy for the big official reception.

It was the first time the big public reception hall, once a Russian prince's ballroom, had been opened to outsiders since the fire.

Accredited as Press, they hurried inside, past a guard of well-drilled Marines in white spats. The conference room was full of densely packed rows of chairs, rapidly filling up. A giant photo-portrait of President Carter looked down from where God presided over a church altar. Again they met the furled Stars and Stripes, which here took the place of the vicar's mace. Marines and flags were everywhere.

Kennedy was an enormous untidy man beside the dapper ambassador.

'Mr Ambassador I do have a question. Can the senator tell us how much the US government is paying per refusenik granted an exit visa by the Soviet Union?'

The ambassador looked to the senator, and the senator was unfazed. 'I don't have a figure right now. I can get it to you.'

It would have been a question for the Soviet side too, how much they received per Jewish life, but it was America's vulnerability that it was democratic and so at least offered to take questions. The ambassador hated Arthur in that moment, but soon the provocation would be forgotten. It was, for better, for worse, part of the process. The two great political superpowers of the post-war era were trading in Jews.

The formalities over, under the watch of marine guards the foreign press drifted towards the drinks and the generous TexMex buffet. Californian wine was poured and re-poured. Russians at diplomatic receptions devoured the food in the first five minutes.

The Italian ambassador was there. People were still commiserating with him over the kidnap and murder of his country's prime minister. He agreed he would never get over it.

Sources within Kennedy's entourage let slip that at a private audience with President Brezhnev the supreme leader had fingered the fine cloth of Kennedy's suit.

'The peasant syndrome again!' muttered Moldy. 'He must think it's expected of him by the proletariat of the world.'

'He's just badly behaved,' said Howard.

Hearing Moldy's story a German reporter went round fingering suits. Soon the whole room of Western journalists was laughing and jeering.

'A proletarian paradise. Who said that first?'

'Someone wanting to humiliate my country, Mr Wilde.' It was Korsakov, with his wife.

'Just stating the facts, Mr Korsakov. I believe that's my job.'

Howard had wondered: 'Could she be in danger too?' What she had done for the *Living Souls* essay was now common knowledge. Gels said: 'He must protect her. He's her husband after all.'

As the days lengthened and warmed—it was not by chance that the happiest Russian political days were named 'the thaw'—it was not only a relief that Marlinsky was still a free man. It even raised the question of a Russia that might start to listen to questions of human kindness. Gels said her favourite time in Russian history was that year 1815, when Alexander I had joined Prussia and Austria and Britain in Paris to celebrate the defeat of Napoleon. Russia had sent Napoleon Buonaparte packing from Moscow, back down the Mozhaisk Road. Unafraid of itself, Russia now opened new liberal schools and even created universities. Fresh writers emerged as representatives of a potentially magnificent country, not of the West but not against it either. 'People felt like that after 1945 too. They loved Russia as an ally. Then Stalin stopped cooperating. Broke up marriages. Broke contracts. Locked his people inside more tightly than ever before. There are documents. Moldy did a story on it once.'

Russia continually falls back. And yet each generation there come forward men and women who believe in a good Russia—a country that can find friends abroad and be reformed. Millions believe it. But they stay quiet. And when it comes to the detail they disagree. Not even Gerasimov and Marlinsky agree.

What must happen for Russia to change? The image has come to many minds, over the decades, and the centuries, of the key in the lock. The lock is rusty but one ought to keep trying (Polly Montenari had believed this all her adult life). The key has been mislaid but surely a new one can be cut (Razumovsky would take that view to the grave). On the other hand has not the devil deliberately thrown away the key? (Howard Wilde had reluctantly reached that opinion). What would it take for the Mozhaisk Road to be cleared for permanent two-way traffic?

What Russia requires of its admirers, whether among foreigners or among its own people, is in the end only one thing: unconditional loyalty. Lovers of Russia must offer total commitment, and ask for no reward. They must be patient, and never lose hope. To be cynical would be to give up. Hostile foreign powers would like people wherever they live to give up on Russia. The lovers of Russia must resist the cynicism. For cynicism is treason. And historical fatalism is laziness and cowardice. If you fail to lay down your life for Mother Russia, and abandon her, you are a traitor; and if not a traitor a parasite; and if not a parasite then a scoundrel. And all these sins follow from the character weakness of plain selfishness—the inability to dedicate oneself to the Russian cause.

Thus The Progress Group passed judgement on their failed recruit, Boris Marlinsky.

'Look at this! They're calling him a Robinson Crusoe. He's a Western individualist. Not a Russian at all.'

Gels read the convoluted essay 'Robinsons in Our Midst' open-mouthed, the thin broadsheet easily folded to a readable quarter of its page size, the familiar wet dog odour of the cheap paper forcing her to pay the mildly disgusting price of ten minutes' concentration. 'I seem to remember Robinson Crusoe couldn't help being shipwrecked.'

'Marx said he was a typical capitalist type. That's enough for them.'

> Who does not know youths and students who believe they are the only people in the world! They will quote you much philosophy to support their case. They think, therefore they are. You can take that way of thinking only so far. Only people in a psychiatric ward believe nothing exists apart from themselves, the German philosopher Schopenhauer once said. Well, sanity and knowledge of the world compel us to be a little more generous.

The tricky words made her head spin. Now Marlinsky was immature and selfish. Now, because he believed in himself, he was a madman—a candidate for the *psykhushka*.

'Howard, they couldn't do that, could they? Put him in a madhouse? After all we've seen? After what the West knows?'

Grisha intervened. 'Bvaaaa.'

> Egoism is …a young man's view, but that does not stop many ageing philosophers clinging on to it pathetically. Occasionally we all experience such colossal moods. Some people are so addicted to the fruits of egoism that they resort to unnatural means, to various kinds of intoxication, to bring about what nature supplies of her own free will in healthier days. I have an immediate antidote to such fantasies: life's real problems. What value is this egoism in the face of a sick child or the death of a loved one or not enough food to feed a family?

'But it's got nothing to do with him!'

'They're creating a profile in his name. This is a version of Marlinsky who doesn't care about the well-being of others. He doesn't need or respect community. That's why he's a *Robinson*.'

'Ra—bin—zone,' in Grisha's booming baritone.

> Towards the end of the feudal period in the West, when capitalism became consolidated, men increasingly believed in the rational ego, claiming that personal interest, rightly and reasonably understood, was the only way to live not distorting human nature and not living out an illusion or a lie. What a defence! We can see with hindsight exactly where it led.

'They're rewriting the history of the world according to their approved character types.'

'Approved character types *were* the revolution. People don't realise.'

'But it's all a Sunday school view of morality and just plain lies.'

These rational egotists got together, understood their interests, found they had many in common, and heh presto! the most reasonable thing in the world was the defence of their socio-economic class. Actually capitalist egoism brought the world enormous moral problems. Voluntary actions, so-called altruism, helped relieve its effects on a small scale, but only Communism was able to solve the difficulties universally. The abolition of private property under socialist conditions deprived this monstrous egotistical system of its universal character as a justifier of social action. Under mature Communism egoism completely disappears. It is that goal we are approaching.

In truth the article, signed K.I. Naumov, didn't mention Marlinsky by name, but it was 'generally known' whom it described, said Grisha. *Obshcheizvestno.*

Some men get left behind by history. Some do not feel the way its spirit moves. These Robinsons live their lives as if they were on desert islands, cut off from the general social-historical tide. Bear with me, dear reader, if I quote you just a few lines from an excellent textbook at this point, for it sums up perfectly their position:

In their case certain 'inner' needs and goals of the individual are fixed on as essentially given. This allegedly makes possible and justifies their activity in society. Marx and Engels...criticised this egoism for neglecting the principle of historicism. They criticised egoists who found only ideological expression for their social programmes. They based their criticism on the correct assumption that each time an insurmountable conflict arises between the needs of society and the 'inner' strivings of the individual, such a way of thinking collapses.

'Tossed by Marx and Engels into the dustbin of history! Damn it! Poor Boris Mikhailovich!'

I often think about these Robinsons, of whom there are not a few in our society, even at our advanced stage of Communism. Some of them are sincere men, with generous plans for society, even if they are misguided as to where the root of social progress lies. As philosophy shows, such men have not understood history, which is the reason why their thinking is limited and in the end pathetic. Well, I feel sorry for these Robinsons. They are indeed cut off by their lack of understanding.

'Meaning they gave him a chance,' she breathed. 'And he turned them down.'

> As we all know, what we are is a product of the society we build in accordance with the spirit of history. Communism does not honour men for what they are as individuals. It honours them for what they do in the community. Men and women who strive, as they claim, 'to be honest with themselves', have no claim to call themselves good Communists of benefit to our country. They also have no right to speak of love. Without involvement in the needs of other men, of our humanity as such, they cannot know what love is. It is only under capitalism that these men who cannot find a place for themselves in the community become heroes.

'They present him as a hopeless case.'

'All because he won't join them. It's like a school report. Or a crime report, written in a peculiar code. Can you write it for the paper?'

'Not as such. It might become background, one day.'

'Sounds ominous.'

'I'm afraid so.'

Grisha made that other strange noise again. Bvaaaa. '*The Kommunarka execution yard is a mass grave site located not far from Moscow. In the time of Stalin it was used for the burial of people shot in the house at Nikolskaya 23.*'

'There, there, old chap! Really, they don't do that anymore.'

The report denouncing Marlinsky was deliberately contrived. No one fit to contribute to a newspaper, even a Soviet newspaper, came up with prose like that. The evolution of Communist society was the topic, and the dying away of what did not fit. It was the occasion to single out one man—as if he were a wrong growth along the way—and prune him from the system. And though you knew there was no truth in it and the author didn't believe a word you had to take it as a bad omen.

'As if this bastard K.I. Naumov were trying to convince himself.'

'Surely he is. To justify his existence. He's the vice-president of the Academy of Sciences.'

The strangest thing was that this history of Soviet society was pure fiction. Written in code, it was a lifestyle constructed, equally, out of code; not out of real people and their real lives, but out of reference points whose force was so abstract and so oblique that no one knew what they pointed to, or if they had once known they had forgotten. They could only be re-quoted, re-cited, represented in yet more obscure language. This official society was like a formalist novel. Its author claimed the autonomy of art for the whole of society. It was a place where language functioned within a meaningful whole, albeit quite different from outside. A place where the author was in sole charge and no one could criticise him, because this was art, and art was a dream and we have to have dreams. He then drafted in millions of people to populate his work, without their choice. Within its covers his capacious tale developed certain themes, housed certain characters, paid homage to significant historical events. It *was* like a sci-fi novel—a version of what might be—and yet all the time its actual people were trapped. They lived expelled from real history. Since the words bringing them into creation had long since lost their meaning, the people inhabiting those words lived in ideological limbo. Nor was their creator an artist. Possibly he was the devil. That's what it felt like to belong to this unique country. No key could open up its meaning. It was a Rosetta Stone for our times. A few experts could write it and read it, but in the end no one could be sure.

Arthur replied to the attack on Marlinsky and his reply was grand.

Fools, Cowards and Dealers run Soviet System without Conscience

Moscow—When a bright young man with a desire to tell the truth finds he has grown up in a country where truth doesn't matter, he becomes a dissident. His personal life takes on a political force.

That has been the case with the Russian, Boris Marlinsky, who began working with dissident Alexander Razumovsky last year and is widely seen as his heir.

At twenty-five his disillusion with a system he told me is run by fools, cowards and dealers has ripened into a philosophy of life that sometimes barely seem to touch the surface of reality.

Against the evils of bureaucracy and public corruption he has pitted art and love.

He told me recently at his home in Moscow, that his spiritual nourishment had come from the world of Russian literature and from the pleasures of life with his parents in the country. He trained as a mathematician at Moscow University before he was expelled for protesting over the treatment of an unconventional student labelled as schizophrenic.

Jobless, and under heavy surveillance by the Soviet authorities, Marlinsky faces a future of which only the degree of bleakness seems certain. Whatever happens to him in the next few months will inevitably contrast with the burst of fame that his connection with Razumovsky has earned him in the West.

Like Razumovsky, a veteran campaigner against abuses in Soviet psychiatry, Marlinsky would like to see more Western political action over the poor state of human rights here. Economic sanctions against the Kremlin, whose agricultural and industrial sectors are already in bad shape, seem to them the obvious answer, together with a major campaign of political and diplomatic pressure in the United Nations and other world bodies.

It is easy to accuse these idealistic men, whose main aim is domestic reform, of being naïve about the realities of world politics, but they have a force of conviction which is persuasive beyond logic, and beyond diplomacy. For them human rights has a significance which is perhaps beyond our grasp. We are not part of the same political and national experience. They argue that the mind is by nature free but in this country in totalitarian chains. It has perhaps its own chains in the West, but they are not interested in the comparison. In reply to my questions Marlinsky spoke of freedom in absolute and personal terms: 'I say that freedom is the space in which the individual defines himself. If the state inhibits that space then we can say we experience lack of freedom.' But he argues that the 'space' may just as often be inhibited from one man to another, so that any programme of reform must be based on individual education.

Like a number of Soviet dissidents he organises small discussion groups and teaching groups where he can further those ideals. Freedom, beauty, goodness, the future of mankind, God, mortality: these were the subjects Marlinsky said they tackled.

Marlinsky has given his politics the force of a personal mission and indeed a confession. 'As a man I care about truth. I feel the lie of our system as a sin. My conscience says I must confess it.' He is conscious of but not explicit about his martyrdom. He knows it can only be a matter of time before he is arrested and tried for his ideas, and his friends along with him.

Twenty-Six

Next day the sky was of such a bright blue, so perfectly compatible with a child's happy dreams, that Moldy said the clouds had been seeded.

'You're just a cynical Brit. You think everything is fake here. Even good weather if it's a special day.'

'Thank you, Gels.' He bowed to her.

On the other hand the annual parade was a party, of a kind, and why shouldn't parties thrown by leaders for their people be perfect at the expense of a little artifice? You want your children to be happy.

Moscow certainly looked the part, cleared from the Army Park to the Kremlin of people and cars. Goons in uniform controlled access to Red Square, and it looked as if the pavements had been swept. She was prepared to defend it, but it frightened her. Formal occasions like this were dress rehearsals for mass conscription.

A sparrow flew by. 'They can't give the birds orders.'

'They can shoot them.'

'That wouldn't look nice, with all the world watching.'

'Thank you, Howard, that really helps me.'

Self-important arm-banded citizens strutted about the empty asphalt looking for incidences of deviance, or rested chatting at the checkpoints. Anyone allowed beyond the Bolshoi Theatre carried an invitation card. Meanwhile Howard and Moldy were discussing the football genius of Brian Clough. Lighten up? All right, lighten up. Gels told Harriet that for the first time this year Britain was also to have a May Day bank holiday.

'I always thought Britain was a socialist country.'

'It might be. But we somehow never quite get there.' Seated on an unforgiving wooden bench, the two women made a joke about their native countries which hung over them in unspoken ways, and they forgave each other because Moscow was like that. You kept having to ask yourself: is yours a good

354

country. Is it a good place to make a life? Harriet produced two inflatable cushions. Americans had everything. Gels said American lives were just *too* comfortable.

'Not all of them, honey.'

'Well, right.' And that took them back to square one, and perhaps they should watch the parade. Banners, athletes, drum majorettes; music with a strong beat and a national pull as the tanks rolled by.

Howard and Arthur took it in turns to survey the other side—the privileged Russian audience, in specially reserved seats—through binoculars. Howard passed them to Gels, from where, he gestured, they should revert to Harriet and back to Arthur.

'Irina Korsakov's still around then,' Gels observed, with a twist of the focus so that she was effectively sitting right next to her. 'She could be the editor of Soviet Vogue.'

'In another universe.'

'Who knows? Maybe one day. If not I'd like to be its editor.'

'Get Daddy to buy it!'

'Howard, will you never forgive me my origins? Have I not done my penance?'

Harriet asked: 'What did happen when they took Marlinsky out there? We don't seem to know.'

'It's as if they swore him to secrecy.'

'*She* must have made an impression on him,' Arthur observed.

'I would have been impressed,' conceded Howard.

'This is men's talk.'

'Politics is never just politics.'

'It's about living together.'

'Thank you, Gels. It's also about who you admire. The kind of people you want to be among.'

'No one can resist beautiful people.'

When the hour came, struck by the chimes of St Basil's, it sounded savage. Honestly those bells were as harsh and cruel as if saucepan lids were banged together before an execution, said Moldy, though he wouldn't tell that to the TV camera.

The thirteen members of the Politburo, one in uniform, the others in civvies, twelve good men, one Judas, who knew, headed by the Chairman of the Party, who was also the luxury-car-loving president, filed on to the upended marble box at the top end of Red Square. The BBC cameraman filmed it, as did the rest of the world's press.

The box contained the preserved body of the First Leader. He was among us and will one day come again.

'It disgusts me.'

'It's just a relic. People don't think about it much anymore.'

'One great leader and then what?'

'Downfall. Where we are today.'

A music of drums and pipes filled the air and the parade began. In a sleek black polo-necked jumper and a grey skirt, a knee-length sheepskin coat worn open over them, and black leather boots, Irina brought style to the rank of shabby granddads above her. Gels had to admire her for it. Down below the ranks of the VIPs, of the rulers and their minions, division after division of tub-thumping washerwomen, spoon-clicking factory workers, beautifully athletic young men and women high-stepping and holding banners aloft, soldiers marching with imperial pride and precision, the whole coordinated rhythmically—an impressive sight—demonstrated what the residue country was made of. Tanks crawled behind, their long guns as if searching for spectators not paying attention.

'They have to show off.'

'If we were part of it we'd feel with it. We all have myths we need to live by.'

'I know something,' said Gels. 'People love this country. They love being part of it.'

'And the ones who criticise it love it most.'

'Razumovsky, you mean? But he's a professor and the people don't care for intellectuals.'

'That's true of Marlinsky too.'

Arthur shrugged. He took a new tour with the field glasses. 'That's the president of the Academy of Sciences in the centre and his deputy to his right, our left.'

'That bastard! That fat pig! All that stupid talk about Robinsons.'

Arthur was all concentration, and as if making notes out loud. 'The anatomy of a nation.'

The banners flashed messages:

DOWN WITH IMPERIALISM!

LONG LIVE OUR GREAT MOTHERLAND!

THE LAND OF THE SOVIETS IS FIGHTING FOR PEACE! ALL HAIL INTERNATIONALISM, LEGACY OF MARX!

'The Korsakovs don't dress like workers.'

'Contradictions, my dear Harriet. They will all be reconciled in the future.'

It helped that the day was warm. Some years you sat banging your feet and unable to think of much else, said Moldy, as the refrigerator assemblers, and the shoemakers, and the watchmakers showed what they were made of and what they could do for their country. They twirled sticks like American cheerleaders. Above them, standing on the mausoleum, the old men nodded like clockwork toys.

And then finally the last division of twirling toilers, in Howard's sarcastic phrase, receded.

'No, oh my God, look!'

A division of 'Workers in Ink' marched past, holding above their shoulders a huge cardboard typewriter. A TYPEWRITER! A banner announced: 'WE ARE THE PEOPLE OF HONESTY, HONOUR AND CONSCIENCE. WE ARE THE TRUE MIND OF RUSSIA.'

Gerasimov strode alongside Marlinsky. Howard's binoculars settled on a disfigured Galya Obolenskaya, translator of Dickens, marching beside them. She was wearing a close-fitting green hat. Malefactors had almost cost her her life. Howard trembled. He wanted to protect these brave people. Their moral zeal disconcerted him. What they brought to the cause was so personal. What they were prepared to lose. Gels sobbed aloud and covered her face with her hands, which was foolish, because she wanted to see them; to keep her grateful eyes on them for as long as she could.

Marlinsky five hundred metres from their gaze marched beside his dear Galya Obolenskaya and his beloved Gerasimov. They linked arms and flanking Galya each man raised the other fist. WE ARE THE WORKERS IN INK. RUSSIA NEEDS US TO TELL THE TRUTH. Marlinsky remembered how his teacher Anatoly Reikhman had been banished. THEY had destroyed him. But no it wasn't their fault. They gave him freedom! Rubbish. Sheer cruelty. Reikhman was too old to rebuild his career abroad and anyway had no money.

Then Marlinsky recalled the demotion of his own father: his removal from his job. He had loved his work on the Russian soil, and derived such satisfaction from the thought that science would help his country if nothing else. His was a country that, in the end, deserved to succeed, for it had so many wonderful people making efforts and sacrifices on its behalf. Glory to the Soviet Union! Marlinsky remembered the removal of his mother from the work with children that she loved; how they deliberately tore her away from an area of life in which she believed she could help make people better. He remembered the death of his friend the poet Shaginyan, who wrote:

The Russian-speaking world has such short sight
Who can make it out—a metaphor? An act?
Tiredness? Courage? Fright?

And, more intimately,

Above the back of a sofa—
A deer flew, not feeling its legs.
This is the life. Suck some seltzer,
Shrug off the calendar.
I accept my entire fate, except…
But that, as the ancients say,
Is a story for another day.
I dream of a quiet hamlet
Not far from the Caucasus.
For now, my memory's light.

A voiced crackled through a loudspeaker. 'Today we report the death of one of our comrades, cruelly incarcerated for the true words he wrote. I will now read from his poems.'

'Isn't that…? Aren't those…?' Arthur's binoculars rested on the artists Zolodei and Zorin.

'The burden of untruth has got to them.'

Harriet reflected with justification that the parts they played in her production of *The Audit* had ended their dependence on Korsakov.

'I want to say, ladies and gentlemen, that I believe in freedom and I won't rest till this country is free. I will now read...'

At which point the police corralled the protesters—who had held a dissident public meeting to rival the great parade. They didn't cosh them because the world was watching, but they shoved them into vans and drove them away.

Not until late afternoon did the bare cobbles of Red Square fall back exhausted from this day-long pageant of productivity, where, as Korsakov put it, a few slackers still insisted on displaying their rotten apples.

Twenty-Seven

When a notice finally appeared on the state news agency service, in Russian, it was in terse officialese easy to miss. When it finally confirmed the arrest of Marlinsky together with his friend Gerasimov, it corroborated something Razumovsky had heard involuntarily. Russia is a land full of rumours, and the rumours endure until someone turns a key in a lock, or picks up an axe. The goons in the yellow Volga parked beneath his window made sure Razumovsky got the news in good time. He rang the LGN office from a callbox, his familiar pile of grey *dvushki* at the ready—the Soviet equivalent of American dimes. He found Howard already filing a brief report on the aftershocks of the parade day. 'Had to be.' The other freelance demonstrators had been released but these two had been held as ringleaders.

Gels heard Howard say 'Don't Alexander Nikolaevich please. We'll have no one left. Please not!' He pulled towards him pen and paper. 'Not so fast, please. Repeat that! I'll read it back to you.'

She raised her eyebrows hoping he would share.

He crashed the cheap plastic phone back on to its cradle. 'They're going on a bloody hunger strike in solidarity.'

'I bet it was Natasha's idea. She's the feisty one.'

'You can't claim her for the women. They belong together.'

'That's not what I meant at all.' But Howard, who could be touchy about feminism, took himself out into the back room, to the teleprinter, where the cool temperature also calmed his inflamed heart.

'We're not to go out there. They don't want to see anyone. Not even us. He's issued a statement.'

'But he might die.'

Protest in Russia was always a calculation.

Gels read parts of the story as Howard typed. 'To quote Razumovsky, …We appeal to the Pope, and to President James E. Carter, and the leaders of the free world to free these innocent men immediately…Until they are freed my wife and I are on hunger strike.'

'He's strong as an ox. What do the Russians say?'

'Strong as an ox. Let's hope.'

Two hours later, as the world's most powerful man responded to the challenge, Washington reporters hammered on their typewriters. 'The president said, and I quote: *We are very worried about the health of Academician and Mrs Razumovsky and are seeking reassurances from the Soviet government.*'

Grisha was securing the story to the clipboard and shaking his head, as Howard filled out the background. Who the Razumovskys were, how they had protested before, how Marlinsky had come on the scene.

'What does the E stand for?'

'Earl. They use it like a patronymic.'

'Gels V. Maybey is what they put on my credit card.'

'The Americanisation of everything.'

Out at Pervomayskaya the community of journalists organised a shift to keep watch. In pairs, for safety's sake, they parked on the hard shoulder and watched for signs that the police, with a medical team, were gearing up to storm the Razumovsky apartment. The Westerners watched the Razumovskys (who didn't want to be watched at all) and the goons watched everyone.

'It takes four days before the body starts to eat itself.'

'Someone threw a bundle up onto the balcony yesterday. Natasha undid it and shook the contents of the tea towel out over the edge. Three apples, a loaf and two pieces of meat. A dog ate the escalopes.'

'Lucky dog. THEY're turning it into a comedy.'

'What else.'

They sat in the car, as if waiting for the action of a play to begin.

'Who was the third apple for?'

'Russians can't count.'

Howard had his binoculars trained on the balcony where Natasha was touching her toes.

'Ah, she's great! She's showing off! Brava, Natasha!'

'They're scientists. They know how the human body works.'

'Raz, dva, tri…' shouted a police wit, standing alongside the regulation yellow Volga. 'And one and two and three…'

'Don't wave,' said Howard.

'And you don't go over there and punch him. Or I wouldn't mind if you did. What a miracle! They've turned their bodies into a political weapon. Plenty of water, and some salt tablets will keep them going for a good while. Pushkin famously said he'd erected a monument. His work. His body. Everything that was him.'

'It must be a comfort to have so much knowledge.'

But sarcastic Howard suddenly got excited. He wanted to tell Gels a tactical truth he'd realised, as they took their turn sitting there in the car, watching over the Razumovskys on their hunger strike. 'Until we can find out what's happening to Marlinsky this is the ideal way to keep the whole dissident story going. Protest continues. Keep your eyes on Moscow, world! Right now the balance of world power is in this flat in Pervomayskaya. It's like leaving the camera running. Brilliant. I salute you, Alexander Nikolaevich.'

The police moved a van into the area with medical equipment and left it open for inspection, because the whole world was watching the fate of the Russian dissidents.

'Where are we?'

'No news except they're not together. The doctors promised to keep them together then took them to separate hospitals.'

'It's for your own sake, Comrades. We don't want you to die on us.'

'I insist you take me to the same hospital as my wife.'

'Haven't you seen enough of her, grandpa? How long have you been married?'

There were no pictures, but descriptions and quotes leaked out. Once Alexander Nikolaevich was hooked up to a drip, and anchored by wires that monitored his vital functions, a nurse whispered, 'If there's anything you need, Comrade…'

In Russia punishment is a birth-right. Inescapable. Compassion is its twin. True Comradeship, you see. It's in our Russian blood. You see what the Party made its own.

He told the nurse he'd like to swap books with his wife. He was quite apologetic. 'I find I read so very fast when I am confined to bed.'

Thus they wrote messages to each other. The messages were to be found in the margins of pages that corresponded to the year of his birth, p.21 and the month, p.10. Her birth year, 32, and then p.5, the month. And then, as necessary they added 10 to all the sequences. No one looked anyway.

'Eat my love, we've done what we could.'

'Eat this junk? You must be joking.'

'I'll send you chocolate. You like chocolate.'

And he did, courtesy of the comradely nurse, who bought three tablets of Shokolad Sputnik.

'I am your companion along the way.'

'I am yours. *Ya tvoi sputnik.*'

While those two disappeared from worldview, Korsakov pondered what next. 'Mr Writer, I'll give you something to fill those blank sheets with.'

Writers are intolerable, with their superiority, and their moralising.

'Mrs Harriet Zimmerman, I'll give you a spectacle to put your view of Russia in perspective.'

Foreigners are sanctimonious meddlers.

Korsakov had tried his best. He too had his vision of a better country. He too longed for affluence to make the daily grind less harsh. It's just a matter of our being slow starters in history. I mean if you read Dickens on England's *Hard Times*, you might think Russia was only now living its version of English nineteenth-century misery. So what? Unpleasant but not wicked.

There are people like Marlinsky and their chief task is to make you feel inferior and irrelevant.

But the *psikhushk*i, Mr Korsakov! Rubbish. You have them too.

But not for our critics! Not for the sanest people of all!

Rubbish. Our whole system is only a little bit harsh because we have to force our people to cooperate to achieve anything at all.

No, Korsakov. I can't agree with you. The system here has taken every last manual worker captive and persuaded them to work for a cause; but in reality to generate some wealth for men like you. It's not right. Gramsci told you so. Polly told you. The people have to be allowed to count. They have to be given respect.

Oh, but signor Gramsci, if they aren't made to work in our country all they do is drink. Sorry Signorina, that is the case.

So, your well-respected Signorina took out the dossier, Korsakov. She didn't respect you, in the end. But then you know that.

Yes. And that was a humiliation. One in the eye for us. It happens. People like to humiliate mighty Russia.

But the problem with Marlinsky, that snooty boy, was he didn't acknowledge the effort Korsakov had made: his diplomacy, and his thoughtfulness. Why, he would have welcomed him as a second son!

Meanwhile The Progress Group, never true allies, but a coterie formed by accident over recent years, only carped. 'He gave him his wife too,' mused Makarenko. 'And all for nothing.'

So now, at least to assert his authority over that rackety clientele, he decided to hang a second Rukhin painting in the dining room, in that lovely villa out beyond the Mozhaisk Road, and insist they gather to celebrate it.

It was called 'Moscow Nights', and it could have been flowers neglected in a window box, or a miniature assembled to show Moscow on fire. That muddy orange streak could have been an exotic blossom or an all-consuming flame: a cause for pride or a folk memory from 1812 now so deeply rooted it made the people morbid and desperate and superstitious; they had set fire to their city to stop an invasion and burnt themselves to a cinder; and again in 1941; but how much had they lost in erecting this barrier with the West, which reduced their own treasure to ashes.

He said only: 'What a painter, eh?'

'It's smudged,' said the Mack, which was true. 'It looks like a kitchen sink.' Indeed. The charred effects of the fire, and the remains of the living plants, were as if carelessly wiped against the whiteish background of a wall or a sink that no one cleaned. The domestic dimension was clear. What it was like to live a human life badly. Without refinement. Without concern or care. Whatever is still alive, just before the moment of painting, is captured here, already withering away.

'I could say a great deal. I could suggest that you are wrong, Comrade, to identify a "smudge" where you would do better to speak of a significant mark. But you are intelligent people. You can see for yourselves.'

'And this is what they pay dollars for in the West? Wo-hay.' That was his own son, Matvei.

'Try a bit harder, Matt,' whispered Lisa. 'It's the real thing. It shows how much we have to learn, stuck here with our schmalzy Soviet sob-stories and icons of national history. This belongs to our part of the twentieth century, at last. At last one of our painters has got there. And how!'

'You think that Marlinsky would have liked it? He's one of them, isn't he?' said Makarenko.

'One of…?'

'The enemies of our state who call themselves artists.'

'Workers in paint!' chirruped Matvei. Lisa giggled.

'Writers are often sensitive to the visual arts. But I don't think it's a conspiracy.'

'You're soft on him.'

'Not at all. I'm just not sure about lumping all our "enemies" together. It seems to me anyway that a painting like this is inimitable. What could a writer come up with to match it?'

But hearing Korsakov almost softening reminded Naumov they had to act decisively where Marlinsky was concerned. The young man had done everything wrong, 'as if he were deliberately provoking us.'

'He resigned from the Komsomol.'

'They threw him out.'

'He was sacked from the university.'

'That followed.'

The Progress Group members continued to peer at the little picture as if the devil himself had hung it in their midst. A chain that bode no one well suddenly disclosed itself on the left side, as if the flower box were a book chained to the wall. Amid the neglected plant life was one wholesome green shoot. Who knows, perhaps the whole could be restored to health. The watercolour painting was intensely rhythmic. Really some marvellous lines caught the aspiration of the plants as they had grown at the height of their season. Or were they lines of smoke rising from the conflagration.

'He is an associate of Razumovsky.'

'Indeed. That is indeed where I felt I wanted to intervene to persuade him otherwise.'

'He's made himself useless here. You should have sent him abroad,' insisted Balabin.

'He's a parasite. And now with his foolish prancing in front of the parade cameras and reciting those so-called poems he's made a fool of us in front of the whole world.'

Round the table they went now, with cheap biros making the occasional note, mostly doodling, on low-grade paper pads. Where earlier they had been free to roam and converse now Korsakov had finally summoned them to the table, and sent Matvei and Lisa packing.

'Ugh.' The mineral water from Georgia was as salty as a cure in Carlsbad.

'What happened to the Borzomi?'

'*Defitsitny.*'

'Coca-Cola?'

'*Oo nass tozhe net.*'

They didn't have that either.

'Too bad we don't make any decent soft drinks.'

'The parade showed that what ex-Comrade Marlinsky wants is revenge against our society.'

The muscles in Korsakov's neck stiffened. 'And what follows from that, dear lady?' He opened a bottle of the salty stuff all the same.

'The doctors advise…'

'Oh no, it was just childish exhibitionism made him parade like that.' For, oddly, in that moment he felt concerned for the man who had briefly been his wife's lover. He did not want him declared insane. That would have removed the issue.

'Exhibition-*ism* is his illness,' Miss Makarenko repeated.

'Or some other -ism,' Balabin muttered. 'You'll think of one.' He had once joked to his students that the system was like a book of mathematical tables. You know how you line up numbers and columns to work out tangents and co-tangents? Well, in our world, *oo nass*, you looked up your -*ism* to see whether it was a deviation or an illness.

'Look up Communism while you're there, my friends,' he had counselled them one Wednesday afternoon, 'the next time you're consulting the mathematical tables. Our country makes a mockery of science.'

'I did say exhibitionism, yes. "A Worker in Ink?" What pretention! What self-importance!'

'He *is* an anti-social element, that's clear.'

'Exactly, Comrade Vice-President. One does so hate these types who won't pull their weight.'

'Robinsons *will* be the death of our way of life.'

'Fortunately you've defined them for us, Comrade Vice-President, so we can be on our guard.'

As the mood of unforgiveness hardened, Korsakov poured them all a brandy.

Irina, who had arrived half-way through, remained looking at the painting. But then she couldn't wait for her latest tipple. She swirled the rich viscous liquid in her glass. Suddenly its chestnut colour reminded her so intensely of Galya's hair she spat it out. '*Mais vous êtes si cruel, mon mari. Pourquoi n'avez-vous détruit ma beauté à moi? Pourquoi fallait-il détruire la beauté d'une femme innocente qui aurait donnée sa vie pour la Russie?*'

In the language of Tolstoy.

Korsakov muttered, not sending the bottle round, because he enjoyed pouring it himself. 'What she did was illegal.' But that was history now.

'It will never be history so long as her friends remember.'

On Marlinsky Korsakov summed up. 'Perhaps you have something to add, my dear? You more than any of us got to know him better when he was here.'

'Where will he be sent?' Irina cried, waving her brandy.

'Why,' said her husband. 'You want to go there too?'

'Can anyone find it on the map, where he's going!' joked the Vice-President.

'We don't have maps, Kiril Innokentevich, as you know. In case they fall into enemy hands.'

'But this isn't right!' She banged the table and slopped the wretched brandy.

Not her husband, who was in pain, but The Progress Group sniggered.

'Volodya, sweetheart,' she cajoled. 'Think of the headlines the Westerners will come up with. WRITER BANISHED FOR CALLING HIMSELF WORKER IN INK.' Are you not ashamed? *Kak tebe ne stydno*!'

'Marlinsky is a bad Comrade. He needs a revision course.'

'Mr Naumov, what do *you* think? Is our Mr Marlinsky guilty? What do *you* think?'

Korsakov continued to reflect silently, Naumov to sit on the fence, Makarenko to fume, and Balabin to pine. Finally Korsakov came out with:

'Our book industry is thriving. Our writers are thriving. No one can accuse us of lack of culture.'

'Our writers are not thriving. Nor are our dancers, nor are our painters.' Irina slammed the door behind her.

'They're mad. That's not our fault.'

'Better to be a dancer. No one knows what you've got in your head.'

'Until you start miming it.'

'Let's all just shut up then,' Korsakov said to the remaining committee. 'Let's have a collective and terminal shutting-up.'

'Professor. You want to break the silence?'

'Marlinsky will need to be removed. For God's sake send him abroad.'

'Prison is the appropriate punishment for a critic of the regime.'

'It won't change his mind. Our poets seem to be able to inherit acquired characteristics, just like Lysenko said our people might. With our poets we've been beating the hell out of them for so long, through so many generations, that our poets are made of rubber.'

> I played the game, and now I'm off the force.
> I've solved your crosswords to the final clue.
> And now I ask for severance, divorce,-
> the right to bugger off to pastures new.

'Where did you get that?'

'One of my students. Samizdat. I thought you might be interested.'

'Put it away! I don't want to hear it.'

Korsakov would win because he had to win. He had to win, with Katya his secretary and the Major and half the Westerners laughing behind his back.

'That's what you get for being nice to scum, eh, Comrade?'

Naumov's eyes had shrunk so deep into his head he resembled Orson Welles in his time of decline.

Dutifully Korsakov called Arthur in on the Monday over his Marlinsky profile. He behaved like the foreign ministry summoning an ambassador to deliver an official reprimand. But he wasn't the foreign ministry and Arthur took his time. He could manage 4pm on Tuesday, he said. He would hang up on that legs-up-to-her-ears secretary if she didn't agree. The stink of her perfume hadn't diminished.

'*Sadites.*'

'*Spasibo.*'

Arthur couldn't help it. If they spoke Russian he felt flattered. He took a seat. Unlike the normal twenty minutes Korsakov kept him waiting he went in almost immediately.

Korsakov started straight in. 'Why you slag off Rasher, Artur?'

He was unwrapping one of those fancy black cigarettes he kept in an onyx box. 'I know you don't smoke.'

The American answered. 'I report what I find and what I find appals me.'

'Marlinsky is a disloyal, unpatriotic citizen. Indeed he is a traitor.'

'He's a discontented citizen. Someone typically fed up with the lies and the absurdities of the Cold War and not allowed to say so.'

'Ah, truth! They say it, you parrot it. Every citizen is allowed to say what he thinks in our country, but through the proper channels. We don't like bad manners.'

'And those channels are?'

'A Soviet citizen knows what they are.'

'You mean every citizen has freedom of speech if he doesn't care what happens to him.'

'I mean slander against the state is not allowed.'

They eyeballed each other across Korsakov's desk, with the grotesque onyx box, and matching lighter and telephone. How couldn't he know what bad taste that was? Was it because Russia had these oriental ways? To match its Byzantine bureaucracy? Surely Byzantium was maligned.

Arthur refocused. 'I'm asking for the last time what are you going to do with Marlinsky.' His interlocutor was feeble. The American, summoned for a reprimand, had easily seized the initiative. 'Be very careful, Korsakov. The whole world is watching you.'

Korsakov silently raised his hands and nodded.

Twenty-Eight

A Cold War criminal. A man or woman guilty of Cold War crimes. Why was that offence never invented? Vladimir Arkadevich Korsakov would by the end of the day be a guilty man.

Still it would be hard to say what the offence was. The law was the law in that corrupt country. The state made sure that the verdicts of the courts played out strictly in the state's interests and the punishment was to move awkward people from one place to another, as if on a chess board. To move them to a remote square, outside the game, or over the edge, where they could no longer play at all. The *psykhushki* played the same role only without appeal to the constitution. Rather they degraded and distorted the human constitution, until there was nothing left. But Korsakov wouldn't have taken that route, unless he had been forced into it. He had too much respect for Marlinsky. You might say Korsakov even wished the young man well, and here was an inclination that, for the first time in years, his wife shared with him. It was not a crime for Korsakov to seek occasion to shine in his wife's otherwise long since averted eyes. But how he made that possible, at the same time as holding on to his job, and his house, and his position in life, entailed such a subtle cruelty that the usual jurisdictions have no name for it.

The Moscow summer was hot. People don't think of Moscow as a dusty desert but by July it hadn't rained for so long that to get to the courtroom was like crossing a dried-up riverbed. It involved traversing a certain *mikrorayon* no one had heard of before and where the metro didn't yet reach.

Howard caught in his hands a few of the little cotton flakes that commonly fell in a Moscow summer, from the poplar trees. 'They call this Stalin's confetti. Nature scatters it to soften the bad news.'

The courtroom was a five-storey brick building. It seemed suddenly to rise up out of nowhere, like an idea someone had yesterday and built today. Architecture had shut down too. The structure had no context. It just stood there.

370

Above were flats with mean windows, the sort of box-like, sense-deadening public housing you could find anywhere, only here with air-conditioning boxes hooked onto outside walls. Bars secured the ground floor windows.

Nor was the entrance to the City People's Court obvious.

'You come to the castle, you actually manage to find it, and then you can't get in. We all know—' They had been walking round the area for a good quarter of an hour.

'There must be some school of design that finds that funny.'

'The concealed door! You'll see, it will become fashionable.'

'For what stupid reason would that be?'

'To keep the façade smooth.'

'To smooth over the contradictions. Remind me in ten years' time, Howard Wilde, if we're still in touch, that it was in Moscow that I learnt to accept contradictions. I'll never believe in them. But I have to accept them.'

When it was proposed, for instance, that modern architecture should provide human beings with machines for living, the suggestion was not for human beings to become machines.

'The evil was when human beings became packaged. That was not a contradiction though. It was a cruel parody of human aspiration.'

'We're all commodities, Gels. The powers that be move us around.'

'Except when we resist. You and I do that, Howard. We resist. Even you.'

They stalked the length of the building's long side and rounded the top corner of a square in the making. Gels felt grim. But just then a handful of colleagues and others waiting in the centre under some skimpy trees came into sight. Arthur in jeans and a shirt with short sleeves was holding a transistor radio to his ear. 'Be right with you!' He looked comically efficient, and decent, and it was such a relief to see a good man at work in that unholy country where the sight of not even friends, just familiar faces, could make you weep.

Howard wore a pale summer safari suit with a white shirt and a red tie. Gels wore a summer dress in striped cotton and sunglasses. They looked like a well-dressed middle-class Western couple on holiday.

Howard said to Arthur: 'You found the bloody entrance then?' It turned out to be a tiny hatch of a door across from where they were facing. Now, with Arthur though, Howard rallied. He found his strength and his presence of mind. He yearned for this big story to happen, and to report it to the world. 'The Razumovskys are here!' He cheered and waved. 'Bravo, Alexander, Natasha!

371

I'm happy to see you here.' Gels followed, smiling slightly, she hoped appropriately, for she had never felt sure of their welcome, as she trailed in Howard's wake.

'Not the ideal occasion,' Natasha said, as if she'd come to a funeral. A christening would have been more welcome. The occasion that day was of that fundamental order but had no name.

Razumovsky's much younger wife looked emaciated but not unwell. She had on a button-through dress in some darkish floral material and her white legs, so recently incarcerated, were bare. Howard had feared the end of that couple; and he was mightily relieved.

Razumovsky cut the usual crumpled figure. But he was still a fine, refined man, tall in stature and good-looking by nature, and though his cheeks were sunken he was in good spirits. Remarkable for a man who had recently been told they would let his wife die if he didn't eat.

This was the Razumovskys' vocation, Gels surmised. They didn't much bother with her because they thought she wasn't of their kind.

'They've brought their own camping chairs,' and she joined Howard in gazing across and starting to walk in their direction.

'Because justice is a spectator sport in Russia,' he replied wistfully. 'You never know how long justice will take and what will be the outcome.'

The Westerners waved half-heartedly and retreated when Natasha poured tea from a flask. Indicating that was exactly her wish she nodded.

'We'll leave you in peace, Natalya Ivanovna.'

From a distance Gels and Howard resumed their watchfulness. The extraordinary couple busied themselves claiming a fraction of the ragged, inhospitable city periphery as a civic space. They occupied it as if it were quite incontestably part of a civilised public life; and that was what you had to do; maintain the old, decent assumptions as if they had never been eclipsed.

'Justice is a good use for a life.'

Whatever was going to happen to Marlinsky and Gerasimov, the Soviet press had been lambasting their *kind* all week; not mentioning them by name; never directly accusing them; but stacking the cards against them. 'Consumerism—a Grim and Uninviting World'! was one headline Grisha had ringed. The West struggles with drugs, alcohol and promiscuity because it tolerates idlers. Who would want to leave Russia for the West? But that wasn't what they wanted, of course. They were patriots if any men were.

Another risky headline was 'The Unbalanced Minority.' Why are people occasionally anti-Soviet? Because they can't see straight. Because they need help.

Meanwhile it was reported that in Leningrad Robinson-minded proselytisers were trying to tempt schoolchildren into joining so-called alternative discussion groups so that they no longer believed in socialism. Robinsons were really terrible people.

'If you disbelieve in everything around you what do you become?'

'You can't judge it like that. You have to start from the end result and work back. A country that produces results like this has got it wrong.'

'They're admitting they've got it wrong?'

'Korsakov knows it but he doesn't know what else to do. Or rather, he built his house here a long time ago. He's not about to raze it to the ground.'

'If they change their ways what will they change into?'

'Exactly. A place without a name. A place no one recognises.'

'The Devil needs his name.'

Some reporters had gathered around Razumovsky and it seemed he decided there and then to give an off-the-cuff press conference. Gels and Howard strolled back over. 'Boris Marlinsky is a brave man, a selfless man, with too much of a conscience for their liking,' Razumovsky was saying. 'They also see him as a kind of foreigner. A man from a place not their own.'

Arthur said: 'The Soviets are always looking for the foreign element. They can't bear it. They're not Communists. They're chauvinists. You have to be Russian their way or not at all'

Razumovsky didn't answer.

A war against foreign ways, yes, that was what this Soviet Communism was. It had been invented to defend Russia, and the way of Russian life was to be intolerant and cruel. The reporters took notes. Arthur did too, holding the radio between his feet.

'No sign of Moldy?'

'He's on holiday.'

'What a time to pick.'

'He didn't choose it. Korsakov made such a fuss about Mary Wormold doing Harriet's play that Patrick either had to leave Moscow altogether or take an unscheduled break.'

'It's just petty.'

'And stupid. The BBC will just send someone else.'

'That's how they do it. They put the West to inconvenience. They've no other way.'

Gels felt more and more grim. 'Good that they're not going to shoot Wormy and Mary.'

Razumovsky continued: 'Marlinsky is an idealist who believes in the sanctity of the human psyche. Our rulers believe the opposite. They will invade anyone's soul.' The observation was too deep to play well as world news, but journalists like Arthur and Howard stored it away for quieter times, when they analysed the decline of the USSR.

'The press has been attacking you too, Sir.'

Razumovsky, an honest and savvy soul, answered with a faint smile. Yes it was true he had received an invitation from a Swiss university.

'The Soviet press reported the West offered you gold, fame and Scotch whisky.'

He laughed a fraction.

Gels said to Howard that it was an interesting reflection of what a Western university had to offer. Korsakov, certainly the source of the misinformation, thought an institution of higher learning could lure the greatest minds in the world with a mixture of booze, wealth and prestige.

'The way Oxbridge is going…'

'Might you accept, sir?'

Natasha Razumovsky interrupted. 'That's not the right question. We don't dare leave.' It was her wish to leave, Howard knew that. She longed for a simpler, happier life, with her husband. But 'They'd never let us back.' It didn't mean she wasn't tired of it.

'Booze, money and status is what Korsakov himself has.'

'Maybe he's grown tired of it.'

Howard paused. 'That's another thing about Soviet justice, Gels. It starts with character assassination and ends with—'

'A bullet? You're not saying they're going to shoot Marlinsky?'

'Grisha keeps chanting: "*The Kommunarka execution yard is a mass grave site located not far from Moscow. It is used for the burial of people shot in the house at Nikolskaya 23.*"'

'Was…not is.'

'It's the system that does it to them. Black is white. Sane is sick. Justice is impossible.'

'It's like one of those little plastic puzzles where you can never get the pieces in the right order because there's isn't enough space to move.'

Razumovsky concluded by declaring himself happy that the International Psychiatric Council had expelled Russia. The news was three months old but the Marlinsky affair was an occasion to recycle it. 'I'll take a break now, ladies and gentlemen.'

Arthur looked at his watch. No one knew when Marlinsky would arrive, and, in truth, whether with Gerasimov or not, for their cases were not the same, nor how long they would have to wait.

Accepting the Razumovskys ought to be left in peace, ahead of a long day, the journalists withdrew to a distance away. On the far side of the square, opposite the court building, a solitary child was careening down a slide in a playground. The reporters all sometime stared at his yellow t-shirt and mused on his innocence. Grotesque, really.

The Razumovskys enjoyed a wafer biscuit and a second tea, and then took out their books.

'Polly!' The Italian woman, Howard's occasional lover, Gels's admired friend, looked fabulous in a crisp white shirt, sleeves rolled up, exposing her tanned forearms, and high-waisted dark jeans. Bizarrely Gels feared for the shirt: that it would mark so easily when blood was spilt.

'I wouldn't normally report a dissident story like this. But this time they've gone too far. Besides, how are you, Gels?' The two women hugged.

Polly listed reasons why she might anyway leave. 'They call themselves Communists, living out there in that damn great pile, full of art and hangers-on. They're like decadent Romans. Even so I keep hoping some better people will step forward.'

The three of them stood chatting and laughing, then Gels said: 'I thought you were helping them rethink their whole approach.'

'Clearly, I failed.'

In the background a TV crew had arrived and a makeup girl was applying panstick to Razumovsky who screwed up his face like a disgruntled pet. Natasha restricted herself to tutting and clucking in disgust. The West was decadent. Everyone knew that.

'Great, that's great, thank you, Sir.' The girl held a mirror up to him for his approval. 'Now if you could just approach the courtroom.'

They filmed Razumovsky as he walked towards the once obscure entrance, now the focus of every camera on site. 'Not open yet,' snapped the functionary who promptly closed the door in Razumovsky's face. The cameras hovered over the black and gold official plaque: Ministry of Justice, Moscow City Region.

Natasha joined him outside the unyielding door, they linked arms, and returned to their base camp.

Polly said: 'We have to hope better people come along. Those Politburo *stronzi* are not immortal.'

'Admit it, Pol, the system's broken.'

'Maybe some will come along who can fix it.'

'You were supposed to fix it weren't you, by teaching them Gramsci?'

'Sounds to me like waiting for the Messiah.'

'Meanwhile step in Senator Edward Kennedy!'

'Like a surgeon letting blood from the diseased body.' Polly shrugged.

Gels said: 'It's all hopeless.'

A 'Black Seagull', an official car, finally drew up in the side road Howard and Gels had first walked along. Simultaneously four men, without uniforms but wearing the armbands of court ushers, spilled from the hitherto closed door. As the reporters dashed over, four more figures got out of the car and two of them in uniform rushed the other two inside the building. It was a good television moment, but less rewarding for the newspaper men, who would have liked a quote. And then they got one.

'Mr Marlinsky, can you tell us if you expect justice to be done today?'

'Can you confirm you will be pleading not guilty to the charges?'

The questions were aimed at Marlinsky who shouted: 'Our great Russian dilemma is how to be modern. Not the European way, heavens no! Our way must be better, more advanced, industrially more efficient, based on a superior science. We will show the decaying West where it has gone wrong. By the way, *ya ne v chom vinovat*.' And with that he disappeared.

He wasn't guilty of anything, he said.

'Mr Gerasimov, how are you? Hasn't there been some mistake?'

The big man grinned. 'Well, it's certain I'm not guilty of anything either.' And he too was ushered from view.

Razumovsky knocked once more on the door, then walked back slowly to the clutch of reporters. 'First it wasn't open and now it's full.' The only persons admitted to the courthouse were the two fathers.

The Russian families had been standing apart, on the far side of a newspaper kiosk. Gels walked across the dry, woolly ground. Beside Marlinsky's mother, who barely acknowledged her, stood a round-faced middle-aged woman, well-kept for her age, and a man of military bearing in his early sixties perhaps. At a slight distance stood a second woman and a girl in her early teens. They didn't welcome Gels. Embarrassed, she took refuge browsing in the kiosk.

Besides all the newspapers—The Red Star, The Tashkent Herald, The Samaran Komsomolets,—academic journals sometimes turned up in kiosks. Razumovsky's report on the *psykhushki* had landed in one of them. Irregular distribution of printed materials was a trick someone risked. Who was going to check in tens of thousands of kiosks across the country for cultural gold nestling amongst the puzzle books and comics and key rings. This kiosk today also had for sale some attractively thick exercise books, provision for the next school year. Two hundred pages at least, tightly bound, in soft covers. 'I'll be needing two of those.' Gels set them aside, amid the *papyrosy*, and wrapped sweets, and an out-of-date calendar dispensing Party wisdom by the day. On a second tour her eyes spied a children's gardening set, dangling from the roof, and then, alongside, a whole roast chicken.

'But it's 32 degrees in the shade, my friend! You can't sell that.' She took off her sunglasses and stared to make her point.

'So what? It's cooked,' said a pale, lethargic, unfriendly youth.

'No, no! Flesh goes off in the heat. It's dangerous. It's a threat to human life.'

'Whatever.' As if the laws of biology were a matter of rumour.

She could feel her face twisting in anger. 'Give me your whole bloody kiosk! I'll buy everything.'

She kicked it. Nothing else was possible. Then she rejoined the others across the other side of the square. 'Here, all the bloody papers from today. I bought the whole bloody kiosk of dreck for us to sit on.'

'Are you all right, Gels?'

'No I'm not.'

But it wasn't the time to draw attention away from the two Russians whose fate they had come to hear.

377

A thin, wispy-haired figure passed by, in open sandals and a cheap patterned t-shirt with a collar. He seemed to be talking to himself. 'I find you a sad spectacle.' Mutter mutter. 'I will write to you from prison.' As he paced in front of the courtroom, the scholarly question Professor Balabin tried to keep at the forefront of his mind was whether in 1816—so quickly after the moment of triumph in Paris, you see—the tsar had read the historian's famous essay and ignored it, thus deliberately rejecting the chance to further Russia's liberal progress; or whether His Majesty Alexander I had already retreated into madness. The project arose out of Professor Balabin's work in the archives of the Korsakov library. It was the closest that timid man came to espousing a cause he might be proud of. It was something of which he might have boasted to Marlinsky, as part of his bid for friendship. For sometimes, in Russia, it had happened before, the decent path could not be taken. Not by anyone. As a famous German philosopher would say in a different context, 'There is no good way to live in a world where everything is bad.' Balabin just needed more time, and more courage. Perhaps.

His skin was almost translucent and he had again lost weight, his legs mere sticks somewhere inside his dusty brown trousers. The eyes were still alert in their small, deep pockets and the fingers pale, bony and long. Expressive of something, but who knew what.

The Westerners talked about the Soviet defence lawyers.

'They perform a semblance of their profession. They have to believe a system of justice exists of which they are part.'

'The trick is not to land themselves in difficulty.'

'Too bad for the client.'

'Farcical.'

Arthur's transistor tuned to the World Service brought the news on the hour. The story in whose midst they stood was already running, with, as its dateline, 'a playground on the dusty outskirts of the Soviet capital.' Moldy's stand-in was doing a good job. Tens of thousands meanwhile were listening in the West and further tens of thousands could tune in in Russia too. All you had to do was find the waveband that wasn't jammed: the one the police themselves used to listen in.

The Western reporters and note-takers needed shade as the day progressed and found it under the trees, where they lounged on those odious smudgy newspapers spread out like groundsheets. Arthur leant against the only tree.

A woman passed with a tiny dog on a lead, with matchstick legs. 'Maybe it will grow.'

'Nah. It's not meant to.' Howard said mini-dogs were all the rage in Russia. As finely bred as possible. Canine aristocrats.

'Something to care for,' said Polly. 'This country is full of displaced loves and hatreds. It would need psychoanalysis, the country I mean.'

'Why not buy yourself an aristocrat on four legs if you can no longer have them on two.'

'Do you know what Gerasimov said once? That he could respect psychoanalysis because it thought people had an inner life. That feels to me true.

'But then he said the founders of this country had developed a weird collective version of psychoanalysis.'

'Russians always have to invent their own version of things,' Howard said gloomily.

'The Bolsheviks believed it was because individual people had secrets that the whole collective project was failing. So they determined to get at those secrets, even if they had to torture people to dig them out. Enter Joseph Stalin. Once the secrets deep inside were culled, purged, aborted, whatever, utopia would be back on track.'

'That's a book. I hope Gerasimov writes it.'

'Can you imagine that he will ever have the chance?'

'I've got a book in mind,' said Gels. 'Take two lives and follow the course of them under interrogation. One would be the life of a political prisoner here, and the other of an analysand back home. Both are offered freedom if they will answer questions about what they think. One is interrogated by a policeman. The other by a psychoanalyst.'

'The stupid *cazzi* who run this country don't have thoughts like that.'

No. But I do.

'So when will the second revolution come, Howard? Please tell me it will come.'

'It will. In the office we've got a newspaper photograph of thirteen men. Grisha's stuck it on the wall with Blu-Tack so we can remember who's who. Some days it seems to me they all look the same and all of them look like Korsakov. But Grisha's written in the names. I take bets against myself which ones are most likely to rise to the top.'

'And?'

'There's a smooth one, the youngest, with a pretty wife. But I won't tempt fortune. Who's to say he would be any better?'

'How is it possible that every third person in this country is a policeman?' Gels wailed. But just then something stirred and they scrambled to their feet.

Marlinsky's father walked towards them with a dignified composure, only raising his head to address them at the last moment. Dr Gerasimov joined him.

The television crew manoeuvred their fluffy microphones into range. Their equipment always made them look clumsy. No, much worse, they looked like predators feeding off human tragedy.

The remaining Russian group emerged from behind the kiosk and linked hands.

'My son Boris Mikhailovich Marlinsky got **two** years for parasitism and slander against the state.'

'Ooo, only two?'

'Well that's —'

'For God's sake, why so mild and friendly all of a sudden?'

'Korsakov must have stepped in for him.'

The skinny professor wept into his handkerchief. But then Dr Gerasimov stepped forward.

'Wait!' shouted Arthur. 'Listen, for God's sake!'

'My son Aleksei Igorevich Gerasimov, Mr Marlinsky's friend and supporter, was sentenced today to **nine** years' hard labour for fomenting social unrest.'

'For God's sake!'

'But that's so twisted!'

Marlinsky senior resumed. 'Both men have said they will appeal. My son's tutor at the university, Professor Balabin, was called as a defence witness but failed to appear. My son and Aleksei Igorevich looked well.'

Perhaps they did. But Ella Gerasimova had fainted, her husband was white and their daughter Katya was crying.

'For God's sake! So twisted!'

'They wanted really to hurt Marlinsky.'

'In a way the world couldn't see.'

'Revenge like an untraceable poison.'

The agency reporters ran towards whatever phone box they had located before the event. The magnetic tapes were already punched in the office, awaiting the last details to be filled in before the latest dissident fates could be broadcast worldwide. Howard alone had time to consider his story. As did Gels, reflecting on what she could *do*.

'Aaah, aaah! Hell on earth!' She had bought all the newspapers but not the chicken. 'Have you still got that chicken, young man? Wrap it up for me. Here's a hundred roubles.'

'What the—'

'Just be happy it's not your supper. Now it's not going to be anyone else's either. At least I can stop a tiny bit of extra harm being done today in this venomous country.'

It was a pitiful gesture. Gels ended with the package under her arm, because if she threw it away some dog or poor person would eat it. Only back home did she turn on the oven and burn it to a cinder.

Her gestures were all so trivial, in the face of what mattered.

What stayed in her mind though was Katya Gerasimova standing reading aloud from a book as the reporters dispersed:

> To wrest life from captivity and wrong
> To start a new world's ways
> We must pipe a song
> From the tangle of our days.

Razumovsky told Howard: 'The Gerasimov girl, she asked me a question while we were waiting. She came over to Natasha and me deliberately. "Do you know the joke about bananas in our country, Sir? Why are bananas in our country like philosophy?"

Razumovsky went on: I shook my head. "Why are bananas in our country like philosophy, young lady?" And she answered: "Because, Nikolai Vladimirovich, there is a word for bananas in our language, but they don't exist. Our justice doesn't exist. This country doesn't exist. That's how we live."

'"Now there's a bright girl!" I said. "You can join us one day."'

Twenty-Nine

In the autumn of 1979, because of the dark things she had experienced, Irina Korsakov fell into a depression. Yet what else does Russian literature serve but to make a return from such misery possible?

И скучно и грустно, и некому руку подать

В минуту душевной невзгоды…

Желанья!.. Что пользы напрасно и вечно желать?..

А годы проходят — все лучшие годы!

… Но кого же?.. На время — не стоит труда,

А вечно любить невозможно.

В себя ли заглянешь? — там прошлого нет и следа:

И радость, и муки, и всё там ничтожно…

Что страсти? — ведь рано иль поздно их сладкий недуг

Исчезнет при слове рассудка;

И жизнь, как посмотришь с холодным вниманьем вокруг, –

Такая пустая и глупая шутка…

When not in yoga poses that somehow mimicked the statues on the terrace, statues which allowed her husband brazenly to imagine an affinity between ancient Greece and Soviet *nomklat*-land, she spent her time translating the poet Lermontov into all the languages she knew.

Over and over the sadness and boredom of life
Oppress me and I reach out a hand to no one
In my distress.
To want something! The eternal return of desire,
What's the point? Meanwhile life, the good years, go lost.

To love…but whom shall I love? To love and end it
Is not worth the effort and eternal love impossible.
I look inside myself and find no trace of the past
Not the joy, not the torment, just nothing…
Passion? Well, you know sooner or later its sweetness
Succumbs to reason. Feeling is lost because words intervene,
And as you look around yourself coldly
Life is this empty and stupid joke.

L'ennui et le chagrin, et une main qui
Faille toucher à une autre dans l'infortune de l'âme.
Le désir? Éternel et toujours en vain.
À quoi bon? Et les bonnes années s'écoulent.
Aimer un autre…mais qui? L'amour brèf ne vaut pas la peine
Et pour l'éternité personne ne le peut.
Interroges-toi! Tu ne trouveras ni la joie ni les tourments
Dans une passé vide, toute abimée, dans ta profondeur.
Même la douce passion cédera
à la raison à la fin,
Et tu regarderas froidement autour de toi: voilà
La vie! Une vide plaisanterie, une farce imbecile.

It wasn't until twenty years later that I, Gels Maybey, learnt what happened to Marlinsky. The open-minded internet had arrived and wily, secretive Soviet Russia had vanished from our planet in the same moment. That coincidence, like the crest and trough of a global wave, was not accidental. Marlinsky's name cropped up on—of all places—a genealogical website designed to recover the lost aristocracy—a place I liked to browse. At least there, on that site, was a Russian history that was not just blood and ashes but had the living texture of human connections and roots. A dream for Russia but now a different dream, as of a place that finally had a noble history. Was it better? Humanly richer for certain, but there was still a tendency to smooth over the contradictions.

In a black-and-white photograph someone posted Marlinsky's finely chiselled face which seemed hardly to have aged. In a linked documentary—and please bear in mind this was now eighteen years on—Irina Korsakov answered the interviewer about the old days with a touch of irritation: '*Off coarse*, the *hwoll* time we were *four-said* to be proletarians we aspired to be aristocrats. In ow-wer manner and in ow-wer soulss. That is why we moved abroad when we could.' She didn't mention Marlinsky, or his case, but the documentary-maker clearly intended the link and would have wished his film to be about something else.

One good thing was that the All-Russia site hardly camouflaged its naked ambition to list every Russian who had ever lived, barely suppressing that old Russian desire to awaken the dead and give them justice, finally. The masthead featured cameo portraits of the last tsar, Nikolai II, and his wife the Empress Alexandra, and was done out, visually, in the kind of red plush typical of prosperous domestic interiors in the wealthy 1890s. Remember when a happier Russia was capitalist, before Lenin and the Bolsheviks reshaped the country in a vicious civil war. Dues were thus paid to a historical shift now passionately lamented and reversed. When the dead arise a real, eternal Russia will inherit the earth.

Marlinsky belonged there by his birth-right. But I knew—and I subsequently learnt—that he wouldn't have chosen it as home.

I entered Борис Михайлович Марлйнский—*imye, otchestvo i familya*— first name, patronymic and surname—into the biggest and best-known Russian search engine and waited for the great digital searchlight to reveal the past. The internet was a cause of such excitement in its early years. It delivered miracles.

Who posted Marlinsky's own brief account of his journey east and his banishment I'll probably never know but I feel he must have sent it to someone wise and responsible. Katya Gerasimova would have been of the age, and have the technical expertise, but I never found an email address for her.

This was that account.

'When I appeared in court they had already decided the outcome. The defence lawyer was just another jailer of a milder sort. Andrei Maksimovich Stavrogin was his name. Preparing me for my appearance he whispered to me that nothing could be done about the sinful ways of men on earth. You also shouldn't expect justice in this life, Boris Mikhailovich. This man also had a function more familiar to consumers of Western justice: to stop me talking unguardedly. Otherwise he just advised me when to stand up and sit down, not to irritate the judge with my disrespect. The judge himself was a headmasterly type, pale, fat, stuffed into his civilian suit, who leant over towards me in the summing-up, as if his task were compassion and the sentence would do me good.

I thought of my sentence and I thought of my friend's and I knew this was their way to kill me.

They held me in prison somewhere in Moscow for a bit over three weeks. I panicked that I would lose my sense of time. I felt intensely that I must keep track of the days. In the WC cubicle I bit into the hem of my prison jacket, and after breakfast each day after I undid a stitch. As the pale strip grew inside my regulation garment I counted the days by the needle holes left empty. I saw myself as travelling backwards along an empty road to nowhere; a long slow monotonous death-in-life.

If my fellow inmates didn't kill me, where would Korsakov send me? I never forgot those immoral, pseudo-elegant and fantastic conversations I'd been made part of out at his villa and wondered how those fantasies would now reshape my life. Or would some bureaucrat simply look up my sentence in a book and run his finger across to a column headed 'corresponding punishments'? 'Corresponding' was one of the words that damned us all, in the old days, the days 'of the system'.

I travelled part of the way by road in one of those lorries labelled 'people' I had sometimes noticed with deep apprehension in my free days, but mostly by train with the windows blackened out. There I felt my punishment begin. I wasn't allowed to see my country out of the window because I didn't love it enough. You see I have this terrible weakness that I DO love my country. To be deprived of the sight of its monotonous panorama and of its timeless, backward, superstitious people seared my heart. But then I loved my friend still more, and they hurt him in my place.

Korsakov made him suffer for me. You know the great idea of our civilisation that Christ died for us? Korsakov staged a parody. He set up my friend to die for me. I gave in in that moment and once I had given in my correction could begin.

You see they, the old men and sometimes not so old men who ran my country wanted us, who pointed out Russia's crimes, who described Russia's terrible carelessness with human lives, to *atone* for speaking out of turn. We had to recognise that it was not heroism that gave us the courage to protest but a psychological weakness which did political harm and brought moral shame on the entire community. We were the guilty ones. And now I certainly was guilty and only a saviour would die for me.

That way our rulers and their *nomklat* servants could still believe in a viable and humane country one day. By sucking our hearts dry. By making the fault ours.

Of course they didn't really believe. Yet they persuaded themselves that they were the ones who had hope and faith, while we were the Judases and the heathens. They were the most dishonest human beings I have ever known. Theirs was the mantra of progress, Western progress even, but they stripped from the hallowed body of that vision all self-knowledge and all conscience. They appropriated words that pointed to human virtue and a grand reward for all mankind if only the world would follow our Communist idea. They hid behind those words their great evil.

They talked of a Russia reborn when every last citizen had the right education. But that meant my education had to be undone.

We—dissidents like me—were spoiling the future. *We* let down our family and friends, our village, our town, our city, the whole project. Hope was our leading institution and I was taking Hope away from them. They persuaded themselves to feel my life as a crime even though Hope was never truly theirs at all. They just salted Hope away, primitive Russian peasant fashion, and produced it for holidays and celebrations.

But amongst us, the few of us who protested, there was true Hope. It was the fuel on which the progress of our dear Russia depended. No one in our country was allowed to give up or complain that we had never in our long Russian history managed to make Hope deliver. They were not believers in me, but I was in them. And when they wounded me so deeply, by making me—if I were a Greek then my friend's nemesis, if I were a Christian the sinner for whom my saviour suffered—I accepted their verdict. I reinterpreted myself in a way that would encourage me to submit and survive.

I was lucky not to get appendicitis, or a kidney infection on the journey. Kidney infections were the worst. They didn't have the antibiotics locally, and the journeys overland broke what resilience we had had because the distances were so great. Transport and fuel weren't easy either. I could have died on the way.

Yet perhaps they took some special care of me because briefly I had received the attention of the West. Had I died it would have embarrassed them.

The great flaw in our New Men and New Women was their inverted vanity. They thought the West was concealing its own failings when it attacked ours. So when a headline appeared in the International Herald Tribune, HUMAN RIGHTS CAMPAIGNER JAILED FOR TWO YEARS, A SECOND FOR NINE, they really thought it was the West camouflaging its own wickedness.

Still when I arrived wherever it was they were sending me and found that a school awaited and not a labour camp I felt that mixture of anger and relief that only Dostoevsky felt on the scaffold. In floods of private tears, I, now a village teacher, trembled with rage at being reduced to a puppet. To hell with them! *Chort s nimi!*

Our conditions in the village were quite primitive. The lavatory was a hole in the ground 100 metres from the house. We lived like clean animals. Out East we were supposed to feel the perverse privilege of being Russian more acutely. And because of the way they had forced my submission, I did.

The trucks that arrived through corridors of compacted snow or trundled along pot-holed roads more or less regularly, but never entirely reliably, relieved the town where we lived, otherwise besieged by remoteness. The occasional low-flying plane overhead made local deliveries or sprayed crops. I thought of it as nudging the system on. Someone in an office somewhere had ordered it; someone who had no idea how or where we lived, in reality.

My punishment was to be made to live viscerally with all the absurdities and illusions that daily held Russia back and still be required to hope. Even to teach Hope. I could see our Soviet plight more clearly in the deep provinces, because I was educated and had come from Moscow University. The intention was that my punishment should be mental torture, and in more ways than one. Thus I atoned and fitted in well.

Think of the vocabulary of a three-year-old American child—aeroplane, house, car, bus, gas station, shop, breakfast, lunch, meat, milk, butter, apple, road, coat, hat, TV, school— Good. Now understand that behind every common noun that—in the West—betokens commonplace things easy to come by, things every little child is familiar with. Every noun in that list was a struggle and a dream and a fantasy for us. To fly, to live, to travel, to buy fuel, to buy food, to ensure that the food nourished and didn't poison us, for the meat to reach our shops and the milk to be available in our milk bars, and not just vodka or nothing, and for our delicious Vologda butter to be on sale somewhere other than the foreigners' grocer's, where the plump, diet-obsessed foreigners already had all they needed; for apples to grow on trees and find their way into autumn pies and for strudels to sit on baking trays, waiting to be ordered by watering mouths in cafés; for roads to lead somewhere; for coats and hats to be made in the right size and appear in the shops longer than a day; for television to entertain and delight and inform, not be an empty gift given by a contemptuous state; for TV to provide adequate human company for citizens who never asked for much, and never complained at being born, and living and dying, in such remote, neglected, sometimes industrially poisoned places, but would have liked a few programmes to laugh and marvel at: I can't account for that elementary deprivation. I threw myself into being a schoolteacher to make a new generation aware nothing could justify it, although, at the time, it was also my duty to teach them how to cope, and I accepted that.

"This is the classroom, Comrade."

The drawings on the wall, in their childlike enthusiasm trumping each other, row above row, I examined closely. When they finally risked encroaching on the framework protecting Our Leader, I smiled, which made Olga Rayeva, my Leader, bare her nicotine-stained choppers at me and narrow her eyes. I was an Enemy of the People. Her lips curled as she took in air. On the other hand we Russians are, as a great spread-out mass of people with no emotional centre to make our lives orderly and moral, we are sceptical and disinclined to judge our fellows. When our masters shunted us this way and that—the ways of the country of my youth—we helped each other. Or we took advantage of the rules when they were slack and we hurt each other.

"We enjoy our work." Olga, a flag-carrier for intense womanhood at work, was my height. Her thick curly grey hair and sturdy figure gave her a solid presence as she presided over her responsibilities, fifteen of them. Hectoring them she had the sweet high Russian voice of a blackbird at dusk.

After a disciplined shedding of coats and boots and hats and scarves, which I watched from behind a half-closed door, the children, the hope of the motherland, lined up to inspect me. It was a Monday morning at the end of October.

"In size formation!" cried Olga, and they formed a perfect line from the smallest Dima to the tallest Valya. Valya, reaching to my shoulders, pale eyes fixed straight ahead, stood like a long-legged calf on military parade, whereas Dima, dark, mystified and easily distracted, was still too small to be harnessed.

"In age formation! Don't fuss, Masha!" Masha was the precocious girl in plaits who wanted my attention as a man. Like Valya she was ten, but some fine-tuning of the months put her second from the top of the line. This time the human finials were a medium-sized serious-looking boy, another Dmitry, who reminded me of myself at eleven, and a little girl called Ala determined to face the challenge of being the youngest. The only other one I remembered straight off was a beanpole called Sasha who had stood next to Valya in the size stakes, and now turned out to be only nine.

I counted them, tapping each one on the head. "Come on, children, count with me!" (It's well known that counting is also a spiritual exercise and it calmed them and made them trust me.) "Odin, dva, tri…" they shouted, and then we did it backwards. "Pyatnadtsat', chetyrnadtsat', trinadtsat'…" We got a nice rhythm going, with the bouncy stresses on the second syllable helping us along. "Right hand out! Now Dima with me! Odin, dva, tri…" I held his shoulders as he numbered off the digits with a smack.

"Again, again," he cried. But it was Ala's turn, this time to sit on my shoulders and pat the heads as we looped to the end of the row. She discovered she could be quite a performer, if she left her anxieties behind. She became the star turn, ending by patting *me* on the head. Everyone loosened up. She clutched my hair like handfuls of new grass.

When we calmed down, the older Dmitry did some fractions on the blackboard and Valya read aloud from Pushkin.

I can still hear Valya reading. She was just like any other child, rushing to the next full stop, refusing to concede a single modulation on the way. Crazy the way children are all the same. You have to single them out and nurture their special ways. Not let them fall into the mincing machine. "Anyone else *like* to read to me?" That was only my first morning but I knew it and Olga Nikolaevna knew it. I would make a good teacher. She slipped away.

In short, I became a primary school teacher in a faraway place where the people were hearty and simple and I was excellent in that role. They believed in what I told them, and they believed in education, and the good of their community. It was far from Moscow but they believed that they were not forgotten and I did my utmost not to let that faith slip. "The lighthouse calling. Moscow speaking," was what we heard when we switched on the radio. I got them to draw that beacon, which they figured as a sun, or a giant microphone, or a watchtower: all things they knew.

It was mostly the little ones who drew a radiant yellow circle on top of a tree trunk or a lamppost, and when I asked them about it they had an explanation. "I'm going to be big like that one day," said Ala. "Then I won't need to climb up to see things." The older Dmitry chose a standing microphone encased in an iron-girdered tower. He was the engineer interested in communication and it was already difficult to read his heart because of the way his imagination hid behind severe images. An element of the watchtower crept into his picture, but then that was also what little Ala wanted, stilts or steps or a ladder so she could *see*, not through a forest of legs but over the heads, even though she loved the heads. Mine she loved.

I took stock of my situation. I needed a wife. My eyes fell on Olga's daughter, home from university for the summer vacation of 1980. Bronya was a trainee teacher in the official mould. There were naiveties I would want to undo. And because this was long ago in an unmodern place she accepted that. She accepted that the man knew best. She looked up to me because I came from Moscow and I was an intellectual.

I never asked after my mother-in-law's husband. In Bolshevik fashion Olga may never have had a husband. In any case our society took for granted the absence of men for whatever reason, eliding the personal and the political in a willingness not to care. Maybe the state killed them directly, maybe it killed them with alcohol and bad food and desperate boredom, maybe they died of their own bad habits. It wasn't normal to distinguish. Whoever my absent future father-in-law was he must have been more of a Slav type, because my Bronya had a contented round face curtained with long dark tresses and angelicised with almond eyes. She was strong and could wrestle my left arm, at least my left, to the ground. That was the first erotic game we played, getting to know each other that summer. We were sitting beside the river watching the water overcome every obstacle to its progress. We cooled off in the knee-high trickle, played our game prone on the rough grass, and that was it, we were lovers, blinking at each other in wonderment at what had just happened.

The older children whom I first knew as willing collaborators in what I was trying to teach them now caught a bus to the only secondary technical school in the region. Some of our psychologists say that children are formed by the age of five. Critics say our Soviet ways made them pliant and characterless in kindergarten, even before the age of red scarves tied with woggles and the chance to be one of a hundred white shirts bulging in the wind on parade. But my friend

Alyosha Gerasimov wasn't like that, and nor, steered by him at a crucial time, around the age of 12, was I.

But now as an educator myself, a reformed criminal no less, I wasn't so dogmatic about steering the children away from the collective. I worried most when in their early teens they became aimless. Even the older Dmitry appeared to have nothing to do but watch Valya and the precocious, now promiscuous Masha try out every poisonous substance.

I decided on a building project, which with her authority Olga could easily get accepted by our local council. It would be a community hut which our young people would design themselves and where they could meet. We had the schoolroom for public meetings and elections, and we had a kind of hotel: that place with the single standing microphone that inspired Dmitri's vision of a new Comintern tower. Bronya and I celebrated our wedding there (of which more in a moment). Our settlement had a playground of sorts for the children, with one swing still intact, and puddles to play in when it rained and a derelict iron bar for balancing. But there was nothing for teenagers who already declined to be patronised. Beanpole Sasha lined himself up with them and was accepted because of his height.

After much hard work, through many voluntary sessions, our enthusiasm unflagging, we celebrated our achievement, which took us two years.

Two months later the authorities demolished it arguing that what we needed was a concrete building, and not something impermanent made of wood. Our own success had shown them what was required.

That moment hit me hard. Someone took an axe to too many branches of my tree and it was not my core strength that was sapped but my will to dream. My reputation shifted from wise man to potential fool. I don't know why but it was at that moment that our wedding party came back to me.

I saw what I saw at the end: the scratched but otherwise intricately crafted parquet dance floor now empty except for a couple of misplaced champagne corks: fabricated toadstools in a plastic-tabled clearing that was the centre of lives. I could make no sense of that place where I had been compelled to arrive and from where, subtly, from the first moment I taught them, I had to encourage the better ones to leave. The fags stubbed out in plates of luxuriant food, the overturned, 'conquered', empty bottles of vodka, the array of tatty magazines and the pathetic reading habits of adult children, the spectacle that poor little Masha, who was neither small nor pretty anymore, made of herself: all this I could only love with an effort of will, and now that I hoped to have children of my own I didn't know what to do.

The authorities did begin work, perhaps someone meant the replacement of our clubhouse seriously, but it was a typical miscalculation that destroyed our faith and disheartened us. I felt very bad. That was in 1982. Misha was two, and my Ala, my All-to-be, was on the way. In my secret despair I drifted back to politics. Some ice of never previously questioned permanence melted when our longtime Leader died (in the year of Misha's birth). On TV we watched them drop the coffin and the room presided over by no one at the microphone erupted in laughter. They, THEY, couldn't even get that right. I felt better about my two years' lost labour reduced to a pile of firewood by thoughtless oafs obeying an order typewritten in smudged purple ink on cheap contemporary papyrus. If the same jobsworths couldn't follow an order signed by the highest authority what could any of us hope for. We defied nature by preserving our First Leader's mortal presence forever. Sixty years on the best we could do was not quite tip out our Latest Leader's rotting remains on the floor, there to be blessed and kissed by a few million fanatics in their tatty wooden armchairs, but also spat at and pissed on in the drunken imaginations of the impotent remainder. Out of two hundred million people there were, say, eighty million impotent men. It didn't bear thinking about. It was also never the case that our old-young rulers were going to change their minds or even, along with most of their subjects, have a mind at all. But perhaps the whole world could now see how they had been poisoned, or some other way emasculated, and take pity on them, not with a view to rescuing them, but for the sake of their children and their children's children in a country that so desperately needed rebirth. So I stayed, all the while fearful I was myself sinking into impotence. Bronya was lucky I didn't drink; unlucky that I tended to depression.

We had two new leaders then, the first a clone of the old, as, like a dying business, they exhausted the old stock; and the second a man said to be an intellectual and who liked jazz… But nothing happened, or they were imitating the succession of the popes in Rome, for whom God developed a fondness so quickly that no sooner were they on the throne than he called them to their eternal home. Another box of ashes was despatched to the Kremlin wall, which must one day fall down from all that weakening. You can't take an unlimited number of bricks out of a wall and replace them with ashes. I can imagine that happening to us, in our capital city. One day the wall of one of our holiest shrines will fall down, and no one will have thought before that there might be a problem.

Instead there arrived on the podium a man with a pretty wife who, both of them, looked a bit different, and the rest you know. But still I stayed, until nine years was up. That had to be.'

(Note: nine years exactly after his sentence, seven years after he had in the meantime become a free man again, Boris Mikhailovich Marlinsky left Russia for the United States, where, classified as a third-wave Russian immigrant and given help to settle, he became a teacher of Russian literature.)

Thirty

Irina Korsakov and her stepson Matvei so loathed Korsakov, and were so hurt over the fate of Marlinsky, that, having rehearsed their escape down the Mozhaisk Road on the day of the trial, they simply drove on early in 1992. From Smolensk to Minsk, they proceeded to Warsaw, from there to queue at the German border beside Frankfurt an der Oder.

Korsakov, buried under so many layers of whatever is the opposite of self-knowledge, shifted his sights so often that where he ended after '91 was perverse. All you need is love for Russia! Once that nation ceased to exist he could sing out his passion with full throat, because now he was simply free: free from all duties and obligations. He was well protected in his shift of views. The young were determined not to suffer like their parents and grandparents. They would build themselves a kinder life, ideally abroad. But many of Korsakov's older kinsmen felt like him that they loved Russia. Russia was everything.

The author doesn't much care for Korsakov, nor, in the end, for the wily Irina. But she would like to know the reason for the cruelty and the arbitrariness that for seventy years held that country together: the one that ended at midnight Moscow time, 2100 GMT, on 31 December 1991. It's not a mystery why the same people abandoned their country on its deathbed with the same cruelty and arbitrariness they had endured all their lives; why they stood, if at all, in the back row of the obsequies, not visible in any photograph taken for posterity. Or just faded into an obscure later life.

But how can we reconstruct from all those negative passions something like the truth?

We've already heard from Marlinsky, who eventually made his way to America. Gerasimov for his part stayed in Russia and, when he was released, returned to his studies and eventually took his place in the profession he had always cherished. His nine years in a camp of correction did not count as a criminal record in the Western sense. Nothing debarred him from public life.

Katya was married by the time her brother returned: she had become a doctor like her father. She lived with her husband but had no children. Somehow a natural in a white coat, she was a selfless, acerbic woman who was a born healer. Both parents were still alive.

Gerasimov quietly picked up where he left off, trying to reform his branch of the healing science from the inside. Never at a loss for women who found him attractive, he married a prominent journalist on the newspaper *Nezavisimaya Gazeta*, 'The Independent Newspaper', and together they enjoyed the whirlwind of 1990s freedom.

And yet those mental hospitals remained cruel and a scholarly article he published in 2004 exposing them as such marked the end of his second, retrieved, career. Having failed to find him on Google beyond that point the author wishes him well and hopes he is still alive.

But let us go back twenty years to how Korsakov, Gerasimov's casual oppressor, restored his own credibility; how that devilish man lasted through the final Soviet decade with his privileges undiminished. Korsakov ratcheted up the torment by having his goons spread the rumour that Marlinsky had cooperated from the outset, to get his own sentence reduced. An imaginary conversation was fed into the minds of the Moscow intelligentsia, at the university and beyond, to poison his memory absolutely. 'You see, Boris Mikhailovich, we've got to know you over these weeks, my wife in particular. You're in a spot of bother and we want to help you. Whereas what use has Russia for another psychologist. We are the only sane country. I'm glad you agree.'

In Howard Wilde's view no one born inside that country could make Russia better. Russia needed a heart transplant from outside. The twentieth century saw a new Germany. Why not a new Russia, truly? Yet, said Howard, Russians would always see that transplant as an invasion, because they cannot accept the fault as their own. Russia had to respect the mind and the honour and the conscience of its honest people. But was there ever a time in history when that country truly *loved* its own people and thought them honest? Some obscure sense of a solution had ignited in Korsakov as long ago as 1968, that as long as—in reverse—the people loved their country that would do. It wouldn't. It was a diabolical parody of the only possible solution: Russia's rulers MUST love their people. He didn't, and, as liberty approached as a prospect, he was too lazy to pretend. He turned the house beyond the Mozhaisk Road into an exclusive international hotel, and, with millions in the bank, stayed on as the gardener.

Razumovsky who did believe in Russia, had the subtler idea of 'the pairs of opposites that hold our society together'. For every Korsakov a Razumovsky. For every villain a good man, and thus a true brotherhood lurking somewhere: a metaphysical dyad in a land where fraternity and fratricide were akin. The brilliant Razumovsky imagined a vivid human dialectic in a suffering land of extremes. Individuals just had to be brave, and keep faith, on the side of goodness, while each generation waited with a strange respect for its villains to die. But be careful, Alexander Nikolaevich! *Ostorozhno!* There is something resembling a political programme here. It may just be waiting for a Naumov—a 'Mr Brainy'—to hollow it out into a few slogans. ONLY WITH THE RECONCILIATION OF OPPOSITES CAN WE MARCH FORWARD. ONLY BY UNDERSTANDING OUR ENEMIES CAN WE UNDERSTAND OUR GOALS. Of course we need to understand our enemies. But in a Russian context most good men and women would question the meaning of 'understanding' and quake in their boots.

Let's go back to that summer of 1979. On the day of the trial Matvei and his mother Irina drove along the Mozhaisk Road all the way to Vyazma to get as far away as they could. Look at that road on the map. It goes all the way to Warsaw and on to Dresden nowadays. Only back then they couldn't cross the frontier, so they simply had a picnic by the roadside and returned. They only rehearsed their own escape. But twelve years later it happened.

Their rage against evil was palpable. There are no dragons and their slayers in this story. In this story there is only protest. But there was much of it. Someone had to stand up for truth.

The day after the trial Harriet Zimmerman drove her car into the middle of Red Square and made a piece of theatre of it. People gathered round as first she stripped it of useful parts like windscreen wipers and wing mirrors—anything she could unscrew—and gave them away, and then set fire to it. Arthur filmed the event with a cine camera. With its living colours now bleached to washed-out pastels, you can see pinkish, greenish, pale fragments of it on the NowYouSeeIt platform. On the audio, Harriet can still be heard saying, in Russian: 'I come in peace. I am a friend of your country. I have tried to understand you,' as she syphoned off her own fuel tank to set her car on fire. Do watch it. Only remember old technology has this awful power to caricature great feeling.

Russian voices crowd into the film, half in horror at the spectacle, half in admiration. 'She comes in peace. She is our friend.' Excited, emotional, the Russians around her talk in their high-pitched language about *druzhba* and *mir*. *Druzhba*, you remember, means friendship, as in the name of the journal that published Okudzhava's novel (Marlinsky's copy of which was last seen gifted to Matvei Korsakov). *Mir* is peace. *Voina i Mir*. War and Peace. But it also means world—*Miru mir*, as the old Soviet slogan went—Peace to the World—and perhaps that is the source of some deep and genuine confusion about the Cold War. Was Russia the cause or the solution? Good people even believed the Russian Revolution of 1917 happened because of that peculiar coincidence in the language; that 'Peace to the World' made the Russian people what they were, for richer, for poorer, in sickness and in health, for thine is the kingdom, the power and the glory, and we are the only people fit to usurp the reign of Jesus Christ, because we come to the world in peace.

When the Zimmermans later showed the film to their friends in the foreign community, in their warm, charming nineteenth-century apartment presided over by the Mundt painting of the fire submerged in the dark landscape, someone even mentioned *Druzhba narodov* and Okudzhava as such a master of disguise that he had got away with expressing views, in 1978, that were roughly in line with Howard Wilde's for all time.

How had Okudzhava got away with it? Either the institutions concerned were so stupid they didn't notice, or they were so wily they knew they didn't have to worry. For who can read a subtle text anymore?

Meanwhile the blackened carcass of Harriet's car, sacrificed on the altar of truth, remained in Red Square. It remained there for a week, where it was much photographed. Not only tourists snapped it with their own Leica and Polaroid and some privileged Russians with their Zenit. Photographers for hire, figures extinct in the West but still to be seen in Russia, with their Brownie boxes, wandered about like tempters of poorer souls. *Vam nuzhna snimka*? They mumbled, or whispered. And you probably did want a record, because you couldn't believe this premonition of the end had happened.

Just as on the day the police were surprisingly slow to arrive—they took as much as twenty minutes, or as much time as to ensure the conflagration was irreversible—so the same authorities were inadmissibly slow at clearing the trail Harriet left behind her. Or—and this is a factor no textbook of political science can encompass—they too, the official loyalists, had their way of conspiring against their country just by being themselves, that is, through tardiness and mismanagement, which sometimes was deliberate and anyway who could tell. It wasn't love, but perhaps it was compensation for lack of love. Harriet was a decent person who accepted that America had to fight against Russia. They were 'similar new countries, after all', despite Russia's long other history. Meanwhile it had become America's reason for existing, to stop Communism taking hold in Europe. France was full of socialists; more than half of Italy considered Communism the only universal post-war solution. Nor in Spain and Portugal did it seem life-threatening. State ownership was a dignified way out of poverty. But the Americans held fast. She knew she was right.

The Brits, as against the Amis, secretly feared, and prepared to admire, a Russian success. Might not a country where money had lost its prestige serve us as a model too? We have so many have-nots; our society is so debased in its core purpose. We don't need slogans and parades, but we do need meaning. Some golden age of pre-industrial England beckoned; or perhaps it was just the proximity of the war which had made a whole generation accept plainness and make-do-and-mend and, seeing that that spirit persisted in Soviet life, applauded it. Here was a people still prepared to make sacrifices. (Don't ask for what.) Back in Russia tourists began to land at Sheremetyevo again, and to drive east again, through Poland, from the end of the 1950s, and when my countrymen and women saw how basic a Russian life was, they thought it made people kinder, and their emotions more heartfelt. There is no wealth but life, as our own John Ruskin had said. Returning to England in 1979, Gels Maybey bought a mangle instead of a washing machine, and a bicycle instead of a car, to set up her new life.

The Amis had a quite different mentality. Their sunshine-haired hippy president talked peace and wanted to engineer a slowed path towards possible war. He was humane, but the approach was that of an economist towards the growth of anything. If something is bad but inevitable then the economist recommends it should at least not grow quickly. That, in America-speak, would be the least worst situation, the growth of something horrific, but so slowly— deliberately slowed—so you wouldn't notice. Let us therefore bring the hostilities between us and the Soviet Union under mutual control; let us exclude the irrational market element of surprise.

Not convinced by this whimsy, the president's tough-minded ambassador continued to count warheads. Ambassador Heffernan reminded commentators of the old nursery rhyme. The king is in his counting-house, counting out the money. The American view, his view, was a financial planner's view of the arms race. It was a financial analyst's assessment of likely conflict, based on the marketplace as driven by self-interest.

Gels Maybey had once wanted to kill herself.

Instead, she became a translator, which is to say a writer of sorts. Galya Obolenskaya used to talk about the challenge of matching a real mind in one language to a hypothetical mind in another. The question was; which mind did the reader of a translation encounter? Neither the author's alone, anymore, nor solely the translator's. Who owns the third voice?

The reader has encountered it here.

Translators always like to think of themselves as worthy of the original. But how do you achieve that? By being faithful, as in a marriage? But what if the spark dies? By being fair to the original? But how can the humble translator judge? Worthiness, fidelity and fairness are the great virtues in the transmission of human messages out of one medium into another. But is the way to achieve them to be inventive? Or to submit to imitation as nearly as possible?

Galya Obolenskaya liked to think of redirecting, towards a new audience, whatever noble and inspired stream of consciousness had come her way out of a different language. She hoped with her work to add to whatever goodness there already was in the universe. That quantity of good couldn't be measured, but many people felt the truth of its existence, without being able to account for it. So she believed.

She was right. You can choose, as a person, to add to the goodness, or the harm, in the world. So I, Gels Maybey, got on with my translations. I might just have led a more original writing life. But since the undoing of Marlinsky that third voice was the only calling left to me. I would 'carry over' certain experiences. Like a mother might carry her child across a swift stream. Like occasionally I have been carried myself by kind souls across troubled waters.

There were many things in Russia I greatly feared.

I was never sure whether Howard shared those fears when for months after the trial he wore a red mark in the middle of his forehead, like a Buddhist, and, after half a year of abstinence, drank himself into a Russian stupor, a zapoi, that lasted a week. But then yes, he did.

I survived Russia because my heart was colder than his and because fiction too is an invading army, with its own vast ambitions of adding to its own empire;

pushing back against experience. It's an aggression and a defence, of a kind, whereas Howard just sacrificed himself.

The translation agency I founded was moderately successful. I didn't need my father's money and he and I could meet, finally, on equal terms. The internet, though, had a bad effect on my business. Thanks to the free services of Google Translate the number of quiet days increased. I filled them chasing raindrops on my basement windows in a chic London Square and wondered again what had happened to the Russians I had known. A browser called Yandex converted my Latin queries into Cyrillic prompts.

One of the easiest names to find was Balabin. He, you remember, was the maths boffin who according to Marlinsky dried up on the only occasion he had to expound dialectical materialism, the one true philosophy of that preposterous invented state, at the university. He had talked about his love of archives instead and so rendered himself vulnerable to students who might betray him. In an accidental act of courage he had told them to look up Communism in a book of mathematical tables to see if it was a deviation or an illness. Another accidental act in the life of this clever but timid man was to fall in love with Marlinsky, who had no regard for him. After 1991 Balabin opened an IT firm, which gave him a decent income and a second wind.

Naumov had vanished. I knew his first name and patronymic, Kiril Innokentevich, but nothing postdating the Communist era came up, except the name of a travel agency, which struck me as too ridiculous. A false trail. Perhaps he had gone abroad. Yet unlike the new rich captains of industry academics like him didn't have access to public funds they could plunder. He couldn't create a lavish post-Soviet life in the West so perhaps he was running a travel agency after all. To travel or not to travel. That is the question. I abandoned my search. *Chort s nim!* Let him look at Italian postcards! The devil take him.

I was more interested in the Korsakov family, although there too initially I drew a blank. I decided to pay a postgraduate student of Russian to investigate on my behalf and suggested her best bet was to pursue Matvei.

Charlene, who had done her first degree at the university of Aloe Vera and had passable Russian, delivered me this report.

Dear Ange, I googled Irina Korsakov, like you suggested. I yandexed Irina Korsakov. I changed Irina to Irena and to Irene because you never know how people are spelling things these days. Nothing came up.

(She emailed me: 'Ange! I just can't find these people.' / 'Keep trying, Charlene. That's what I'm paying you for.' I imagined her fetching a caramel latte and staring at her screen.)

Here I go again. Maybe a different spelling for the surname? Korsakoff. Korsakow. There are different ways to spell Russian names apparently. Korsakow? Korsa Cow maybe? No one writes it like that but it's how dummies back home actually say Russian names.

('But you and I have degrees in Russian, Charlene! We shouldn't be too hard on people.')

Korsakoff, DJ, pioneer of Powerrave. DJ Korsakoff does hardcore music that unleashes the beast. Heh! But Nope. DJ Korsakoff's website showed that she was a woman. Or posing as. As good as. Not a guy. Not normally.

Korsakov, Sergei d.1900. Early Russian neuropsychiatrist, pathbreaker. Discovered brain syndrome caused by severe alcoholic abuse. Palsy, ataxia, psychosis.

(Yes! I wrote in the margin. The condition Alyosha Gerasimov's father diagnosed in the bus driver and treated in the hospital. I read alcoholics are impotent, Charlene replied. Ange? Does that mean the Russians will die out? Jesus Christ!)

Korsakow... I was about to give up on Korsakow. Absolutely nothing was coming up, which was crazy. I mean it's weird when you scrape the bottom of the web. It's as if you've bumped up against the edge of the world. So our universe is finite, after all.

(Try one f, Charlene.)

I did a search with one 'f', Prof! Korsakof, right? *Nada*. Zilch. Finally I got to think outside the box.

(Brilliant! That's what it takes to succeed in life.)

I tried Korsak—and left the final syllable blank. Wo-heh, that did it! Matt Korsak, proprietor of a *Gesellschaft mit beschränkter Haftung* called Matt Ka. Matt Korsak, company director, wrote just the first letter of his surname, K, pronounced it Ka, and got himself a new life in German. Matt Ka Musik GmbH, Partys, Happenings. Allerlei Vergnügungen. *www.mkm.de.*

(You only can't sue him if he goes bankrupt, the unpronounceable stuff means. Still, you write to him Charlene, it would sound better coming from you.)

So I clicked Contact and sent him a mail:

Dear Herr Korsak,

Excuse this intrusion if you are not the son of Vladimir and Irina Korsakov, last heard of living in Moscow. I was trying to contact your mother concerning her role in the treatment of the dissident author Boris Marlinsky. If you can help I'd be very glad to hear from you.

Yours sincerely, Charlene Esposito, MA.

I got the top of my old class to repeat the mail in Russian when I got no answer. *Uvazhaemyi gospodin Korsak, Matt Ka, I ishchu vashu matku.* Finally I wrote it out by hand and posted it snail-mail.

Still no bloody answer.

So I phoned Matt Ka, Party Specialist, in Berlin. That took some guts, I can tell you. I went for a run first to psych myself up.

'*Matt am Apparat.*'

'Is that Matt Korsak?'

'*Hab ich eben gesagt.*'

'Matt, could you please speak English? My name is…'

'Walk On By, Babe.'

'Please.'

'Tschschsch! Whatcha need, babe?'

'Where your mother lives.'

Burp burp burp burp.

Would you believe, Ange, I had to take my vacation in Berlin just to get that guy to speak to me! But, heh, what a cool city! I loved it. Lots of happenings. Buzzy places. Theme bars. History. Her-story. Forty per cent of the world's transvestites live and love in Berlin. That's ok with me. The more love the better. War is insane. People seventy years ago were nuts to fight a war!

There's a really sad broken-down church right in the middle of Berlin and they left it a ruin so people would remember. Now that's so cool.

(Ange, Matt Ka runs a shop renting out theatrical outfits under the El bridge at Kreuzberg. Hawking tattoos, working up disguises, playing with carnival masks, and providing *Musikaffin*. Musical caffeine! Clever! Perfect. Go and see him, Charlene. I'll pay your expenses.)

What an area of Berlin that was! I really felt like I'd arrived somewhere when I got out at that subway.

But Jesus, it was like underground in Matt's shack! Not sure I'd call it a shop. There was this guy just sitting there at a table, with a reading light and everything else was dark. He was mostly hairy, but patches of white skin on his face lit up the space around; and he had glasses, and the light bounced off them. Get some non-reflectors, dude!

'Cool music!'

'It's Chaliapin singing *Boris Godunov*.' He looked me up and down. 'You come to get inked, girl? You ready to suffer for my art?'

(I was wearing my college sweat, Ange. I guess he could work out something from that. Also I'd written to him, hadn't I, bloody twice, and called! Of course we didn't need introductions. *Bon courage*, Charlene. *Forza*!) His arms, bare to the ripped off sleeve tops of his sweatshirt, writhed with purplish arabesques. It was as if all the snakes in Arizona had taken up residence just under the skin of Matt Ka. Matt Ka, I read outside on the pavement. Body Modifier.

'Are you Matvei Korsakov? Is Moscow where you were born? I've come to ask you some questions, if you don't mind.'

'I totally mind. Get out of here!'

'But Mr Korsakov, I've come all this way.' Big soupy tears fell from my eyes. Like *I* was going to steal *his* freedom? 'Doesn't the name Boris Marlinsky mean *anything* to you anymore?'

'Jesus Christ!'

'Boris Marlinsky is like Jesus Christ to you? Oh wow!'

He jerked his head, that fuzzy thing with the patches of white skin.

(Ange, I hoped for the life of me it wasn't a weirdo I was shut away with in that dark back room with Chopin singing his heart out.)

Matt Ka's skin was like one of those Eastern carpets, twisting and turning. I heard it takes years of study to know what all those writhings and weavings mean.

'Matt, I have to ask you. I've come all the way from London on behalf of a certain lady. How can I find your mother?'

A face with wind-puffed cheeks snapped at me in lurid yellow and red from his inside wrist.

I guess he was like forty? He had glasses, and man was he hairy. I liked his scarf. Like a knotted necktie. Cool against bare skin and tatts.

'Matt Ka?' I had to keep checking I had the right person. 'MattKa?' I repeated.

(You did great work, Charlene.)

He made two fists on the desk. All that wind shut in a cave! 'What do you want with my mother?'

'When your country ended—'

'When it *ended*—'

'Where did your mother go?'

'Did she have to go somewhere?'

'My lady in London says your mother always longed to go abroad. Now she was free to go.

You too, Matt. She told me you longed to leave. Look where *you* ended up.'

Me and him sat in silence, our eyes glancing away from each other, you know, like not communicating.

'You know, I would like a little tatt,' I conceded.

('You'd make a good journalist, Charlene. You were ready to go the whole hog.' It's all very well you saying that, Ange, but as he took up that engraving tool I had really to pray to God he wasn't a weirdo.)

'Can you do me a loveheart in the hollow of my collarbone?' I thought it would be cool, instead of a choker. If you've got a round face like me, a choker can be, well, quite provocative, I've been told. Like you're into bondage. Like you don't mind being strangled. I do actually, but that's the sort of thing you confess when you're further down the line.

'In your *collarbone*!' He put the tool down and came on to me like the doc at college when I said I wanted smaller boobs. 'Watcha doin this for babe?'

Weeping was an option, but I decided to speak. I was up for being honest, in that moment, to tell the truth.

'I'm here to suffer for your art, Matt.'

(I was lying of course. I was into all this for you, Ange. And I'm grateful, Charlene. There will be a bonus.)

Honestly I didn't much fancy his needle at my throat, but I'd come all this way, so there had to be a *narrative*.

He fetched a schnapps bottle and poured me a shot. I sipped. 'Nice, really nice. It tastes of pears!'

'All the women like it. It relaxes 'em.'

Oh my. Besides, I wasn't all women, I began. Really that's not the way a man should-

But he was in a groove. 'So, tell me why, hon. *Pochemu,* babe?'

'Heh, that's Russian.'

'Sure is. *So, warum, Liebchen?* What's up? *Zachem, golubchik? Wozu?*'

Zachem was a nice word. It sounded like a piece of fruitcake, if that makes sense.

Here was the moment for my narrative. 'I'm just trying to get a life. You know?'

'I know. Get a tatt and live for it. Really get something to live for.'

He shone his bright work lamp on me and I tensed and tried not to. But then he stopped and sat back in his chair again. 'It's just, babe, your aesthetic insults me. You want a loveheart, a fucking loveheart, in your clavi-crater!'

There was a chart on the wall showing the various parts of the body on which tatts were best displayed, and those parts had funny names.

'Ok, ok, I hear what you say. I'm not cool.' I sniffed. 'Where do I go from here?'

He suggested a vagina in my armpit. Yikes! Does the moon have, well, a tunnel? He said he'd ink in ants emerging out of it! Now that's seriously diseased. But the ants would be killing a dragonfly on my shoulder.

How impressive would that be!

I thought, how many ants does it take to kill a dragonfly? He'd make me look like I'd got some venereal rash in my armpit.

How would I explain that to anyone I got so far with? Matt spent some time laughing at me.

(I'm sorry to hear that, Charlene.)

I laughed too, Ange. Actually I cried a bit more. This guy was really working me over.

'My ma married again.'

'Oh, Matt, thanks, thanks!' I got out my notebook.

'She doesn't live *there* anymore. No of course not. No one does. They opened the doors and *everyone* left.'

'Everyone? Collective exodus? Jesus.'

'She lives in Prague.'

'Oh wow! Is that Pow-land?'

'Next door.'

'You mean?'

Next country along, moving West. Like California is next to Colorado.'

'Yeah!'

Finally we agreed on a little peace dove. Bunches better than a loveheart. What's more, and this pleased me, as I lay back on the couch, like at the dentist's, and Matt Ka leant over me, his hand was absolutely still, from which I drew two conclusions. He kept himself pure for his art and probably wasn't impotent.

All the same I didn't fancy him and to tell the truth I was quite glad to get out of there. I went back to the main drag they called the KooFirstTenDam and had a caramel latte in sight of the ruined church. Little pricklings kept making me think of my vagina and the ants emerging. My mum had a diamond necklace. I have ink and pricklings. Now that's a thought. Matt gave me some cream. He said the rash would die down. Please God.

Body modification is both art and science, I'd say. *Körperumgestaltung* they call it.

After Charlene endured this remarkable adventure on my behalf I paid her generously and resumed my searching alone.

I wrote to Irina briefly, by post.

She was gracious enough to reply, longhand, again through the post. All that took the best part of a month, but she told me a little of what I wanted to know.

Volodya Korsakov had been far too attached to Russia to leave. He now gardens in that hotel 'which is what my father's lovely house has become'. Well, yes I knew that.

'They've dug out the nineteenth-century history. The architect was Domenico Ghillardi. It's all printed in panels for guests to read, and the Greek reproduction statues have been given helpful legends beneath, so visitors can say they've seen Il Spinolo. "The boy with the spine in his foot."' Good to know.

Irina for her part had formally divorced Korsakov and remarried. But what I didn't know was her new husband was an American businessman retired from the CIA, and they were living in Prague. She must have been proud of him, to tell me all that.

Curious to see where Irina had settled, I took a cheap flight to Prague, stayed in an even cheaper hotel, and stalked her. I saw her twice, as I wandered around the gracious early twentieth-century neighbourhood where she had resettled. Grand villas led their peaceful existences all around, as if high bourgeois turn-of-the-century society lived on untarnished. I didn't ring at the door but I could see she and her husband were flourishing in some expat style.

Prague of course was the new centre of a united Europe, and it was natural also for me to gravitate there. The city was spacious, historic and beautiful, not yet overrun by tourists, and the rents were cheap.

One evening I met a young Russian woman on the bus from the airport. I heard her speak Russian to her child and joined in. She too was exploring Prague, but only by night. That way she didn't have to pay for a hotel. She couldn't afford to travel otherwise. I tried to imagine that: seeing the sights of the rest of the world, outside Russia at last, but only being able to see them by lamplight: the illuminated castle, the river all dark but for orange stripes left by the lamp glow, the majestic bridges, free of traffic. On the other hand you don't need money to reinvent yourself. You just need imagination. The Charles Bridge anyway lived all night, crammed with visitors from east and west, and trinket sellers and ticket touts and pickpockets who never slept. Somewhere there, beside a medieval statue commemorating the patron saint of safe travel, my Russian visitor and her little girl would pause to eat their middle-of-the-night meal. The bridge was not awash in neon illumination but enough light to stave off the dark. The meal would be bread and butter, eaten with a boiled egg, both two days old but no matter. A boiled egg could keep a Russian tourist going for a long time. They had water in a bottle. What a trip!

One day I saw Howard Wilde's byline in *The Times*. He must have gone freelance. I rang up the office on the Isle of Dogs. He was living in Helsinki. He worked for a radio station that broadcast the world news in Latin. *Hodie unio sovietica delenda est.*

After the grand imperium that was Russia fell apart he moved into the happy interim place that was Finland. The crucial thing is it was nearby.

I checked into a small hotel with an inviting Art Nouveau façade, impeccable cleanliness and English-speaking staff.

There he stood when I walked down the stairs: windblown and untidy, a vast black puffa unzipped in response to the indoor warmth, and a ponytail.

'Gels! Did you fly?'

'I wasn't in a hurry. I took the train.' Not an easy journey on the map, up through Denmark and Sweden, but Scandinavian efficiency finessed it and I believed in saving the planet. 'Heh but you report the news in Latin! Hodie…dixit.' I did my best.

'Over dinner I'll tell you.'

The waterfront and the main roads were brightly lit, but there was an almost rural quiet and a lack of disturbance recalling Moscow all those years before.

He went ahead down a narrow staircase. Since I couldn't afford any better in London I've learned to like basements. Small tables lit from the wall and picked out with individual tea-lights were pushed together under vaults of brick. The heating was generous and the music loud.

'I know that one, don't I?'

A medley of Russian folksongs played, hardly in the background. 'Esli by vy znali ka mne dorogi podmoskovnye vechera…'

'I love that song. Moscow Nights.'

It recalled picnics by the Moscow River, under the stars, and, frankly, unlike Galya and her Petya, Petya something, the fact that Howard and I had never made love.

'We thought Russian suffering could teach humanity to the whole world,' Howard asseverated grimly, as if he would have preferred not to remember. 'Did you hear? The old cow who ran the library had a nervous breakdown when the system collapsed.'

'No one misses her. Plenty of Russians here, by the way, all around us.' If you knew the language, your ears pricked up at the lilting voices.

'I suppose that's why you brought me.'

'Nostalgia. You can understand. I feel it too.'

We ate the Siberian pasta dish called *pel'meny* and drank at enormous expense a bottle of Chianti. I wanted to pay.

'Does Latin pay? Translation doesn't.'

He shrugged. 'Leave it to me. Special occasion. *Na zdorovie*!'

The waitress had taken our plates when the lights dimmed and a white screen descended on the far brick wall.

'The floor show. At nine every evening.'

'Is this why you brought me here?'

'Of course.'

Naturally. The strange logic of our shared Moscow existence was now about to be resolved in an artistic performance.

A piece of film featuring a flock of birds began to run. All the birds seemed to be flying out of derelict brickwork at the same time. They crowded each other and their number never diminished. How could there be room for them all to flap their wings? They were all flying forward towards the camera and the sound was raucous. The little airborne creatures were excited and screaming and calling, and who knows if they were not discussing some crisis left behind or some destination now to be reached, with renewed effort and concentration.

Against this background, a bird-man started to dance. 'Zolodei!'

'Our souls,' declared the dancer, as he took a bow. '*Vam vsego dobrogo*. I remember you.'

We came out beside the sea, where, offshore, small shallow islands basked like sharks in the freezing moonlight. Helsinki's icy charm was growing on me. From the waterfront you could turn and take in the variously lit cityscape, with the great white Russian cathedral, symbol of the giant neighbouring power, and the blackly forested hills behind. Turning back seawards, the geometric outlines of the masts of the fishing boats, lit by occasional lamps in every direction, stuck out against the sky.

'London's full of Russians these days.'

'They're here too, as you've seen.'

'Like you, they want to be close.'

'That's nonsense.'

'But you said you felt nostalgia.'

'That's different. I feel it on their behalf.'

The backstreets were more sheltered and the sky no longer black but dark blue. I was wearing Howard's greasy fur hat, having failed to bring one of my own.

'No bullet hole in the front?'

'Those were the days.'

Indeed, when he'd drawn one in with red ink on his forehead. 'Novorossisk, Novosibirsk, Novopetrovsk, Novoselinsk,' I chanted. 'Ever new attempts to get it right. Doesn't it make you weep?'

We had cried together, after the trial.

Howard had a nice flat without pretentions at the top of a tower block. We squeezed into the lift, made happy enough by the Chianti. I presumed he had long since resumed drinking in moderation, though I could never be sure. There was a small balcony which if you stepped out offered a panorama of white lights like occasional stars, and otherwise blackness. Artificial grass made it possible to stand there in my socks. I stood there for a while with my mug of coffee.

'Can you see Russia?'

'On a clear day.'

I didn't believe it for a moment. I turned back into the room, where he was fixing some music.

It had rankled with me since that moment in the foyer of my hotel. 'Won't you cut your hair? I don't like a ponytail on a man.'

'Won't you grow yours? You're not Jean Seberg anymore.'

You'll think I took flight at not being admired enough. But we just didn't feel for each other in that way.

'I should go.'

'I'll walk you back to your hotel.'

Our outerwear disguised us. Otherwise, we had dressed similarly for the evening, in well-fitting black jeans (even his) and black t-shirts. Only our different body contours distinguished us until I added a silk scarf and he a pale jacket. It was like that, sartorially, with most men I knew. I liked it.

My relationship with Howard wasn't exactly a failure. It just didn't happen.

Meanwhile the fashion that possessed us belonged to the perceived end of the age of something else, not just Soviet Russia. Anyone could be anywhere, us included. I think it was the end of the bourgeoisie. The idea was to hover over the cities of the world, descending here and there to enjoy peculiar local charms, whoever you were, playing by your own rules. I lived like that myself, with pleasure and endless curiosity.

The bad dark Russia we remembered was the opposite.

'The BBC often wasn't jammed, despite what people say.'

'But it was hard to know the truth.'

'The old men were ambivalent, by that stage. They got to like being the stars of the show. They liked hearing their names on world radio.'

'If they could make head or tail of them.' I mimicked some funny pronunciation of Razumovsky and Gerasimov and Shaginyan, the ones that used to stand out.

'You used to tell me you wanted to work for the BBC Pronunciation Unit.'

'I still would. It would have been my mission. Basic mark of respect for other people's tongues.'

'The old men only didn't like Marlinsky shouting out "hello, hello" into the world to attract attention. Mayday, Mayday. This is the truth speaking.'

'Truth was just a rival attraction for them then. Just as it is for us now. Truth is just another performance now we don't have the Russians to keep us in order. Do you buy what I have to say, audience? Maybe you do, maybe you don't.'

After that weekend, when Howard also introduced me to the wonderful ahistorical films of Kaurismaki, I returned happily to London, which was now my home. Howard stayed in Helsinki, eternally on the Russia Watch, whatever he said. I offered him not a formal 'until we meet again' but a friendly, casual, 'whatever happens in the meantime.' *Poka.*

Alexander Razumovsky had long since died, still in Moscow. But you can verify that for yourself.

The poems quoted are as follows: on page 193, 'Klik and Tram' (Osip Mandelstam); on pages 195, 196 and 368, 'It's nice to chat', 'Just think of that' and 'I played the game' (Boris Slutsky, translated by G.S. Smith); on page 319, 'The Last Toast' (Anna Akhmatova); on page 358 'The Russian-Speaking world...' (unknown); Shaginyan borrowed 'Above the Back of a Sofa' from Sergei Gandlevsky, 'Twilight came late', translated by Philip Metres, *Modern Poetry in Translation*, Winter 1996); on page 381 'To wrest life from captivity and wrong' (Osip Mandelstam, from 'The Age'); on page 252, 'You left foreign parts' (Alexander Pushkin); on pages 382-84, the translations of Lermontov's 'I skuchno i grustno' are Irina's own.

The painting referred to on p. 110 is by Mundt. The paintings of Zorin, including *Lenin Descending a Staircase*, last seen hanging in the VIRILE Institute in Vilnius, Soviet Lithuania, and the collage *Twentieth Century*, bought by an American collector in 1992, are also his own. This story has been as faithful (pp. 183 and 186-87) to the work of Alfred Manessier as lies in the author's gift to render a likeness in words. The works alluded to on p. 308-09 ('The Lock') and p. 364 ('Moscow Nights'), and bought by Vladimir Korsakov, among others, belong to the brilliant Evgeny Rukhin (1943-1976).